Eumeswil

Eumeswil

Ernst Jünger

Translated by Joachim Neugroschel

Edited and with an Introduction by Russell A. Berman

Telos Press Publishing
Candor, NY

Printed in the United States of America
19 18 17 16 15 1 2 3 4

Translated by permission from the German original, *Eumeswil*, in Ernst Jünger, *Sämtliche Werke*, vol. 17, Stuttgart 1980. © 1977, 1980 Klett-Cotta—J. G. Cotta'sche Buchhandlung Nachfolger GmbH, Stuttgart.

ISBN 978-0-914386-52-0

Library of Congress Cataloging-in-Publication Data

Jünger, Ernst, 1895–1998, author.
[Eumeswil. English]
Eumeswil / Ernst Jünger ; Translated by Joachim Neugroschel ; Edited and with an Introduction by Russell A. Berman.
pages cm
ISBN 978-0-914386-52-0 (pbk.)
1. Dystopias—Fiction. I. Neugroschel, Joachim, translator. II. Berman, Russell A., 1950- editor. III. Title.
PT2619.U43E9313 2015
833'.914—dc23
2015019025

Cover design by Amanda Trager and Erik Moskowitz
Cover painting: Adrienne Rempel, *Bear Claw Mountain (an encounter with the sublime)*, mixed media on paper, 11 x 15 in., 2010

Telos Press Publishing
PO Box 811
Candor, NY 13743

www.telospress.com

Contents

INTRODUCTION

The Anarchic Imagination in *Eumeswil*

Russell A. Berman

"We fail not because of our dreams but because
we do not dream forcefully enough."

Ernst Jünger's *Eumeswil* is a post-apocalyptic novel that combines elements of science fiction and dystopia with a sustained philosophical reflection on the predicament of the individual in the face of the intrusive powers of the state and technology. It points toward opportunities to pursue an elusive freedom, but it provides no guarantees, no reassuring metaphysics of progress or redemption. The complex vision of this novel, first published in 1977, speaks directly to conflicting aspects of our twenty-first-century condition: the prospects of ecological catastrophe and nuclear conflict, the threat of global warfare, and the exhaustion of cultural traditions. Yet the novel is equally contemporary because of its persuasive articulation of a libertarian sensibility in Jünger's language of imaginative brilliance and crystalline intelligence.

Eumeswil is the name of a fictional city, somewhere on the North African coast. (While working on the novel, Jünger traveled several times to Agadir in Morocco.) It is named after Eumenes, a Greek general who played a central role in the Diadochian Wars that carved up the Macedonian Empire after the death of Alexander the Great. Ancient history and futuristic vision overlap in *Eumeswil*: just as Eumenes, the general, navigated through the collapse of an ancient empire, the novel takes place, temporally, in the wake of a future catastrophe. The precise character of that antecedent destruction is never fully spelled out, not unlike the sparse treatment of post-apocalypse in Cormac McCarthy's *The Road*: a major destruction has taken place, but its history is less important than its consequences. Nonetheless, there are plenty of hints spread throughout the novel that can allow us to piece together the backstory. After a "final period of wars between nations, a time that heralded great coalitions," a "first world-state cast its shadow." Yet that universal regime faced the same fate as Alexander's empire: a "world civil war" broke out with "great devastations," nuclear war and environmental catastrophes. In the aftermath, a shattered world remains. Eumeswil is a small city-state, ruled by a dictator, the Condor, and defined by its post-historical situation. Heroism belongs to the past, including any heroism of ideals: "... the surfeit of a late era is involved here. The catalogue of possibilities seems exhausted. The great ideas have been eroded by repetition; you won't catch any fish with that bait.... People no longer demonstrate publicly for ideas; bread or wine would have to cost a lot more...." The mood in Eumeswil is as post-historical and postmodern as in our own. Jünger surely modeled his epigonic city-state on provincial West Germany, in the shadow of World War II; it can speak to us today, however, in the wake of 9/11, as a sense of limitation and the mentality of aftermath replace grand strategies and ambitions.

In *Eumeswil*, Jünger scrutinizes a world in which ideas and ideals, commitment and aspiration, have dissipated, replaced by a culture of generalized mediocrity, populated by "the last man" whom Nietzsche had predicted. At the same time, however, this is a world of visionary technological achievement, especially with the luminar, a hybrid combining aspects of a computer that can draw on an enormous archive, a holograph, and a time machine, capable of calling up scenes from other eras: the protagonist travels easily to moments in the distant past to understand the background to his present. We also read of the phonophore, a sort of smartphone, the capacities of which Jünger described with uncanny prescience: "Anyone in possession of a phonophore—in other words, nearly everyone—is always solvent. His account is kept up to date automatically.... through the phonophore, I pay more quickly and more easily than with a check." However the distribution of the device carefully reflects differences in social status. On that point, Jünger anticipated not only the technological developments with which we are familiar today but the digital divide as well; access to technology is highly stratified. The deployment of these new tools enhances human potential, but they also maintain the dictatorial order. Nonetheless, "people were skeptical about everything but science. This was the only thing that developed unswervingly and worldwide.... Science managed to do something that had been reserved for the Great Titans, who had existed before the Gods, indeed created them." Jünger invokes a mythological framing of our metahistorical condition, a battle between Titans and Gods, leading ultimately to the tipping point of the Second World War, designated as the "final triumph of the technician over the warrior." Myth and faith have succumbed to machines: *Eumeswil* is a study on how to live in this condition.

The historical circumstances of the novel are described most precisely in the words of one of the novel's most important characters, Vigo—Jünger's hardly concealed stand-in for Giambattista Vico (1668–1774), the political philosopher and historian: "The world-state is shattered into its parts, just as Boutefeu [Jünger's Nietzsche—RB] predicted. We are left with Diadochic realms and epigonic city-states. The keynote proclaimed by the nineteenth Christian century was a permanent, indeed qualitative growth; this seemed to be realized by *Homo faber* in the twentieth century. Next, new distinctions split off from progress—and they can be roughly described as the differences between economists and ecologists. The former thought in terms of the history of the world, the latter the history of the earth; the former thought in terms of distribution, the latter in terms of administration. Conflicts erupted between the human milieu and the natural environment, and they were exacerbated by the apocalyptic atmosphere that recurs at the end of every millennium." Through Vigo we encounter Jünger as cultural diagnostician. The historical optimism of the nineteenth century adulated growth, which transformed into the ambitious development schemes of the twentieth century: industry was expected to accomplish anything. Yet a fundamental tension erupted between the economic expectation of ever greater consumption and an ecological awareness of limited resources. Today the awareness of this tension is greater than ever, but writing in the 1970s Jünger was one of the first far-sighted thinkers to extrapolate from the oil crisis and the ominous predictions of the Club of Rome.

The novel is the first-person narration of an inhabitant of Eumeswil, Martin Venator, a historian and an offspring of a prominent family of historians. It consists of short passages, fragments, and aphorisms, often in the nature of diary entries. Martin's historian father and his brother, Cadmo, still feel allegiance to the liberal regime of the "tribunes" who preceded the dictator, but Martin in contrast has found his way into the inner circle around the Condor. His family treats this collaboration with contempt, while Martin views their nostalgia for an earlier era as obsolete. One can recognize this conflict within the Venator family as an echo of Jünger's own biography, reminiscent of his conservative revolutionary phase of the 1920s, when he emphatically broke with the old-fashioned world of the pre-war era. (One important document of that period in his life is the essay *On Pain,* which Telos Press has published.) Yet that phase in Jünger's career is best understood as just the German version of the ambiguities inherent in the larger field of twentieth-century modernism, with its characteristic insistence on abandoning the categories, political as well as aesthetic, of the liberal or bourgeois nineteenth century. The Victorian (or in the German context, the proper term is Wilhelmine) world, with its dedication to progress, individualism, and reason, faced profound challenges from thinkers as diverse as Marx, Ibsen, and Nietzsche, as well as from the bitter experiences of industrialization, urbanization, and especially the devastation of the First World War. Modernism, in its multiple varieties, tended to reject the bad and seemingly antiquated world of the parents' generation while reaching for new values and new political agendas, both on the left and the right. Embedded in Martin's conflict with his family is a retrospective evaluation of that generational divide at the moment of modernism, which then therefore gives *Eumeswil* a distinctly postmodern perspective. It is this stance too that imbues the novel with such a contemporary feeling today.

The element of family conflict in *Eumeswil*—the effort on the part of the son to escape the stranglehold of the father's old-fashioned worldview—points to a subtle indication of the specific genre. Underneath the hallmarks of the post-apocalyptic dystopia, one can recognize vestiges of that premier German novelistic form, the bildungsroman, or novel of education, which excelled in tracing the growth of a hero from childhood to maturity. That genre, perhaps more than any other literary form, expressed the self-understanding of the era of liberal individualism, and it found its paradigmatic expression in Johann Wolfgang Goethe's *Wilhelm Meister's Apprenticeship* of 1795. More than a century later, Thomas Mann's *The Magic Mountain*, published in 1924, embodied the novel of development in the era of modernism, where the erstwhile ideas of individualism and progress faced profound challenges from psychoanalysis, new understandings of time, and the traumatic experience of the world war.

Eumeswil inherits that tradition and reshapes the genre again, exploring the possibility of the bildungsroman in the era of a postmodernism fundamentally antithetical to developmental narratives (and by implication hostile as well to economic agendas of development, hence the widespread postmodern affinity for environmentalism as well as its aversion to capitalist modernization). Instead of the classical liberal individualism of the traditional genre, *Eumeswil* describes Martin's origin, his birth scene so to speak, twice over. At the outset, we learn that his father gave him his "Christian name," Martin: "he calls the newborn baby by his name while picking him up and letting him prove his existence by bawling his lungs out." Yet we also learn how Martin entered the employ of the Condor, working in his domicile, "the Casbah, the citadel," as night steward, and there the dictator renamed him "Manuel," in part out of his "extreme musical sensibility, which is offended by [the harsh consonant in the middle of the name—RB] 'Martin'"—the Condor displays an aesthetic refinement that the grim father lacks—but in part as a sign of his power, as his prerogative to rename his servant. At first Martin was christened, but then he was born again when he was renamed by his benevolent godfather, the dictator.

This shift between the two naming scenes and the two identities takes place so effectively because the son feels little more than contempt for his biological father, a contempt which takes the political form of the critique of the father's liberalism but which in fact has a prior, more powerful source. As a budding historian, fascinated by documents and sources, Martin had discovered the correspondence between his father and mother during their courtship, and it is there that he learned of the father's unsuccessful efforts to persuade his fiancée to abort the foetus. "My father hounded me when my life was frailest. This may be our most exquisite time. My mother concealed me from him in her womb, like Rhea hiding Zeus in the grotto of Ida to shield him from the clutches of a voracious Cronus. Those are monstrous images; they make me shudder—conversations between matter and time. They lie as erratic boulders, uninterpreted, beneath surveyed land." No wonder Martin often avoids referring to his father with that designation or any other term of endearment, choosing instead to label him with cold functionality as his "genitor," his *Erzeuger*, merely the sperm donor who would have preferred to eliminate the son before the birth. Some dissonance between father and son often features in novels of development, but in *Eumeswil* it is particularly acute.

A further feature of the bildungsroman genre is the prominence of education: the novel describes encounters with his teachers, mentors, and colleagues, especially the aforementioned Vigo, the historian, Bruno, the philosopher (Jünger's figure of Giordano Bruno), and Thofern, the grammarian who provides crucial commentary on the decay of language. As in *The Magic Mountain*, this bildungsroman too turns into a novel of ideas, and the reader benefits from Jünger's erudition and intelligence, his historical depth as well as his zoological and botanical knowledge. At the same time, however, the academic milieu of the novel provides an opportunity to characterize the venality and corruption of professors in this post-apocalyptic context, where, as we have seen, ideas have surrendered their former importance. Thus for example the biting description of one of Vigo's professional adversaries, Kessmüller, whose "ideas are as nonexistent as his hair; he is a bon vivant and a gourmet, and has a sense of humor.... His talent has gotten him through various, even antithetical, regimes as a king-of-the-herrings, which shines on the surface. He has an instinct for conformity and for irresistible platitudes, which he stylizes in a highbrow manner. He can also reinterpret them, depending on which way the wind is blowing." Martin's antipathy to Kessmüller results from the latter's persecution of Vigo, but it is also Kessmüller who is more representative of academic life than are the exceptional Vigo and Bruno. In an era devoid of compelling ideas, the life of the mind degenerates into crowd pleasing, which then leads to a particular opportunism on the part of the professoriate, combining verbal radicalism and comfortable job security.

Jünger is no doubt thinking here of his contemporary German university of the 1970s, in the waning days of the student movement, but he also participates in a skepticism toward academia that dates from Nietzsche, at the latest, and still resonates today. Consider his parody of the professor as political activist: "Incidentally, I notice that our professors, trying to show off to their students, rant and rail against the state and against law and order, while expecting that same state to punctually pay their salaries; pensions, and family allowances, so that they value at least this kind of law and order. Make a fist with the left hand and open the right hand receptively—that is how one gets through life." Although this corruption of academic authority belongs, in Martin's account, more definitively to the past era of the Tribunes, a world of liberal greed, it continues in the novel's present as well and contributes to the general mood of cultural decline, one of the primary targets of *Eumeswil.* Nor can one deny some resemblance to parts of the contemporary academic world. Placed in a distant future, the novel offers trenchant commentary to us today.

Eumeswil describes a process of cultural atrophy, particularly affecting language quality and historical knowledge, which uncannily anticipates what we today think of as the crisis in the humanities. Points of cultural orientation have disappeared, and the inhabitants of Eumeswil face a ubiquitous alienation and malaise: "In a period of decline, when it was considered glorious to have helped destroy one's own nation, the roots of language were, not surprisingly, likewise pruned, above all in Eumeswil. Loss of history and decay of language are mutual determinants; the Eumenists championed both. They felt called upon to defoliate language on the one hand and to gain prestige for slang on the other hand. Thus, down below they robbed the populace of language and, with it, poetry, on the pretext that they were facilitating speech; while on the heights they presented their 'mugs.'" In the name of emancipation, the poor are denied access to cultural traditions through educational reforms that keep the elite in power. Jünger's own prose is an antidote to these conditions, with its linguistic precision and his historical knowledge. Still, building on a critique of linguistic decline that derives from Karl Kraus, Jünger presents a tableau in which this process leads to a society of vast conformism. The preconditions for this conformism include both the degradation of language and a systematic elimination of encounters with the past.

The city-state of Eumeswil is the dystopia of the managed society. Not only do the dictator and his apparatus maintain a system of extensive surveillance, but the inhabitants themselves participate eagerly in their own oppression. Thus "one often has the impression in Eumeswil that it is not the person but the swarm that answers." Individualism has disappeared, and if there are answers given they are provided by "swarms," i.e., the many who act as if they made up part of a mass cohort of animals. At the same time, that mass can be divided and conquered through the powers of technology, through the phonophore, with its explicit class distinctions, and even more through television. The Domo (short for Majordomo), a regular companion of the Condor, recognizes its value: "He also thinks that the best police force, like a good housewife, is the kind that is least spoken of. He is relieved of some of his worries by television; here, too, games and melodramas are more popular than politics. Besides, the masses are thus divided among their households." A core function of that mass media form was, at least in Jünger's view, to break up the masses and keep them at home, in front of their screens.

This dispersion and the corresponding conformism in opinion contribute to a depoliticized culture that nonetheless generates broad loyalty to the regime. Opposition is minimal. On the contrary, there is widespread support for the Condor and his regime, despite the lack of freedom and governmental transparency. "Gullibility is the norm; it is the credit on which states live: without it, even their most modest survival would be impossible." The mendacity of the powers that be, in other words, poses no threat as long as the population remains credulous; if however that popular appreciation were to be lost, if the population were to grow critical, no technology of domination could maintain the regime and its security. The core issue in the politics of Eumeswil therefore is not the behavior of the sovereign but the acquiescence of the population to the Condor's rule. Understanding this apparatus of subordination and navigating among strategies of resistance make up the core of the novel.

Privately, Martin may be the black sheep of the Venator family for having taking up with the dictator. Professionally, he is a historian as well as the night steward at the Casbah. However his primary identity, the self-understanding that he underscores repeatedly, is as the "anarch," the emphatic individual who refuses any ultimate allegiance, maintaining his inner freedom and always reserving the option to decamp. In the figure of the anarch in *Eumeswil*, Jünger fashions one more of the major archetypes in his own oeuvre—after the soldier, the worker, and the forest fleer: this is the "forest rebel" in Jünger's *The Forest Passage* of 1951, also published by Telos Press. With the anarch, Jünger has added to the list of existentialist heroes of modern literature, akin to the narrator of Dostoevsky's *Notes from the Underground*, Kafka's Joseph K., Camus' Sisyphus, and the protagonist in Ellison's *Invisible Man*. "As an anarch, I am determined to go along with nothing, ultimately take nothing seriously—at least not nihilistically, but rather as a border guard in no man's land, who sharpens his eyes and ears between tides." Existence is replete with danger; hence the need for perpetual agility: "Such is the role of the anarch, who remains free of all commitments yet can turn in any direction." His experience as a historian contributes to this perspective, since looking back across time, like Epimetheus, he understands that all regimes decline. "The special trait making me an anarch is that I live in a world which I 'ultimately' do not take seriously. This increases my freedom; I serve as a temporary volunteer." Every arrangement is only provisional, and with every choice, the anarch seizes freedom. Martin insists furthermore on distinguishing emphatically between the anarchist and the anarch. "It is especially difficult to tell the essential from that which is similar to and indeed seems identical with it. This also applies to the anarch's relation to the anarchist. The latter resembles the man who has heard the alarm but charges off in the wrong direction." Through their commitment to establishing a new order, anarchists slide into ideology and a repetition of domination; in contrast, the anarch strategizes to maintain independence in the face of the challenges of existing order. "[The anarch] is not for or against the law. While not acknowledging the law, he does try to recognize it like the laws of nature, and he adjusts accordingly. When it is hot, you doff your hat; in rain, you open your umbrella; during an earthquake, you leave your house."

Skepticism toward any regime results in a consistent and radical libertarianism as a political philosophy. "Flags have meaning for him, but not sense." The anarch can understand the political exigencies of the moment, and he can even act opportunistically (which is what his father and brother accuse him of doing), but he also understands the provisional status of all political meanings. After a revolution, "the May Day celebrations will survive, but with different meanings. New portraits will head up the processions." Each new state system develops its own discourse of propaganda, even as it recycles the symbols of the past. For the anarch, it is at most a matter of a change of costumes: "For the anarch, little is changed when he strips off a uniform that he wore partly as fool's motley, partly as camouflage. It covers his spiritual freedom, which he will objectivate during such transitions." No doubt sentences like those could be read as retrospective apologetics, Jünger's reflection on his own personal agility across German regimes during that country's troubled twentieth century. Yet Martin's point is somewhat different: in contrast to the anarch who preserves an internal freedom in situations of duress in order to "objectivate" it when the opportunity develops, the fundamentally ideological anarchist, opposed to this order only for the purposes of establishing another one, ends up making matters worse because, "objectively unfree, [he] starts raging until he is thrust into a more rigorous straitjacket." That paradoxical inversion, when the activist's aspiration for freedom flips over into a new oppression, reappears throughout the novel, perhaps most saliently when Martin reflects on the ironic proximity of the death of the famous anarchist Peter Kropotkin in 1921 and the Bolshevik suppression of the Kronstadt revolt, the uprising of sailors and soldiers against the repressive policies of the Leninist regime: "There is a brief intermezzo between the fall of the legitimate powers and the new legality. Two weeks after Kropotkin's funeral cortege in which his corpse had followed the Black Banners, the sailors of Kronstadt were liquidated."

This invocation of Kropotkin and Kronstadt takes place in the context of an extended meditation on the history of anarchism and socialism. Thanks to the luminar, Venator can visit Jacob Hippel's wine garden in Berlin—94 Friedrichstrasse—in the 1840s, where the young Karl Marx engages in verbal battle with the left Hegelians, an Ur-scene of the long conflict between socialism and anarchism. The novel also integrates material from the American anarchist Benjamin Tucker, while it devotes special attention to Max Stirner and his 1845 volume *The Ego and Its Own*, a foundational text of individualist anarchism. These passages are the crux of *Eumeswil* as a novel of ideas and a treasure trove for engaging with the nexus of individualism, libertarianism, and anarchy: Martin insists that "my study of anarchy... is my secret focus."

While the futuristic technology of the luminar brings the reader to the scenes of these historical debates that would turn out to be foundational for subsequent revolutionary thinking, it also provides Martin with corroborating evidence supporting the melancholy view of the history of permanent dictatorship as the grand narrative of the past. In order to understand the condition of the Condor and his tyranny in Eumeswil, Martin the historian searches for comparable cases: "Through the luminar, I was presented with a wealth of types and also of eras in which these types were concentrated: Greek and especially Sicilian cities, satrapies in Asia Minor; late Roman and Byzantine caesars; Renaissance city-states, including, over and over—on Vigo's behalf as well—Florence and Venice; then the very brief and bloody uprisings of the *okhlos*, nights of hatchets and long knives; and finally the prolonged dictatorships of the proletariat, with their backgrounds and shadings." Nearly all history was a history of dictatorship, but the scandal of Jünger's listing should not be passed over too quickly: the equation of the Nazi "night of the long knives" with the Communist dictatorship of the proletariat. The thesis of the proximity between the two modes of terror, familiar since Hannah Arendt's *Origins of Totalitarianism* (1951), remains a provocation for those who may still want to rescue Communism as a good idea just poorly implemented, rather than a fundamentally flawed vision. Martin offers us a more sobering view by equating red and brown terror, framed moreover with the suggestion that both extremisms represent the will of the mob, the *okhlos*, the oppressive majority as the motor of modern power. Yet we have already heard that in Eumeswil it is the swarm and not the individual who speaks. It is the Condor who rules, no doubt, but is there not also a subjective side, as the Hegelians would have said, a "rule of the swarm"? The compulsory membership in the collective of the class or the race, or the obligatory participation in received opinion forms the structures of unfreedom from which the anarch endeavors to escape—these are the constituents of shared experience in societies that eliminate the space of personal freedom.

As Martin describes this claustrophobic situation, he is suddenly gripped by concern with the threatening possibility of an imminent revolt or some other unspecific political disorder from which he would have to escape. Political danger lurks everywhere, even if it is never specific, and a free-floating anxiety results as well as the desire for some safe haven. The most lyrical passages in *Eumeswil* invoke scenes of potential refuge where one might flee to hide and evade the unnamed threat: here Jünger's prose, for all of its cool intelligence and adventure, gestures toward a utopia of genuine happiness and protection. For example, in a reverie sequence, Martin imagines himself a mouse in the wilds preparing a hideaway for hibernation. "Now let the snow fall; the wolf season was beginning. I could lay myself to rest with drawn knees and a sunken head. My breath would not stir a feather, my heartbeat would be barely perceptible. I was the child in its mother's womb. Why could this not last forever?" The image of intrauterine safety recalls the paternal threat of the abortion: natural history (the mouse), family history (the parents), and political history (tyranny) converge in the description of escape.

Yet the mouse passage was only Martin's dream; in fact, he begins to construct a clandestine bunker outside the city, not unlike the mouse's nest, where he would hope to flee to safety in the case of an uprising or a palace revolt. That his refuge would be located in the forest is consistent with Jünger's imagery since *The Forest Passage*: nature as a location of archaic freedom. It follows then that *Eumeswil* also alludes to a paradigmatic literary flight into nature from the medieval Icelandic saga of Grettir—"the longest forest flight in Iceland was carried out by Grettir, the strongest man on the island: he feared no human being, but he did fear ghosts"—and this Nordic imagery recurs in the vision of a strange island in the ocean with a mysterious "Gray Castle of Transiceland." Although *Eumeswil* is placed in a science fiction future, we have already seen how it invokes the distant past of Mediterranean antiquity through the reference to Eumenes; here it is a different archaic stratum, the medieval North that Jünger integrates into his diagnosis of the present.

Martin appears convinced that he will sooner or later be compelled to flee to his bunker. The regime is structurally unstable, not because it is the Condor's dictatorship—he is hardly the worst tyrant—but because power is always destined to collapse, as the luminar teaches. "The best one can expect is a modest legality—legitimacy is out of the question. The coats of arms have been robbed of their insignia or replaced by flags." It would be a mistake to treat this remark as a vestigial monarchism nostalgic for a Kaiser, with the legitimacy of a coat of arms, since Martin continues, "Incidentally, it is not that I am awaiting a return to the past, like Chateaubriand, or a recurrence, like Boutefeu; I leave those matters politically to the conservatives and cosmically to the stargazers."

Eumeswil therefore enters no plea for counterrevolution, but, rather, it appeals to an existential dimension that surpasses the political as it has ever been previously known. "No, I hope for something equal, nay, stronger, and not just in the human domain. *Naglfar*, the ship of the apocalypse shifts into a calculable position." Naglfar—from Norse mythology, the ship of the dead who will battle the gods—signifies here a breakthrough into dimensions of freedom beyond political ideologies and regimes.

Yet before he takes refuge in his bunker, Martin receives an invitation to accompany the Condor and his advisors on a "Great Hunt" that will penetrate the ominous forest that lies beyond Eumeswil, specifically as the "Xenophon," the historian of the expedition—once again, the ancient past erupts in the midst of futuristic vision. Previously the forest simply stood as the extreme alternative to Eumeswil, the unknown beyond. All that we have learned of it comes from accounts provided by Attila, another member of the Condor's inner circle, who has gone on "ventures beyond the boundaries: into the polar sea, the great deserts, the forest." The account of Attila's journey provides more insight into the post-apocalyptic condition of the planet after one of the previous nuclear catastrophes, euphemized as "great devastations." "The caravan trails were lined with human and animal skeletons. The bones gleamed like opals in the sun; they were calcined. It was not decay that had bleached them. The flesh must have been devoured instantly." Attila sees "plants and animals, including some that were new to me. A few of them evoked pictures in old fable books, as if a demiurge had patched them together," suggesting post-nuclear mutations. Then suddenly at the edge of the desert: "The forest stood like a rampart; no axe could ever have touched it. The cataclysm must have intensified the growth of the forest, as if the breath of the fire and the subsequent deluge had liberated its primal energy." Entering the forest, Attila encounters a world of the imagination realized, bizarre forms of life absolutely beyond the realm of normalcy. "The snakes that traveled the trees overhead were also huge. They seemed neither to glide nor to fly; the edges of their skin were shimmying. They were obviously demonstrating the transition to dragons." Within the framework of *Eumeswil*, these bizarre phenomena suggest, on one level, the consequences of nuclear radiation, but the prose also invokes the imagery of hallucinations—Jünger experimented with psychedelic drugs—as well as religious visions: "In a clearing, a sunbeam fell upon a ramlike shape. Its left front leg was propped on a lamb with a human face. Both dissolved in light as if the vision were too powerful."

Before departing, Martin pays a final visit to his mentor, Vigo, who encourages him to participate in the expedition. Vigo understands that his protégé has always preferred the forest. Because of his anarchic aspiration to independence, Martin has maintained a subterranean opposition to the normalcy of any regime. While Attila treats the forest as an adventure, and the Domo denigrates it as fiction, Martin understands it as a "passage," a forest passage to a realm of freedom. Vigo endorses the undertaking with the blessing: "A dream comes true in each of our great transformations. You know this as a historian. We fail not because of our dreams but because we do not dream forcefully enough." Is the alternative to tyranny the anarch as dreamer? The "Great Hunt" is the enigma that marks the limits of the novel, the venue of some profoundly different life, a promise of an adventurous alternative.

But *Eumeswil* has one more surprise for us. In the short epilogue, we learn that years later, Martin has been declared dead, the Condor is long gone, and a new regime has come to power. Cadmo, Martin's hostile brother, has taken control of the literary legacy, editing some of the writings and adding the final words to the text before us. Since it includes damning comments on himself and their father, Cadmo finds himself in a difficult position. "Reading these pages has thrown me into an inner conflict—between the private man and the historian. My brother did not love his family. Such was his peculiar character. But we loved him. His presentation is larded with judgments and, in my opinion, misjudgments that would justify my burning it as a private person; I have thought about it." Instead of destroying the pages, however, he acts as the meticulous historian that he is and preserves the documents. Was this an act of restitution to his brother? Did he try to reach out across their political and existential divide? Hardly. Cadmo's closing gesture is more akin to an assertion of property rights and unmitigated triumph over the deceased. For regarding "these notebooks," the text of the novel that we hold in our hands, Cadmo does not edit them: he withholds them. "There is an archivist's conscience to which a man must sacrifice himself. I am submitting to it by sealing these pages and storing them at the institute."

Martin/Manuel Venator has not returned from the Great Hunt, from the expedition into the imagination, from the pursuit of freedom in a forest passage. In Eumeswil, the city-state, the self-satisfied culture of the tribunes has been reestablished, where the erstwhile advocate of freedom of the press, the brother, consigns Martin's words to the impervious silence of the archive. He has sealed the writings away, ensconced them in an archival tomb, where, he presumes, they can do no harm, raise no doubts, and encourage no pursuit, neither of anarchy nor of art. Yet the text has, inexplicably, escaped that incarceration. We have it before us, Jünger's magnificent novel, *Eumeswil,* a study of tyrannical conformism as well as of the potential for every one of us to pursue very different lives.

Eumeswil

The Teachers

1

My name is Manuel Venator: I am the night steward in the Casbah of Eumeswil. My appearance is unobtrusive. In athletic contests I can expect third prize, and I have no problems regarding women. Soon I will be thirty; my character is regarded as pleasant—which is already inherent in my profession. Politically, I am considered reliable if not especially committed.

So much for a brief personal description. My information is sincere, although still vague. I will gradually make it more precise; as such, it contains the outline of an overall account.

*

To make the vague more precise, to define the indefinite more and more sharply: that is the task of every development, every temporal exertion. That is why physiognomies and characters become more distinct as the years go by. The same applies to handwriting.

The sculptor at first confronts the raw block, the pure material, which encompasses any and all possibilities. It responds to the chisel; the latter can destroy or it can release water of life, spiritual power from the material. All this is indefinite, even for the master: it does not hinge entirely on his will.

Vagueness, imprecision, even in invention, are not the falsehoods. They may be incorrect, but they must not be insincere. A statement—imprecise but not untrue—can be interpreted sentence by sentence, until the thing finally rebalances and swings back into the center. But if an utterance begins with a lie, so that it has to be propped up by more and more lies, then eventually the structure collapses. Hence my suspicion that Creation itself began with a fraud. Had it been a simple mistake, then paradise could be restored through evolution. But the Old Man concealed the Tree of Life.

This touches upon my sorrow: irremedial imperfection, not only in Creation, but also in my own person. It causes hostility toward the gods on the one side and self-criticism on the other. Perhaps I tend to overdo these things; in any case, they both weaken my actions.

But not to worry: I am not trying to pen a treatise on moral theology.

2

Right off, I must specify that while my last name is indeed Venator, my first name is actually Martin and not Manuel: Martin is, as the Christians phrase it, my Christian name. In our country, the latter is given by the father; he calls the newborn baby by his name while picking him up and letting him prove his existence by bawling his lungs out.

Manuel, in contrast, has become my nickname during my employment here in the Casbah; it was bestowed on me by the Condor. The Condor, being the current ruler of Eumeswil, is my employer. For years now, he has been residing in the Casbah, the citadel, which, some two leagues beyond the city, crowns a bare hill that has been known as Pagos since time out of mind.

This relationship between city and fortress can be found in many places; it is the most convenient tie not just for tyranny but for any one-man regime.

The tribunes, toppled by the Condor, had resided inconspicuously in the town, ruling from the *municipio*. "If there is only one arm, it has a more powerful effect on the long lever; if many people have a say, they need fermentation: they infiltrate whatever exists, like yeast in bread." Those words were spoken by Vigo, my teacher; I will come back to him later.

*

Now just why did the Condor want and thus order me to be nicknamed Manuel? Did he prefer the Iberian flavor, or did he have something against Martin? That was my initial conjecture; and indeed, there is a dislike of certain first names or at least an irritability that we do not sufficiently take into account. Some parents encumber a child for life with a name that expresses their wishful thinking. A gnome walks in and introduces himself as Caesar. Other parents choose the name of whoever happens to be at the helm, just as there are now little Condors here among rich and poor. This, too, can be harmful, especially in periods without a sure succession to the throne.

People—and this is true for the majority—pay scant notice to the harmony between the given name and the last. Schach von Wuthenow: that is strenuous—it is almost a phonetic imposition. In contrast: Emilia Galotti, Eugénie Grandet—this combination floats, light and well balanced, through acoustic space. Naturally, the German form, Eugenie, should have a Gallic and not a Germanic stress: *Öjénie* with a weakened Ö. Similarly, the people here have ground down the name Eumenes: it dwells in Ömswil.

We are now getting to the crux of the matter: the Condor's extreme musical sensibility, which is offended by "Martin." His reaction is understandable, for the middle consonants sound hard and jagged, they grate on the ear. Mars is the patron saint.

Such delicacy is, to be sure, bizarre in a ruler who owes his power to weapons. This contradiction dawned on me only after some long observation, even though it casts its shadow on everyone. Each person, you see, has his day side and his night side, and some people become different at twilight. In the Condor, this distinction is unusually salient. His appearance remains the same: a middle-aged bachelor with the slightly stooped shoulders of a horseman. Plus a smile that has charmed many people—friendly joviality.

However, the sensorium changes. The diurnal raptor, the grasper, who peers into the distance, following remote movements, becomes nocturnal; his eyes recover in the shadows, his hearing grows finer. It is as if a veil had dropped away from the face, opening up new sources of perception.

The Condor sets great store by visual acuteness: seldom does a candidate who wears glasses stand a chance with him. This is particularly true for command positions in the army and the coast guard. The applicant is invited for a chat, during which the Condor sounds him out. His study, towering above the flat roof of the Casbah, is a round, swiveling glass dome. During the interview, the Condor usually convinces himself of the aspirant's visual strength by pointing to a ship or a very distant sail and questioning him about its type and direction. Of course, all this is preceded by rigorous examinations; they are to be confirmed by the Condor's personal assessment.

*

With the transformation from diurnal to nocturnal raptor, the taste shifts from dogs to cats, both of which are raised in the Casbah. For reasons of security, the space between the fortress and the ring-shaped bailey is kept flat and unplanted—in other words, it is meant to be a field of fire. Brawny mastiffs slumber there in the shade of the bastions or frolic on the flat terrain. Since the animals can easily become a nuisance, a bridge leads from the square, where the cars halt, to the entrance of the Casbah.

Should I have any business on the terrain, I never set foot there without one of the guards; I am astounded by their nonchalant way of taking hold of the animals. I am already repulsed if they nuzzle me or their tongues slurp my hand. In many respects, the animals are smarter than we. They obviously whiff my malaise; and it could intensify into fear—at which point they would leap upon me. One never knows when they might get serious. This is a trait they share with the Condor.

The mastiffs—dark Tibetans with yellow noses and yellow eyebrows—are also used for hunting. They go wild with joy when they hear the horn at dawn. They can be sicced on the most robust adversaries; they attack the lion and the rhinoceros.

This pack is not the only one. Remote from the Casbah, but observable from the heights, a complex of stables, coach houses, aviaries, and open and covered riding courses stretches along the beach. It also includes the kennels for the greyhounds. The Condor loves galloping along the very edge of the sea with his minions; the party is surrounded by the swarm of steppe dogs: they are used for hunting gazelles. Their style of running evokes the racers and ball balancers who triumph in the arena here: intelligence and character have fallen victim to speed. Their skulls are narrow, with truncated foreheads; their muscles ripple nervously under the skin. In a long chase, they run their quarry down, indefatigable, as if a spring were uncoiling inside them.

Often the gazelle could escape if it were not brought to bay by the hawk. The sparrow hawk is unhooded and tossed aloft; the hounds and, behind them, the mounted sportsmen follow its flight, which guides them to the game.

This hunt across vast areas covered only with halfa grass offers a grand spectacle; the world becomes simpler while the tension grows. This is one of the best gifts that the Condor offers his guests; he himself enjoys it festively, and a verse from the edge of the desert seems tailored to him:

> A good hawk, a swift hound, a noble steed
> Are worth far more than twenty women indeed.

Needless to say, falconry, with all the ins and outs of bagging, bearing, and taming, is held in high esteem. Peregrines and sakers are caught in clap nets throughout the land; others, including snow-white creatures come from the far North. Every year, the Yellow Khan, his most stellar hunting guest, brings them as presents for the Condor.

Falconry is practiced through ample areas on the banks of the Sus. The riverside location is favorable for the training. Countless water birds nest in the lowland forests; they gather to fish on the inundated sand banks. The heron is the most suitable bird for training hawks to hunt wildfowl. Other breeds of dogs are also necessary: long-eared spaniels, which like going into water; their fur has white spots allowing the marksman to recognize them in the reeds.

The chief falconer is Rosner, who obtained a degree in zoology and then, out of passion, turned to hunting. And he did the right thing, for while any number of professors can be found in Eumeswil, such an extraordinary falconer is a windfall.

But he is also a professor. I frequently see him in the Casbah and at his institute and occasionally run into him during solitary strolls in the hunting area. Once, during the migration of the peregrines, I accompanied him to one of his blinds. There, where the steppe borders on a towering clump of broom bushes, the fowler hid in their shade. A dove on a long string served as decoy. Whenever a hawk approached, Rosner jerked the string, making the dove fly up. Once it was grabbed and held by the predator, the two birds could be pulled effortlessly to a ring through which the thread ran and where the clap net dropped.

The process was thrilling as a model of intelligent snaring. There were circumstances that exceeded the boundaries of human sight and seemed almost magical. Thus, the dove must soar up at the passing of a hawk that eludes even the sharpest human eye. For this purpose the falconer uses as his lookout a dappled, thrush-sized bird, which he ties up near the dove; not quite recognizing the sparrow hawk at an incredible distance, the bird more likely senses it. Then it warns with a shattering shriek.

This hunt has a magical impact, for it seems to feather the world. In the bewitchment, the hunters become one with their prey; they alight in their wiles. It was not just the dark trapper, who had dedicated his life to this activity; the scholarly ornithologist likewise turned into a Papageno and took part as a somnambular dancer. I myself was overcome with the deep and rapid breathing of passion.

It should, however, be noted that I am no hunter—indeed, despite my last name, I find hunting repulsive. Perhaps all of us are born to be fishers and fowlers and killing is our mission. Fine, then I have transformed this desire. During a heron hunt, I feel for the victim rather than for the hawk that kills it. Over and over, the heron keeps trying to gain altitude, and over and over, it keeps getting outsoared, until at last its plumage flies.

The gazelle is one of the tenderest of creatures: pregnant women like to keep them at hand, their eyes are celebrated by the poets. I saw the eyes of the gazelle break at the end of the chase while the hawk fluttered in the dust and the hounds panted. Hunters delight especially in killing beauty.

*

However, we are talking about the Condor and his day vision and not the eyes of the gazelle. Still, I will have to deal with hunting again, and in various dimensions at that, but qua observer and not qua hunter. Hunting is a regale, a prerogative of rulers; it captures the essence of rulership, not just symbolically but also ritually, through the spilled blood on which the sun shines.

*

My job involves taking a greater part in the Condor's night side. One then sees bespectacled palefaces, often as if they were gathering in an owl's nest—professors, literati, masters of unprofitable arts, sheer hedonists who contribute to comfort and coziness. Acumen has now shifted to the ear. Allusions lie not in the words but in the sounds alone, or even in the mimicry—at such moments, I have to prick up my ears. Other topics, chiefly artistic ones, are debated, and the hunt, it seems, only in a strangely enciphered manner. This must be observed.

The room is quite noiseproof; it is my job to attune the sounds. At such times, the Condor finds loud and harsh speech repulsive, even painful. That is why he has given nicknames to some of the regular convives and officials, making sure that these new cognomens form an overall euphony. Attila, say, his physician, who barely leaves his side, is called "Aldy." Should the Condor wish to have me perform some service for Attila, he says, "Emanuelo—Aldy"; that sounds smooth.

When I, like anyone having business in his proximity, was introduced to the Condor, he picked out his name for me. "Manuel, Manuelo, Emanuelo"—depending on the phonetic context. His way of distinguishing and modulating deepens the effect when he addresses people. In the agora, the how is even more important than the what, the delivery more powerful than the facts that it can alter, indeed create.

"Currying favor": that, too, is an art. This idiom was presumably coined by someone resembling the fox with the grapes. However, once the currier has joined the cabinet, things change. The crowd, like a beloved, joyfully recognizes the lord and master after admitting him into the tiny chamber.

*

I was presented in my service garb, a snug-fitting, blue-striped linen suit, which is changed daily since no underwear is worn. Plus babouches of yellow Safian leather. Their soft soles are comfortable and noiseless when I move behind the bar, where there is no carpet. Finally, the ludicrous cap, a small skiff that perches at a slant. The whole outfit is something between an official uniform and a jaunty getup; my appearance is supposed to combine assiduity with cheerfulness.

At the presentation, the Condor, in order to check my haircut, removed my skiff. While so doing, he punned on my name, but I have forgotten the exact wording. The gist of it was that he considered it possible and to be hoped for that some day *Venator* would become a *senator*.

*

One has to mull over the words of the powerful. The Condor's were open to various readings. In terms of the substance, he may have wanted to indicate the importance of my job. Of course, considering the ranks and honors to which some of his minions have risen—and why not?—they would not be so pernickety with a night steward. After all, Sixtus IV made his ephebes cardinals.

However, the Condor may have meant it more personally. The positive attitude of the Venators, at least of my father and brother, toward the tribunes is well known in Eumeswil. While neither was politically active, both have always been republicans out of conviction and inclination. The old man still has his position; my brother was removed from his because of impertinent remarks. Perhaps the allusion to a senator was meant to imply that my family should not rub off on me.

Manuelo: this establishes a kind of godparenthood. At the same time, I received the phonophore with the narrow silver stripe, which identifies a post that is subaltern but within the tyrant's immediate entourage.

3

So much for my name and its variants. I also ought to go into detail about my profession. While it is correct to say that I am employed as night steward in the Casbah, my job fills only certain gaps in my life. This can, no doubt, be inferred from my diction. It might prompt an attentive reader to surmise that I am basically a historian.

A penchant for history and a vocation for historiography are hereditary in my lineage; this aptitude is based less on professional tradition than on genetic makeup. I need only cite my famous forebear Josiah Venator, whose magnum opus, *Philip and Alexander*, has long enjoyed prestige as a seminal contribution to the theory of social milieu. His tome has gone through numerous editions and was just recently republished here. Its preference for hereditary monarchy is undeniable; hence, Eumeswil's historians and specialists in public law do not praise it unabashedly. Of course, the glory of Alexander the Great is supposed to reflect on the Condor as well, but his genius, like the phoenix, allegedly rose from the ashes.

There are different reasons why my father and my brother—typical liberals—deal gingerly with Josiah. First of all, and this is understandable, they are perturbed by the way their ancestor is customized to fit current politics. Furthermore, an outstanding personality makes them squirm. Alexander strikes them as an elemental phenomenon, a lightning bolt that is sufficiently explained by the electrical charge between Europe and Asia. There are bizarre congruences between liberal and heroic historiography.

*

Thus, for generations now we have been producing historians. By way of exception, a theologian may come to the fore or else a bohemian whose trail vanishes in obscurity. As for me, I managed to obtain my master's degree in a normal way, I was Vigo's assistant, and now, as his right arm, I deal with collaborative and also personal works. Moreover, I lecture and supervise the doctoral candidates.

This may take a few more years; I am in no hurry to obtain tenure or become senator because I feel just fine. Aside from occasional depressions, I am well balanced. So one can comfortably let time pass—time itself provides enjoyment. Therein, presumably, lies the secret of tobacco—indeed, of any lighter drug.

*

I can work on my topics at home or in Vigo's institute, or even in the Casbah, which I prefer because of its unsurpassable array of documents. I live here in the lap of luxury, and I would not be drawn to the city if the Condor tolerated women in the stronghold. They are not to be found even in the kitchen, nor can any laundress, with whom one might have same discreet dalliance, get past the guards; there are no exceptions. The married men have their families in the city. The Condor feels that the presence of women, whether young or old, would only promote intrigue. Still, it is hard to reconcile the rich diet and leisurely life-style with asceticism.

*

My father did not like my studying under Vigo rather than under him, as my brother had done. But from our mealtime conversations I know what the old man has to offer, and besides, I regard Vigo as a far better historian. My genitor carps at him for being unscholarly, even journalistic; he thereby overlooks the true root of Vigo's strength. What does genius have to do with scholarship?

Now I am not denying that the historian must rely on facts. But Vigo cannot be accused of neglecting them. We dwell here on a sheltered lagoon, where enormous masses of flotsam and jetsam from shipwrecks have been washed ashore. We know better than earlier generations anything that has ever happened anywhere on our planet. The material is stored in Vigo's mind down to the nicest details; he knows the facts, and he is able to teach his disciples how to evaluate them. In this respect, too, I have learned a lot from him.

*

If the past has thereby been brought down to the present and re-erected like the ramparts of cities whose very names are forgotten, then we may say that decent work has been done.

But Vigo, it must be pointed out, does not spirit anything into history. Rather, he leaves the ultimate questions open by presenting the questionable nature of events. When we look back, our eyes alight on graves and ruins, on a field of rubble. We are then inveigled by a mirage of time: while believing that we are advancing and progressing, we are actually moving toward that past. Soon we will belong to it: time passes over us. And this sorrow overshadows the historian. As a researcher, he is nothing more than a burrower in parchments and graves; but then he asks the fateful question, with the skull on his palm. Vigo's basic mood is well-founded sorrow; it appealed to my conviction that the world is imperfect.

*

Vigo has a special method of cross-cutting through the past—that is, going nonchronologically. His is not so much the hunter's eye as the gardener's or botanist's. Thus he views our kinship with the plants as deeper than that with the animals, and he feels that at night we return to the woods, indeed all the way to the algae in the ocean.

Among the animals, he says, the bees have rediscovered this kinship. Their mating with the flowers is neither a forward nor a backward step in evolution, it is a kind of supernova, a flashing of cosmogonic eros in a favorable conjunction. Even the boldest thinking has not yet hit on that, he says; the only things that are real are those that cannot be invented.

Does he expect something similar in the human realm?

*

As in every organically evolved work, his, too, contains more that is tacit than formulated. His reckoning has an unknown quantity; this places him in a predicament vis-à-vis people for whom everything works out evenly, including his students.

I clearly remember the day that brought me close to him: it was after a lecture. The topic was "Plant Cities"; the course went on for two semesters. He compared the scattering of cultures over land and sea, over coasts, archipelagoes, and oases, to the flight of seeds or the washing-up of fruits along tidemarks.

When lecturing, Vigo usually holds up or simply clutches small objects—not as proof, but as vessels of a substance related to his topic: sometimes just a shard or a tiny fragment of brick. That morning, it was a faience plate with an arabesque motif of blossoms and handwriting. He pointed to the colors: a faded pattern of saffron, rose, and violet, and above it a shimmer created not by the glazing or the brush, but by time. Such are the dreams of glasses that were salvaged from Roman debris, or even tile roofs of hermitages that blazed and blazed during a thousand summers.

Vigo had arrived here by a tortuous path: he had started out from the coast of Asia Minor, which is so favorable to such a rooting in new soil. This had been demonstrated by the Phoenicians, the Greeks, by the Templars, the Venetians, and others.

He has a preference for mercantile societies. Early on, they had blazed trails through deserts and oceans: for salt, amber, pewter, and silk, and later for tea and spices. In Crete and Rhodes, in Florence and Venice, in Lusitanian and Netherlandish harbors, the treasures had accumulated like honey in combs. These treasures were transmuted into higher standards of living, into blisses, buildings, and artworks. The gold embodied the sun; its hoarding enabled the arts to unfold and blossom. A touch of decay, of autumnal surfeit had to be added. And Vigo held the plate on his hand as if awaiting alms.

How had he hit on Damascus and then the leap to Spain, through which Abd-ur Rahman had escaped being murdered? For almost three centuries, a branch of the Omayyads, who had been exterminated in Syria, flourished in Córdoba. Along with mosques, the faiences testified to this branch of Arabic civilization, a branch long since withered. And then there were the castles of the Beni Taher in Yemen. A seed fell into the desert sand, managing to yield four harvests.

The fifth Omayyad, an ancestor of Abd-ur Rahman, had dispatched Emir Musa to the brass city. The caravan traveled from Damascus through Cairo and the great desert, into the western lands, and all the way to the coast of Mauretania. The goal was the copper flasks in which King Solomon had jailed rebellious demons. Now and again, the fishermen who cast their nets in the El-Karkar Sea would haul up one of these flasks in their catches. They were closed with the seal of Solomon; when they were opened, the demon spurted forth as smoke that darkened the sky.

Emirs named Musa also recur subsequently in Granada and other residences of Moorish Spain. This emir, the conqueror of Northwest Africa, may be regarded as their prototype. His Western features are unmistakable; of course, we must bear in mind that the distinctions between races and regions vanish on the peaks. Just as people resemble one another ethically, indeed become almost identical, when approaching perfection, so too spiritually. The distance from the world and from the object increases; curiosity grows and with it the desire to get closer to the ultimate secrets, even amid great danger. This is an Aristotelian trait. One that makes use of arithmetic.

It has not come down to us whether the emir felt any qualms about opening the flasks. From other accounts, we know that his step was risky. For instance, one of the imprisoned demons had sworn to himself that he would make the man who freed him the most powerful of mortals; he had spent hundreds of years thinking about how to make him happy. But then the demon's mood had soured; gall and venom had concentrated in his dungeon. When a fisherman finally opened the flask centuries later, he would have suffered the fate of being ripped to shreds by the demon had he not resorted to a trick. Evil becomes all the more dreadful the longer it is deprived of air.

In any case, Musa, needless to say, could not have recoiled from the unsealing. This is already evidenced by the uncommon boldness of his expedition through the wastelands. The aged Abd-es Samad, who possessed *The Book of Hidden Treasures* and could read the stars, guided the caravan to the brass city within fourteen months. They rested in deserted castles and amid the graves in decaying cemeteries. At times, they found water in wells that Iskander had dug while trekking westward.

The brass city was likewise dead and was enclosed by a ring wall; it took another two moons for blacksmiths and carpenters to build a ladder all the way to the battlements. Anyone who climbed up was blinded by a spell, so that he clapped his hands, and crying "Thou art beautiful!" plunged down. Twelve of Musa's companions perished, one after another, until at last Abd-es Samad succeeded in resisting the witchcraft by incessantly calling out Allah's name while clambering up and, after he reached the top, reciting the verses of salvation. Under the mirage as under a watery surface, he saw the shattered bodies of his predecessors. Said Musa: "If that's how a rational man acts, what will a madman do?"

The sheik then descended through one of the turrets and, from the inside, opened the gates of the necropolis. However, it was not these adventures—although they have their secret meaning—that prompts the mention of Emir Musa; rather it was his encounter with the historical world, which becomes a phantasm vis-à-vis the reality of the fairy tale.

The emir had the poet Thâlib read aloud the inscriptions on the monuments and on the walls of the deserted palaces:

> Ah, where are they whose strength has built all these
> With unbelievably lofty balconies?
> Where are the Persian shahs in castles tall?
> They left their land—it did forget them all!
> Where are the men who ruled the vast countries,
> Sind and Hind, the proud hosts of dynasties?
> To whom Sendge and Habesh did bend their will
> And Nubia when it was rebellious still?
> Await no tiding now from any tomb,
> No knowledge is forthcoming from its womb.
> The times changed, weaving death from every loom;
> The citadels they built brought naught but doom.

These verses filled Musa with such profound sorrow that life became a burden for him. As they wandered through the rooms, they came to a table carved out of yellow marble or, according to other reports, cast in Chinese steel. There, the following words were notched in Arabic letters:

> At this table, a thousand kings have dined whose right eyes were blind and a thousand others whose left eyes were blind: they have all passed on and now they populate the graves and catacombs.

When Thâlib read these words aloud to him, everything went dark before Musa's eyes; he shrieked and rent his garment. Then he had the verses and inscriptions copied down.

*

Seldom has the historian's pain been captured so vehemently. It is the human pain that was felt long before any scholarship, accompanying man ever since he dug the first graves. Anyone who writes history would like to preserve the names and their meanings, indeed rediscover the names of cities and nations that are long forgotten. It is like placing flowers on a grave:

> Ye dead and also ye nameless—princes and warriors, slaves and evildoers, saints and whores, do not be mournful: ye are remembered lovingly.

But this thinking, too, is limited by time, to which it succumbs; every monument weathers away, and the wreath is cremated along with the corpse. Why is it that we nevertheless refuse to give up this ritual? We could make do with Omar the Tent Maker, join him in drinking the wine of Shiraz down to the dregs and then tossing away the earthen beaker: dust to dust.

Will ever any custodian open their graves, any cockcrow wake them to the light? It must be thus, and the historian's sorrow, his torment are among the indications. He sits in judgment over the dead when the merrymaking that roared around the powerful has long since hushed, when their triumphs and their victims, their grandeur and their infamy are forgotten.

And yet only an indication. The torment, the anxiety of the historical human being, his tireless labor with imperfect means in an ephemeral world—this could not be felt, could not be achieved without a directive to create this indication. The loss of perfection can be felt only if perfection exists. This is the goal of the indication, of the trembling of the quill in the hand. The compass needle quivers because a pole exists. In its atoms, the needle is kin to the pole.

As the word is weighed by the poet, so, too, must the deed be weighed by the historian—beyond good and evil, beyond any conceivable ethics. As the muses are evoked by the poem, so, too, must the Norns be evoked here; they appear in front of the table. Now the room grows still; the graves open up.

Here, too, there are grave robbers who, for the sake of the market, falsify poems and deeds; so it is better to carouse with Omar Khayyám than to join them in violating the dead.

4

At this point, there was a scraping of feet in the auditorium. I could already half-hear it from the corridor, for I had softly opened the door in order to leave. Afterwards, in the library, Vigo asked me about it:

"So, did you also find what you were hearing too antiquated?"

I shook my head. On the contrary, the lecture had moved me too deeply; it stirred my own preoccupation, my own torment. I do not know whether I have sketched it correctly. Vigo has an enormous supply of images, which he weaves into his speech as though plucking them out of thin air. They envelop his train of thought without disturbing it, thereby recalling trees that bear their blossoms directly on their trunks.

I contented myself, as I have mentioned, with shaking my head; it is better, especially among men, for emotions to be guessed rather than verbalized. I sensed that he understood me. This was the moment that established out friendship.

Evidently, my fellow students had not noticed what had seized hold of me. This happens when a circuit closes between two human beings. They had laughed at certain points—for instance, upon hearing the word "moons." They are quick to laugh; it makes them feel superior.

They regarded "moons," like all of Vigo's lecture, as antiquated. For them, timeliness is of the essence. No doubt they had failed to realize that Vigo was quoting from an old text based on Galland's translation of *The Thousand and One Nights.* Aside from that, "moons" is, of course, phonetically, grammatically, logically preferable to "months." "Moons" is now tainted because trivial writers have flogged it to death. I would therefore avoid using it. Vigo is above such qualms; he could restore the prestige of language. In any other time but ours, when people no longer take one another seriously, his true rank would have been recognized despite some crotchets.

While strict and unyielding about facts, he is personally quite sensitive. Naturally, he could say anything in any way, even the grossest drivel, if he were "with it." But his substance prevents him; it forces him to be honest. He could not, even if willingly, twist the facts to his advantage.

Whenever a highly cultured man has harmonized with the Zeitgeist, it has always been a happy fluke, a rare exception. Nowadays one had best stick with the ancient sage:

> To keep from falling victim to a thief,
> Conceal thy gold, thine absence, thy belief.

This is practiced even by the rulers: they don the little smocks-of-all-trades. The Condor, though able to take all sorts of liberties, is likewise cautious; a night steward can judge this.

*

A teacher does best, as things stand, to limit himself to the natural sciences and the realm of their practical applications. In anything that goes further—say, literature, philosophy, history—he is on thin ice, particularly if he is suspected of having a "metaphysical background."

These are the suspicions with which two sorts of faculty members operate here: they are either crooks disguised as professors or professors posing as crooks in order to gain popularity. They try to outdo one another in the race for infamy, yet there is honor among thieves. Still, should a genius like Vigo wander into their circle, he is treated like a magpie; they close ranks against the intruder. It is bizarre the way they band together as if threatened with annihilation.

The students, though basically good-natured, get their watchwords from these teachers. I do not wish to go into *quisquiliae*. In the analysis of history, two main perspectives crystallize, one of which is directed at men, the other at might. This also corresponds to a rhythm in politics. Monarchies, oligarchies, dictatorships, tyranny as opposed to democracies, republics, the *okhlos*, anarchy. The captain as opposed to the crew; the great leader as opposed to the collective. For insiders, needless to say, these antitheses are necessary yet also illusory; they are motives serving to wind up the clock of history. Only seldom does a Great Noon shine, making the antitheses dissolve in happiness.

*

After the Condor's triumph over the tribunes, "men" are once again held in high esteem here. In this respect, the Condor himself acts more liberal than the professors, who try to fawn on him at any price: the younger ones out of sheer stupidity, the older ones (who taught during the Tribunate) out of well-founded prudence.

One can do studies here as in a waxworks. For example: a young lecturer is presented with a theory that is alien to him, perhaps even unpleasant. Fashion compels him to deal with it. He is won over—we could not object, though his conversion per se is not quite decent. But then he starts behaving like an adolescent who fails to distinguish between when to enthuse and when to think. He takes on authoritarian and soon also dangerous characteristics. The university is filled with such half-wits, who poke their noses everywhere and make mischief giving off a repulsive stable stench whenever they get together. Once they hold the reins, these lecturers ignorant of what power is about, lose all sense of moderation. Eventually, the army boot arrives.

At present, they are held in check by the Condor and his majordomo and so they limit their hunting to victims whom they believe to be in disrepute. Vigo is one such target. Since "men are making history" again, his preferences—say, for merchants who hire soldiers—are considered decadent. But those people fail to see that his ideal is cultural achievement. Thus, the Carthaginians, although they, too, had mercenaries do their fighting, are not to his taste. Basically, it is beauty that he serves. Power and riches should be its thralls. Perhaps in this respect he is more closely related to the Condor—or at least his night side—than he realizes.

*

Vigo, being, as I have said, sensitive, takes this professorial infighting tragically, although it is no threat to his safety. To be sure, extremely importunate persecutorial types thrive in our putrid lagoon. "Each student is a viper nursed in the bosom," Vigo once said to me in a gloomy moment when speaking about Barbassoro, who, granted, belongs more to the species of purebred rats.

The purebred rat is highly intelligent, obliging, hard working, flexible, and endowed with subtle empathy. This is the luster of its life, predestining it as a teacher's pet. Unfortunately (and this is inherent in its nature), it cannot resist the lure of the pack. It hears the whistle—and even if the prey is the venerated master himself, the rat joins the throng that pounces on him. The rat is especially dangerous because of its knowledge and the intimate wisdom it has gained by associating with the master. It becomes the lead rat.

*

Vigo's critique of the Zeitgeist is so intricately encoded as to be virtually indecipherable. By the way, "critique" is not quite accurate. Rather, it is his character that is considered almost opaque. If everyone is moving, and in the same direction at that—whether right or left, whether up or down—the stationary person is in the way. He is taken as a reproach, and since people collide with him, they brand him as the offender.

Motion seeks to transform facts into opinion, then into conviction; and anyone hewing to the facts themselves is shown, against his will, in an adverse light. This is quite possible in a faculty where after every overthrow; world history is to be rewritten for the sake of the moment. Textbooks wear out, they no longer grow obsolete.

To make someone with Vigo's mind vulnerable requires a certain intelligence. His sheer existence is felt as an immediate nuisance. The blockheads have an unerring instinct for such things. All they need do is prove that this nuisance is insignificant and yet also dangerous. Such evidence is presented by scholars of Kessmüller's ilk. These are the truffle pigs that grub up the delicacy. Then the rats pounce upon it.

*

Kessmüller, a bald-headed homosexual, has studied Vigo thoroughly. Kessmüller's ideas are as nonexistent as his hair; he is a bon vivant and a gourmet, and has a sense of humor. As a Eumenist, he is "above suspicion": he could also earn his money as a master of ceremonies at the Calamaretto and he plays the entertainer at academic soirees. His talent has gotten him through various, even antithetical, regimes as a king-of-the-herrings, which shines on the surface. He has an instinct for conformity and for irresistible platitudes, which he stylizes in a high-brow manner. He can also reinterpret them, depending on which way the wind is blowing. A hedonist; materially, he feels more at home with the Condor; materialistically, with the tribunes.

In his lectures, he seldom neglects to quote Vigo, whereby his face is voluptuously transfigured. A good comic appeals by his very appearance—by the comical per se. Kessmüller can transform himself like a chameleon, slipping out of the pedagogue's costume into the Pantaloon's with no other transition than a brief silence. It is as if he were performing at a Mardi Gras. An expectant mood spreads through the auditorium before he so much as opens his mouth. A few of the students can barely choke back their mirth.

I attended his course if only to study this sleight of hand; oddly enough, he scarcely twists his face. The audience laughs; one is reminded of telepathy. Kessmüller is an orator who knows the secret of pauses.

Then he begins to quote Vigo—a sentence or even a paragraph—from memory. Sometimes he acts as if he has just had a brainstorm; he pulls out a book to read aloud, which then sounds—to use the apothecary's term—"casually compounded," but is actually well prepared. He moves his finger to and fro, apparently seeking the passage which he has carefully marked. Vigo's name is not mentioned, but everyone in the auditorium knows what's what.

The excerpts, though wrenched out of context, are presented verbatim. Kessmüller is aware of his responsibility to scholarship. Nor does he act as if he were quoting from a comical text; at most, words like "moons" are stressed pleasurably. He also likes emphasizing "high" and "higher" in this fashion, and "beautiful," like a clown putting on a red nose.

This borders on persiflage, which ranges from slight parody to crude nastiness. Kessmüller cultivates it as an art. Nor is it a coincidence that he extracts passages from Vigo's texts that I particularly love. At a cabaret by the wharves, there is a lampooner who recites poems farcically as if they were being yiddled by Rabbi Teiteles or squeezed out by someone sitting on a toilet. He chooses classical texts, twisting his mouth like Kessmüller. Oddly enough, the listeners seem familiar with the poems; they must have learned them at school, otherwise there would be no cause for merriment.

*

I owe to Vigo one of the geological findings in Eumeswil: fellah-like swamping on an Alexandrian foundation. The substratum was Alexandrian knowledge on a classical foundation.

Thus, values keep growing more and more shallow. First they were present, then still respected, and finally annoying. For Kessmüller, the very word "value" is suspect.

Before our times, they still had an afterglow. But the stove is cold; it no longer even warms the hands. No salvation comes from exhumed gods; we must penetrate deeper into substance. If I take a fossil, say, a trilobite, in my hand (marvelously preserved specimens are found in the quarries at the foot of the Casbah), I am transfixed by the impact of mathematical harmony. Purpose and beauty, as fresh as on the first day, are still seamlessly united in a medal engraved by a master's hand. The bios must have discovered the secret of tripartition in this primordial crab. Tripartition then frequently recurs, even without any natural kinship; figures, in transversal symmetry, dwell in the triptych.

How many millions of years ago might this creature have animated an ocean that no longer exists? I hold its impression, a seal of imperishable beauty, in my hand. Some day, this seal, too, will decay or else burn out in cosmic conflagrations of the future. The matrix that formed it remains concealed in and operative from the law, untouched by death or fire.

I feel my hand warming. If the creature were still alive, it would perceive my warmth like the cat whose fur I stroke. But not even the stone into which it was transformed can escape this; the molecules expand. A bit further, a bit more strongly: it would stir in my hand as in a daydream.

I cannot vault the barrier, but I sense that I am on the right path.

5

This harassment was repulsive, but Vigo overly dignified it by letting it get to him. Sometimes, when I ran into him at the library or dropped by in his garden, I found him pale and shunning the light, like an owl hiding in a hollow. If it ventures out into the light, the crows will pounce upon it. I tried to raise his spirits by highlighting his prowess and his mission. I did not lack for arguments.

Vigo must have realized—and also knew from his eminent command of history—that this sort of cheap persecution underscored the opponent's weakness and Vigo's strength. His freedom is a rebuke, a thorn in the flesh of these half-cadavers, who therefore never tire of dealing with him even though he is devoid of any aggressivity. He did not endorse the Tribunes, nor does he now support the Condor; he is irked by both. He will not fall in with any regime. Forms of government, for him, are like thin skins that keep scaling incessantly. The State as such, independent of metamorphoses, nay, bringing them about, is a great entity, a criterion for him.

He favors certain polities without committing himself to any, especially a current one; in contrast, he is fascinated by the way they replace each other out of the substance of history. Men and powers have followed one another as if the world's spirit has gotten fed up with each in turn after exhausting it, always unsatisfactorily. Here, doctrines, ideas, ideals; there, more or less clearly defined individuals. Highly advanced civilization—a lull as if the will were fading—has always been possible, both here and there: cosmetic beauty broke through the structure, above all before it hardened or after it developed cracks. Both the overture and the finale concentrate the motif.

The second possibility appears to stimulate Vigo more strongly because the gods are no longer so powerful. Their variety, and that of the states, are more advantageous. Here, the palette; there, monotony. The Romans are exemplary for the state, the Greeks for civilization. Rome had the Colosseum; Greece, the Parthenon.

"Why do you want to impress Kessmüller, much less debate with him? It will only provide him with material for his comedy."

The Domo's materialism is realistic, that of his predecessors was rationalistic. Both are superficial, meant for political use. Hairsplitters could get more under the tribunes; that was why Kessmüller harmonized with them more easily.

However, his deft contortions in adjusting to the Condor are notable. My brother and my genitor were less successful. This touches upon the distinction between the threadbare liberal and the shallow doctrinarian who lives on promises. Everything becomes evolution, progress turns into the earthly paradise. It can be extended ad infinitum.

"You should also regard such figures as temple custodians, whose grimaces at least keep the worst blockheads away from you. Would you like this smug complacency to spread through your courses, too? Such minds have to be sought in the places of their belief, among their gods. That is where a rouged workaday routine and the clay feet become obvious."

Vigo—like my genitor, incidentally—presumes that people still venerate objective knowledge. But how can that be, amid the universal loss of respect? He still lives in times when a theater, a parade, a bestowal of honor, an act of parliament, even a lecture, could be a celebration—how would this be possible without a delight in celebrations? Then there is Vigo's pedagogical passion, which is utterly lacking in me even though presumably I, too, will someday become a full professor.

Not that I do not consider myself capable of that. I could afford to be tenured, like a man who becomes a general because that has been customary in his family since time immemorial. He possesses the required technique, he knows how to train troops, he has the hang of it. That is why he can occupy that rank in any regime, even completely antithetical ones, and why he suddenly shows up on the enemy side, as is virtually the rule among revolutionary generals. His passion remains untouched—as was the case with Jomini, who, in the thick of battle, cried out: "Damn it all, now I wish I were commanding on the other side: what a festival that would be!" The same goes for the historian. The less committed he is, the less biased his judgment; Eumeswil is good soil for that.

A man who knows his craft is appreciated anywhere and anytime. This is also one of the means of survival for the aristocrat, whose diplomatic instinct is almost irreplaceable. I must thrash this out with Ingrid for her postdoctoral dissertation, after one of our Icelandic embraces.

*

The vaguer the substratum on which he moves, the stronger the expert. No more bonds, no more biases; the power rises from the base to the exponents. The man with the least amount of ethical and ethnic baggage is the matador of quick spins and chameleon-like transformations.

The great spy is the one who embodies this most purely; this is no coincidence. With every master spy, a counterspy, too, is born; this lies deeper than race, class, or country. One senses it and also expresses it wherever things are still halfway intact—Schwarzkoppen viewed Esterhazy only through his monocle, and Prince Urusov refused to shake Azev's hand.

*

Inner neutrality. A man is involved wherever and for as long as he likes. When the bus is no longer comfortable, he gets out. Jomini, if I am not mistaken, was Swiss, a condottiere as in the Renaissance, a high-level mercenary. I intend to pinpoint the details at the luminar or ask Ingrid to do so.

A general is a specialist insofar as he has mastered his craft. Beyond that and outside the arbitrary pro and con, he keeps a third possibility intact and in reserve: his own substance. He knows more than what he embodies and teaches, has other skills along with the ones for which he is paid. He keeps all that to himself; it is his property. It is set aside for his leisure, his soliloquies, his nights. At a propitious moment, he will put it into action, tear off his mask. So far, he has been racing well; within sight of the finish line, his final reserves start pouring in. Fate challenges him; he responds. The dream, even in an erotic encounter, comes true. But casually, even here; every goal is a transition for him. The bow should snap rather than aiming the arrow at a finite target.

"General" stands here for the individual who goes into action, whether freely or forcedly. Since anarchy offers him an especially favorable charge, this type is permanent today. Thus, "general" has a universal rather than a special meaning. It can be replaced ad libitum. It refers not to a profession but to a condition. The latter may also crop up in a coolie, in which case it is particularly effective.

*

Vigo has great reserves at his disposal, but he does not deploy them correctly. He fritters them away by trying to get them across and then expects their true value to be requited. Does anyone flash money in obscure taverns? It looks suspicious, yet a tip is gratefully accepted; a pittance suffices.

He is not unaware of his own worth, but he cannot translate it into currency of the realm. A prince in the domain of the mind rummages through his pockets, looking for change.

When I became his assistant and then his friend, my chief task, as I saw it, was not in serving the luminar but in forming a circle around Vigo, a circle where not everything would be dropped—a small group worthy of him.

He who seeks shall find; nor does Eumeswil lack spiritually homesick people, if only one in a hundred or in a thousand. Three, five, or seven students were enough for an afternoon in the garden or an evening symposium, at which Vigo felt fine. Ingrid, who took over my job, also joined in.

We attempted to keep these things a secret—invitations to tea, to an outing, a chance encounter among the graves, not even thought of as a private tutorial. Nevertheless, the rumors could not be avoided, as always when a few people cut themselves off. I was approached by individuals who were curious or else eager for knowledge, so I could pick and choose.

*

There were hours when the portals of history were flung wide, the tombs opened up. The dead came with their sufferings, their delights, the sum of which always remains the same. They were conjured up to the light of the sun, which shone on them as on us. A ray struck their foreheads; I felt its warmth as if the trilobite were stirring in my hand. We were allowed to share their hope; it was the eternally dashed hope that is handed down from generation to generation. They sat among us; often friend and foe were barely distinguishable, we could thrash out their quarrels. We became their advocates. And each one was in the right.

We shook hands; they were empty. But we passed it on: the wealth of the world.

*

We were sitting together in the garden—it was late; the full moon loomed behind the Casbah, which sliced into its disk like a signet. The dome and the minaret were sharply inscribed. Now and then, one of us would leave the circle for a breath of air, as I did after the lecture on Emir Musa and the brass city.

At last, it seemed to overcome even Vigo—not exhaustion, for his face was aglow; he rose to his feet: "Children, let me be alone."

6

Until now I've spoken about my name and profession. I now ought to go into detail about my political reliability. It is indisputable; how else could I be employed in the Condor's innermost circle—within his reach? I carry the phonophore with the silver stripe.

Naturally I was probed and grilled, picked out and sieved out. While I have little regard for psychologists, indeed for technology in toto, I must admit that they know their business. They are cunning fellows who never fail to catch anyone with oblique ideas, much less oblique intentions.

They start out in a comfortable, leisurely fashion after the physicians have scrutinized the candidate's *physis* and the police his background; this investigation goes all the way back to his grandfathers. While the psychologists chat with him over a cup of tea, others listen to his voice, observe his gestures, his face. You grow chummy, you come out of your shell. Your reactions are registered imperceptibly: your heartbeat, your blood pressure, the shock with its pause after a name or a question. Furthermore they have psychometers—that old Reichenbach would have envied, they develop pictures on which yellow or violet auras radiate from the forehead, the hair, the fingertips. The borderline areas that were metaphysical for the ancient philosophers are parapsychological for them—and they find it praiseworthy to get at them with numbers and measurements. Needless to say, they also resort to drugs and hypnosis. A droplet in the tea, which they also sip, a speck of pollen—and we are no longer in Eumeswil but in the mountains of Mexico.

Should friendly neighbors, say, from Cappadocia or Mauretania, smuggle in an agent or even an assassin, he would be exposed within three days. Far more dangerous are the wily emissaries of the Yellow Khan and the Blue Khan; there is no way to prevent them from settling at the harbor or in the city, haunting those places until they eventually make a careless error. But they never penetrate the interior of the Casbah.

*

My case did not cause the committee any headaches; there was no problem. I am, if I say so myself, anything but oblique, I am as straight as an arrow: going neither right nor left, neither up nor down, neither east nor west; I am perfectly balanced. Granted, I deal with these antitheses, but only in history, not in current events; I am not committed.

It is well known that my father and my brother sympathized with the tribunes, albeit moderately and also not without discreet criticism. That was the rule in Eumeswil; there was virtually no exception. And why should there be? After all, a baker, a composer, or a professor has more important concerns than making political waves; above all, he wants to ply his trade, practice his art, do his job without losing the best years of his life; he simply wants to survive by hook or by crook. Moreover, he is easy to replace; others are already lurking in the wings.

Aside from that, such types are also more useful to the successor than the "upright souls who remained true to the idea, holding the banner aloft," and generally merit the praise that has passed from military lingo into the jargon of civil war. They cut their finest figure in their obituaries. As survivors, they soon become unpleasant again.

The examiners know that; enthusiasm is suspect. Hence, I earned points by expressing myself objectively, as a historian, in regard to the Condor. I believe that under the influence of a hard drug, I said: "He is not a leader of the people; he is a tyrant."

They know that unconditional devotion is dangerous. A politician, an author, an actor are venerated from a distance. At last you get to meet your idol—and as a person he cannot live up to expectations. Your mood then easily swings. You have had an incredible stroke of luck, you have succeeded in gaining admission to the diva's bedroom, and disappointment is not long in coming. With clothes, divinity also drops away. Eros is strongest in the unexpected, the unforeseen.

They found no mischief in me. I remained normal, however deeply they probed. And also straight as an arrow. To be sure, normality seldom coincides with straightness. Normalcy is the human constitution; straightness is logical reasoning. With its help, I could answer satisfactorily. In contrast, the human element is at once so general and so intricately encoded that they fail to perceive it, like the air they breathe. Thus they were unable to penetrate my fundamental structure, which is anarchic.

That sounds complicated, but is simple, for everyone is anarchic; this is precisely what is normal about us. Of course, the anarchic is hemmed in from the very first day by father and mother, by state and society. Those are prunings, tappings of the primordial strength, and nobody escapes them. One has to resign oneself. But the anarchic remains, at the very bottom, as a mystery, usually unknown even to its bearer. It can erupt from him as lava, can destroy him, liberate him.

Distinctions must be drawn here: love is anarchic, marriage is not. The warrior is anarchic, the soldier is not. Manslaughter is anarchic, murder is not. Christ is anarchic, Saint Paul is not. Since, of course, the anarchic is normal, it is also present in Saint Paul, and sometimes it erupts mightily from him. Those are not antitheses but degrees. The history of the world is moved by anarchy. In sum: the free human being is anarchic, the anarchist is not.

*

If I were an anarchist and nothing further, they would have easily exposed me. They are particularly geared toward detecting anyone who tries to approach the powerful with mischievous intent, "with a dagger in his cloak." The anarch can lead a lonesome existence; the anarchist is sociable and must get together with peers.

Like any other place, Eumeswil has its share of anarchists. They are divided into two sects: the good-natured and the ill-natured. The good-natured are not dangerous: they dream of Golden Ages; Rousseau is their patron saint. The others have pledged their allegiance to Brutus: they convene in basements and garrets, and also in a back room of the Calamaretto. They huddle together like philistines drinking their beer while nurturing an indecent secrecy that is revealed by a giggle. They are listed in the police registers; when cells have to start forming and chemists get to work, they are watched more sharply. "The boil will soon burst." Those words are by the majordomo major, nicknamed "Domo" by the Condor; I retain the abbreviation. Before an assassination can take place, either arrests are made or the conspiracy is steered. Against an opposition that is gaining a foothold no weapon is more potent than blaming the group for an assassination attempt.

The anarchist's hazy idealism, his goodness without sympathy or else his sympathy without goodness, makes him serviceable in many ways and also useful for the police. He does sense a secret, but he can do no more than sense it: the tremendous strength of the individual. It intoxicates him; he spends himself like a moth burning up in a flame. The absurdity of the assassination attempt lies not in the doer and his self-assurance, but in the deed and its link with the fleeting situation. The doer has sold himself too cheaply. That is why he usually achieves the opposite of what he intends.

*

The anarchist is dependent—both on his unclear desires and on the powers that be. He trails the powerful man as his shadow; the ruler is always on his guard against him. As Charles V stood on a tower with his retinue, a captain began to laugh; when interrogated, he admitted to thinking that if he embraced the emperor and plunged down with him, his name would be forever recorded in history.

The anarchist is the antagonist of the monarch, whom he dreams of wiping out. He gets the man and consolidates the succession. The *-ism* suffix has a restrictive meaning; it emphasizes the will at the expense of the substance. I owe this note to Thofern, the grammarian, a hairsplitter par excellence.

The positive counterpart of the anarchist is the anarch. The latter is not the adversary of the monarch but his antipode, untouched by him, though also dangerous. He is not the opponent of the monarch, but his pendant.

After all, the monarch wants to rule many, nay, all people; the anarch, only himself. This gives him an attitude both objective and skeptical toward the powers that be; he has their figures go past him—and he is untouched, no doubt, yet inwardly not unmoved, not without historical passion. Every born historian is more or less an anarch; if he has greatness, then on this basis he rises without partisanship to the judge's bench.

This concerns my profession, which I take seriously. I am also the night steward in the Casbah; now, I am not saying that I take this job less seriously. Here I am directly involved in the events, I deal with the living. My anarchic principle is not detrimental to my work. Rather, it substantiates it as something I have in common with everyone else, except that I am conscious of this. I serve the Condor, who is a tyrant—that is his function, just as mine is to be his steward; both of us can retreat to substance: to human nature in its nameless condition.

*

When, in the course of my work at the luminar, I was reviewing public law, from Aristotle to Hegel and beyond, I thought of an Anglo-Saxon's axiom about human equality. He seeks it not in the ever-changing distribution of power and means, but in a constant: the fact that anyone can kill anyone else.

This is a platitude, albeit reduced to a striking formula. The possibility of killing someone else is part of the potential of the anarch whom everyone carries around inside himself, though he is seldom aware of that possibility. It always slumbers in the underground, even when two people exchange greetings in the street or avoid each other. When one stands atop a tower or in front of an oncoming train, that possibility is already drawing closer. Aside from the technological dangers, we also register the nearness of the Other. He can even be my brother. An old poet, Edgar Allan Poe, grasped this geometrically in "A Descent into the Maelstrom." In any case, we watch our backs. Then comes the thronging in the catastrophe, the raft of the Méduse, the starving in the lifeboat.

That Englishman boiled it down to a mechanistic formula. Experience with civil war contributed to it. This leads further down than Descartes. The zoological operates still beneath the human, and the law of physics operates further down. Ethics, instinct, and sheer kinetics dictate our actions. Our cells are composed of molecules and the latter of atoms.

*

I want to indicate this only insofar as it concerns my service. In any event, I brought this knowledge into the Condor's range, into the inner sanctum that Monseigneur described as his "Parvulo." I can kill him, dramatically or discreetly. His beverages—he especially loves a light red wine—ultimately pass through my hands.

Now, granted, it is unlikely that I would kill him, albeit not impossible. Who can tell what astrological conjunctions one may get involved in? So, for now, my knowledge is merely theoretical, though important insofar as it puts me on his level. Not only can I kill him; I can also grant him amnesty. This is in my hands.

Naturally, I would not try to strike him just because he is a tyrant—I am too well versed in history, especially the model that we have attained in Eumeswil. An immoderate tyrant settles his own hash. The execution can be left to the anarchists; that is all they think about. Hence, tyranny is seldom bequeathed; unlike the monarchies, it barely endures beyond the grandson. Parmenides inherited tyranny from his father "like a disease." According to Thales, the rarest thing he encountered in his travels was an old tyrant.

That is my basic attitude in performing my job, and perhaps I do so better than any number of others. I am his equal; the difference lies in the clothing and the ceremonies, which only blockheads despise; you doff your clothes only when things start getting serious.

My awareness of my equality is actually good for my work; I am free enough to perform it lightly and agreeably—as if dancing. Often it gets late, and if things have gone well, I pat myself on the back before closing the bar, like a performer whose act has succeeded.

The powerful appreciate this mood, especially at the Parvulo. The free and easy atmosphere in the space increases their enjoyment. Of course, this atmosphere must be dosed out. Needless to say, I do not imbibe, even if I am offered a drink, which happens if the Yellow Khan is our guest—at which time caution is in order.

I also let the conversation pass over me, although I follow it attentively and am often enthralled. My smile is detached; it is part of my job, but I do not join the mirth triggered by a punch line. I weave a tapestry.

I may presume that the Condor is satisfied with me. His "Good night, Manuelo," when he leaves the bar, sounds benevolent. At times he inquires about my studies. He has historical sympathies—say, with the era of the Diadochi; this is natural in Eumeswil. He also seems fascinated by the history of maritime battles; before coming to power, he briefly commanded the navy. The overthrow started with the bombardment of the city from the ocean side.

The intermezzo left him with a kind of dilettantish passion for seascapes. At the Casbah he seems to feel as if he were on a ship sailing through time. I order the beverages from the galley, stewards do the serving in the mess hall. The dome of the Casbah resembles a captain's bridge; there are no women on board.

He began his career in the infantry; his father was a corporal, a soldier of fortune. I once heard a conversation between him and the Domo, who always sits at his right. They were discussing the reliability of the troops; the prize, they said, went to the foot soldiers. Next came the cuirassiers; there was no banking on the hussars. These comparisons extended to the sailors and the aviators. The Domo, in charge of security, had obviously also pondered this issue in theoretical terms.

"The faster someone can move, the more closely he has to be watched."

7

The conversation was also theoretical in that there is scarcely such a thing as troops here. Eumeswil, with its territory and its islands, forms an oasis between the Diadochian kingdoms of the great khans and some epigonic city-states. In the north, our territory borders on the ocean; depending on my mood, I sometimes believe it is the Mediterranean and sometimes the Atlantic. Toward the south, our territory vanishes in the desert; this area is patrolled by scouting parties.

The desert is followed by steppes, tangled chaparral, jungles, which have grown even denser after the sudden bursts of fire, and finally the ocean again. There are different types of hunting in these regions. It is mainly owing to the abundance of game that the Yellow Khan keeps his hand over Eumeswil. He comes annually with a large retinue; the preparations for his visits are the most important aspect of our foreign policy.

A hunt must be staged through every zone, all the way to the big game of the steppes beyond. We also have to think up interludes, surprises for a jaded ruler with an iron constitution and an insatiable lust. "I fill the quiver with strenuousness and exhaust it with enjoyment."

*

There must be a close kinship between the chased and the chaser. The hunting masters have totem heads; the *grand louvetier*, the master of the wolf hunt, has a wolf's face. One can guess who hunts the lion, the buffalo, the boar. Not to mention the movements and the stature. I do not wish to generalize, however, for aside from correspondences, there are also complements. Thus, the Yellow Khan opens the elephant hunt by sending out dwarves, who sneak up to the animal with naked blades. On the whole, his venery is archaic, almost without powder or optical aids. Though cruel to human beings, he observes noble rules in regard to game.

The Great Hunt ends at the impenetrable southern jungle. The latter supposedly harbors species of game that have never been sighted by human eyes and that one hears about only through rumors. Most people consider them the mirages of adventurers who dared to enter the wilderness and returned with a deadly fever.

However, it appears that this is precisely where the khan dreams of crowning his venery. He hires scouts, especially those dwarves, who are unsurpassed in reading tracks; plus scholars who do not fit in at any faculty—half mythologists, half interpreters of dreams, who are derided not only by Rosner as a zoologist, but also by my genitor. He compares them to the alchemists who once offered to make gold for rulers. The simile is not bad; in either case, transmutation means the great hope, the ever-frustrated dream.

There can be no doubt that surprises lurk in the jungle; now and then, new fauna and often new flora are brought in from its outskirts. They have confirmed a number of rumors that have been treated as fables since the age of Herodotus. But that is not the point. Scholars used to believe that after the Great Floods, there were not only new species emerging but also new genera. The role of water has now been taken over by fire; blazing curtains separate the metamorphoses.

*

When I am at the luminar, skimming through tomes that were printed before the time of the great Linnaeus, I stumble upon creatures that obviously existed only in the imagination, yet were so deeply entrenched as to be depicted—say, the unicorn, the winged serpent, the satyr, the mermaid. Scholars suspected the forest, in particular, of harboring strange things, and they described them. Thus, a certain Doctor Gesner wrote about the forest demon, "a wondrous creature": a quadruped with spurred heels, a wreath of breasts, and a human head. Supposedly, he was captured in a Salzburg diocese during the year 1531 of the Christian Era, but died within days because he refused all nourishment.

This reminds me of an adventure that frightened Periander, who strikes me as sharing a number of features with the Condor. One of Periander's herders showed him a creature that he was carrying under his cloak. It had been foaled by a mare: a colt with a human head. Periander sent for Thales and asked his opinion. Thales advised him not to have the horses tended by herders—unless they were married.

Back then, the mythical age was not so remote that people were skeptical about the possibility of such births—and today in Eumeswil, knowledge has brought them close to us again. It is as if the snake were biting its own tail.

*

These notes are no quaint digression; they are directly relevant. For their sake, I have to keep an eye on Attila (who sits at the Condor's left), especially late at night: if anyone knows what goes on in the woods, it is he.

Apparently, he has also gained intimacy there with drugs and remedies. Previously he had already mastered their synthetic structure. As cupbearer, I have to deal with him when he prescribes certain admixtures for the Condor or his guests. He resorts, I notice, to wonder drugs that, being attributed to superstition, have long since vanished from the dispensaries. Thus, I have to blend certain drinks in the shell of the *coco de mer*, a palm fruit that drifts ashore in the coves of Sumatra and was once said to come from a tree that grows on the ocean floor. Others opined that the griffin carried it there. Goldsmiths would mount such a shell as a drinking vessel; it was regarded as an infallible specific against even the strongest poison.

Attila seems to believe in the virtue of the unicorn as well; this could be his totem animal. Today it is known that the twisted stern belongs not to a white horse concealed in the darkness of the woods, but to a whale in the North Sea. The stem was preserved in treasuries. When the physicians had left a dying man's bed, a pinch was shaved off this horn and served to him in a cup of wine.

The mandrake, with which I deal more often, is considered no less precious. It serves as an outright miracle drug, especially for increasing virility. Supposedly, the Yellow Khan in particular is indebted to it for herculean achievements in this area. It is a treat for *grand seigneurs*, since extensive precautions are required for finding roots of the proper size and substance. The wild plant—the only potent kind—grows sporadically in the wildernesses around Kukunor; there it is called ginseng. Anyone who knows of an occurrence keeps it a secret; he marks the spot and digs up the mandragora at the right time under a full moon.

Here in the bar, the root is kept under lock and key, for the Chinese cooks crave it the way opium eaters crave their stuff. I have a code word for the cocktail to which I add it. When the khan asks for it late at night, then the lupanars on the western periphery are in for a Mongolian storm.

8

While I was still wavering about accepting the position, it was Vigo who strongly urged me to take it.

"Martin, you will see things that will be inestimable for you."

He was referring to the observation of the manner in which power issues are weighed and played out—immediate insight into the methods as demonstrated on a practical model. A spectacle was beckoning to the historian, especially at the Parvulo.

Vigo distinguishes between the surgeon's eye and the anatomist's: The one wishes to operate, the other only delves into the condition.

The former's time is measured, while the latter has all the time in the world. Eumeswil is particularly advantageous for the historian because no living values are left. The historical material has consumed itself in passion. Ideas have become untrustworthy, and the sacrifices made for them are disconcerting.

On the other hand, images can be recognized more sharply; no wishful thinking distracts anyone. If, say, the Condor played out a life that vacillated between enlightened despotism and tyranny, he would be opening his eyes upon distant pasts. I should, Vigo told me, scrutinize this closely as an experiment and shift the accent; in standing behind the bar, I would be nearer to reality than one who, precisely by taking it seriously, merely simulates it.

I was able to follow my master that far, and so I took the job with that goal in mind. I am not saying that this was my only reason, for such decisions are complex. In addition, there was what is known as the emoluments: a lot of free time for my own work, the luminar, a good salary, the phonophore with the silver stripe, the ruler's aura.

I soon noticed that the historical view did not suffice. As an ahistorical person, one becomes freer; but the powers one served in bondage are incalculably transformed. At certain midnights when I am working at the Parvulo, the mood gets eerie. People thrash out topics that Vigo did not care to know about, much less enter into, just as I tried not to for the longest time. If the masters fall silent, the room seems more heavily charged than when they half-whisper words that they are evidently reluctant to pronounce even if they are among themselves. At such moments, the Domo waves his hand. I have to heighten the ambiance and lower the resonance.

The subject, no doubt, is the forest. It must contain trophies and perils that recall the voyage of the Argonauts rather than the heydays of historical and even prehistorical hunting.

*

When I began my job, my genitor behaved like a true liberal: on the one hand, he was embarrassed by my working as a waiter; on the other hand, he felt politically strengthened in his security. For Cadmo—that is my brother's name—I am simply the ruler's menial. The old man is a speechifier, the boy a permanent anarchist, albeit only so long as things do not get hot. Degrees of freedom in which one can commit or omit everything are alien to both men.

I stay with them when I come from the Casbah; our mealtime conversations are unpleasant. They can steer clear of neither the political nor the social. I prefer being out in Vigo's garden; I also have a pied-à-terre in the city—the attic of an old seaside house that used to be part of the bastion. From here, I could throw out a fishing line, but the fish that indolently move their fins down there fatten on the sewage of the Subura and are not sought after. Sometimes a gull rests on the windowsill. On the ground floor, a wine dealer runs a roadside shop, a *salumeria* that carries snacks.

A bare garret: the walls, internal and external, are crumbling and encrusted with sea salt. I go there in order to meditate and gaze at the ocean, all the way to the islands and beyond—especially at sunset. A table, an armchair, a mattress lying on the floor. A washbasin on a rack, beneath it the water pitcher. Plus a chamber pot that I empty through the window, since, especially after drinking, I am tired of climbing up and down the stairs. No pictures or books on the walls; instead, a mirror over the basin as a concession to Ingrid, whom I bring here after we have worked at the library or visited Vigo outside the walls. She remains barely an hour; this is a sort of obligation, a debt of gratitude to the mentor.

*

Thus, I show up at home only for meals, and not so consistently at that. Even our professional discussions are unproductive, based as they are on irreconcilable standpoints: a metahistorian who has left the space of history, conversing with people who fancy they are still rooted in it. This leads to temporal lags between our reflections: the two of them wallow in a cadaver that, so far as I am concerned, has long since petrified into a fossil. Occasionally, things turn funny—when they get worked up over values that are at best parodied in Eumeswil. To that extent, they are even to be taken seriously: as typical of the era.

*

If I like referring to the old man as my "genitor," this does not mean that I do not hold fathers in high esteem. On the contrary—except that mine does not fill the role, or at most as a ham actor pasting on a Santa Claus beard. A fisher, a day laborer, a longshoreman do a better job of it. It is curious that precisely these free spirits command respect within a hierarchy that was shattered by their grandfathers.

My genitor was married twice. Here in Eumeswil it is customary for a man on the ascent, say, a Party man, to simply take whatever he finds. Once he makes it, the first wife no longer suffices for him—she is neither young and beautiful nor presentable enough. He trades her in for a status symbol. Here, for example, in our melting pot, one recognizes this development partly in the shift toward a lighter complexion.

The man who starts out on a higher level tends to behave differently; his chief concerns are career and outer circumstances. It is only when he is firmly in place, midway through life, that other wishes burgeon in him. Now Aphrodite demands a late sacrifice. He often stumbles terribly. Recently a three-star general was trapped by a notorious hooker. In the Casbah such things are taken humorously. I was on duty at the Parvulo when the Domo reported it to the Condor. The Condor laughed: "Then he won't have any shortage of brothers-in-law!" As for the Domo, what used to be called "blots on the escutcheon" suit him just fine; he turns moralistic when necessary.

The professors tend to take a female student—one of those who sit in the front row and are enthralled by intellectual demands. This can work out nicely. For my genitor, it was his secretary; he got divorced for her sake. His first wife still lives in the city. He fathered Cadmo with her; they parted on amicable terms—now and then he visits her to refresh some memories.

My mother died young, during my early school years. I regarded the loss as a second birth, an expulsion into a brighter, colder foreign land—this time consciously.

The world was transformed by her death. The house became inhospitable, the garden bare. The flowers lost their hues, their fragrances. It turned out—not gradually but immediately—that they lacked the maternal hand. The bees no longer alighted on them, the butterflies stayed away. Flowers sense human attachment not less but more finely than animals, and they requite it with affection.

In the house, in the garden, I sought out the nooks. I often huddled on a stairway leading to the attic, a dark oubliette. I was unable to weep; there was a choking that closed up my throat.

*

Pain is like the major illnesses; once we recover, we are immune. We are vaccinated against the serpent's venom. Scar tissue does not feel the bite. A numbness has remained. At the same time, fear was reduced in me. I grasped my surroundings more sharply the more my involvement waned. I could gauge their dangers and their merits. Later, this was also beneficial to the historian. It must have been back then, as I huddled in the darkness without finding a way out, that I formed my conviction of the imperfect and peaceless nature of the world—a conviction that still haunts me. I remained a stranger in my father's house.

The pain must have worn on for a year or longer. Then it began to cool off like lava, which develops a crust one can walk on. That was the scar tissue; I grasped the rules of the society that surrounded me. I began advancing at school; the teachers started noticing me. Then came my hours at the piano.

My genitor felt more and more benevolent toward me. I could have gotten close to him, but I actually felt embarrassed when he put his arm around my shoulders or acted more familiar than necessary.

Nonetheless, I was a child of love, unlike my brother, with whom he harmonized more intellectually and who regarded himself as the legitimate heir and me as a kind of bastard. I am willing to admit that his opinion was based not only on jealousy; however, they had put the divorce through quickly so that I could arrive at a conventional time. Besides, people are not so pernickety in Eumeswil.

*

My mother had been the world for me; she gradually became a person. In later years, when my genitor was attending a congress, I had an opportunity to delve into my background. A historian is inconceivable without archival tendencies, and he preserves certain things that other householders tend to destroy once a process is completed. Almost every death is followed by a burned offering.

My genitor, too, would have done better to burn the correspondence he had exchanged with my mother during the critical quarter-year. He evidently could not part with those letters and so he stored them in the attic. There, rummaging through a jumble of papers, I fished them out and, in the dimness, I buried myself in the first few months of my existence.

That was how I found out the time at which it began, and also the place: the map room at the Institute of History. I know that room; almost nobody ever goes there, and the maps offer a fine shelter for a casual seduction. Still and all, I would not have thought my old man capable of such impetuousness.

There must be women who know instantaneously that a spark has flown. This cannot be explained physiologically; my mother was such a woman. She stated cryptically yet unmistakably that I had appeared, or at least made myself noticeable. This did not quite make sense to my old man. He tried, at first theoretically, to talk her out of having me—during the third week, when I already had the form of a mulberry and was starting to differentiate subtly. I was no bigger than a grain of rice, yet I could already distinguish between right and left, and a heart stirred inside me like a hopping dot on a screen.

When I could no longer be thought away, he tackled me physically. I do not wish to go into detail. In any case, while floating in the amniotic fluid, I was menaced with dangerous adventures, like Sindbad the Sailor. He tried to get at me with poisons and sharp instruments and also with the help of an accomplice on the medical faculty. But my mother stuck by me, and that was my good fortune.

According to my brother's version, my birth was her way of getting her hands on the old man—that is quite possible, but it was merely the practical side of an elemental attachment. As a mother, she wanted to have me; as a person, she had the right to watch out for herself.

*

On the whole, one must judge such a relationship in all its intricacy. That I am able to do so I owe not only to Vigo but also to Bruno, my philosophical mentor.

I remember a course in which he lectured on the mythical aspects of time and space. According to him, the father represents time and the mother space: in cosmic terms, he the heavens and she the stars; in telluric terms, he water and she earth; he creates and destroys, she receives, conceives, and preserves. Time is astir with insatiable disquiet, every moment snuffs out the previous one. The ancients depicted time as Cronus, who eats his own children.

As a Titan, the father devours his engendered son; as a god, he sacrifices him. As a king, he squanders him in the wars that he instigates. Bios and myth, history and theology offer any number of examples. The dead return not to the father, but to the mother.

*

Bruno also went into the differences between cremation and burial. I do not know whether I have quoted him correctly. Thus, water strikes me as really peculiar to the mother; the Christians identify it with the spirit. These are questions of category, which have unleashed interminable wars. Cyrillus regards water as the most important of the four elements and as the stuff of the great metamorphoses. The findings of space travel seem to confirm that *ex negativo*.

People well-versed in mythology know that the incredible vastness of the sea is only in its manifestation. In Eumeswil, where for generations now people have been thinking in purely quantitative terms, that notion is inconceivable. I read in the memoirs of a Russian pilgrim that the sip of water we hold out in a cupped hand to a man dying of thirst is greater than the Seven Seas. The same holds for amniotic fluid. In many languages, the words for "ocean" and "mother" sound somewhat alike: *mer* and *mère*.

9

In any case, I am willing to acknowledge that my genitor, in going after me, was behaving naturally. And as an anarch, I have to admit that he was protecting his rights. To be sure, this is based on reciprocity.

Our city teems with sons who have escaped their fathers in a similar way. Usually, this remains obscure. The Oedipal relationship is reduced to a malaise between individuals. The loss of esteem is inevitable, but people get along with one another.

Moreover, I am troubled less by my background than by the respect that my old man demands on the basis of his paternity. He cites a credit that is not his due: the fact that fathers, rulers, professors once lived and deserved this name. Nowadays, that is nothing but a rumor.

When he swaggers, I sometimes feel like reminding him of the map room and the tricks he harassed my mother with. She sheltered me from him in her cavern just as Rhea shielded her Zeus against the gluttonous Cronus.

Naturally, I avoid making this chess move; I am aware, here too, of imperfection, which torments me. There are truths that we must hush if we are to live together; but you cannot knock over the chessboard.

I owe my restraint partly to Bruno, whose course also covers magical and even practical conduct. He said: "If the words are about to flee your lips, then reach toward the left side of your chest for your wallet. You will then save your joke; it will accrue to your capital. You will feel your heart."

That is how I act with my dad. At such times, I am even overcome with benevolence. This is also my advice to Vigo when he wants to parry hateful criticism by giving tit for tat.

*

The fact that I forgo having a father precisely because I do not recognize him as my genitor is an altogether different matter. I seek a man for whom I can feel respect. This is possible even in Eumeswil, albeit exceptional. One finds spiritual foster fathers. The bonds one forms with them are stronger than those of blood.

Of course, such a statement must be handled with care, for a material substratum will always be present. In this respect, one owes one's father the link to an infinite network. In the act of procreation, he celebrates a mystery that is unknown even to him. His intrinsic nature might perish in it. Thus, we could be more closely related to an uncle or a distant forebear than to him. Genealogists and also biologists are familiar with such surprises; they often shatter their system. The genetic burden is endless; it reaches all the way into the inanimate world. It can bring forth creatures that died out long ago.

*

This digression may indicate why I prefer adoption to natural kinship. The fatherhood becomes spiritual; we are chosen relatives and not natural ones. Thus, Eros must also prevail in spiritual kinship; adoption is a more sublime repetition of godfathering. We pick the godfather, the *pater spiritualis*; and he recognizes himself in us—he accepts us. That is a contact to which we owe life, albeit in a different, an—I dare say—immortal manner. I do not wish to speak of the heart; this is not the right place.

My birth and the surroundings in which I was put may explain why I felt this kinship with three academic teachers, three professors. If I had had a vocation for craft, art, religion, war, I would have had different models—and different ones again had I opted for a criminal career.

During the tuna fishing, I watch the rais and his fishermen performing the drudgery; their obedience is simply the equipment of the trust that binds them to him; he is their leader, they have elected him. More fatherhood is to be felt here—even when he treats them severely—than when I sit with my old man, who swims in stagnant waters.

*

A philosopher is expected to have a system; in Bruno, you would seek one in vain, even though he is well grounded in the history of thinking. His course on the development of skepticism since Heraclitus runs for an entire year; he is precise, and that is the basis of his reputation. This course covers the practical part of his theory—the handiwork, so to speak. Anyone who attends it has spent his tuition wisely; he will be satisfied. Gifted students who have already become teachers themselves get a great deal out of it. The person who teaches us how to think makes us lords over men and facts.

While there is more here than meets the eye, this need not concern them; it would actually confuse them. To be sure, the things he conceals are not without an impact on them too; they light up the rationality of his lectures. Authority is more powerful in silence than in words; this obtains both for the monarch, who may be illiterate, and for the teacher of a high intellectual rank.

When I had the good fortune of becoming intimate with Bruno, certain things remained tacit in the background, even on the nights when we had drained a glass or two. He loves wine, which, rather than subduing him, always leaves him more and more aglow.

Bruno is short, with broad shoulders and a full, slightly ruddy face. The bulge of his eyes lends them an intense shine. When he speaks, his face can take on a penetrating boldness; it then grows ruddier. His ironic passages are accompanied by a smile that is almost imperceptible yet as charming as a compliment. His maxim was a taste sample like that of an exquisite wine: reserved for the connoisseur. Thus, I often saw him facing me with a light, free gesture as if he were lifting the curtain on a wordless realm when the angel of silence entered. Concurrence then supplanted comprehension.

*

Bruno, too, considers the situation in Eumeswil favorable: the historical substance is used up. Nothing is taken seriously now except for the gross pleasures and also the demands of everyday life. The body social resembles a pilgrim who, exhausted by his wanderings, settles down to rest. Now images can come in.

These ideas also had a practical meaning for my work. Vigo had advised me as a historian: I would obtain glimpses of historical models that kept recurring without their having to move me, much less inspire my enthusiasm. That is how one studies the style of coins that have been withdrawn from circulation. Although worthless as legal tender, they fascinate the amateur.

Bruno rounded this out by adding an insight: a wall with its limewash already flaking off would reveal idols that, albeit long forgotten, were slumbering in private—graffiti of proto-, nay, prehistoric power. That would be the limit of scholarship.

*

Thus, my attentiveness when I stand behind the bar goes in three temporal directions. First of all, I am devoted to the comfort of the Condor and his guests: that is the present. Next, I follow their conversations, the development of their objectives, the interweaving of their political plots. All this may be topical for them; for me, in Vigo's terms, it constitutes a model that is more sharply defined in small states than in great empires. Florence was enough for a Machiavelli. I am certain that the Domo has studied him; a few of his maxims sound as if they were borrowed from *Il principe*.

After midnight, when they have been drinking, I grow more alert. Words, sentences are spoken that obviously refer to the forest: I join these splinters into a mosaic. Larger pieces, fragments are offered by Attila's memories; having lived in the forest for a long time, he is lavish with anecdotes. They are hard to pigeonhole in terms of time and authenticity; they demand the mythologist's flair rather than the historian's. A forest hermit lives as if in a feverish dream.

I track these conversations like a hound, all the way into the mimicry, the gestures, and the depths of the silences. Then there is a stirring in the thicket—is it the wind, or is an unknown quarry about to emerge into the clearing? The desire to capture the moment in a note is overpowering; this is an instinct that lives in every historian. I have ways of doing it:

My duties include keeping the mess log; any beverages and collations passing from the galley through the bar have to be entered. The point here is not so much bookkeeping as security.

Thus, no one notices when I pick up the pencil and make my accounts. To be sure, the Domo asks to see the log. He is interested in such things as the tastes and habits of the individual participants. He cannot possibly spot a secret writing in the text. I introduced a dot system and I imperceptibly emphasize certain letters. My goal here is not so much to capture my impressions as to mark the focal points. Here I come back to the meaning of silence. I also have to control the ambiance, and at those times when I sense there is something in the room, I indulge in certain liberties by charging those moments with significance.

I finally succeeded in making do with the ductus alone; I scrutinize my handwriting like a mirror of time. I would have ignored a detail in this context if it did not point to Bruno's methods:

The fact that penmanship communicates things, from a simple household budget to intellectual realms, is a commonplace; and every graphologist knows that it reveals an image of character to the knowledgeable observer. But Bruno went further: for him, handwriting is a mirror that traps and releases the moment when we engross ourselves in it. Why were the tablets of Mount Sinai taken along during the wanderings? Everyone knew the text by heart anyway. And yet the tablets expressed something more than and different from the Commandments: the commanding power. That was why the high priest secretly perused them before the sacrifice—and probably touched them as well.

Bruno—I say this making all due allowances—advanced in that direction. The mirror played a large part in this: "Primal image is image *and* mirror image." Apparently, he expected unwonted results from my nightly reconnoitering and also felt I had the proper sensibility. As for my notations, I owe to him the luminous pencil that contains several refills. If a conversation turns ardent, bringing the forest closer, a finger squeeze makes certain refills, meant for this purpose, spring out of the reserve—as if I were releasing the safety catch on a gun. I do not need to make any special entries, I simply continue the list of consumed beverages.

It may be my imagination—yet what is imagination?—but once I look at these written columns, the conversations seem closer than when I heard them. It is as if their background were opening. Words then have the power not only to communicate but also to evoke. In retrospect, I saw the faces freeze as if during a ritual sacrifice. It was eerie.

What might conjure up this effect? One could readily speculate that this lead refill was inoculated with one of those substances that carry us beyond the limits of perception. They work even in the tiniest doses, unweighable like wind-wafted pollen.

Bruno frequently experiments with them, but allows no adepts to watch. Once, when I walked in unannounced, I found him completely absent. Behind the glass mask, I saw a face whose gaze I could not endure. A propos, he clearly does not recall that visit.

At any rate, I do not regard him as a magician. His path includes a not indelicate magical phase. It is meant only as an approach—the way a course in logic introduces the study of philosophy. Problems of passage arise here: magical lore must be forgotten, for it will be deceptive once the cosmic chase begins. That is the reason why the gods ultimately depend on human help. I suspect that Bruno has nevertheless opted for the underworld.

*

At New Year's, some firms in Eumeswil offer their customers modest promotional gifts, usually mechanical pencils. These are reminders of the firms and their achievements. I assume that Bruno brought back the mechanical pencil as a similar reminder from one of his visits in the catacombs.

A mere toy. It is probably meant to indicate the level of technology that has been attained there and to inspire if not fear then respect. And is *technology* the right word? *Metatechnology* would, no doubt, be more fitting. It applies not to the perfecting of means, but to their sudden transformation into a different quality. When a runner reaches his top speed, running turns into flying. A sample was supplied by that sparkling script; verbal communication no longer sufficed.

Once, people got fed up with pure dynamics, and so technology declined in the larger areas. This was matched on the other side by its plutonian concentration in the hands of a small, now autonomous personnel.

10

I see them as my spiritual fathers: I owe to Vigo an unbiased view of history—a view that works only when we are no longer involved in the pros and cons. That is the historian's delight; he takes part in the squabbles as Zeus does in the battles of gods and men. From under the varnish with which they were dimmed by the Enlightenment, the images emerge in their glory.

Bruno gave me glimpses of the backgrounds that belong neither to history nor to the natural realm—indeed, they are independent of the human presence in the universe. He was able to snuff out the historical consciousness and its torment.

Why is it that I cannot distinguish the two of them clearly enough, despite their differences? Presumably because they do meet and unite somewhere—for example, in me. Thus, all disciplines—say, a biologist's and a physicist's—meet where antitheses are transcended in the atoms. I do not choose this simile at random. Vigo is turned toward the gods and Bruno toward the Titans; one toward the forest, the other toward the underworld.

*

Vigo peers into the world as into a picture book. The objects are charged under his eyes and they pounce on him. One evening, when we were sitting in his garden on the edge of town, he pointed to an araucaria.

"Martin—do you see anything special about it?"

It was a beautiful specimen of this tree, whose silhouette lends an austere touch to our coast; yet nothing about it struck me as unusual. Vigo provided the explanation:

"Seven years ago, its tip was broken. Perhaps a bird wanted to rest on it, or an insect nibbled on the bud. A blemish—I almost chopped the tree down. It is good that I refrained. For what happened? One of the side branches straightened up and formed a new tip, like a soldier presenting a bayonet. Several years later, no trace of the injury could be seen. What is your opinion?"

"I would call it the restoration of appearance through shape."

"I see you have learned from me. You must bear in mind not only that this ninety-degree turn repairs the morphological damage, but also that the anatomy is modified all the way into the discrete structure, into the scarring, which the forester calls the 'wounded wood.'

"You can also view this genealogically. When the whorl straightens up, an offshoot takes over the task and the supremacy. The forests contain our elementary models, the gardens our social models."

He then examined my response:

"What is manifested here? Nothing but Paracelsus's Inner Physician; he straightens the creature up again even after a decapitation. In my opinion, the mere sight of this tree is salutary."

I can listen to Vigo for hours, and also join him in hours of silence. The moon hung over the Casbah; the tree stood out against the pale nocturnal sky; its slender twigs were studded with round cones like a series of musical notes with heads.

*

Just as Vigo wants to lead us beyond history, Bruno wants to lead us beyond knowledge; the one beyond the will, the other beyond conception. This is treated by the guild as either regressive or utopian; both men are considered unserious. I like them both, although and precisely because I have often enough heard my genitor and my brother poke fun at them during meals.

"The unnavigated seas lie beyond the Pillars of Hercules. Herodotus and Heraclitus are their publicans."

They did not like hearing such maxims, which I brought back from Vigo's seminar. They do not find them sober enough. Yet idealism is far from my mind, even though I have made sacrifices to it. I, in turn, feel it does not suffice to grasp facts according to their weight but not their eros. Matter is concentrated in eros; the world becomes exciting. For this path, both teachers were helpful to me. They gave me what my genitor was unable to give me since his love and his lore were inadequate.

*

Although an anarch, I am not anti-authoritarian. Quite the opposite: I need authority, although I do not believe in it. My critical faculties are sharpened by the absence of the credibility that I ask for. As a historian, I know what can be offered.

Why do people who leave nothing unchallenged still make demands of their own? They live off the fact that gods, fathers, and poets used to exist. The essence of words has been diluted into empty titles.

In the animal kingdom, there are parasites that clandestinely hollow out a caterpillar. Eventually, a mere wasp emerges instead of a butterfly. And that is what those people do with their heritage, and with language in particular, as counterfeiters; that is why I prefer the Casbah, even from behind my counter.

*

"At universities there are always groups of teachers and students who view the way of the world together and not without pleasure. The content varies, the mood remains the same; it recalls the mood of sectarians within cults—and it always involves error."

That was Vigo speaking. And Bruno: "This applies to every intellectual expenditure. But it is nothing to crow about. For where does it ultimately lead? People convince one another that the world is imperfect. Then they send out calls for help and flash beacons of hope. It makes no difference whether Hercules cleans out the Augean stables or a mailman his pigeon house. And the stars do not draw closer no matter what pedestal one gets up on."

Similar things can be heard when the wind wafts from the desert. But there are also euphoric moods.

11

"There will always be people who speak better than the rest."

The auditorium greeted this statement with *ohos.*

"There will even be people who speak well."

The disquiet increased. They had not come willingly to this supplementary lecture series that the Domo had foisted on them; it was a required course given by Thofern, the grammarian.

Like a number of other directives from the Domo, I was able to follow this one from its inception; such insights are among the joys of my profession. I am curious by nature; this is indispensable for the historian. A man is a born historian or else he is boring.

Saint-Simon went to court not because he was a courtier but because he was a born historian. His being an aristocrat helped to facilitate his task. Those are roles—had he played the part of valet de chambre, then perhaps better, even tinier fish would not have escaped him. More important than the *grandes entrées* was his familiarity with the *derrières*—the fact that he was on good terms with Bloin and Maréchal. Not only did the prince witness that dreadful scene in Marly one evening, when the monarch was beside himself because his favorite bastard had failed in battle. The prince had also heard the preceding conversation with the bath servant.

*

This is no digression. I am speaking about my sideline, that of night steward in Eumeswil. In that capacity, I had mentally followed a conversation between the Condor and the Domo; they were talking about the judgment in a civil proceeding. The Domo had the court transcript brought from his office, and he read a few sentences aloud.

"Are you satisfied with the decision?"

"A question mark should be put here."

He reread the passage, shaking his head.

"No, an exclamation point—the fellow's botched up the imperative."

He examined the signature:

"And not even a stenographer—just a paralegal!"

*

The Domo, unlike the Condor, is no soldier of fortune; he is descended from one of the old families. It verges on the miraculous that such names outlive the chain of upheavals; they owe their endurance to aptitudes that have developed through the generations, becoming instinctive—especially the diplomatic talent. The foreign service offers a number of survival options, I do not wish to go into detail. At any rate: if anyone in the group that I serve can be thought to have historical substance, it is the Domo. Of course, this is something he probably tries to conceal rather than flaunt.

His relationship to power can likewise be seen as both "primitive" and "late." The former view is held by my genitor, the latter by Vigo, my teacher. Vigo sees further and he therefore knows that these two possibilities are not mutually exclusive. He also has an apt image for this:

According to him, the primitive element is the basic stock of the individual and his communities. It is his bedrock, on which history is established, and which is exposed once more when history withers away. Humus with its flora piles up on the rock and vanishes again, in whatever manner—it either dries up or is swept away by tempests. Then the bare tuff emerges; it contains prehistoric inliers. Say: the prince becomes a chieftain, the physician a shaman, the vote an acclamation.

This implies that the Condor stands closer to the start of the process, the Domo closer to its end. The end is dominated by the elemental, the start by the rational mind. There are historical examples of this—say, in the king's relationship to the chancellor, or the commander-in-chief's to the chief of staff. In short, wherever business is divided between character and intellect, or between being and doing.

*

My genitor strikes me—to maintain Vigo's image—as someone who delights in dried bouquets, in flowers from Rousseau's herbarium. I can even sympathize with this as an academic. On the tribune, my old man's self-deception becomes a deception of the populace.

On the other hand, my interest in the Domo's squabbles with the tribunes is metahistorical; I am absorbed in the model, not the urgent issue. At the luminar, I studied the particulars of Rousseau's visit with Hume, plus the misunderstandings that led to Hume's invitation.

Jean-Jacques's life leads from disappointment to disappointment to solitude. This is reflected in his successors, down to the present day. It hints that something human was touched at the core. The great ideas spring up in the heart, says an old Frenchman. One could add: and are thwarted by the world.

*

I consider it poor historical form to make fun of ancestral mistakes without respecting the eros that was linked to them. We are no less in bondage to the Zeitgeist; folly is handed down, we merely don a new cap.

I therefore would not resent my genitor for merely believing in a fallacy; no one can help that. What disturbs me is not error but triteness, the rehashing of bromides that once moved the world as grand utterances.

Errors can shake the political world to its very core; yet they are like diseases: in a crisis, they can accomplish a great deal, and even effect a cure—as hearts are tested in a fever. An acute illness: that is the waterfall with new energies. A chronic illness: sickliness, morass. Such is Eumeswil: we are wasting away—of course, only for lack of ideas; otherwise, infamy has been worthwhile.

The lack of ideas or—put more simply—of gods causes an inexplicable moroseness, almost like a fog that the sun fails to penetrate. The world turns colorless; words lose substance, especially when they are to transcend sheer communication.

*

I have to occupy myself with the Domo's political standpoint insofar as it is significant for my studies. Anything beyond that—say, affection—I must avoid, like any kind of whirlpool.

This does not interfere with my pleasure in hearing him speak; nor do I lack the opportunity. If the Yellow Khan or other important guests are not being served, then the night bar is peaceful; often only the Condor is present with Attila and the Domo, plus the minions on duty.

I perch on a high stool behind the bar; it makes me look as if I were standing by in full dress. My close observation of the guests is part of my service; I anticipate their every wish. To this end, I have an obliging smile at my disposal. I test it in the mirror before going on duty. I have already mentioned that I make notes on whatever is consumed. The minions wait on the tables, doing the actual serving.

That is the raised blind from which I observe my game. If I say I like hearing the Domo, then my primary reason is a negative one—namely that he lacks the grand utterances, with which I got fed up once I learned how to think for myself. Still and all, I must admit that at first his diction had a sobering effect on me, accustomed as I was to a style that replaces arguments with claptrap.

The initial sobering effect is due to the economy of his expression: few adjectives, few relative clauses, more periods than commas. The howlers are absent; evidently, correctness carries more weight than beauty, and necessity more than morality. This is not the kind of language with which orators address an assembly in order to sound agreeable and obtain agreement; rather, it is the kind of language aimed at preaching to the converted. Usually, the wording reassures the Condor in whatever he is wishing anyway.

Thus, it is the language of a man who knows what he wants and who transfers this wanting to others: *Dico*: "I speak"; *dicto*: "I speak firmly, dictate." The *t* concentrates.

I soon got accustomed to his diction, as to an older school—say, in painting. A tree-lined riverbank was seen, as interpreted by the late nineteenth century of the Christian era: light, movement in the foliage, an interplay of general, changing impressions that developed through detailed transitions since Rubens. I could decompose it nicely at the luminar. Now comes another room, the Florentines, circa 1500, after the banishing of the Medici. The air grows dry and transparent. The trees motionless, unhazy; here the cypress, there the pine. This is matched by the faces, the laws, the politics.

*

For a long time now, the army has been producing all those who boast that they can clear up the mess whenever things are mired in the mud. The situation then gets more dangerous—for them, too. There was a transition during which they formulated ideas that were the spit and image of those of the tribunes. This is no longer necessary in Eumeswil. Incidentally, the Domo does without cynical remarks; this can be attributed to his strength.

However, it is well known that military men do not move things much further than anyone else. Changes seem to have been taking place here since antiquity, since Marius and Sulla; in each case, an advance payment of faith, of good will, or simply of vitality has been used up. The world spirit loves blank pages; once they are written on, they drop away.

*

I sidestep, as I have said, any affection, any personal sympathy. As an anarch, I have to steer clear of such feelings. Working somewhere is unavoidable; in this respect, I behave like a condottiere, who makes his energy available at a given moment, but, in his heart of hearts, remains uncommitted. Furthermore, as here in the night bar, work is a part of my studies—the practical part.

As a historian, I am convinced of the imperfection—nay, the vanity—of any effort. I admit that the surfeit of a late era is involved here. The catalogue of possibilities seems exhausted. The great ideas have been eroded by repetition; you won't catch any fish with that bait. In this regard, I behave no differently within my framework than anyone else in Eumeswil. People no longer demonstrate publicly for ideas; bread or wine would have to cost a lot more, or there would have to be a rumpus with the racers.

*

As a historian, I am skeptical; as an anarch, I am on my guard. This contributes to my well-being, even to my sense of humor. Thus, I keep my property together—albeit not for myself as the only one. My personal freedom is a perquisite. Beyond that, I stand ready for the Great Encounter—the irruption of the absolute into time. That is where history and science end.

*

If the Domo's language pleases me more than my genitor's, then this is relative. His language is more concrete, but, compared with, say, Attila's, it seems defoliated. One views the embranchment, the bare boughs, which, however—I must add—indicate the roots. The latter are mirrored in the branches. There is a depth from which logic ascends into language—I don't mean the logic taught here in Eumeswil, but the kind that establishes the universe and that, by rising into the ramifications of the universe, constantly keeps reorienting it.

*

"He who cannot speak should not judge." I have often heard that maxim from the Domo. So, I was not surprised that he was irked by the crude blunders in that court decision. The immediate consequence was Thofern's required course, which he imposed on the law students. The professor is regarded as our best grammarian.

12

After incurring displeasure in the auditorium by giving his introductory lecture on qualitative linguistic distinctions, Thofern resorted to a diversion which garnered mirth and applause.

"Last night, when I was sitting in the Blue Egg, with nothing wicked in mind...."

It must be noted here that Eumeswil has no shortage of low dives. There is something to tickle even the most devious fancy. That is the fruit of the Domo's liberality, which is supported by the Condor. "To each his own"—this motto is interpreted broadly here.

The Domo said, "Whatever a man does in bed or even in a stable is his own business; we do not interfere. *Bien manger, bien boire, bien foutre*—by giving our blessing to all that, we relieve the police and the courts of an enormous workload. This way, aside from lunatics and gross criminals, we only have to deal with do-gooders, who are more dangerous.

"Our people in Eumeswil do not want a better life in some vague future, they want a good life right now. They do not want to hear a coin clink; they would like to have it in their pocket. They prefer a bird in the hand to a bird in the bush. We can even give them the chicken in the pot."

The Domo banks on facts just as my genitor does on ideas. That is the difference between liberalism and liberality. As a historian, I must comment: Everything is correct in its time. The Domo's methods presume the existence of our fellahlike condition. The great ideas for which millions got themselves killed are worn out. Distinctions have largely vanished; circumcised and uncircumcised, whites, yellows, and blacks, rich and poor no longer take themselves so seriously in their qualities. At most, they take to the streets if there is a cash crisis, or during Mardi Gras. All in all, a man can do or not do as he likcs.

Though a tyrant, the Condor, discreetly accompanied, moves like a common man in the marketplace and on the waterfront; he likes talking to people: "Kârim, you old scoundrel, still up and about—I bet you're still doing it, aren't you?"

Such were his words to the rais of the tuna fishermen, a white-bearded man who is going on eighty. And the oldster replied, "Condor, do you mean during the week or at night?"

*

The Blue Egg is a saloon frequented by criminals and flipped-out types. Vigilantes keep the Domo posted about anything occurring in the *bas-fonds*; theirs is a risky profession. Barely a month passes without the night watch stumbling on the corpse of a man who's been stabbed to death.

So, needless to say, Thofern's mention of a place avoided by even the better sort of pimps was greeted with merriment. What he supposedly heard there did indeed involve a stabbing. The crooks were trying the case themselves. Having more to do by night than by day, they while away an occasional afternoon by sitting in on court trials. This is entertaining and also instructive for them.

Here at the Blue Egg, they had been discussing a murder indictment that had fallen flat. The victim was an opium dealer; this traffic, though tolerated, is not without its risks. Indeed, tolerance is one of our watchwords; there are lots of things here that are prohibited yet seldom prosecuted, which leaves a semidarkness on the outskirts of legality, consistent with the dreamlike mood of this tavern.

In this twilight domain, the kickbacks are unlimited. People profit from this both in the Casbah and in the underground. There are scandals, due less to poppy than to hemp; the former dazes, the latter rouses. A man runs amuck through the streets, brandishing a cold knife; a student burns to death in her bed. When the Domo thereupon summons one of the major dealers and appeals to his conscience, he need not add anything to stimulate the man's charity; nor do such donations leave any trace.

The underworld, likewise, gets its tithe. The dealers, distributors, and saloonkeepers are especially vulnerable to extortion, to which they resign themselves. They pay regularly and count it as overhead; this, too, leaves no trace.

In the matter at hand, the dealer had risked a struggle for power that he could not handle. The affair had taken its nasty course; after sending him threatening letters, they had planted a grenade outside his door, then riddled a bodyguard with bullets, and finally sicced the rats on him. It was high time he left Eumeswil; he managed to reach a ship lying under sail in the harbor. He was, no doubt, planning to seek refuge with the Yellow Khan, relying overly on his protection.

The rats are no laughing matter; once they are set on the trail and have picked up the scent, their job turns into a greedy passion. As the dealer was mounting the gangway, a crate came loose from the hoisting crane, missing him by a gnat's eyelash. The crate was so heavy that it smashed through the gangplank. Unscathed, he reached his cabin, a *camera di lusso* with bath and salon.

But when the *facchino* arrived with the baggage, he found the passenger lifeless in front of the vanity mirror. The ship's doctor, who was already on board, could only ascertain his demise. Heart attack—the excitement had obviously been too much for him, as it was for the horseman who galloped across a frozen Lake Constance without realizing it until he reached the other side.

No seaman likes having a corpse on ship. There was still time to get rid of it. After filling out the death certificate, the physician returned with the porters to supervise the transport. The dead man lay barechested on the bed. That had been his position when the doctor had examined him. The doctor could therefore state under oath that the stiletto had not yet been thrust into the left part of the torso. Now its handle was sticking out.

The stab had been dealt with professional self-assurance, and indeed in the brief span between examination and transport. No blood had flowed; the blade had bored through a dead heart. This was confirmed by the autopsy, which was also attended by Attila. I had therefore learned about the case from the conversations in the night bar.

Policemen came aboard; there was a terribly annoying delay. Passengers and crew were interrogated, as indeed was everyone who had been present on deck or below. Attention focused on the *facchino*, who seemed to know more than he cared to admit, although he obviously had nothing to do with the crime.

When threatened with having to testify, people prefer to conduct themselves like the temple monkeys of Nikko, which cover up their eyes, ears, or mouth—and with good reason. But for the police, this is right down their alley; no matter how ensnarled a thread, once they get hold of one end, they unravel it all the way.

It therefore did not take them long to get something out of the porter: he had noticed an irregularity. He confessed this all the more easily since the intruder had been a *facchinaccio*. These are the boys who sneak aboard vessels in the turmoil of departure, trying to wangle tips and watch out for opportunities. Working without a license, they are, needless to say, a thorn in the side of the *facchini*.

This put the police hot on the trail: the phony porter, a hired killer, had done the stabbing. Like a shadow, he had slipped into the cabin where the dead dealer was lying in the penumbra just as the physician had left him; then the intruder had carried out his task in a split second.

*

That had been the topic of the conversation that Thofern had eavesdropped on at the Blue Egg, or claimed to have eavesdropped on—I was not sure which. I felt as if I had already read that embroiled plot in a novel or seen it in one of the gangster movies that form the bulk of entertainment here and are soon forgotten. The manhunt, with all its ins and outs, is one of those themes that never lose their charm and that go through infinite variations. At the luminar, I occasionally view shortened versions from the Pitaval and by other authors. As for the murdering of a corpse, I found a similar recipe in Day Keene, a classic writer in this genre. It is one of the recurrent variants insofar as it touches on a nightmare that has been haunting us since the days of Cain. We believe we have murdered someone in a dream; awakening restores our innocence.

But why did the professor go into such detail? After all, he was teaching a course in philology, not law. However, Thofern showed he could live up to the Domo's expectations.

*

"Gentlemen, the court had to decide on criminal charges for a capital offense. The defense moved for acquittal and won. Let us follow up on the defense by probing the verb 'to stab.'

"If we assume that the dealer was still alive when the stroke was dealt and that it killed him, then that would have been a clear case of homicide—with obvious intent to kill. Had the stroke not been deadly, then the defense attorney would have pleaded bodily injury. But neither was the case. A cadaver can be neither killed nor injured in this sense. Otherwise the anatomist who dissects it would also have to be punished.

"Thus, the defense attorney had to prove that the dealer was not *slain*, but merely *stabbed*—that is, that the action that had taken place did not entail any criminal liability. The *facchinaccio* would have been incapable of such rationalizing because it went beyond his linguistic ken; the defense attorney had to feed it to him.

"Gentlemen, the difference between these two verbs, *slay* and *stab*, seems nugatory; but here you have an example of its scope—by varying just two consonants."

Thofern smiled: "You can do a lot with that. A sound or two can make all the difference in the world. Anyone with a smattering of trigonometry can calculate the distance to the moon; He has *estimated* it—this is common property, which he shares with the rest of society. But he alone can *esteem* it."

The professor then came to a different issue. "We might also suppose that the dealer fell victim to a gang and did not live to experience the final stroke. In such a case, this is not the continuation of an action, but a continued action.

"The distinction is not so much in the reproachability as in the punishability. The exact time of the deed must be pinpointed by the judge. If the tenses do not suffice, then precision must be achieved by paraphrase."

He provided examples.

*

Thofern was, no doubt, intent chiefly on presenting himself, which he succeeded at nicely. This opening lecture was meant to indicate a linguistics course that he offered as a puzzle of etymological detective work—exciting and, for me as a historian, even thrilling. He then examined the *facchinaccio*'s intention, citing classical examples in order to differentiate various kinds of unlawful intent.

For instance: Had the dealer been only seemingly dead after the stabbing, and had the perpetrator, in order to dispose of the corpse, thrown it into the sea, thereby precipitating death by drowning, then the defense attorney would have been faced with a less simple task.

"Success would have come from a series of causal yet not logically linked actions, which the ancient jurists would have classified under the heading of *dolus generalis*. Nowadays, we get off more cheaply—for better or worse: because it has become more difficult to distinguish the real from the possible and the latter, in turn, from the desirable. This involves a loss of verbal forms, which cannot be made up for by psychological speculations. I will deal with this subject when we get to the conditional tense."

*

This was an idea that vividly haunted me, too—albeit in a different way—since in Eumeswil we live in a city where nothing seems real anymore and anything seems possible. This levels distinctions and promotes a chiaroscuro in which day and dream blend into each other. Society is no longer taken so seriously—this adds a new touch to dictatorships; it is no accident that Vigo so frequently points to echoes of *The Thousand and One Nights*.

A fisherman, a coolie, or a dyer does not only fancy marvelous things in his dreams, he ascends from them like a *grand seigneur*. No barrier remains between wish and fulfillment. This recalls the possession of the magic ring; the cobbler who found it rubs it, and a demon spurts from the wall. "I am the servant of the ring and its bearer. Master, order me to put up a palace overnight, wipe out a nation, or burn down a city."

At least, the fairy tale says so—and yet the nation is wiped out, and its far eastern city burns down to its very foundations. This was ordained by a textile merchant. The historians tried to comprehend it, but in vain; it was beyond their scope.

Bruno is right when he classifies this as magic, which is developing into a *scienza nuova* as a subcategory of science. Technology has a subsoil. Now, it is starting to feel queasy about itself. It is approaching the immediate realization of thoughts, as is achieved in dreams. Only a tiny step appears to be missing; this step could emerge from the dream itself as if from a mirror. Eumeswil lends itself to this possibility.

A door should no longer be touched; it should spring open on its own. Every desired place should be reached in the twinkling of an eye. Any world is drawn from the ether or, as at the luminar, from the catacombs.

That is the comfort side. Thofern derives "comfort" from *conferto*—"I fortify, I strengthen." But comfort can become too strong.

*

Starting with that introduction to the course for law students, I regularly attended Thofern's lectures and also his seminar. There I met few and nearly always the same people; grammar is a dead science. That is why it is studied more seriously within the framework of the extinct languages than the current ones.

However, the Domo wanted law students to master language as a logical instrument in order to be able to pass judgments; nothing is further from his mind than aesthetic or even artistic sentiments, with the exception of music.

Tyranny must value a sound administration of justice in private matters. This, in turn, increases its political authority. The latter rests on equality, to which tyranny sacrifices freedom. Tyranny is intent on overall leveling, which makes it akin to rule by the people. Both structures produce similar forms. They share a distaste for elites that nurture their own language and recognize themselves in it; poets are even hated.

As a grammarian, Thofern sets great store by the verb "to nurture," and it is here that I, as a historian, concur with him. The historian's task is a tragic one; ultimately it has to do with death and eternity. Hence his burrowing in rubble, his circling around graves, his insatiable thirst for sources, his anxious listening to the heartbeat of time.

What could lie hidden behind such disquiet?—I have often wondered. How understandable the terror of the savage who, upon seeing the sun disappear, fears it will never return. The man who stored the mummy in the rock hoped for the mummy's return, and we rob it of its bindings in order to confirm his—no, our—hope. When granting life to the past, we succeed in conquering time, and a subduing of death becomes apparent. Should the latter work out, then it is conceivable that a god will breathe new life into us.

13

"The decay of language is not so much a disease as a symptom. The water of life is dwindling. Words have meaning still, but not sense. They are being replaced largely by numbers. Words are becoming incapable of producing poetry and ineffective in prayer. The crude enjoyments are supplanting the spiritual ones."

That was what Thofern said. In the seminar, he went into detail: "People have always delighted, more or less clandestinely, in the argots, the books sold under a coat or read with one hand. Then they are praised as models. The Third Tone dominates."

By the "Third Tone" he meant the lowest level for naming things and activities. They are addressed in a lofty, a current, or a common manner; each manner is good in its place.

"If the common becomes normal in colloquial speech or even in poetry, then it involves an assault on the lofty. Anyone who likes to gobble and boast about it forestalls any suspicion of viewing bread as a miracle that is celebrated in the Supper.

"Profanation sets off lower forms of merriment. A head can ascend to a crown, a face to a countenance, or it can twist into a mug. Profanation can provoke merriment when it appears in Pandaemonium; the gods, too, laugh at Priapus. The merry-andrew has his place in the intermezzo. But if he rules the boards as a *buffo assoluto*, then the stage becomes a distorting mirror.

"At the *opera comica*, I always saw a few spectators departing once the laughter began to roar. This is more than a question of taste. There is such a thing as a collective gusto, also a jubilation, announcing imminent danger. The good spirits leave the house. In the Roman circus, the effigies of the gods were draped before blood flowed."

*

Now and then, I, as a student of history, was permitted to help Thofern prepare his lectures. Thus, when dealing with the decay of language, he asked me to gather material about the contributions of the Eumenists.

Those things go back quite a way, and it may be said that no one cares two hoots about them anymore. At the luminar, however, the number of titles that I tallied up was enormous, even for the limited area of our city. As in any work on a scholarly apparatus, the main issue was to survey the cardinal points. Whatever has moved the Zeitgeist cascades in a chaotic flood; one has to catch the historical meaning concealed behind opinions and events.

The linguistic decay that the professor was talking about occurred during the final period of the wars between nations, a time that heralded great coalitions. First, the regional gods had to be disempowered worldwide; the fact that the father was also affected indicated a planetary agitation.

The disempowering of the father endangers the heavens and the great forests; when Aphrodite bids farewell, the ocean goes dim; once Ares is no longer in charge of wars, the shacks of flayers multiply, the sword becomes a slaughterer's knife.

In a period of decline, when it was considered glorious to have helped destroy one's own nation, the roots of language were, not surprisingly, likewise pruned, above all in Eumeswil. Loss of history and decay of language are mutual determinants; the Eumenists championed both. They felt called upon to defoliate language on the one hand and to gain prestige for slang on the other hand. Thus, down below they robbed the populace of language and, with it, poetry, on the pretext that they were facilitating speech; while on the heights they presented their "mugs."

The assault on evolved language and on grammar, on script and signs, is part of the simplification that has gone down in history as a cultural revolution. The first world-state cast its shadow.

*

Well, that lies behind us now. In this area, we have been released from wanting and wishing and can render unbiased judgment to the extent of our abilities. In Eumeswil, this applies, I feel, to Vigo, Bruno, and Thofern. Different as they are, these three are able to have a conversation without promptly serving up the trendy claptrap. One often has the impression in Eumeswil that it is not the person but the swarm that answers. Of course, there are raised platforms, as with my dear father, and also flounders of the deep, which unite in schools.

Also common to all three teachers are their direct roots in mythology, which, unlike the psychologists, they have not sterilized and secularized. In this way, they can still test the very substance of the gods. By moving away from time, they approach the basic structures reiterated by events.

Vigo describes the world-state as one of the permanent utopias that the stewards of history more or less succeed in depicting.

"This is already inherent as a kind of hunger in natural history; say, in the formation of macromolecules. Of course, these are also more threatened with decay—perhaps they are even its portent. The further the state expands, the more it depends on equality; this occurs at the expense of substance."

At the same time, Vigo sees the striving for maximum size and the inevitably following decadence as an overall pulsation: "Even a jellyfish moves by unfolding and then closing its umbrella. Thus, in the course of history, the desire for largeness alternates with the desire for smallness. Boutefeu already knew—and we, too, have learned—that the world-state both culminates and disintegrates overnight. The leviathan's limits are not so much spatial as temporal."

*

I have already mentioned Vigo's penchant for periods of decline. This has less to do with decadence than with the late maturity of highly advanced civilizations after the first frost. Hence, for him, Athens and Thebes are "greater" than Alexander's universal empire—all in all, he loves city-states:

"In the city-state the landscape crystallized, while in the empire it is leached out, degraded to a province. Asia Minor was a wonderland before Alexander and still under the satraps. Herodotus and even Ovid provide us with some notion of that."

Incidentally, for Vigo, Alexander rightfully carries the predicate of "the Great": "Perhaps this greatness would have been embodied more purely had it been limited to the human. He had more than historical power, he had divine might. That was why he was one of the last men to enter mythology."

"What about Christ?"

"That was no longer a myth."

For Vigo, the struggles of the Diadochi likewise demonstrated the uniqueness, the singularity of Alexander. They provided the model for the destiny of great empires. Vigo had then delved into Eumenes, the Greek among the Macedonians, our favorite Diadochus. Eumeswil is his namesake; any further citing of him is fellahlike arrogance.

"When the empire falls apart, as after Alexander's death, the old tribes try to isolate themselves again, each citing its own distinctive character. Yet this is precisely what they have lost by passing through the empire, like grain ground by a mill. All they retain is their names, akin to the Greek cities of the Roman era. Yet Alexandria blossoms.

"There, civilization resides no longer in the blood, but in the head. The period of the polyhistors, the lexicographers, the connoisseurs and collectors begins. The prices of antiquities and artworks skyrocket. Echoes still resonate in Eumeswil. They resemble the growing interest in the animal world during the very times that it begins to die out. That is how rooftops shine at sundown."

*

That was more or less what Vigo said. I am quoting from memory, and roughly at that. As a historian, Vigo sees the course of the world as cyclical; hence, both his skepticism and his optimism are limited. In any period, he would find a small spot warmed by the sun, even in Eumeswil.

Bruno, in contrast, views the world as a magus. Now and again, the earth shows its totem, that of the ancient Serpent, by casting off or pulling in its limbs. This explains the world-state, the atrophy of civilization, the dying-out of animals, the monocultures, the wastelands, the increase in earthquakes and plutonian eruptions, the return of the Titans—say, Atlas, who embodies the unity, Antaeus, the strength, and Prometheus, the cunning of the mother.

The fall of the gods was tied to all that. They returned—they who had driven their father from his throne; that which had once been the diamond sickle that emasculated him was now reason and science. Bruno pointed out the underworldly character of technology, its feeding on ore and fire, the plutonian glare of its landscapes.

The serpent regained its power; those were birth pangs. In Eumeswil, people, as if on an island or on a shipwreck, lived off the cargo—for how much longer? The gods were already mocked by schoolchildren. And why not? They would soon have new dolls, the supply is endless. And why gods? Surprises were in the offing.

Bruno has access to the catacombs and, in regard to knowledge of the real powers, resembles Vigo less than he resembles Attila, who has lived in the forests.

*

Bruno withdrew from the field of history more resolutely than Vigo; that is why I prefer the former's retrospect but the latter's prospect. As an anarch, I am determined to go along with nothing, ultimately take nothing seriously—at least not nihilistically, but rather as a border guard in no man's land, who sharpens his eyes and ears between tides.

I therefore cannot consider returning. This is the final refuge of the conservative who has lost all political and religious hope. To him, a thousand years are now small change; he bets on the cosmic cycles. Some day, Paraclete will appear, Emperor Frederick Barbarossa will rise from his enchanted sleep and step forth from the mountain.

But meanwhile, development still exists here, and so does time. Temporality returns, forcing even gods to do its drudgery—that is why there may be no Eternal Return; that is the paradox—there *is* no Eternal Return. Better, the Return of the Eternal; it can take place only once—time is then captured.

Thus, in Vigo's garden, I had come out of myself while the moon hung over the Casbah.

"Look," he said, "we have discovered a sore point."

He said that to me, whose skin is nothing but sores.

The idea of the Eternal Return is that of a fish that wants to jump out of the frying pan. It falls on the stove plate.

*

Above all, Thofern feels loss. His suffering is that of the artistic person in an unartistic time. He knows the values and also the criteria;

his disappointment is all the more acute when he applies them to the present. I suspect that he was moved by a poetic instinct, but expression fails him. In a godless space, he resembles the fish whose gills keep quivering after the surf has hurled it upon the reef; that which was pleasure in its element is turned into pain. The Age of Pisces is past.

For me as a historian, such torment is all too familiar. In our guild, it has given rise to famous works. The mood of the wasteland is part of it. In a vacuum, structures advance in a surreal way. A stimulant, a foretaste of death—that is the magic of the Brass City.

The man who opens the tombs with awe finds more than putrefaction, indeed more than the joys and sorrows of bygone eras. This is precisely why the historian suffers less than the poet, whom no knowledge avails and to whom the deserted palaces no longer offer shelter.

*

I would have liked to get closer to Thofern, as I had done with my two other teachers, but I soon realized that it was not possible. His fear of contact is extraordinary. He avoids even the sun; the law students have nicknamed him "The Paleface."

If, as a professorial duty, he has to receive a student, he avoids shaking hands and he offers him a chair in the farthest corner. His hands are inflamed from frequent washing, which includes thorough brushings.

It seems peculiar that he has risen to the rank of professor. History was his minor subject, and Vigo says that it took trickery to examine him. Offering Thofern a ride, he had engaged him in conversation; but when Thofern realized what was going on, he jumped out of the car, injuring himself. He passed all the same.

Such anxieties spring from his almost skinless sensitivity, which, on the other hand, make him receptive to the finest shadings. It is a delight to participate in one of the exegeses in which he exposes the body of a poem, gingerly following its movement, feeling its pulse. He never explicates the euphony, he quotes it as if inviting the poet in.

His delivery is both subdued and passionate, interrupted by pauses that reach deeper than words. Not even the law students can resist. He scans with his fingers, casually beats time with his arm. Whenever possible, he secures the manuscript or has it photocopied at the luminar. I noticed that, albeit holding the page in his hand, he nevertheless recites from memory—what he cares about is the poet's presence. A magical trait, which delighted Bruno when I told him about it.

On the other hand, Thofern's sensitivity to language brings him less joy than sorrow. Even in a casual conversation, breaches that no one else perceives disturb him as shirt-sleeved affronts.

For all that, the self-assurance of his delivery is astonishing—he then speaks ex cathedra. In so doing, he resorts to irony, the classical weapon of the underdog.

*

So much for my teachers, to whom I feel closer than to my genitor, for I prefer kinship of spirit to that of blood. It would, of course, be lovely if the two overlapped: in the old days, that was known as "one heart and one soul"; back then, "soul" was still synonymous with "spirit." But even my brother is alien to me.

As I have already said, I have nothing against authority, nor do I believe in it. Rather, I need authority, for I have a conception of greatness. That is why, although not without skepticism here too, I associate with the top rank.

To be fair, I will not conceal that I also owe something to strata that might be called the humus of education. In teaching, there is an eros that is reserved for simple minds. Their knowledge is a patchwork; yet it is received and handed around like bread. Showing something to children—say, a clock, and explaining how the hands work—will delight them, as if they were raising a curtain or drawing a circle on a blank page. There is enchantment here.

Isolation and Security

14

The days in the Casbah are fairly uniform. I can barely distinguish between work and leisure. I like them equally. This is consistent with my principle that there can be no empty time, no minute without intellectual tension and alertness. If a man succeeds in playing life as a game, he will find honey in nettles and hemlock; he will even enjoy adversity and peril.

What causes the feeling of constantly being on vacation? Probably the fact that the mental person liberates the physical one and observes his game. Far from any hierarchy, he enjoys the harmony of rest and motion, of invulnerability and extreme sensitivity—at times even authorship. He writes his text on a blank page and vanquishes destiny; the world changes through writing. This is the marriage of dance and melody.

*

On the other hand, I am also constantly on duty. This applies not only to my mental participation in everything that occurs in the Casbah and in the night bar, but also to the everyday banalities, as prescribed by the rules. There is nothing special about that: many professions require constant preparedness—particularly if they involve danger.

The preparedness is geared to the possibility that something might happen—thus, it is a form of service in which nothing or little happens. If, however, something does occur, all hands are needed. This recalls the precautions for possible fires or catastrophes at sea. With a drill at the start of the voyage, they make sure that everyone knows his function and his lifeboat. He is to find it like a sleepwalker when the siren wakes him up.

Thus, the Casbah has a quarterly drill for coping with domestic unrest. This is little more than an armed stroll—otherwise, my days are my own, and often enough my nights, for the Condor does not always feel like going to the bar after mess. Nor is it always an extended session: often, a Turkish coffee, a flute of champagne, or a digestive suffices. I scarcely need emphasize that the nights that stand me in good stead are precisely those involving long and hard drinking.

Sometimes a whole week can go by before I don my skiff. A bed of roses—at least for most people, and even more so for me because of the intellectual pleasure.

*

"That's the fly in the ointment." So says my dear brother, who, just like my genitor, sees me doing things that are unworthy of a university teacher. To his mind, I am waiting on the tyrant in his indulgences and assisting him in his oppression. "A man who shoots at the populace—and without even having to do so. Old Josiah is turning in his grave."

My good brother forgets that I sometimes got him and the old man out of hot water when they ventured a bit further than their usual pussyfooting. And what does a fly in the ointment mean during a time when a movement is successful only if oblique? We play on slanting chessboards. If some day his pontiffs—and I do not doubt it—topple the Condor, then Eumeswil will once again celebrate *liberazione*—the transition, that is, from visible to anonymous power. For a long time now, soldiers and demagogues have been spelling one another.

Although I have often studied this issue at the luminar, I feel that our scholarship has not managed to draw an adequate typological distinction between tyrant, despot, and demagogue. These notions overlap, and telling them apart is difficult, since they designate a deeply rooted human faculty, which changes iridescently in individuals. This is demonstrated in practice, since anyone who "seizes power" is initially hailed and cheered.

Man is born violent but is kept in check by the people around him. If he nevertheless manages to throw off his fetters, he can count on applause, for everyone recognizes himself in him. Deeply ingrained, nay, buried dreams come true. The unlimited radiates its magic even upon crime, which, not coincidentally, is the main source of entertainment in Eumeswil. I, as an anarch, not uninterested but disinterested, can understand that. Freedom has a wide range and more facets than a diamond.

*

I pursued this part of my studies ad hoc in order to visualize the Condor's condition. Through the luminar, I was presented with a wealth of types and also of eras in which these types were concentrated: Greek and especially Sicilian cities, satrapies in Asia Minor; late Roman and Byzantine caesars; Renaissance city-states, including, over and over—on Vigo's behalf as well—Florence and Venice; then the very brief and bloody uprisings of the *okhlos*, nights of hatchets and long knives; and finally the prolonged dictatorships of the proletariat, with their backgrounds and shadings.

The days and nights at the luminar take me into a labyrinth where I am afraid of getting lost; life is too short for that. But how tremendously time and times expand when one enters them through a strait gate. It is fascinating; I need no drugs for that, or barely the beaker that I hold in my hand.

Say, Matarazzo's chronicle of Perugia, the history of a city among cities in a land among lands—I cross-fade pictures of Etruscan gates, Pisano's choir, paintings by Baglioni, Pietro Perugino, by the twelve-year-old Raphael. Even this tiny section snowballs ad infinitum—as does every source, every point that I touch in whatever has been handed down. I sense a crackling, then a shining: that is the historical charge in its intact and undivided power. Friends and enemies, perpetrators and victims have contributed their best.

I spend the actual, the fully exhausted time in front of the luminar, whether in the Casbah or down in Vigo's institute. The mood then infects my work up here or my strolls in the city. This does not mean that I lead a literary existence like an epigone; I actually see the present more sharply—like someone looking up from the carpet on which he has said his prayer. The warp is supplied by the centuries, the woof by the day. This creates a distance for nearby things; people and facts gain a background. They become more bearable.

*

How, then, shall I classify the Condor? Among the tyrants—though not to be doubted, it says little. According to linguistic usage, tyrants find a more fertile soil in the West and despots in the East. Both are unbounded, but the tyrant follows certain rules, the despot his cravings. That is why tyranny is bequeathed more easily, though at most to a grandchild. The bodyguard is likewise more reliable, as is one's own son. Despite profound disagreements, Lycophron, the son of Periander, rebels against his father only in spirit but not in deed.

According to the classical scheme, the Condor is not one of the older tyrants, who attained power by fighting the aristocracy or murdering the king. In Eumeswil, this has been out of the question for some time now. The old tyrants, to be sure, did preliminary work as "blenders of people," not only by destroying the elites and egalitarianizing the demos into a mass, but also by deporting people and filling the gaps with foreign mercenaries and workers. From decade to decade, this reduces any domestic resistance that evinces quality. The upheavals become chronic, but alter nothing. The types that follow one another are all alike, especially in their will power. They also use the same big words, as a kind of fireworks that drowns out the live shooting.

Regardless of his South American tinges, the Condor recalls the older tyranny only in that he has taste. As a soldier, he read little; he tries to make up for this lack by having artists and philosophers in the Casbah, and also men of science and intelligent artisans. I benefited from this proclivity when he set up the lavish luminar for me.

On some evenings in the night bar, I enjoy reminiscences of Sicyon, Corinth, Samos, and especially the Syracuse of the ancient potentates—I won't deny it. One consequence of the worldwide entanglement is that "solitary men" appear, talents not rooted in one specific landscape or tradition. They loom up from the plain as "lonesome peaks." Granted, no style can develop in this way. There is no place, no exchange among lofty peers, no gaudy colonnade, no master's workshop. At times, it seems as if the surface tension were being discharged through a fireball.

Scarcely linked to place and time, the important individual turns generous. Major and minor potentates try to bind him; they adopt him. The Yellow Khan prefers planners, architects for Asiatic residences;

his pendant prefers artists and metaphysicians. They can be seen in Eumeswil, though not as permanent guests but as infrequent visitors in retinues or in transit. Still and all, I am satisfied with the discussions between the Condor, Attila, and the Domo. Incidentally, one also hears astonishing answers from the minions when they are addressed. I am thinking of the smooth-haired pages, whose profiles are virtually carved out of carnelian. Later on, many of them advance to high offices.

*

A late Diadochus, then? It is not for nothing that we dwell in Eumeswil. Of the character traits that were indispensable for a Diadochus, this Eumenes, according to one historian, lacked odiousness; the same might apply to the Condor. He also lacks cruelty; he even finds it repulsive.

But I wonder why I myself cannot reach a satisfactory comparison. It must be the fault of the dilution, like a beverage that has been constantly brewed and rebrewed from the same leaves. We live on depleted organic substance. The atrocities of early myths, Mycenae, Persepolis, the ancient and the younger tyrannies, the Diadochi and the epigoni, the decadence of the western and then the eastern Roman Empire, the Renaissance princes and the conquistadors, plus the exotic palette from Dahomey to the Aztecs—it would seem as if the motifs were exhausted, sufficing for neither deeds nor misdeeds, at most for faint reminiscences.

As a historian, I know how to elude all that by moving through history as through an art gallery, surrounded by masterpieces—I am familiar with them through my studies. However, once released from any attachment, I know its rank. I grasp the human quality buried deep in its strata: in Cain *and* Abel, in the prince as in the coolie.

15

Thus, I am always on duty, both in the Casbah and in the city. When fully back to teaching, I am exempted from my obligation up here; but people think of me as a "sympathizer," and I am known as such not only to the Condor and his staff but also to his opponents. This I must reckon with, although, as I have already explained, there are limits to my sympathy.

I tend to distinguish between other people's opinions of me and my own self-assessment. Others determine my social status, which I take seriously, albeit once again within certain limits. Nor am I dissatisfied with it. In this respect, I differ from most Eumeswilers, who are dissatisfied with their positions or their standing.

I could just as easily say that I neither am satisfied with my position nor take it seriously. That would obtain for the overall situation of the city, the absence of any center, which puts every office under obligation and gives meaning to every action. Here, neither oath nor sacrifice counts any longer.

Nevertheless, when anything is possible, one can also take any liberty. I am an anarch—not because I despise authority, but because I need it. Likewise, I am not a nonbeliever, but a man who demands something worth believing in. On this point, I am like a bride in her chamber: she listens for the softest step.

My demand is based, if not entirely, then to a large extent, on my education: I am a historian, and as such I know what can be offered in terms of ideas, images, melodies, buildings, characters.

*

My current situation is that of an engineer in a demolition firm: he works with a clear conscience insofar as the castles and cathedrals, indeed even the old patrician mansions have long since been torn down. I am a lumberjack in forests with thirty-year cutting cycles: if a regime holds out that long, it may consider itself lucky.

The best one can expect is a modest legality—legitimacy is out of the question. The coats of arms have been robbed of their insignia or replaced by flags. Incidentally, it is not that I am awaiting a return to the past, like Chateaubriand, or a recurrence, like Boutefeu; I leave those matters politically to the conservatives and cosmically to the stargazers. No, I hope for something equal, nay, stronger, and not just in the human domain. *Naglfar*, the ship of the apocalypse shifts into a calculable position.

*

I cannot fail to regard myself with a certain sense of humor when I lecture to an auditorium that jumps only at the most bromidic and faddish bait. The serpent becomes an earthworm here. My sense of propriety gets more of its money's worth when, in my steward's uniform, I wait on the Condor and his guests.

Thus I take my duties seriously within an overall context that I reject for its mediocrity. The important thing is that my rejection actually refers to the totality and does not take up within it a stance that can be defined as conservative, reactionary, liberal, ironic, or in any way social. One should avoid changing one's work shift in the ever-increasing corvée of the civil war.

On this premise, I can, to be sure, take seriously what I do here. I know that the subsoil moves, perhaps like a landslide or an avalanche—and that is precisely why relationships remain undisturbed in their details. I lie aslant on a slanting plane. The distances between people do not change. I actually see them more sharply against the deceptive background. Their standing so close to the abyss also arouses my sympathy.

At times I see them as if I were walking through the streets of Pompeii before the eruption of Vesuvius. This is one of the historian's delights and, even more, his sorrow. If we see someone doing something for the last time, even just eating a piece of bread, this activity becomes wondrously profound. We participate in the transmutation of the ephemeral into the sacramental. We have inklings of eras during which such a sight was an everyday occurrence.

*

Thus I am present as if Eumeswil were a dream, a game, or even an experiment. This does not rule out personal sympathy, which, after all, we do feel when we are moved by a play at the theater.

Given my brand of observation, I would rather associate with Vigo and Bruno than with my genitor and my dear brother. Were I to behave like them, I would be rooted in an agitation that does not appeal to me in any way, whether I view it from above, from below, from the right, or from the left.

The Condor would then be "the tyrant" for me not just factually but also morally. Tyrants must be hated, so I would hate him. Or else: he embodies the will to power, as extolled by Boutefeu; a great navigator, he steers us through the waves and storms of the struggle for life, I then model myself after him, I follow him without giving it a second thought, I idolize him. Be that as it may: these are feelings that I ward off.

When I, as a historian, view us *en famille*, it strikes me that I dwell one story higher than my father and my brother: in rooms where one lives more unabashedly. I could come down at any time. That would be the historian's descent into politics—a change that might have good and even noble reasons, yet would in any case entail a loss of freedom.

*

Such is the role of the anarch, who remains free of all commitments yet can turn in any direction. A customer sits outside one of the famous cafés whose names have gone down in literary history. I picture him as, say, Manet, one of the old artists, might have painted him: with a short, dark beard, a round hat, a cigar in his hand, his features both relaxed and concentrated—that is, silently yet attentively at ease with himself and the world.

In those days, great personal freedom must have been possible. The café is near the Chambre des Députés; well-known contemporaries pass by—ministers, deputies, officers, artists, attorneys. The waiters are starting to reset the indoor tables for the evening customers; the *écailler* comes with the oyster baskets, the first streetwalkers show up.

Ambiance: around this time, the big cities begin dreaming; the night casts out its veil. The customer sees familiar and unfamiliar people, who try to involve him in a conversation, a business deal, a pleasure. But no matter how many people go by, he ignores their overtures. Otherwise the treasure accumulating in him would be frittered away in small change. Their images move him more profoundly than their fleeting presences. If he were a painter, he would store their images in his mind and liberate them in masterpieces. If he were a poet, he would revive the mood for himself and for many others: the harmony of the people and the houses, the paling of the colors and the awakening of tones with the thickening night. Everything flows into everything else and melds.

Tout, jusqu'au souvenir; tout s'envole, tout fuit
Et on est seul avec Paris, l'onde et la nuit.

All things, and even memories, flee out of sight,
And you're alone with Paris, and the wave and the night.

Like any pleasure, this one, too, is whetted by abstinence. Sensibility and, with it, the sensations, are heightened into an incredibly keen scent. Invisible harmony flows more and more intensely into visible harmony until it dazzles. The café customer could enter reality at any time. If he withholds himself and lingers in non-desire, then this means that the offer is as yet inadequate for the hypersensitive suitor. Now the figures writhe in more and more violent throes; they want to be recognized.

The rock awaits Moses, whose staff is about to touch it.

16

Now, how about that fly in the ointment? This is the way my father and my brother refer to my service, particularly during domestic turmoil, when they hole up in our little house, not reemerging until the worst is over. They have two flags in the attic, not just in theory but also in fact, and they hang them out according to the weather. If the Condor has stood fast, they can flaunt their white vests; should his enemies triumph, then my father and my brother have always supported them. Perhaps they once attended a course on Giordano Bruno; they now blow it up into a heroic deed. Every historian knows what antithetical lights can be projected on men and powers.

I never cease to be amazed at how unabashedly my genitor tries to dovetail his basically praiseworthy theories with our slanting reality. I, in contrast, know that I lie aslant within a slanting reality, and I believe it is precisely this knowledge that gives thought some integrity. When acting, I, by the way, do so not aslant but obliquely: consistent with the situation and devoid of self-pity. A distinction that can no longer be taken for granted in Eumeswil.

*

The Condor sticks to Machiavelli's doctrine that a good military and good laws are the fundaments of the state. One might add that our daily bread has to be assured. Such is the case; and the butter, too, especially at the games. It is precisely here, at the athletic contests, in the market-places as well, and more seldom in the law courts, that tumults may erupt. The police quell them easily, the Domo prefers to let them simply run their course. "They feel worn out once they've done enough rampaging." He also thinks that the best police force, like a good housewife, is the kind that is least spoken of. He is relieved of some of his worries by television; here, too, games and melodramas are more popular than politics. Besides, the masses are thus divided among their households.

Furthermore, the Condor enjoys popular favor. So domestic turmoil is seldom to be expected, although possible at any time. It then catches us unawares, like an earthquake. For a long time now, the classical revolutions have been supplanted by military putsches, which spell one another. Even the tribunes require a general above all. This is a truism; the predecessor's corruption is a leitmotif. In this, too, they are nearly always right.

There are variants when the new rulers present themselves: a few cite the populace and its will; the others, like the Condor, are satisfied with the power of facts. In some cases, there is a joviality that inspires confidence.

Either way, both the police and the military have to be watched over: this includes generals and praetorian guards. Cliques of guard officers, like those from which the Orlovs ascended, are hard to imagine in the Casbah; still, the Condor's father was a simple sergeant. The Domo has confidential agents all the way down to the battalions, and then again others who watch over those agents. This should not be regarded as espionage; the current method is more casual.

"My dear sergeant, you know the Condor's high opinion of you." At parades, he is addressed by name and has the opportunity of distinguishing himself; no wonder he is also ordered to attend the report session. A capable soldier, an open adherent—there is no secrecy involved, no hint of snooping. And it goes without saying that the Domo "stays in direct contact with the troops." I see one or another of the boys when the Condor takes him along to the night bar after mess—a special distinction. Open faces, thoroughly uncritical, gullible. That is a third variant of conduct in Eumeswil: failure to recognize the slanting situation, which I accept as a task while my genitor misjudges it.

Gullibility is the norm; it is the credit on which states live: without it, even their most modest survival would be impossible.

*

Thus, domestic turmoil is unlikely; but when riots erupt, they go for broke. They would also start right in with serious actions—naval mutinies, occupation of radio stations, proclamations by officers, and, above all, an attack on the Condor. That was how he himself seized power.

Attempts of this ilk can seldom be fully hushed up. Something usually leaks out. Many uprisings have succeeded only because the rulers failed to take the early symptoms seriously. And the symptoms are prefaced by an incubation period.

It is unlikely that the Domo could be caught by surprise; the intelligence system runs perfectly. The morning bulletin apprises him of anything special that has occurred during the night. Once a day the chief of police comes with his report, in which, *inter alia*, the postal surveillance and the *chronique scandaleuse* play a role.

There is no essential difference between the police and the military. To the extent that we can speak of war between our fellah states, this is usually a fire encroaching on foreign territories. After all, they are dependent on the empires.

Tyranny goes by the law of the hunting preserve; if any of the young harts thinks he can defy the royal stag, they engage in a test of strength. Then all hell breaks loose. The Domo puts out a Red Alert, first for an entire minute, then at repeated intervals. This is followed by a message to the phonophores: a normally silent frequency is now opened—of course only on apparatuses that, like mine, are suitably equipped.

The units gather at the alarm posts. Every man knows what he has to do.

17

If I happen to be in the Casbah when the alert comes, I first get into my fighting gear, which, like a life jacket on a ship, lies packed up beneath my bed: comfortable overalls with boots and a cap. Everything is dyed the reddish shade of the castle cliff. Iron rations, bandages, and such fill a sack; not even the small flask of cognac has been overlooked. The armory is in the cellar; from there I fetch guns and ammunition. Two cabin stewards report to me. Since they work for me in the Casbah, I know them from our everyday dealings.

The three of us then descend one of the paths that meander down to the city, and we station ourselves at midcourse. There used to be a small watchtower here, but it collapsed during the great earthquake. A stump has survived; covered with reeds, it resembles one of the shacks that were built for duck hunting down below on the Sus. There we settle in. First I send the other two a bit further down, to a sign that says NO TRESPASSING. They tear off the metallic foil, and a death's head appears in phosphorescent paint.

The Domo expects the police to refrain from using their firearms; even shooting in self-defense has to be justified in subsequent reports. If, however, they are authorized to shoot, then he demands that they aim at the individual and with intent to kill.

My two assistants set up the preliminary warning sign and then come back. I assign the guard schedule and discuss the possibilities with them. The cabin stewards switch off with one another; probably one of the Chinese cooks who also serve as waiters and a Lebanese named Nebek are part of our unit. The cook has a long name; his fellow workers call him Kung. A fat fellow wouldn't be of much use; his girlfriend, Ping-sin, lives in the city.

I can picture them: the Lebanese listens in joyous expectation; since he likes to shoot, he hopes that it will be our crew that gets attacked. His vocabulary is rich in aggressive expressions, especially up in the Casbah when he has not visited his ladylove for weeks on end. "Shoot, hit, mow 'em down!" The Chinese sits back comfortably, folding his hands on his belly.

In reality, nothing much can happen here. It's an excellent position. Anyone passing the warning sign would be courting suicide. By day, the sign could be spotted from far down on the slope, and by night, the outpost would alert us with signal flares and through the phonophore. It is impossible to leave the path, for the castle cliff is covered over with a prickly euphorbia which the populace calls "more venomous than a mother-in-law." An attack could be mounted only on the paved road and not without military arms. A lot must happen beforehand.

*

I ponder my mission from three points of view: first as the Condor's night steward, then as a historian, and finally as an anarch.

It occurs to me that my instructions overlook, or rather ignore, one possibility, a very crucial one, which they must have taken into account. I am referring to the eventuality that attackers might advance on us from the rear. Should that occur, then the Casbah would have to be in their hands already. Presumably, this would be done stealthily, for if it followed an assault, we would notice it. From our shack, we can view a bend in the access road and thus contribute, albeit modestly, to the defense.

So that would be the classic case of a palace revolution. All it takes is a few shots, perhaps a dagger. The relationship between the ruler's seat and the capital is one of the problems of comparative historiography. The citadel can stand either inside or outside the city. The inner location offers the advantage of immediate proximity; a revolt can be nipped in the bud. The outer location, in contrast, provides latitude for reflecting and then for pressing the long arm of the lever. The distance from the capital should be precisely calculated. Eumeswil can be surveyed from the Casbah, which, in turn, is hard to climb up to. Capri is very far from Rome; nevertheless, from that island, Tiberius, through diplomatic maneuvering, succeeded in thwarting Sejanus's dangerous conspiracy. Yet he kept ships ready in the harbor in case he had to flee.

We know of ancient Oriental palaces that stood inside the city walls; each, however, had an underground escape route. In hereditary monarchies, a residence outside the capital can assume the character of a *château de plaisance* or a summer villa. The tyrant, in contrast, must always be prepared. He would do well to have eyes in the back of his head; at the night bar, the Condor and the Domo sit with their backs against the wall. Mirrors are installed in other rooms, even the corridors.

That is why I think they cannot possibly have failed to take a palace revolution into account. On the contrary—this is one of the notions haunting the tyrant even in his dreams, perhaps intensifying into forms of madness that can be highly dangerous, especially for his intimates. Such an obsession can even destroy a good character, like that of Tiberius. No wonder the historians have such conflicting opinions of him.

Another reason why my employment in the Casbah is pleasant is that the distrust does not transcend the boundaries of objectively justified caution. The overall tone is terse, not without a benevolence that can become almost warm at night. Mutual respect is seldom violated. The level sinks only when the Yellow Khan visits with his people. But such moments offer a great deal to observe.

*

I do admit I would not mind serving a Tiberius. That would be closer to the historical substance whose final infusion I am tasting here.

The period following Actium opened up tremendous prospects, of which only some were realized. Vigo pointed out the background: the destruction of Mark Antony's fleet in the shadow of the arcana. On the one side, Isis and Osiris; on the other, Apollo. Octavian to his brother-in-law: "Thy name should be Serapion, not Antony." Asclepius was also present. Mark Antony's ships were made of wood from the grove that was sacred to the god on the island of Kos. After the victory, Augustus had Publius Turullius executed for that sacrilege.

I must not go into detail, otherwise I may start dreaming. The African assaults on Europe are almost as thrilling as the Asiatic ones and, by their very nature, more colorful. But I was discussing Tiberius, who, I find, lost some grand opportunities by moving to Capri. This error was repeated historically on a much smaller scale when, say, the duke of Orleans, as regent, wanted to devote himself entirely to his debaucheries with his roués, and so he unloaded all business on the abominable Guillaume Dubois.

Tiberius is remarkable for his character; the sheer fact that he, virtually as a private citizen, could hold on to the reins for such a long time verges on witchcraft. Nor were magical features lacking in him. Even today, when shepherds on Capri talk about "il Tiberio," their intonation has a strange lilt. He lingers in the rocks.

I have often summoned him to the luminar late at night. Some of his days are registered there virtually minute by minute. Now and then such details are important, because historiography is forced to rely on abbreviations. But I also want to know when, for how long, and in whose company such a man was bored—I want to participate in his boredom. In this respect, the historian is akin to a good actor, who identifies with his role.

*

Naturally there are different conceptions. They are unavoidable; even a brilliant composer will not find a conductor who interprets him historically. Of course, sharp deviations often distort less than imponderable ones. If the background of the notes, their own existence and instinctual life, are grasped through congenial improvisation, then the time of destiny triumphs over the time of history.

I was reckless enough to broach this topic at the family table, only to reap an answer worthy of my genitor: namely, that the invention of the phonograph has rendered such speculations null and void. The inventor was, I believe, an especially disagreeable American, a disciple of Franklin's named Edison.

After all, as things stand—but it was sensible of me to avoid any rejoinder—not only is technology changing, but so is the human ear. So even if a recording is perfect, we hear differently—aside from the fact that even the best machine cannot replace an absent orchestra.

To be sure: with that invention, jukeboxes began to invade music. This led to the first universal musical style and therewith to the generalizing and vulgarizing of folk tunes—and also, incidentally, to an arsenal of extremely hideous instruments. I often listen to them; each style has its own content—the era of warring states managed to bring forth almost nothing but nostalgic reminiscences. And the physicians had to treat more patients who had gone deaf in the musical infernos than in the wars.

Now, I am not putting down the universal style as one of the anarch's hopes. A new Orpheus could do justice to the world along with its heavens and hells.

*

I can enjoy "Intuitive Improvisations" at the luminar; for generations, important minds must have hoarded and shaped the material of world history in the catacombs.

Such things are possible during long periods of security, especially when they are played as a game. A passion for the archival and a eunuchlike chinoiserie add to the fun—as does fear of annihilation and also of universal wars. The archives of the Vatican would fill only a niche there.

I often wonder what this archivistic instinct is aiming at. It seems to transcend any historical intention. Perhaps it is laboring for an Emir Musa of future deserts and wastelands.

Where was I now? Oh, yes—Tiberius. And I was wondering how I would have served him on Capri—my job here in the Casbah helps me chiefly as a historical model. I believe I have a certain knack for dealing with great men. As with moons and satellites, a mean distance is the most favorable. If you get too close to Jupiter, you burn up; if you keep far away, your observation suffers. You then move in theories and ideas instead of facts.

Res, non verba—whatever you commit or omit, it is generally good to be informed about physical laws. This is an important maxim; it guides the elephant, which tests the ground before taking each step. Once, at the night bar, Rosner started talking about this animal; he told us, among other things, that when it finds itself sinking into quicksand or a bog, it never hesitates to swing up its trunk, lift its rider from his seat, and thrust him under its foot like a piece of wood. The Domo, who has a mind for such anecdotes, said, "The fault lies with the driver who demands the impossible. This could never happen to an experienced mahout." He was probably correct; if you ride an elephant, you have to know what you are doing.

Keeping a proper distance from a power wielder takes restraint; one must avoid approaching him on one's own, even with good intent, like that fisherman who had caught a gigantic sole and, when he brought it as a gift to Tiberius, reaped a nasty reward. The same thing happened to the centurion who was supposed to show the way to the bearers of Caesar's sedan, but wound up in a cul-de-sac. Caution is necessary, as when one is dealing with explosives; I am thinking of that stargazer who, when ordered to predict the hour of his own death, had enough presence of mind to slip his head out of the noose. He said, "As I see, I am momentarily in great danger."

The best job is one in which you see a lot and are seen little. In this respect, I am content with my work; at the night bar, I often fiddle around like a chameleon, as if melting into the wallpaper. Compared with Capri, these are small fry that I catch here; meanwhile I dream about Tiberius chatting with Macro at the triclinium as I refill the beakers of the Spintrians. Now a fateful name is spoken: "Germanicus."

*

The work, even if subordinate or, as my brother says, "unworthy," causes me no headaches; it is the substratum of my observation. As a chauffeur, an interpreter, or a secretary for trivia, I would still do my job. Anything occurring on the side—a stifled smile, a backstage cue—yields more than the grand receptions and the speeches at the Forum, where the potentates stand on their buskins. That is grist for Plutarch's mill.

I therefore prefer the history of courts and cultures to that of politics, and I prefer Herodotus to Thucydides. Action is more easily emulated than character; this is borne out by the bromidic reiterations in world history. Eumeswil may be a city of epigoni and also fellahs, but at least there is no sounding off for posterity—even in the Casbah. Minor everyday weal and woe are the stuff of conversation.

*

People say I thrive on my work, and I do live up to this reputation. My day flows by agreeably; I have plenty of time for my studies. But when the waves surge high, as during the Yellow Khan's visits or at banquets, I volunteer for cabin service, and I also wait tables, which is not normally part of my job. My efforts are rewarded and known to everyone all the way up to the Domo. This provides me with leisure when Emanuelo turns into Martin at the luminar.

My about-face is not as simple as it may look at first glance. For one thing, I have to succeed in treating my work as a game that I both play and watch. This gives even dangerous places like the duck shack a charm of their own. It presumes that one can scrutinize oneself from a certain distance like a chess figure—in a word, that one sees historical classification as more important than personal classification. This may sound exacting; but it used to be required of any soldier. The special trait making me an anarch is that I live in a world which I "ultimately" do not take seriously. This increases my freedom; I serve as a temporary volunteer.

*

In regard to self-distancing, I owe Bruno a thing or two; he also taught me techniques for overcoming fear. The soldier participating in an attack knew he might get wounded or killed; that was part of the job, it was even laudable. A hit here on the duck shack would be simply a fact unconnected to king or country—an industrial accident. This is something I have to reckon with; I am fascinated by the tactical situation and not its meager ideology. The Domo is aware of this; after a clash, the Condor hands out not medals and decorations but donations of land and money. Also, the phonophore may be raised to a higher level.

A more difficult problem is maltreatment, which involves deeply rooted notions of honor. The stroke that knighted a man was the last to be dealt with the flat of the sword; after that, only the edge was considered acceptable. The officer wounded in a national war was decorated. If he was slapped in a social context without getting satisfaction, he would have been socially disqualified. Thinkers with a cynical streak have always made fun of that: the cavalier who limps away with a smile after being kicked by a horse wants to see blood when an ass has banged him in the head.

The world civil war changed values. National wars are fought between fathers, civil wars between brothers. It has always been better to fall under the father's hand than into the brother's; it is easier being an enemy of another nation than another class.

I do not wish to expatiate. It is enough for me to be at the luminar and, say, compare the situation of prisoners-of-war in the nineteenth Christian century with the situation of social prisoners in the twentieth, plus the differences between political vernaculars. According to Thofern, the debasement of these jargons has run parallel to the increase in mass pressure. If humanity is written on the standard, then this means not only the exclusion of the enemy from society, but the deprivation of all his human rights. This explains the resurgence of torture in vast areas, the deportations of whole populaces, the mercantile conception of mankind, the official and criminal forms of hostage-taking, the batteries of cannon. Plus the grand words—it reminds me of my genitor, who has one foot in Periclean Athens and the other in Eumeswil.

*

Playing the gentleman here would be possible only for actors; nor would anyone consider doing it anymore. Rather, people, such as my genitor and my brother, feel like martyrs. Half of Eumeswil is inhabited by types who have suffered for an idea or at least claim to have done so. They stood true to the flag, offered heroic resistance—in short, the worn-out military claptrap has reawakened. Upon taking a closer look, one sees that, with rare exceptions, they tried to save their hides just like anybody else. But one turns a blind eye to all that, so long as they do not overdo it.

The anarch sticks to facts, not ideas. He suffers not for facts but because of them, and usually through his own fault, as in a traffic accident. Certainly, there are unforeseeable things—maltreatments. However, I believe I have attained a certain degree of self-distancing that allows me to regard this as an accident.

*

We are still dealing with the duck shack—what am I to conclude from the fact that my instructions mention no possibility of a palace revolt? Such an event usually takes only minutes, ending with the destruction of the attacker or the attacked. Evidently the Condor and the Domo have not considered the possibility of fleeing. And that fits in with my image of them.

Thus, there is no need to instruct the outposts. This does not absolve me of judging the situation for myself. Being mowed down from the back and *en passant* is a peasant's fate and has little appeal. So I have to know what is happening at the Casbah while we observe the access roads. Events would scarcely be altogether soundless.

We can rely above all on the dogs; they can scent violence, participating in it with their howls. They also herald death with a peculiar whimpering. The dogs perceive it even from far away, and not through scent alone.

Aside from that, I dispatch one of my sentinels up to the Casbah at regular intervals in order to forage or "maintain contact," as the primer for sentry groups terms it. I keep abreast, and I would be one of the first to learn that the Condor had been toppled. That would gain me some time.

After such an overthrow, the city starts teeming like a beehive—half as before a wedding flight, half as during the killing of the drones. At home, Father and Brother confer on whether the old flag should be hung out. Rashness can be fatal. Perhaps I may have enough family feeling to inform them from up here. They would then be the first to know that the Condor was lying in his own blood, and they could take their advantage.

For the anarch, little is changed; flags have meaning for him, but not sense. I have seen them in the air and on the ground like leaves in May and in November; and I have done so as a contemporary and not just as a historian. The May Day celebration will survive, but with a different meaning. New portraits will head up the processions. A date devoted to the Great Mother is re-profaned. A pair of lovers in the woods pays more homage to it. I mean the forest as something undivided, where *every* tree is still a liberty tree.

For the anarch, little is changed when he strips off a uniform that he wore partly as fool's motley, partly as camouflage. It covers his spiritual freedom, which he will objectivate during such transitions. This distinguishes him from the anarchist, who, objectively unfree, starts raging until he is thrust into a more rigorous straitjacket.

*

The two sentries whom I previously commanded on behalf of the Condor are now immediately subordinate to me—that is, I subordinate them. I order them to unload their guns and get the ammunition to safety. Then I can confer with them, not because I need their advice, but because it makes a better impression. I have studied such debates. They involve a lot of talking, but there is always someone who knows what he wants and who has a cudgel in his sack. Things drift toward this cudgel.

I will probably check once more on how far things have developed up in the Casbah and down in the city. Nothing is more dangerous than relying on mere rumor; one easily gets into the role of the donkey who ventured out on the ice too early. "La journée des dupes"—this, too, is a recurring figure.

The Chinese is quietistic—I will send him into the city; he will not stand out. Nebek has aggressive tendencies; he is more in place at the Casbah. He will have to tell me whether he has seen the corpse. And: "Did you see not just the boots, but also the face? Above all: Who is now in charge up there?"

Perhaps he will already do a bit of looting up there; that is his due. I also have to reckon with his making a fuss. The Chinese, instead of coming back, may sell his gun in the city and stay with Ping-sin. That is likewise his due, and I will be rid of him.

I will probably dismiss both men; they can contribute little to my safety and are more trouble than they are worth. The fact that I regard almost everyone as a potential traitor is one of my failings, but it has stood the test. Most of them need not even be tortured to talk. Indeed, torture appears to stimulate them; they talk for nothing.

*

Presumably I will have enough time to ferret out what game is being played and to what extent we can expect purges. Be that as it may, it will be imperative to go underground for a while. Every sensible person in Eumeswil reckons with this possibility. He changes homes, even if only for one night. He "is in the country," he has a secret bank account. They vanish like frogs, resurfacing after several days, months, or years. They hibernate until a new springtime brings a new May Day.

As for me, I do not foresee a long absence. After all, a night steward is not a big fish. However, he, too, had best remain invisible for now. Of greater concern is the fact that I am also suspect as a historian. Whole gaggles of impotent professors have shifted into political persecution. Even if I had nothing to fear from them, their sheer proximity would be unendurable. I would much rather wash dishes.

It is also possible that I may strike my tents indefinitely. If things heated up in the Casbah, people might even think I was dead. Such a form of disappearance is especially favorable to resurrection.

18

Disappearing is even better than submerging; I prefer the tactic of mice to that of frogs. I am thinking not of the black and the gray mice in houses and gardens, but of the tawny mouse in the bush forest, the one that resembles a tiny squirrel. It feeds on nuts that it gathers in early autumn to store in its winter nest. There, safe and sound, it hibernates for six months or longer while the leaves settle on the forest floor and the snow then covers them up.

Following the mouse's example, I have planned ahead. The muscardin is a kinsman of the dormouse; in my childhood I already pictured the lives of such dreamers as highly comfortable. It is no coincidence that after my mother's death I lost myself in this protective world. Lonely as I was in the attic, I became the muscardin. For years, it remained my totem animal.

On the outskirts of the forest, I sought out a nook for my lair. The entrance hole was not to be located on level ground; it would be better in a hollow trunk or a cleft in a rock. From there, I began digging the tunnel, a bit deeper each day; scraping out the soil, I scattered it so that no trace remained.

Once I got deep enough, I dug a second tunnel, which led upward as an escape route. With every entrance, you have to provide an exit; with every road, you have to think of the road back—that was already clear to me even then. The work had to be done quietly and prudently. From above, the sparrow hawk was a threat by day and the owl by night; on the ground, there were hostile creatures, especially the viper—a muscardin is always menaced. That is the tribute it pays to freedom.

Once the tunnels were dug, I started the dwelling, a cozy chamber, not too small, not too big. It never occurred to me that there might also be a female. Nor did I have to provide for my mother; she was omnipresent, she was the cavern itself.

Once the chamber was set up and its oval smoothed out, I dug the tap tunnel to the storeroom. The latter was bigger and arched like a cake; with such a pantry, there would be no want. Not to be forgotten was the toilet; the muscardin is praised for its cleanliness. It does not smell like other rodents, though in springtime it gives off a musky fragrance. During the winter, the toilet would fill up with black kernels; here, too, I thought of not only the mouth but also the exit.

After the construction, I went on to the furnishing. In a camp for mooning away the winter, the finest downs were just barely fine enough. I knew places where the selection had already been made: the nests of kitty wrens and marigold finches. I tracked them down whenever I heard the "zi-zi-zi" of the finches; that is their cry when their brood has taken wing. I had already spotted their nests while they were still building them. The muscardin climbs cautiously through the branches. Up there, I discovered the downs that the birds had plucked out, the tiny fibers that they had gathered in, and I took my tithe.

On the edge of the woods, the clover dodder twines up in the nettles and scabious herbs. It deserves its German name, *Kleeseide*, "clover silk," for it forms cushions of silky-soft threads that desiccate in early autumn. I knew how to harvest these, too; I wove them into my lair and I added briar rose apples and hawthorn.

I enjoy working; I held the fibers with my feet, I wove them with my hands and mouth. It was easy, though it took place in the dark. When fabrics are supple and feel pleasant, the work can become a game; the material pleasure turns into a spiritual one.

That was my mood in the construction, and I became even more joyful when the first nuts were falling—with thuds that I could distinguish from all other sounds. It was a knocking, a heralding. That is my favorite kind of prophecy. Not an empty promise, but a phenomenon, a small handsel, something material. I am like Saint Thomas: Show thy wounds! Then I stand firm.

Soon the nuts were falling en masse; when the wind blasted through the foliage, they sounded like hail. The nuthatches likewise tossed them down—stymphalian birds with iron wings, swarms of them whirring in from the north, where they had spent the summer in the forests of the Yellow Khan.

I raked in some of the abundance, carrying down the best nuts in my mouth, but always cautiously. Other fruits also stood me in good stead: the three-sided beechnut, the rose hip, the hawthorn, the rowanberry, and all kinds of seed grains.

My storeroom was quickly filled. Nor did I neglect my immediate rations, since the supplies you bring in your paunch are even more important for hibernation. "Winter, we'll sleep you out; we are brimming with blossoming fat"—those are the words of a Roman poet who celebrated our life.

A small dormouse's hunger is soon appeased. The imagination, by contrast, is insatiable; it feasts on the world's abundance. I enjoyed being with my provisions—a tiny cellarer with a crammed belly. I arranged my stores by types, piling them up. Let winter come, the harsher the better; I had planned ahead.

When the leaves fell more densely, the outdoors became inhospitable. One morning, the leaves were rimy. I reexamined my lair, tugging and twitching it aright. Then I stopped up the entrance with dry hay, and also the exit, though less solidly. Now let the snow fall; the wolf season was beginning.

I could lay myself to rest with drawn knees and a sunken head. My breath would not stir a feather, my heartbeat would be barely perceptible. I was the child in its mother's womb. Why could this not last forever?

*

Why is it that my reveries stopped when I reached this point? A dream culminates; it grows too strong—we have to break off. We await the beloved, from far away we make out her vehicle among all the others. It stops outside the house, and now the game of doors commences: the door of the vehicle, of the garden, of the house; now she is mounting the stairs. The final door is about to open.

19

Children's games are as disparate as their characters; their playing foreshadows what they will do as men and women. The leitmotif recurs at every age. And that was what happened to me with the muscardin and its refuge in Eumeswil. For that, I have to go back a little.

Even before the Condor shelled the harbor, one could sense the uneasiness that usually precedes such actions: there is a lot of talking and also whispering; people who used to barely exchange nods get together now and confer.

In my genitor's home, too, there were meetings of people who, like him, hoped that the tribunes would hold out and who more or less had reasons for their hopes. They tried to raise each other's spirits; they heard more or less sensible things. I could judge them from my perspective as an anarch, who, although personally indifferent to the whole business, found it fascinating as a historic issue. Moreover, I may have been the only person who was not afraid. I relished what I was listening to, like Stendhal on such an occasion. I appreciate him also as a historian.

Now, I am not putting down fear. It is a foundation of physicality, indeed of physics. If the ground wobbles or if the house so much as threatens to collapse, one looks for the door. This, too, creates a selection—say, of those people who did not fall into the trap. In this respect, Odysseus is one of our greatest models—the whiffer par excellence. Fear is primary: the instinctive whiffing of danger. It is joined by caution, then canniness and also cunning. Odysseus' caution is so extraordinary because he also has courage and curiosity. He is the harbinger of Western man's intellect, boldness, and inquiring mind.

*

Their fears demonstrated a better assessment of the situation than any words they uttered. The Condor was already the center—invisible to his enemies, visible to his partisans. They clung together, from Cato the Younger to the traitor Ganelon. The Condor dictated their thoughts, then their movements. Could one, should one adjust to him or even fall in with him?

On such eves, a tyrant needs friends; but equally indispensable are enemies. Blood will flow—that is the consecration he cannot renounce. The populace expects it of him. "There's the glutton, the gimp! Drag him on a hook, the patricide—throw him into the Tiber!"

And what about the proscription lists? Some people are more or less incriminated, but the fellow traveler will also be charged. Accusers who have kept silent develop an astounding sense of justice. Still, the very prospect of losing one's job is harsh, so you put up with a thing or two. The best job is a modest one, where you don't act big. But even here, the envious are not lacking.

So they calculated their chances, weighed the issues of time and space. In cases of doubt, vanishing is advisable, even for one night. The absence can be drawn out. Meanwhile water flows over the dam; anyone can resurface eventually.

"Dear friend, where have you been? We haven't seen you in ages."

"I've been living."

*

Regarding a space, it is good to plan ahead during periods when there isn't a cloud in the sky. Several of my genitor's friends had relatives abroad; in those days, a bungalow on the northern edge of the Mediterranean was also popular. Another friend had made emergency arrangements with his girlfriend. There are women who kept a lover hidden for years behind a jib door or in a garret. He could take breathers at night.

That was more or less how they thought and planned in the background, while I rubbed my hands. Man is a rational being who does not like sacrificing his safety to theories. Placards come and go, but the wall they are pasted on endures. Theories and systems pass over us in the same way.

"Nothing fazes you," my brother once said during one of our useless debates; I took it as a compliment.

*

Incidentally, it was not as bad as they had expected, although it did not come off without violence; every revolution demands blood. Not much more flowed than at bullfights.

Naturally, prudence is always called for; there is a gap during which imponderables occur. For days and nights, the underworld has a free hand. The new rulers do not interfere—these are shortcuts. They fit in with their plans. The Lebanese once said to me: "You know, when we got the first news of the terror, the time of flowery speeches was over." In a woodland near Nahr-el-Kalb, they had found corpses that no one gave two hoots about—least of all the police. A clairvoyant was also killed. One-eyed people get off more easily.

*

Almost everyone is scared for his job. Others, however, may look forward to being promoted out of turn; accordingly, the denunciations swell. This also tends to happen when majorities succeed one another legally. They push their party men even into the tobacco shops.

During an overthrow, one must also reckon with types who tell themselves, "It would be best if he never came back." The higher a predecessor stood, the deeper his fall and the more certain his death. But even the little fellow traveler out in the suburbs is threatened with a settling of accounts. He pays for his daily bread a second time.

There are strata that abut on the magma, becoming too hot for the historian, too dense. Perhaps that is the source of my disgust at the obtuse reiteration of events. If a Shakespeare has mastered the material, then that should suffice once and for all.

*

We should act either instinctively, like animals, or reasonably, like cerebral beings. In that case, there would be no remorse. Here in Eumeswil the soil is too leached out to put forth a Saint Bartholomew's Night or a Sicilian Vespers; the ground can only nourish infamy. On the other hand, one must consider liquidation through administrative channels. This is taken care of quite dispassionately, cozily, by bureaucrats sitting on their behinds, in their offices—frequently types who cannot even watch a chicken being slaughtered.

*

These views are partly retrospect, partly prospect. "Remission" is what the doctors call the temporary abatement of an illness. However, the body remains susceptible. For now, there seems little to fear; the Domo even exaggerates the judicature. This, too, is a suspicious symptom. Our model is not the courtroom but the traffic accident. A driver overlooks a stop sign or a right of way and burns up with a hundred other people.

My genitor and nearly all his friends actually kept their jobs; only my brother was slightly plucked. Soon they were sitting together again as the Seven Upright Men.

*

Incidentally, I notice that our professors, trying to show off to their students, rant and rail against the state and against law and order, while expecting that same state to punctually pay their salaries, pensions, and family allowances, so that they value at least this kind of law and order. Make a fist with the left hand and open the right hand receptively—that is how one gets through life. This was easier under the tribunes; it is also one reason for my dear brother's nostalgia for their splendor. Yet he himself helped to saw off their branch.

*

The Condor feels like, and presents himself as, a tyrant; this entails fewer lies. For me, nothing basic has changed; my character, that of an anarch, remains intact. For the historian, the yield is actually richer in that it becomes more vivid. The political trend is always to be observed, partly as a spectacle, partly for one's own safety. The liberal is dissatisfied with every regime; the anarch passes through their sequence—as inoffensively as possible—like a suite of rooms. This is the recipe for anyone who cares more about the substance of the world than its shadow—the philosopher, the artist, the believer. In this respect, I feel that the Jews were wrong when they refused to hail Caesar. Saluting was purely a question of form. To be sure, one must overcome one's inner resistance before agreeing to something.

At first, as after every change of regime, there was a period of fair weather, even a certain upsurge due to reforms; new brooms sweep clean. Then came disturbances of a mostly personal nature. I will return to this when discussing capital punishment.

It was in the city and not in the Casbah that I sensed I might get involved in the turmoil. At the institute, I was viewed with greater reserve, they grew more reticent with me in conversations, though almost imperceptibly. Such caution is heralded by a lessening of candor, the emergence of taboos. Thus, in my presence, they avoided any allusion, even humorous ones, to the ruler—or, if they did venture to allude to him, it sounded forced. In the street, this was clearer. Unknown people who saw my phonophore turned away as if they had spotted something unpleasant. Others glared at me with unconcealed repulsion.

The phonophore is generally carried in such a way that its edge sticks out of the left breast pocket. The classes are marked on it. If we can even speak of classes here, they are of a potential and dynamic nature. Equality and distinctions of the ahistorical masses are reduced to motion. The social function is mechanically encoded and integrated in the hierarchy. The Condor controls the monopoly on addressing the people and he doles out the opportunities as he sees fit. The phonophore guarantees what the Jacobins strove for as an ideal: the perpetual forum, "deliberation *en permanence*."

Rarely is the gold phonophore seen; its carriers seldom walk in the city. My silver phonophore, of course, is merely that of a minor trabant—but notable insofar as it is attached to the Red Network. This has its pluses and minuses. I can be mustered as an auxiliary policeman at any time.

*

Changes in profound strata announce themselves on the surface as delicate ripples. One becomes sensitive to variations in the weather; perhaps the temperature has dipped one tenth of a degree.

It is not pleasant when a group of acquaintances obviously change the subject the instant one enters. Back then, I noticed that in certain places or on certain occasions I would cover my phonophore with the flap of my breast pocket. At first, this was purely a reflex action, yet it was already the beginning of a camouflage. A short time later I pondered my safety: It might become advisable for me to withdraw from society for an indefinite period.

This does not mean that I was thinking of simply deserting; such a demarche would flout my rules. A game, whether one starts out with white or with black, is played to its end. This end was, no doubt, considered by the Condor, and that was why his instructions ignored the possibility of a rear assault on the duck shack. The tyrant wishes to remain true to himself And to that extent he can count on me. This loyalty is not to be understood as vassalage. It is a question of personal integrity.

20

There was something appealing about the prospect of taking a complete holiday from society and being my own master for a while. I even had to avoid wishing for the catastrophe, much less promoting it with my limited powers—this would not have been altogether far-fetched. *Carnevale*—this madness breaks out even when a year draws to its close, not to mention a millennium.

Now it was time to locate a place for my molting—which brings me back to the muscardin. The mouth of the Sus is shallow and sprawling; sandbanks emerge at low tide. Troops of flamingos gather on them, and also herons, bitterns, ducks, ibises, and cormorants; in short, the delta is transmuted into an avian paradise. The hunters, fowlers, fishermen, and naturally also ornithologists like Rosner, feel fine there. Rosner sits on the shore in front of his flock of birds, observing them while keeping his journal and banding the feet of those he catches. Occasionally I accompany him—either for pleasure, since this is a life as in the garden of Eden, or in a semiofficial capacity when the Yellow Khan is about to visit and the Great Hunts have to be prepared. The falconers then train their birds to seize, the hunters train their hounds to fetch.

That was where I began my reconnoitering. No one notices if you move about with a bird gun and provisions. Reed jungles spread out just above the estuary. They would be impenetrable if animals had not beaten their trails: shadowy corridors in the elephant grass. Going through them is dangerous; I may have to dodge into the rushes at any moment, especially at dawn or dusk. Also, prior to every step, I have to test where to set foot. Then again, I scarcely have to worry about being followed.

Further upstream, the reeds become sparse; the swamp becomes treacherous. Most treacherous of all are the alluvial sandbanks deposited by the high tides. Even if you sink only knee-deep, you are doomed. The tide has left sloughs and basins enjoyed by the reptiles. It took me a long time to mark out a safe path.

In the midst of this labyrinth, a flat cap swells up, scarcely larger than a medium-sized golf course. Not even a Bushman would dream of venturing to the top, for it is densely overrun with a copse of hand-long thorns, *Acacia horrida*. A slope for shrikes—in order to reach the peak, I had to slash a path for myself. At the top, a surprise was waiting.

*

As a historian, I have to deal with the geomantic power that imbues many places, especially hills. It is primarily of a material, physical nature. That is the source of its strength. Every nook harbors a cave. Novalis: "The bosom is the chest risen to the rank of mystery." That is good. "*From* the rank of mystery" would be even clearer.

My model was Lugdanum, a Gallic city that I care about. A stronghold and sanctuary for tribes and nations that followed one another from the days of those whom the archaeologists puzzle about until the tourist swarms of the third Christian millennium—would all fill more than one book. Roland, too, resided there. A hill, visible far and away, also commanding far and away. The cathedral was built from its stone; the rock rose from the rank of mystery. Under its foundations: crypts and catacombs; there, mystery dwells more densely than above, in the forest of columns. I had to think of it when, scratched by thorns and punctured by mosquitoes, I reached the crest of the hill.

*

Historically, this coast has always lain in shadow—under foreign masters who carved it up into provinces and colonies or retreated here during civil warfare. Mauretanian earth; soldiers have fought on it with horses, camels, and elephants, with chariots and tanks.

This hill offered itself to anybody who wanted to survey the lowland all the way to the sea and beyond the river. The last time must have been after the Second World War—that is, after the final triumph of the technician over the warrior. Just as flames keep blazing on the edges after vast conflagrations, isolated feuds keep going after peace treaties. Such feuds rarely leave names or dates behind; for the historian, these are dry spells, which, at best, constitute oddities—and even these are mostly repulsive. One advantage of the luminar is that, quick as lightning, you can pick out details from huge old tomes such as *History of the Medieval City of Rome*.

Up here, a sultan must have planned a fortified lookout, a bunker whose crenelations were all that loomed from the ground. The place had been completed, but obviously never used, for concrete mixers and other equipment had not been cleared away. They were rusting in the bushes. The bunker had a green dome; the acacias had seeded it long ago. No pilot, however low he flew, would get suspicious. Smoke, of course, must not rise during the day.

Thus, I had already taken possession of this place, and at first glance to boot. It struck me as quite favorable for the forest flight even over a longer period. A hole led down to it; I slipped in after using a candle to test for gases and a Geiger counter for radiation. The door was armored and still intact. A few drops of oil would be necessary. The interior, designed for a commando team, was neither too large for me nor too small.

*

This reconnoitering launched a yearlong labor, on which, thorny as it was, I look back fondly. The planning occupied my leisure hours in the Casbah; the execution filled out my free time and a long vacation.

The task was simple, the performance complicated. The chief reason was that I treated it as a game. As everyone knows, we devote far more zeal to such games than to any breadwinning. This applies, say, to fishing, riding, playing ball, putting up a bungalow, and to all diversions and collections. For thousands of years, warfare, hunting, horses, theater, and splendid buildings were regarded as princely pastimes. Technology put an end to that. We observe that, at the very latest, since the invention of gunpowder, the warrior accepted the more effective weapon only reluctantly because it spoiled his fun.

*

The problem I had to solve boils down to a simple formula: "How does one make oneself invisible for a while?" This was not only my personal concern; in Eumeswil, everyone thinks about this more or less earnestly. These are thoughts that occur automatically during a civil war. They hover in the air, are dictated by atmospheric conditions.

A palace revolution, a military revolt are possible at any time. One morning, occupiers can knock on your door. If you stand out even slightly, your name will be on a list. The police have developed a great cunning along these lines, and some private individuals even maintain files. One cannot be cautious enough.

The participation in certain processions and assemblies, the refusal to perform certain tasks, to accept certain honors, indeed to employ certain forms of greeting, are discerned in a seemingly inattentive way or even with liberal benevolence—but, as Thofern once put it, these things are not only noticed, but also noted down. There is a hole in the card, and the system of these punchings sketches what is known as "conviction."

I endeavor to have no conviction, and so my dear brother regards me as lacking conviction. "Being free of conviction" would, of course, be the better term. I set great store not by conviction but by a free disposition of myself. Thus, I am at someone's disposal to the extent that I am challenged, whether to love or to war. I value not the conviction but the man. *Je regarde et je garde.*

*

From a remark made by the Domo at the night bar, I gathered that he maintains a register of the subscribers to *The Wren*. This *Wren* is, albeit to a rather modest degree, the opposition gazette of Eumeswil. It is tolerated, though not according to the motto of a weak Prussian king: "I love an opposition with conviction." Presumably, however, the little gazette owes its existence precisely to that official register. A touch of honey and the flies gather for the feast.

The editors venture out only on tiptoe. But under the circumstances, even the subtlest hint has an effect. The ears become sharp enough to catch even the drop of a pin. Such gazettes live on an anonymous popularity. Everyone has read them; people refer to them *sub rosa* as if to a taboo.

Napoleon III had a far more severe pursuer, who hounded him with a journal, *La Lanterne*. The cover was printed in a cheap ink; it gave the readers rosy fingertips. Flaunting them was considered chic; even the emperor would coyly show his. This explains why *The Wren* has a tiny subscription list despite its large circulation. People buy it at stands or from street vendors. So I was not caught unawares by the Domo's remark—I am on the alert.

*

On a sloping plane, one deals more thoroughly with questions of personal safety. Nor am I different from anyone else. I began taking practical precautions when I noticed that passersby were glaring at me. Ferreting out the bunker was the preparation; then came the setting up.

My goal was to find the best solution for vanishing as thoroughly as possible for an indefinite period, so I approached this problem in my own way, taking my time. When society involves the anarch in a conflict in which he does not participate inwardly, it challenges him to launch an opposition. He will try to turn the lever with which society moves him. Society is then at his disposal, say, as a stage for grand spectacles that are devised for him. If he is a historian, history becomes a presence for him. Everything changes; the fetter becomes fascinating, danger an adventure, a suspenseful task.

In my case, flight was transformed into the luxury of solitude. Living as a monk in a cell, as a poet in a garret, as Robinson Crusoe on his island: everyone has had those dreams. For me it was the muscardin, the totem animal of my childhood, that revived in my memory. When we have to make a dream come true, we spare no effort; and that was what happened here.

21

In order to describe these efforts, I would have to ramble on and on; let me therefore content myself with the preliminary arrangements. Others could benefit from this, for it is a general problem.

A year's provisions plus extensive equipment had to be hauled inconspicuously through swamp and thicket—a task that seemed almost insurmountable for a lone man; yet it had to be performed without assistance. If even one person knew about it, then the security would be questionable from the very start.

The site itself offered a number of resources. Since I could expect to find the concrete depressing, I covered the walls and the ceiling with the bamboolike reeds that proliferated in between the acacias. The deep yellow color of the canes was pleasant—almost orange. Aside from that, I would be spending most of the day outdoors. The bushes shielded me from prying eyes. Still, their feathery foliage was so sparse that enough rays came through for sunbathing. The bed was taken care of with the help of moss and halfa grass.

But now for the transport from the city. If an enterprise is to be concealed from society, there is a proven method: you secrete it in some undertaking that society approves of, indeed regards as commendable. For example: A father is pleased to see his son studying the Bible. His pleasure would vanish if he realized that this zeal is focused solely on tracking down the risqué passages. Or: a master spy sets up a photography shop, and so forth.

As for me, ornithology came to my aid: I camouflaged myself as a bird-watcher. Rosner was delighted. I gave him the wording for the appropriate instructions. There are still a few birds left that are little known to scholars, or even new for them. Thus, just recently, some of the Yellow Khan's hunters discovered a forest peacock beyond the desert. Rosner had a similar windfall on the upper Sus when he tracked down a breed of chicken whose nearest kin live in the Australian bush—a creature with bizarre habits. He said, "This beast invented the incubator long before the Egyptians hit upon it." There is simply nothing new in the cosmos; otherwise the universe would not deserve its name.

This fowl assigns its incubating to the elements by piling up mounds of foliage, where it conceals its eggs. The warmth caused by fermentation does the hatching. The bird only has to make sure that the heat is kept within the right limits. For this, the moisture must be regulated. To capture water, the bird hollows out the top of the mound during rainfall and covers this cavity in sunshine. In so doing, the bird knows how to prevent the interior from getting too warm; it thereby also anticipated the thermostat. All in all, we may assume that our intelligence is nothing but a reduced instinct, a branching-off from the Tree of Life with a selection process that has been intensifying for thousands of years. This conjecture is not new, but with the decay of history—metahistorically, that is—it takes on new meaning. Among other things, the animals could demand from us the same sacrifices that we have inflicted on them. On this basis we can judge the banality of the savants who wrestle with the question of whether animals have intelligence.

*

In its own way, this bird can also function as a model for a familial problem—insofar, that is, as only the male works. The male is distinguished by his feet—powerful scrapers that tirelessly rake the leaves together. It is only when the wattles swell on his naked throat that the female appears for mating. After ceremonial bowing and dancing, she lets him tread her and then she lays eggs in the nest. It is the husband who looks after the eggs until they hatch. The chicks then flutter off like quail and are able to perch on trees during the very first night.

Rosner regarded this enrichment of our fauna as a sensation. He drew up a catalogue of questions. The remoteness of the habitat was probably the cause of this atypical behavior. For me as a historian, this raised matriarchal issues. I summoned Bachofen to the luminar. We got into a lively conversation. It automatically followed that I offered to observe the fowl in my free time. Rosner praised my zeal; the Condor himself was informed about it and vouchsafed me an appreciative word as he left the night bar.

This solved the transport problem. The biotope had a favorable, almost inaccessible location; the entrance to the acacia thicket lay nearby. That was where I rigged up my lookout post. It was obvious that the job, with interruptions, would take at least one season.

There was no great distinction between setting up this stand and what I was planning for my bunker. Anything I needed was driven down to Rosner's flocks of birds on the lower Sus and then lugged on muleback through the elephant grass. There the porters built my shack. Once they left, the actual labor began; I brought the stuff for the bunker up through the acacias. For this, I kept one mule. To enable the animal to squeeze through, I had to widen the access trail. This did not bother me, for acacias grow quickly. Soon after moving in, I would be as snugly cocooned as in Sleeping Beauty's castle.

The shack for observing the scraper chicken had roughly the same significance for me as the pressure chamber for a diver: he pauses there with his equipment before venturing down to a new depth. The shack also had a political advantage: that of a relay station. Whenever trouble might be brewing in Eumeswil, I could plausibly retreat to the shack and eventually go home in fairer weather. I would then have worked for Rosner. If things changed, I would move to the hermitage. First I would become less visible; then I would become invisible.

*

Rosner, incidentally, was not shortchanged. I had enough free time for observing his scraper fowl. I used the mounds for concealing small apparatuses to register the temperature at various levels, and I set up others to record the clucking of the mating call. One of the things I observed was that the fowl has a nasty enemy in the wild dog; I managed to shoot a few of them. Their presence alone makes the region appear unsafe.

Above all, I could confirm that this fowl was in fact a new breed. Rosner was enraptured; he absolutely insisted on naming it after me: *Alectura venatoris*. I had a hard time dissuading him. After all, despite everything, I had tricked the good man. However, one of the anarch's emoluments is that he is distinguished for things that he has done on the side or that go against his grain.

*

Needless to say, I took weapons along to the bird stand. Not only did I have to catch birds for Rosner's museum, but I also had to protect myself against predators and big game, especially the red buffalo, a highly dangerous creature that pops up unexpectedly. I therefore armed myself with hunting and military weapons. The anarch wages his own wars, even when marching in rank and file.

For the shotguns, I stocked up on ammunition, from birdshot to buckshot, plus hollow bodies for short-distance shooting. As for my rifle, I needed to fire bullets without cartridges—Unedo brand: "One's enough."

A man who wears the silver phonophore does not need a gun permit. I purchased two identical sets of weapons in various shops; one set remained in the lower hut, the other was stored in the bunker. Thus I was armed not only for defense, but also for hunting fresh meat. A large antelope, whose venison makes for excellent drying, crosses near the bunker. It provides meat for a year.

*

Unbidden guests were scarcely to be feared; nevertheless, they had to be taken into account. I cleared the final stretch of the acacia trail in a straight line. At night, I would replace the rifle's telescopic sight with a spotlight to shine on the intruder. The ray would be immediately followed by the shot.

I would have heard the bloodhound before he entered the line of fire. In Eumeswil, fine acoustics has almost reached perfection. There are areas where one does not even dare whisper. You would be risking your life.

Rather than lose myself in details, I merely wish to mention that I rejected mines from the very outset. "One shouldn't even start with them," an experienced sapper once told me. This was thoroughly borne out by my study of guerrilla warfare.

The mine, as the Russian says about the bullet, is a "blind fool," a true Pandora's box even for the man who plants it. Aside from the earthquakes in our region, a mine can be set off by an animal's footstep, or it can blow up an innocent person. One's own forgetfulness can also be fatal.

A mine is anonymous, a crude weapon. Partisans like using mines because of the peculiar nature of their struggle, which makes the landscape uncertain. The anarch is not tempted by them, if only because he is oriented to facts, not ideas. He fights alone, as a free man, and would never dream of sacrificing himself to having one inadequacy supplant another and a new regime triumph over the old one. In this sense, he is closer to the philistine; the baker, whose chief concern is to bake good bread; the peasant, who works his plow while armies march across his fields.

The anarch is a forest fleer, the partisans are a collective. I have observed their quarrels as both a historian and a contemporary. Stuffy air, unclear ideas, lethal energy, which ultimately put abdicated monarchs and retired generals back in the saddle—and they then show their gratitude by liquidating those selfsame partisans. I had to love certain ones, because they loved freedom, even though the cause did not deserve their sacrifice; this made me sad.

*

If I love freedom "above all else," then any commitment becomes a metaphor, a symbol. This touches on the difference between the forest fleer and the partisan: this distinction is not qualitative but essential in nature. The anarch is closer to Being. The partisan moves within the social or national party structure, the anarch is outside it. Of course, the anarch cannot elude the party structure, since he lives in society.

The difference will be obvious when I go to my forest shack while my Lebanese joins the partisans. I will then not only hold on to my essential freedom, but also gain its full and visible enjoyment. The Lebanese, by contrast, will shift only within society; he will become dependent on a different group, which will get an even tighter hold on him.

*

Naturally, I could just as well or just as badly serve the partisans rather than the Condor—a notion I have toyed with. Either way, I remain the same, inwardly untouched. It makes no difference that it is more dangerous siding with the partisans than with the tyrant; I love danger. But as a historian, I want danger to stand out sharply.

Murder and treason, pillage, fire, and vendetta are of scant interest for the historian; they render long stretches of history—say, Corsican—unfruitful. Tribal history becomes significant only when, as in the Teutoburger Wald, it manifests itself as world history. Then names and dates shine.

The partisan operates on the margins; he serves the great powers, which arm him with weapons and slogans. Soon after the victory, he becomes a nuisance. Should he decide to maintain the role of idealist, he is made to see reason.

*

In Eumeswil, where ideas vegetate, the process is even more wretched. As soon as a group has coalesced, "one of the Twelve" is bound to consider betrayal. He is then killed, often merely on suspicion. At the night bar, I heard the Domo mention such a case to the Condor.

"He could have gotten off more cheaply with us," he commented. "Muddleheads—I'll take the gangsters anytime: they know their business."

I entered this in my notebook. In conclusion, I would like to repeat that I do not fancy myself as anything special for being an anarch. My emotions are no different from those of the average man. Perhaps I have pondered this relationship a bit more carefully and am conscious of a freedom to which "basically" everybody is entitled—a freedom that more or less dictates his actions.

*

The most important consideration was water; this was hardly a problem. Any bunker in our area was built with a sloping roof, which fed a cistern during the rainy season. I cannot rely on that, however, since the surface of the roof has long since been overgrown. Luckily, a bend in the Sus is located nearby. The marshes do dry out in the summer, but scattered pools always remain full. Moreover, fish and turtles survive in them. These pools are unapproachable from the river; the quicksand in between does not bear the slightest weight.

And so, pushing first through the acacias once more and then through the reeds, I will break a path which can also serve as an escape route; that is to be my initial task. It will provide access to water.

Nor will there be any lack of wine; I have put in a large supply, at least one bottle per day. I must remark, however, that our local wine is very strong; the vines creep over the hot earth, producing true Caleb grapes. I am familiar with the vintages; as steward, I join in the tastings prior to every purchase for the Casbah.

As I have mentioned, I plan to live chiefly by hunting. For this reason, I had to obtain salt and pepper as well as other spices; our cooks have a spice for almost every roast. Nor will I lack vegetables; I have brought up a stock of seeds. Lettuce, radishes, a type of climbing bean grow amazingly fast here. I have also planted several clusters of cassava; they propagate without your even glancing at them.

Tea, coffee, chocolate are packed in airtight containers. They could be deposited in mummy tombs, and future archaeologists would be delighted. Cane sugar and maple syrup, crystallized honey for tea.

Vessels—first my silver goblet: I will not bring it until my final trip. Flatware, not to mention the corkscrew; then everything required for cooking and roasting. One pot suffices, the kind that the Arab women use here and that would have pleased Rumohr, the gastrosopher. They assemble it out of perforated components, which they fill up with various kinds of meat as well as millet, greens, legumes, and tubers. The ingredients enrich one another almost alchemically.

Though there is plenty of dry wood lying about up there, I plan to avoid building fires because of the smoke. Heating has not been a problem since the invention of the thermal rings; the device, which produces any degree of warmth up to white heat, was a relatively recent development. The rings are expensive; possession of the silver phonophore is a prerequisite for buying them. Supposedly, further surprises can be expected from the catacombs.

So much for provisions. I could elaborate. Any reader would find this itemization long-winded; and rightly so. I got lost in a fantasy game, as I had done in my muscardin role in the attic. Only this time I was closer to reality; I could, if I wanted to, make the dream come true. The same holds for my jottings. They suffice for attesting to my freedom in soliloquy.

*

Diversions are the least of my problems, since my nature is such that I never get bored. As a child, in order to enjoy myself, I had to retreat to the most out-of-the-way nooks. Today this is no longer required. Bruno helped me in this respect, too; let me briefly add the following.

The view that external things like rank, money, and honors bring happiness has frequently been criticized, but it is not necessarily incorrect. After all, these things belong, as Aquinas would have it, among the "accidents." *Accidens* is the unessential, which includes the body. If one manages to separate essence from flesh, if one manages, that is, to gain distance from oneself, then one climbs the first step toward spiritual power. Many exercises are geared to this—from the soldier's drill to the hermit's meditation.

However, once the self has been successfully distanced, the essential can be brought back to the accidental. This process, resembling a vaccination with one's own blood, is initially manifested as a reanimation of the body. The physiognomy takes on the kind of features seen in paintings by old masters. They added something of their own. They blended it into the pigments. This also applies to objects; they were meaningful, now they gain a sense. A new light shines on things, they glow. Anyone can manage this; I heard the following from a disciple of Bruno's: "The world seemed hollow to me because my head was hollow." But the head, too, can be filled. First we must forget what we have learned.

On this score, I am still a novice. The goal also leads beyond Bruno. "Could I expel the magic from my path"—but ennui is banished. The play has not yet begun; the musicians are tuning their instruments, there seems to be a stirring behind the curtain. In front of the mirror I practice the removal of my self. Its return, however: that is the problem.

*

Up in the bunker, I will also have time for fishing and hunting. There will even be notes for Rosner. During my first exploratory outing, I had noticed an acacia; it grew in the type of clearing that emerges when a tree collapses. The bush, like a gallows, was hung with skeletons. Although the skeletons were small, I recoiled at first glance.

This sometimes happens to us when we unexpectedly stumble on nature's cruelty. Rosner views this as resentment. He compares nature to a festive kitchen where everyone both consumes and is consumed. Nothing perishes; the equation works out. "Everything fertilizes everything else," as the farmers say. If I am to believe Rosner, we live partly on the beings that we produce in our innards in order to digest them. That is how one might picture the demiurge: up there as a world spirit, with Olympian serenity, delighting in the raging of animals and the warring of men; down here as a pot-bellied man, who benefits from every consuming and from every being-consumed.

This, of course, releases me from pain as little as it does the grenadier whose leg is shot off for the greater glory of the king. As an anarch, I also have to steer clear of martyrdom. And for the historian, the issue of pain is fundamental.

Incidentally, the historian must avoid not only the biological or the economic reading of history but also the philosophical; his scholarship aims at the human; history, like man, can be neither explicated nor sublimated. Look into your own eye.

*

The skeletons on the gallows were those of birds, frogs, and lizards. The birds must have been the size of unfledged to full-grown sparrows. This was plainly a shrike's hunting ground. The shrike is also popularly known as the nine-killer, nine-murderer, or butcherbird. It lingers near thorn hedges, setting them up as pantries. There it skewers any prey that it does not consume immediately. Whenever necessary, it returns in order to gulp down smaller animals at one bite or tear the flesh from the bones of larger ones, as I saw here at its Golgotha. A miniature image, but eerie.

There is a lot to observe here. When the shrike brings its victims, are they dead or still alive? And how does it impale them? Presumably, like a good householder, it makes sure that they remain fresh as long as possible. Rosner knows of similar examples. A wasp, by stinging the ganglion, paralyzes its prey—a caterpillar that is to serve as food for the wasp's young. The victim can still chew; the maggots then live on it by skimming off its extra weight.

Perhaps some little-known butcherbird was at work here. Further down, in the reeds, a huge kingfisher, the pied kingfisher, does its hunting. In these climes, this bird is ubiquitous along our coasts and rivers and seldom timid; you can almost touch it with your hand. Once, when I was fishing on the Sus, a bird, holding a fish it had caught, alighted next to me on a post and nodded at me. I would have nothing new to report on it, but that is not the point.

Rosner knows infinitely more about these creatures than I do. But, if I may go back to what I was saying, he limits himself to the accidents.

*

Aside from a calendar in which I cross out the days, I will take no printed matter along. The prospect of a year in which the mind is utterly relieved of reading is pleasant. A temporary break from reading can be as beneficial to mental health as a fasting cure to physical health.

The absence of the luminar will also be benign. Not only is the transformer stored in the rock under the Casbah, but it could be moved only by truck. I will miss inquiry not as an anarch, but probably as a historian. Aside from rare conversations, as with Vigo, this magical and often brilliant evocation of time from the catacombs fills the only hours in which I am entirely devoted to my work. I have often wondered if it is the temporal distance that transforms events into history; but I would rather presume that this interval clarifies whatever is hidden as essence in the foam and froth. History then becomes a subject for the poet as well. On the other hand, Eumeswil, even should a thousand years go by, can never become an object of history in this way. Eumeswil is without history, and expectations are therefore different.

*

There is a paraplegia that slices through the nerve of history. It terminates tradition. The deeds of the fathers can survive only in spectacles or tragedies, but not in action. We must resign ourselves. This has been going on in Eumeswil for generations.

To be sure, custodians have also survived here, dream-towners who convene as phantoms. Their séances bear a certain resemblance to those of the anarchists. They put flags on their regular tables and buy drinks for young men who make fun of them. Naturally, revolutions, too, can offer material for tradition. I recall one of those groups and its vapid idealism—the Storm Companions of Socrates. My dear brother introduced me there.

For the historian, such phenomena are more ghostly than epigonic. Long periods are meager, anemic, barren. Tradition is preserved wherever it bottoms out—gets to the bottom, that is—with its final stewards, and not where, as with the Western caesars, it drowses away in a twilight state. Of the Eastern caesars, the last one fell in the breach of the city wall. The great cities become transcendent in the flames. I am thinking of Hasdrubal's wife, a woman I venerated and loved. She preferred fire to submission.

*

I have brought a small televisor up to the bunker. I will occasionally switch it on for news. The news is telecast toward sundown and generally received in such a way that an individual viewer cannot be spotted around this time. The supervision of the network is precise; not only are partisan nests tracked down, but their planning is often followed in detail.

It is incredible how frivolously young people with good backgrounds plunge into such adventures. Their imagination outsoars their intelligence. Though certainly bold enough to challenge society, they lack the know-how. That is why they always start out with the same mistakes; all the police need do is wait for them to fall into the trap. There is no hurry.

"Let it come to a head." This is one of the Domo's maxims that I hear in the night bar; I then prick up my ears. That is how deliberations in the cabinet end, yet a hint or two may be dropped in passing. The upper Sus is not considered a partisan area; of that I can be certain. It would be highly unpleasant if dilettantes settled there, bringing the police down on me.

As I have said, I have nothing to do with the partisans. I wish to defy society not in order to improve it, but to keep it at bay no matter what. I suspend my achievements—but also my demands.

As for the do-gooders, I am familiar with the horrors that were perpetrated in the name of humanity, Christianity, progress. I have studied them. I do not know whether I am correctly quoting a Gallic thinker: "Man is neither an animal nor an angel; but he becomes a devil when he tries to be an angel."

*

Normally I will receive news through my transistor; but it might become necessary to confirm it with the televisor—say, in cases of doubt regarding the deaths of rulers or the lives of hostages. One must wait until the heads are displayed.

Should anyone be missed, the search begins with an appeal through the phonophore. If a response follows, then one knows the man is still alive, and also roughly where he is. So I will keep the phonophore off for a long time. Our social existence is exhausted in switching and being switched. Its ideal is the switch to conformity.

Incidentally, the way the discovery and utilization of electric power corresponds to social consciousness is a story unto itself. To find anything comparable, one must hark back to prehistory. That is one of the topics that Ingrid is working on. Franklin as a key figure.

*

I have done some serious cogitating about the reasons for the failure of the forest flight. This issue haunts many people—indeed, everyone who plans the "perfect crime." Nearly all these types surrender to a misplaced optimism.

The forest flight confirms the independence of the anarch, who is basically a forest fleer anywhere, anytime, whether in the thicket in the metropolis, whether inside or outside society. One must distinguish not only between the forest fleer and the partisan but also between the anarch and the criminal; the difference lies in the relationship to the law. The partisan wants to change the law, the criminal break it; the anarch wants neither. He is not for or against the law. While not acknowledging the law, he does try to recognize it like the laws of nature, and he adjusts accordingly.

When it is hot, you doff your hat; in rain, you open your umbrella; during an earthquake, you leave your house. Law and custom are becoming the subjects of a new field of learning. The anarch endeavors to judge them ethnographically, historically, and also—I will probably come back to this—morally. The State will be generally satisfied with him; it will scarcely notice him. In this respect, he bears a certain resemblance to the criminal—say, the master spy—whose gifts are concealed behind a run-of-the-mill occupation.

I assume that in great men whose names I dare not mention, the anarchic element was very powerful. You see, when fundamental changes are to succeed in law, custom, and society, they presuppose a great distancing from established principles. And the anarch, should he take any action, is capable of working this lever.

I have summoned a few of the great movers and shakers to the luminar in order to look behind the revolutionary façade—less by delving into their private lives than by tracking down their intellectual foundations. Things that are spoken and noticed peripherally, unintentionally, without slogans, are often more revealing than the program itself.

"Greatness" is secondary for the anarch, often fortuitous. This explains why these great men considered their own achievements inadequate or even repugnant. Last words: "And so much to do." They do not like being pinned down. Such qualms are posthumously reflected in their followers. More and more new schools and sects that cite the master keep germinating.

*

The forest fleer and the partisan are not, as I have said, to be confused with each other; the partisan fights in society, the forest fleer alone. Nor, on the other hand, is the forest fleer to be confused with the anarch, although the two of them grow very similar for a while and are barely to be distinguished in existential terms.

The difference is that the forest fleer has been expelled from society, while the anarch has expelled society from himself. He is and remains his own master in all circumstances. When he decides to flee to the forest, his decision is less an issue of justice and conscience for him than a traffic accident. He changes camouflage; of course, his alien status is more obvious in the forest flight, thereby becoming the weaker form, though, perhaps indispensable.

Needless to say, I thoroughly studied these issues in the luminar and at the library. Here I stumbled on the possibility of an error in the other direction. Let me quote a sentence I found in the introduction to an ancient work on Germanic pre- and proto-history. A certain Professor Kiekebusch wrote: "To live as a serving link in the whole is both a duty and a reward. The supreme goal of every individual's labor and striving is the good of the collective."

This is in the style of the eschaton of the warring nations, when exploitation changed its face. A few generations earlier, during the wars of liberation, this would have been expressed in a more fiery manner. The spirit passes over the flesh like a wind that keeps moving new generations. Enthusiasm follows it and vanishes after it. In Eumeswil, such statements have long since become so historical as to be rarely quoted in seminars.

For the anarch, things are not so simple, especially when he has a background in history. If he remains free of being ruled, whether by sovereigns or by society, this does not mean that he refuses to serve in any way. In general, he serves no worse than anyone else, and sometimes even better, if he likes the game. He only holds back from the pledge, the sacrifice, the ultimate devotion. These are issues of metaphysical integrity, which have little clout in Eumeswil. By the same token, one does not chitchat with men who think there is plenty of room for improvement here or who actually promise you a heaven on earth.

I serve in the Casbah; if, while so doing, I died for the Condor, it would be an accident, perhaps even an obliging gesture, but nothing more.

*

I will allow myself a glance, albeit brief, at the weather. Every born historian knows the terror sparked by facts that, while traditional in their breadth, have become senseless. Just why did they sacrifice themselves? This can extend to man's conception of the world. Sir Richard Burton, the great traveler, wrote:

How Life is dim, unreal, vain,
 like scenes that round the drunkard reel...
A drop in Ocean's boundless tide,
 unfathom'd waste of agony;
Where millions live their horrid lives
 by making other millions die.

There is a degree of senselessness and glaciation that, in terrifying the eye, brings out contrast. Reality becomes suspect, and so phantoms draw nearer. This may be why the sight of a skeleton dismays us in a more precise manner than the sight of a corpse. The same holds true for purely mathematical conceptions of the world. This effect was the basis for a school that can be looked up in art history under the name of Surrealism. It flourished shortly before the first lunar landing.

A house is not just untenanted, it has also died out, petrifying into the sarcophagus of the mind, the mausoleum of a charred world. No mortal emerges from the doorway.

A volcano can be regarded as extinct since time immemorial; the very first neighboring inhabitants viewed it as dead. Yet if an eruption is in the making, the atmosphere turns sinister. This is sensed by few people in Eumeswil.

*

The forest flight resembles the perfect crime in both its planning and its failures. Nothing is easier than opting for autonomy, nothing is harder than bringing it about. Man has forgotten how to stand for himself—on his own two feet, which grasp the ground directly. He does not like doing without helpers and accomplices. They introduce the first cracks into the system.

The longest forest flight in Iceland was carried out by Grettir, the strongest man on the island: he feared no human being, but he did fear ghosts. When Gudmund advised him to settle on an untakable cliff, Grettir replied: "I will try. But I am so scared of the dark that I cannot be alone for the life of me."

To which Gudmund rejoined: "That may be true. But trust no one as much as yourself."

Grettir took along his fifteen-year-old brother, Illugi, and that was good; but he also took along Glaum, his slave. Illugi perished at his side while Glaum betrayed him. I have put up a memorial to Illugi on the acacia hill.

*

Here in the south, the unhoused have also made a name for themselves—islanders like those of the north and, similarly, shepherds and killers. The shepherd is bolder and freer than the cowherd; he is less tied to the soil, he grazes the wastelands. The plow, the yoke, the fence, the house were invented by the cowherd and are thus degrees of servitude and profit. These are phenomena; behind them are the great signs of the Ram and the Bull.

Such observations are useless in a city where people can no longer distinguish between ground and cause. The cause has a ground, but the ground no cause. The cause explains, while the ground is grounded on the unfathomable—but all this merely in passing.

Whenever I was at the luminar to follow the destinies of Corsican and Sardinian brigands (say, a Tandeddu), forest dwellers who often kept a huge throng of policemen at bay for an astonishingly long time, I found that nearly all of them were doomed by a woman: not that they were betrayed by her like Samson, but simply because of her complicity. The woman, usually the only person who knows the location of his hideout, steals up to her spouse or lover. Eventually, the gendarmes with their hounds succeed in following her trail, and the game is up.

Thus, I had my reasons for not letting Ingrid in on my plans. After all, we were often seen together in the city and at the institute, and she is no doubt mentioned as a contact in my file at the Casbah. Granted, I can count on her silence—but what does that mean, in the end? The police only need to know that someone knows something—and then they are fully informed.

*

Whenever tyranny is discussed, the word "torture" automatically springs up. There is no question of torture in Eumeswil. The police are much too good for that—which, to be sure, does not mean good-natured. They are obliged to work with gloves, which, on the other hand, does not mean kid gloves. Their grip has to be firm, but not too harsh; their response—to quote the Domo—"must fit the provocation." This implies that, as people used to put it, "Blood should not stain the land."

When I stand behind the bar, usually waiting rather than waiting on, I have plenty of time to observe the Domo. He is incapable of brutalities. He is not nervous, but he does have fine nerves. The motions of service are to blend harmoniously. The minions in particular are trained along these lines. If noises or voices displease him, his face sharpens imperceptibly; I have studied the engrams. He particularly seems to dislike the baying of hounds outside the Casbah on moonlit nights.

So when he puts his red *I* on the margin of a file in case an interrogation has to be repeated, this does not indicate secret horrors. On the contrary—the more important a matter, the more pleasant the style of the proceedings. Occasionally, a fat military judge pops up in the night bar and sits cozily with the defendant, making sure, if I understand correctly, to keep the mood within certain limits.

It is common knowledge, though not shouted from the rooftops, that severe torture is still or again being practiced in the territories of the Yellow Khan. Both the Condor and the tribunes are discreet on this score, albeit with very different motives.

*

In Eumeswil, the regime is tyrannical but not despotic. The despot enjoys degrading people; it is innate in him—he therefore acts on this instinct even beyond *raison d'état* and his own advantage. Judging by deeds that are constantly tried in courts here, I conclude that this instinct occurs in an especially pure form in certain regions, but is not regionally limited. Young men accost a passerby at night, overpower him, and take him to a lonely place. There they start torturing him and eventually kill him—although the victim has done them no harm and they do not even know him; yet that intensifies their rage.

Such attacks do not occur at the waterfront, where bloody fistfights break out every night; they take place in the neighborhoods of the prominent citizens and for the pleasure of their offspring. There is also such a thing as a de luxe criminality, an art for art's sake. "Grounds," says Vigo, "are merely the skin on the groundless."

*

So if I keep my secret to myself, I do so partly for safety's sake and partly because I do not want to burden anyone else. Ingrid knows only that should I disappear, she might receive a call from me. She is familiar with the bird shack to which I would summon her, but not the acacia grove. That is where my own domain actually begins.

I do not intend to stir for another six months; my phonophore is switched on for reception only during the quarter hour of news. This measure, too, is prompted solely by caution, for I am not curious, since the politics in Eumeswil cannot possibly improve.

Living without a woman for six months should not be difficult; in the Casbah we are trained along these lines. I have noticed that dreams are not only refined but also more vivid if a man puts restraints on himself. The coins of the realm are exchanged for gold—this is not meant to sound ungallant.

*

Basically, I am a small fish here, though perhaps a groundfish—a trabant in the tyrant's retinue, like almost everyone in this city. Strictly speaking, there are only tyrants today; their methods of padding their cudgels differ only in color, but not in cloth. Their similarities, down to their choice of words, show that of the three great principles equality has triumphed. Freedom was consumed for the sake of equality. The tyrant is the equalizer; everyone recognizes himself in him.

Fraternity means that the father no longer sacrifices the sons; instead the brothers kill one another. Wars between nations have been replaced by civil war. The great settling of accounts, first under national "pretexts," led to a rapidly escalating world civil war.

All that is behind us. We play it through in dreamlike repetitions because nothing better occurs to us, but also—though this applies only to certain individuals—we are waiting.

Why am I, as a small fish, a groundling, going to all this trouble? It would probably suffice to take refuge with *pater peccavi*, my genitor, who, together with a dozen deceased or still living nullities, would be hailed as a luminary of scholarship.

Incidentally, most revolutionaries suffer from not having become professors. The Domo knows this, too: once, at the night bar, I heard him telling the Condor: "We'll make him a professor—that should take him off our backs."

So why then all the trouble? My safety does not demand it. On the contrary—I find that danger actually makes life here bearable. Hence the thriving of crimes, addictions, the lottery. I prefer getting out when things grow boring, not dangerous. If I play the Condor's game to the very end, it is not because I am bound by any vassalage or allegiance, much less any party loyalty. It is really my own integrity. That is why I become more reliable in the end game.

I regard a change of power as an intermezzo—two forms of domination, of whose inadequacy I am convinced, spell each other. I thereby enjoy a recess that clarifies the very fact that I am taking a recess.

If I live on the hilltop like Robinson Crusoe on his island, I will be no freer than the man serving in the night bar. And I am no more autonomous as a doer than as a historian. However, things become more palpable in the doing. Inner freedom is demonstrated. Perhaps I will start by bringing about a private Cannae in front of the duck shack.

22

The anarch differs from the anarchist in that he has a very pronounced sense of rules. Insofar as and to the extent that he observes them, he feels exempt from thinking.

This is consistent with normal behavior: everyone who boards a train rolls over bridges and through tunnels that engineers have devised for him and on which a hundred thousand hands have labored. This does not darken the passenger's mood; settling in comfortably, he buries himself in his newspaper, has breakfast, or thinks about his business.

Likewise the anarch—except that he always remains aware of the relationship, never losing sight of his main theme, freedom, that which also flies outside, past hill and dale. He can get away at any time, not just from the train but also from any demand made on him by state, society, or church, and also from existence. He is free to donate existence to Being, not for any pressing reasons, but just as he likes, whether out of exuberance or out of boredom.

Why do so many people strive for the career of petty functionary? No doubt because they have a sensible notion of happiness. They know the rules and their taboos. They sit in their chairs while others file past with their wishes or tributes. Time flows by nonchalantly. You are already half way to Tibet. Plus the security. No state can do without minor officials, no matter how high the waves may surge. Of course, you have to keep a low profile.

*

As a historian, I must acknowledge that there have been long stretches in history, especially prehistory, when the ride was so satisfying that there was little reason to get off. Things generally became unpleasant with monotheism; on a single track, there is no swerving aside. The palette becomes more meager.

Equality is based, as we have seen, on the possibility that anyone can kill anyone else. This awareness alone is enough to help us see through the swaggering of the superpowers—or, as here in Eumeswil, to help the historian study human behavior.

*

So much for equality. Freedom is based on the expansion of that maxim: on the anarch's awareness that he can kill himself. He carries this awareness around; it accompanies him like a shadow that he can conjure up. "A leap from this bridge will set me free."

That is more or less how I regard the care I am taking in the acacia forest. The anarch, as I have expounded elsewhere, is the pendant to the monarch; he is as sovereign as the monarch, and also freer since he does not have to rule.

The hilltop bulwark is the chapel of my freedom, whether or not I enter it. It will serve as my stronghold when I change into a warring power and obtain my freedom against the demands of society—my exact courage against their exactions.

*

I began with the respect that the anarch shows toward the rules. *Respectare* as an intensive of *respicere* means: "to look back, think over, take into account." These are traffic laws. The anarchist resembles a pedestrian who refuses to acknowledge them and is promptly run down. Even a passport check is disastrous for him.

"I never saw a cheerful end," as far back as I can look into history. In contrast, I would assume that men who were blessed with happiness—Sulla, for example—were anarchs in disguise.

*

Regarding in particular the rules for "Conduct during Domestic Unrest," I have mentioned only the case of an alarm while I am in the Casbah. But the phonophore transmits the Red Alert in the city, too. One must then expect unpredictable things—especially if the weapons have not yet been distributed.

Sometimes I play similar scenes at the luminar—say, from the history of the caesars, or the Russians before and after the revolution. I close the door, draw the curtains; I am in the abyss.

Then I take over the role of the monarch—say, Nero, once he is notified that his bodyguards have left. This is one of the final omens. Now the palace becomes very lonesome, eerie. None of the friends, none of the powerful respond. Only a few freed slaves have remained; they hope he will put a swift end to it all.

The caesar is the person who can least conceal himself in this world. Strange how now, alone in the universe, he becomes similar to the anarch. Even though his mortal fear is breathing down his neck, he manages to get out a few significant asides. Even as the hoofbeat announces the arrival of pursuers, he quotes the appropriate Homeric verse: "Thundering into my ear…." And then the brilliant "*Qualis artifex pereo*"—"What a great artist perishes with me!"

He is too weak, too clumsy to stab himself; his secretary, Epaphroditus, guides his hand. Incidentally, that was why Domitian had this benefactor executed.

I would like to avoid getting mixed up in such quarrels by hearing, say, the Condor tell me, "That is loyalty," as Nero told the centurion whose behavior was dubious.

*

In case the alarm is sounded while I am in the city instead of the citadel, things will be easier—and not only because I can retreat to my own citadel whenever I like. I will also have less to think about, since I will find sealed orders, namely at the central bank; there the envelope is kept for me in a safe-deposit box. My phonophore contains the encoded password that will open it.

When I receive the call, I will interrupt my activity or my leisure and head to the bank. If the newsstands are open, I will buy a copy of *The Wren* and tear it in half en route, throwing both pieces away at the next intersection.

I am noting these *quisquiliae* because, like so many others, they demonstrate the Domo's rational organization. There is no doubting that *The Wren* will become cantankerous when "the banner of freedom is unfurled"; I would be willing to bet that my dear brother keeps a copy of the proclamation, albeit encoded, in his desk.

If a torn copy of *The Wren* is now lying on the sidewalks of intersections, then thousands of people will go past it; the image will implant itself in their minds. It is not the Condor who is at work here; this comes from below, from the nameless, a passerby has done it. It is also a warning, a disdainful greeting. A tug on the "ribbon on which it fluttered."

Night Bar Notes

23

If my dear brother had any inkling of what I toss away en passant, he would be through with me for good. I would have laid hands on his most hallowed treasure. "Freedom of the press" and "capital punishment"—I usually give these phrases a wide berth at the family table, for were I to voice even the slightest criticism, the game could be up for me altogether.

He would never get it into his head that freedom begins where freedom of the press ends. "Freedom of thought"—this means that he would never test his stale ideas in a state of primeval freedom. I am willing to grant that he is rooted in liberal traditions, although they are more diluted and mitigated in him than in my genitor. Even good ideas have their time. Liberalism is to freedom as anarchism is to anarchy.

Cadmo, to enlighten me, often takes me along to his "Storm Companions." I am not really welcome there—perhaps they even regard me as an agent of the Domo, who, by the by, knows about their meetings but considers them irrelevant, indeed almost useful. "A barking dog never bites."

The main reason I have a hard time getting along with these men is their indecisiveness. They feel when they ought to think, and vice versa. All they have inherited from Socrates is skepticism; but, unlike Xenophon, they would not hoist him on their shoulders and carry him out of the fighting. Convinced as they are of the temporal and finite nature of things, they shy away from pain, sacrifice, devotion.

*

My dear brother, even after much soul-searching, has not become an anarchist like, say, Zerrwick, who edits *The Wren*. Zerrwick's ideas flow glibly from his lips and his pen; he converts them into the "ferment of decay." I am using this image, a favorite of the conservatives, because I enjoy it—for the anarch, however, decay is a process like any other; and for the historian, this Zerrwick is more informative than my genitor and my dear brother. One could regard him as an antechamber councilor or even a doorman who steps away after performing his task, for that is what it is. There is also something of the lackey about him; he belongs to the ruler's entourage and he vanishes with him. He hides in the Condor's plumage, living for the moment when he can soar beyond him.

If ever I should write an essay on this type, I will start with Beaumarchais, who, after engaging the "nobles, whose sole effort is being born," eventually was himself defamed for being a courtier. Defamation to the point of character assassination is the usual livelihood here.

*

Such ponderings repeatedly make me aware of the limits to the writing of history or, rather, to its contemplation. The suffering begins the instant we take pen in hand.

I agree with my teacher Vigo that we succeed only in achieving more or less sharp-edged perspectives—lanes through the grown forest. Above all, we have to disregard the will, disregard partisanship. The true historian is more of an artist, especially a tragedian, than a man of science.

When I, as I am doing here, examine the powerful man's relationship to his opponent, I stumble upon the antithesis between the person who lays claim to freedom of action and the person who lays claim to freedom of thought. These are figures that recur not only in history but in myth as well, all the way into the animal kingdom. Fable lives on them; the lion is powerful, Reynard the fox is cunning.

Fine, the antithesis lies deeper: within matter itself. The ruler embodies stasis; he is painted, like Zeus, sitting or standing. His adversary is nimble—there is hardly a more agitated sculpture than the bronze statue that the Athenians put up for the tyrannicides Harmodius and Aristogiton; both paid with their lives for the assassination.

That is the classical ending when blood flows; I played a series of examples at the luminar, from the assassination of Julius Caesar to the one in Sarajevo. These two murders were similar insofar as each provided the oriflamme for a world war.

If we delve all the way into the atoms, differences vanish—like the ones between Caesar and that insignificant Austrian prince. Both men, like their assassins, were subject to the same constraint. In this, too, I go along with Vigo's idea that the historian has to supply images, not explanations. Nonetheless, the atomic reality has to shine through in color and drawing, in deeds and characters.

Naturally, our Zerrwick cannot be placed on the same level as Harmodius. Nor is that an issue for me. Aside from the fact that as an anarch I strive to remain free of value judgments, Eumeswil suffices for my studies precisely because I am impartial. The night bar is my aquarium: the fish have fins and teeth like those in the ocean. Bruno peers into a crystal ball, where he sees the kings campaigning with their armies.

*

Zerrwick, as I have said, bodies forth the disquiet with which a moving object circles a static one, trying to drive it from the center. That is a law of nature. If the Condor were to fall, the tribunes would soon have an equivalent satellite in Zerrwick; this is based simply on the fact that every regime, even the best, finds its opposition, and with it a public that, if not hailing the assault, at least enjoys it as a balancing stunt.

Indeed, Zerrwick has something of the tightrope walker in him. Then again, he also resembles a balladeer, the kind who performs in a cabaret as a master of double-entendres, who, when one tries to grab him, slips away. At times, he is also as daring as the picador who riles the bull, making its blood boil, and who could easily be tossed on its horns at any moment.

Recently, when I was at the luminar, participating in a parade on Berlin's Tempelhof Field, a certain incident reminded me of Zerrwick's trapeze acts. The king of Prussia was taking his good time; a cobbler's lad, who was sitting in a tree, called out, "Ain't the creep comin' yet?"

A policeman yanked him down. "You goddamn brat—who did you mean?"

"My brother, of course—who else?"

At last, the king came and reviewed the troops. Afterward, the cobbler's lad went over to the officer of the peace: "Officer—who did *you* mean?"

This roughly corresponds to the winks in Zerrwick's essays. Many people are surprised that the Condor puts up with him; his tolerance, too, runs a gamut; for, depending on the weather, this scribbler can develop from a court jester, to a thoroughgoing nuisance, and finally to a dangerous man. At present, he is in the middle range, so he could still be gotten rid of without any scandal. After a change, at which point I would retreat to the acacia grove, he might be the great man in Eumeswil for a few weeks.

Even his opponents have to admit that he is eminently gifted as a journalist. The Domo himself reads every issue of *The Wren* hot off the press—and, presumably, not only as police chief, but with gusto. He does, moreover, have a sense of clean prose and logical precision.

*

During dinner, I stand by in the bar. I check the air, the temperature, the vaporizer, the glasses in front of me on the counter, the bottles behind me on the shelves. I ask the pantry downstairs whether it is well provided. Most of the dishes come up ready to be served; I order them by means of key words.

The dinner, as a rule, is simple; it lasts for three quarters of an hour; a trio plays at the start, after the appetizer, and during dessert. The dining room is known as the "mess hall" or "refectory." Once the Condor rises from the table, several of the convives, always including Attila and the Domo, accompany him to the Yellow Salon, where mocha and liqueurs are served. Smoking a cigar is permitted, though the Condor finds it disagreeable. Depending on his whim and mood—by no means always—the Condor may feel like going next door, to the night bar. Anyone who wishes to (à la "Sire, Marly") may join him. The Domo notifies me; the minions take their seats.

*

Before dinner, the Domo has delivered his report to the Condor; after that, there is to be no shoptalk, although dribs and drabs inevitably filter in. I find them more instructive than if I had been present during the report—tidbits for my insatiable appetite. Let me repeat that I prefer the history of cultures to the history of states. That is where humanity begins and ends. Accordingly, I value the history of royal courts and even back courts over that of politics and parties. History is made by people and at most regulated by laws; that is why it is so inexhaustible with surprises.

*

I do not wish to digress too much from Zerrwick. Granted, his name never crops up at the night bar; he is deliberately ignored. Yet it is obvious when some dust has been kicked up by one of those articles that my dear brother reads gloatingly. Just recently, for instance, when the diners emerged from the Yellow Salon, the Domo said, "I've checked the Meidinger." The Meidinger is our encyclopedia, a truly Alexandrian opus.

The Domo favors a precision that almost transcends the limits of necessity; he wants to grasp not only the strict meaning of a word, but also its subliminal sense. To do so, one must delve into both its etymology, like Thofern, and the magic of its sounds, like Bruno.

In the Domo, such probing is astonishing in that he offers no hint of aesthetic inclinations. Rather, I would suspect a need for legalistic exactitude. If the word is to hit home, it must home in. I have already mentioned the waterfront case, a life-and-death matter that hinged on the judge's allowing a distinction between *stab* and *slay*.

The Domo's great musicality may be consistent with a decidedly rational character. We have surgeons, architects, even fairly disreputable policemen with aesthetic interests. Perhaps their houses have only this one spiral staircase leading down to the foundations. "Whenever my husband picked up his violin, he became a better person." This was a woman testifying in a sordid trial, and I liked what she said, although as an anarch I would have expressed myself differently. Be that as it may: one cannot fully fathom the ground of a character. And precisely this failure has its grounds.

*

The Domo's meticulous use of language contrasts strangely with the way it is routinely mangled in Eumeswil. Hackneyed phrases are all that we hear—as well worn as pennies tossed to beggars; and, indeed, they come more from academics than from the harbor or the market. This has not always been so; the farmer, the artisan, the hunter, the soldier, the crook knew how to animate powerful images.

The fellah period has made a clean sweep of such talents. Eumenists of Sperling's and Kessmüller's cast have done their bit. The goal was the annihilation of correct language. "*Le style, c'est l'homme*"—this notion was revoked; intellectual rank was no longer to be identified by a mastery of language. The result is a banal chitchat defective in both its heights and its depths.

To be sure, there were errors in calculation. Even in times when there are no cabinetmakers left, one still distinguishes the well-built armoire, or even a planed board, from all the others. Similarly, when elites have grown rare or shrunk down to a few individuals, the clear, unadulterated word convinces the uneducated man—indeed, precisely him, the non-miseducated man. He senses—and this puts his mind at ease—that the ruler still observes rules despite his power. *Caesar non supra grammaticos.* A solace in periods of decline.

24

Far be it from me to liken the Domo to Caesar; but, as I have already said, the study of fish in our lagoon is useful for looking back in history.

What had he checked in the Meidinger? I was to find out immediately, for, after the minions had adjusted the chairs of their masters, and they sat down, he continued: "So far as I can tell, the vulture has been honored in both the Roman and the German nations—at least in times that were not so sterile as ours."

He launched into etymological niceties. *Vulture* comes from Latin *vultur*, which is probably cognate with *vellere*, "to pull, pluck," and also with *vulnerable*. The German word for *vulture* is *Geier*, which is related to *Gier*, "greed, avidity" (in its earlier form, *gihr*); the adjective *gierig*, "greedy, avid," refers to someone who will not give up his prey. *Carrion* goes back to Latin *caro*, flesh; the German equivalent, *Aas*, used to mean simply "food" and is cognate with the English *eat*; it meant the bait employed by the hunter. The Roman *vultur* hints at a swift turn, *volta. Volturnus* was a raging river in Campania, the Volturno. Language has not only frayed out, it has also moralized itself.

*

So much for the Domo with his collectanea. When I heard the word *vulture*, I knew what was biting him. It was my first day on duty after my vacation. In the morning, I had come from the city, purchasing a *Wren* on the way. I do so now and then with half-disgusted curiosity in order to keep abreast of the overall mood—but I get my copy at the newsstand.

I believe I have already noted that the number of actual subscribers to the magazine is tiny, although nearly everyone reads it. The subscription list is, of course, available at the Casbah. Being on it would not be incriminating; but, together with two or three other names, it could draw the circle tighter around you. In my case, for instance, my family would be linked to me. That was precisely why Zerrwick began mailing me free copies several years ago—which was almost worse. I therefore politely asked him "not to send me any further issues." It is my old complaint: getting caught between parties whose quarrels I find cumbersome and often repugnant. At times I have one party on my back, at times the other, and occasionally both at once.

*

The current issue included a pseudonymous article that bore Zerrwick's unmistakable stamp: "The Raptors." Zerrwick had costumed himself in a professorial style. First he went into the zoological classification of the diurnal birds of prey and their habits. It boiled down to a comparison of eagles and falcons with vultures. The former were proud creatures that attacked live prey, the latter were scavengers. The vultures of the New World, all listed by name, were described as colossal shredders. The condor was missing although he, needless to say, was the target. As a true polemicist, Zerrwick knew that omission provides the best emphasis. The *centre d'attraction* had to remain camouflaged.

Whatever Zerrwick thinks or writes, he always means the Condor. This will be so even if he survives the Condor; he will remain Zerrwick's topic for decades. Zerrwick would then become a scavenger himself. Pursuer and pursued are always made for each other.

The article gave me food for thought, albeit differently than for my dear brother, who, no doubt, must have been absolutely elated. In depicting the royal eagle and the peregrine falcon, which he cited as epitomes, Zerrwick's diction took on a heraldic loftiness. This could have been penned by a Chateaubriand, who, to be sure, was already an equivocal figure.

If Zerrwick can pick at the Condor, he will stop at nothing. As a nihilistic conjuror, he pulls whatever he likes from his top hat: liberty caps or crowns and scepters. I mention this because it fits in with a New Year's mood that is spreading through the tyranny. Each man nurtures his own ideal, which barely makes it past the surging of jubilation. I once thought of a hundred-year calendar with the *journée des dupes* as one of the recurrent red-letter days.

The anarch nurtures no expectations. He stakes on no one but himself. Basically, people remain pied pipers, whatever melodies they play to introduce themselves. And as for the rats—that is a chapter unto itself.

*

The snare was cunningly set, even with regard to its timing. In dictatorships there are two phases that demand particular caution. One phase comes right after the seizing of power: "New brooms sweep clean." The second announces the end. The ruler tries once again to forge ahead, but he lacks a consensus. This makes him even more dangerous. A man must now be on his guard if he is not to get caught in the last-minute throng.

In between, there are lulls, during which one can indulge in all sorts of things, like this foray into zoology. In eras filled with rich images, fables served that purpose, just as scholarship does here. Yet Zerrwick did not lack the "epigrammatic pointedness" that Lessing calls for. Still, his portrayal of the vulture's meal went beyond the boundaries; his quill had been guided by pure hatred. Anyone conversant with the internal affairs of Eumeswil found material galore to interpret.

Every polemical analysis of a seizure of power distinguishes between "those who blaze the trail" and "those who come along for the ride." The trailblazers that Zerrwick cited were a species of raven or carrion crow—small, nimble, hungry blackcoats. They scent the weakness of a large animal before it even drops; perched on the branches of bare trees, they watch its agony. Since their tiny beaks are incapable of tearing it up, they must wait for the vulture to perform this task. Meanwhile they busy themselves with the eyes and the anus.

It is the agitation they spread through the atmosphere that first alerts the king vulture. He then swoops down and does the carving. Next come the fellow travelers, big and small, each according to rank. "Order is restored."

With an obvious "sense for the nasty," Zerrwick lovingly dwelt on the details of this gruesome repast. Especially graphic was his description of a turkey vulture, which, sporting a hooked beak and a wrinkly, bluish-red throat, pokes its head into the body openings and dabbles in the tripe—a striking portrait of the minister of finance, whom I often observe up close at the night bar.

*

Zerrwick knows his craft—of that there can be no doubt. When reading such excursuses, I, as a historian, keep my distance, not only from their tabloid polemics, but also from their timeless verities. Zerrwick has grasped the mechanics of coups d'état for the succession of dictatorships, which have long been the only kind of regime to maintain relative order here. Even the tribunes need their general.

Zerrwick sees this as a journalist, not a historian. It therefore escapes him that he is describing the methods of not only the Condor but also his predecessors and successors. Furthermore, Zerrwick is painting a self-portrait, for he is one of the carrion crows.

If, rather than an anarchist, he were an anarch without moralisms or prejudices, he could make a name for himself as a historian. But, like all men of his ilk, he prefers to take the cash and let the credit go.

*

The historian's sorrow and his transformation into an anarch derive from his insight that the cadaver cannot be cleared away and that more and more swarms of flies and vultures regale themselves on its flesh. Thus, all in all, they are based on the world's imperfection and on the suspicion that something is inherently wrong.

Seen politically, systems follow one another, each consuming the previous one. They live on ever-bequeathed and ever-disappointed hope, which never entirely fades. Its spark is all that survives, as it eats its way along the blasting fuse. For this spark, history is merely an occasion, never a goal.

One more item about the cadaver: Zerrwick's interviews are feared; he knows how to ask trick questions. Say: "How do you feel about the fact that your opponents call you the gravedigger of the tribunate?"

To which the interviewee, a high-ranking magistrate, replied, "Before the gravedigger comes, you have to have a corpse."

*

Zerrwick also serves as a showpiece for the Domo, demonstrating his liberalism. Still and all, the excursus on the vultures was a bit much: "The guy's trying to make fools of us."

The mood was blatantly sour; when they had taken their seats, Attila, to the Condor's left as usual, said, "We do have an expert: Rosner. He could help us out."

The Condor: "Right, let's send for him. I'm curious to know what kind of bird I am."

The Domo passed the order on to me: "Manuelo, telephone him. After all, you watch birds for him."

True enough; I also knew that the professor could still be reached in his institute at this time of night. Incidentally, the Domo's remark once again showed me how well investigated I am.

Half an hour later, Rosner was in the Casbah; the guard announced him. Upon entering, the bespectacled professor looked like a startled night bird himself, but he regained his composure upon hearing what it was all about. The Condor motioned toward a seat and assigned him a minion, who snuggled against him. I wondered how Rosner would manage to wriggle out of it: the expert as a dubious figure.

The Domo turned to him: "Professor, we have summoned you because of that concoction about eagles and vultures in *The Wren*. I assume you are familiar with it?"

"Sorry, Your Excellency, but I never read pulp. Besides, my work leaves me no time for such things. Still, I would gladly help with factual information."

Not a bad start; he was sure to do well. After being filled in, he got down to the gist. First of all: what is a scavenger?

"We must avoid judging such matters anthropocentrically—in terms, that is, of human taste. After all, we, too, never consume animal protein *in statu vivendi*, with the exception of oysters. If that were to constitute a criterion, then bloodsuckers like mosquitoes and vampire bats must dine more nobly, as must the woodpecker, which hacks maggots out of the heartwood.

"Fresh meat strikes us as less palatable, so we let it age—often till it becomes quite gamy. Nor should we forget dairy products like cheese, whose advanced putrescence is revealed by its very smell. And yet it titillates our taste bulbs.

"Incidentally, the biologist places no value judgment on the process of decay; the bios passes through a series of stations in the vast digestive tract of Nature."

*

Rosner's statements, I felt, were not bad; they dovetailed with my views on the changes of polities.

The endless succession of dynasties and dictatorships is not explained by their imperfection alone. A peristaltic movement must play a role. It does not lead upwards; rather, the sum total of suffering remains constant. Indeed, a knowledge hidden in matter seems to be corroborated. This is already indicated by the naïve fervor with which all revolutionaries utter the word "movement." It is their fateful word, with which they rise and fall.

Rosner is a materialist of the purest water and as such too intelligent to be a Darwinist. One could describe him as a successor to certain neovitalists. A touch of anonymous piety, such as distinguishes the classical naturalists, is nicely fermented and sublimated in him. Aside from needing him for my private war, I have often enjoyed conversing with him—both about issues pertaining to his field and about other things as well. Ornithology has a special magic, a depth of perception, that links homeland with immensity. Moreover, it focuses on the wealth and splendor of life. The eye rests on the richness of the palette; it is satisfied not in hope but in the "here and now." No progress: *universalia in re*.

*

Incidentally, the anarch can usually converse nicely with the unrelenting materialist. Many years ago, Hippel's Wine Garden in Berlin was a fertile soil for such conversations, a crucible in which, to be sure, only amalgams succeeded. It was a gathering place for the "Free Men," who styled themselves "an isolated volunteer corps of radicalism." I have summoned them to the luminar, and I will go into detail later on. Initially, I saw them as a typical Germanic coven, huddling at the trunk of the cosmic ash tree and "dreeing their weird." Whenever we track down the great turning points, we wind up in one of their universities—Tübingen, Königsberg, Göttingen—but who is familiar with those names today?

*

What Rosner had said about viewing putrescence non-judgmentally seemed to have stimulated Attila, too—the unicorn was stroking its beard: "A spark remains, although in disreputable circumstances. I can confirm this as a physician. We ought to return the spark to the gods."

He looked at the Condor and took his hand. I noted this and stored it in my memory, like anything else said in the bar. It was not until the Great Hunt was approaching that this remark struck me as more meaningful than a casual maxim.

Rosner said, "That is not within my area of expertise."

The conversation now took a different turn, insofar as "nonjudgmental observation of putrescence" had also given the Condor food for thought.

"I will note that for the next exhibition. I prefer a dungheap by Hauser to a Madonna by Cario. Would it not at least be possible to have a jury free of value judgments?"

To which the Domo, at whom the question was directed, replied, "That is impossible, if only because it contradicts logic. The jurors are supposed to judge. It is best to let them do as they like, provided they do not interfere with politics. Yet it is impossible to uproot this propensity."

*

The Domo's aesthetic taste is confined to music. His opinions on style and language are grounded in the classics. I would not claim that he has no understanding of the fine arts, but he will always side with the draftsmen and not the colorists. His private domicile is appointed in classical style—a spare, sober elegance. It is neither too warm nor too cold, and one speaks softly there rather than loudly. The walls boast a single painting, a Vermeer rescued from the great fires, with contrasting planes of lemon and ultramarine. Only the bull's-eye windowpanes are iridescent—as if the master wanted to provide an example of his command of the intermediary tones.

The Domo has a standing desk there, from which he dictates, should he summon a scribe after dinner. He may do so late at night, even though reading is more of a diversion for him. I once had to classify his bedside library: plays and histories, no novels or poems, instead a collection of maxims from Heraclitus to Montaigne and Lichtenberg. His own maxim, incidentally, is: "First the chessboard, then the game."

In his office he sits at his desk and receives people with a terse ceremony geared to the specific visitor. The huge window faces the city; a televisor can bring in all parts of the city, even the hidden ones. A second apparatus receives news uninterruptedly; a small bell jingles only when the moderator believes that the news deserves special attention.

Just as he does not appreciate paintings in which the color dissolves or even annihilates the forms, so, too, does he hate an emotional emphasis of political facts. "Feelings are a private matter."

He finds enthusiasm suspect, even if it is for the Condor. "Human beings are ungrateful—especially when they are spoiled. So we reckon with this from the very start."

When the Condor had shelled the city, the Domo occupied the town hall, where he was told by several of the deputies who had not fled: "We will yield only to force."

"That is sensible, and here it is," and he pointed to the sailors standing behind him in the door.

*

That should suffice to indicate that the Domo could not be comfortable with the drift of the conversation. Rosner now wanted to go into the relativity of smells.

"For many animals, if not most, scents become attractive only when the putrescence is fairly advanced. On the other hand, dogs can fall ill from smelling perfume. Often this is a question of dosage; thus, the delicious fragrance of attar of roses conceals a hint of skatole—the substance that gives excrement its fecal odor."

*

I followed every word of Rosner's lecture while mixing him his orange juice with a shot of gin, noting the consumption, and taking care of other obligations required by my job. This affords me, as I have said, a certain pleasure, and I would be a good barkeep even if I had to do it full time for want of something better.

In this activity as in others—driving, selling, teaching, informing, operating—it is crucial to take it very seriously for a while and do it thoroughly until it is mastered. It is then performed either automatically or playfully. One has thus gotten past the period of thinking. For example, I know a croupier on Place Hassan who slides the chips so elegantly across the table that the bettors scarcely notice whether they have won or lost.

In fact, most types who deal a lot with money have a fluid vein: this is shown by the way they flip through bank notes or strew coins across the counter. Here in Eumeswil, where payments are made with gold, this is a poem. Such people are recognized simply by the way they don a hat or walk through a door. Magic is involved or at least a touch of legerdemain.

This makes for self-assurance, as expressed in the litheness of my motions behind the bar. The guests like it. They would be less edified if they knew what else I was thinking about.

These are, en passant, three dialectical stages: first the personal and material task, then its transcendence through exercises, and finally the liberation leading to universal—which, for me, are historical—perceptions.

*

In this respect, Rosner's explanations are an example of how to be at ease in society. Since he could not possibly exclude the vulture from the scavengers, he tried at least to ennoble its food or present it as fairly common. Furthermore, Rosner could also point to categorial distinctions—say, the fact that there are puny eagles and mighty vultures. The

Domo seemed to expect as much; he said, "Professor, do not draw out the preamble. We would like to hear all about the condor."

25

Rosner was able to report marvelous things; he sketched an impressive picture of this bird, which has a greater wingspan than any other feathered creature. The condor soars without beating his wings over the loftiest peaks of the cordilleras, over the icy tops of smoking volcanoes. Though invisible to the sharpest eyes, the condor notices anything happening in the narrow gulches, the *quebradas*, or the atmosphere. If the lower vultures start circling, which means they have spotted prey, then he swoops into the depth, and no creature dares contest the meal, much less approach him before he is sated.

The tyrant, having listened more and more benevolently, now wanted to know whether this bird was completely dependent on carrion. By no means, if one cared to believe the professor: the powerful take what they like. Shepherds on the Sorata claim—and scientists have followed suit—that the condor, by beating his wings, terrifies the animals in the high mountains, the alpacas and guanacos, until they hurtle from the precipices. Then he plunges to the bottom of the abyss and feasts on them.

One recognizes the *grand seigneur* chiefly by his banquets. The beach is his table, on which the ocean leaves huge morsels: seals, sea lions, and dolphins, even a whale, which, if stranded, is crushed to death by its own weight.

The professor went further into the condor's habitat, calling it his "biotope." Most ornithologists are well traveled; Rosner had obviously done some studies in cordilleras, for he described such a mountain range, with its rows of volcanoes and gigantic walls, like someone who had hiked through it from the seashore to the high plateaus. He knew it from the jungles on its flanks to the edge where glaciers push into the ocean. Rosner also reached beyond his science.

"A colossus that keeps its majesty a secret by covering it with mass. Its impact is immediate, deriving from its sheer weight. However, we must remember that our initial sight of it is upward, from sea level, so that we view only half of it."

Passion, devotion to the subject, arouses the sympathy of even detached outsiders—as if these matters had found a mediator, a mirror that reflected their light as heat. Of course, not everyone feels it; the courtiers in Berlin dreaded the evenings when Humboldt entertained one of the Prussian Wilhelms with the marvels of the New World.

Attila harked back to the image of the stranded whale: "The condor cannot possibly take care of it alone."

"No, but he tears it open. Then huge swarms of gulls, ravens, lower vultures, and even land animals come thronging up."

"So one could say he lives off leviathan?"

Rosner did not care to indulge in such speculations. "A poet could phrase it like that. I believe that this is more properly the domain of my colleague Vigo."

But Attila dug in his heels: "In any case, one cannot deny that the condor has myth-making strength? You must have heard about it from the highlands all the way down to Mexico City."

*

In the course of my evenings and especially my nights behind the bar, I had concentrated on Attila. Only little by little did it dawn on me that the standards I am used to applying as a historian do not suffice. I have to reach back to archaic things, not only their temporal extension but also their spatial depth, which is always present. This is virgin soil for me, and I am primed for surprises.

As a historian, I am trained to *decipher*; here, I must *guess*. That is the difference between a rational and a numinous approach. The hieroglyphs were deciphered roughly around the time when Alexander von Humboldt climbed the peak of Tenerife and the Chimborazo with his instruments, while heraldic figures were being replaced by colors and national borders were solidifying. In the twenty-first century, when they were wiped out first by economic, then by intellectual principles, the legacy of the Nahuatl tribes was revealed to idle elites. Deciphering was not enough. Such encounters are mutual; they involve an ascent. Likewise, the preceding archaeological disquiet would be inconceivable without plutonian energy. At the propitious moment, the treasure, as in fairy tales, rises to the surface.

That is precisely what strikes me about Attila: a sudden glow from the depths. The old man must have seen a lot, must know a lot that he keeps to himself. My task is to guess what it is. Attila is the counterpart of the Domo, the policy director of the Condor, to whose left he sits as the physician of his body and, even more, of his mind.

*

Attila conceals his knowledge because it wishes to be guessed. Just what did he mean with his question about the "myth-making strength"? The contemporary man provides only fact-making strength. He is quantified as a vote, as a payer and payee, as a species that survives in the registers of government offices and ministries. Any memory of him sinks into the grave with his grandchildren.

Anecdote-making strength is greater; it is historic. It concentrates the species with its characteristics; it leaves its stamp for centuries. A mountain chain is recognized in a crystal, and a metal in a coin. This is no privilege for rulers and popes; a monk, a peasant, a buffoon can knock more noisily.

Myth-making strength, by contrast, is ahistorical, not subject to any derivation or development; it effects history incalculably and unpredictably. It does not belong to time, it creates time.

That is why in periods of decline, when the substance of history is exhausted, unable to guarantee even the zoological place of the species, a dull, tacit expectation has adhered to myth-making strength. Theology peters out—it yields to theognosis; people no longer want to know about gods: they want to see them.

Needless to say, a historian who despairs of his function becomes sensitive to myth and all the more alert, because he rejects whatever can be offered by the people around him—he conducts himself, that is, as an anarch.

*

Attila must have spent a long time in the great forests beyond the desert. It would seem as if he wanted to take the Condor in a different direction, while the Domo wishes to keep an iron grip on the status quo—with some latitude, but nevertheless within his limits. Both men regard tyranny as the sole framework for keeping the atomized masses in shape and delaying the free-for-all battle. The Domo is a pragmatist, devoid of any transcendental stirrings. The day must teach the day. Better to navigate with a red sail until the ship is wrecked than to drift inactively in the Red Sea.

Yet power seeks cosmic fulfillment; otherwise it will die of its own voracity. Power was not enough even for the caesars. The sea approached one of them in his dreams and whispered its secret to him; another saw gods appear to him as his equals before the battle.

*

If day is dawning and I am exhausted, I see them hieroglyphically: the Condor in the middle as the king vulture and, to his left, Attila as a unicorn with a silver beard. Only the Domo still has human features, though modified; that is how Odysseus is depicted on ancient vases. He, too, is bearded; a fringe of coppery hair curls from his temples down to his chin. It actually sharpens his profile. But I notice that Attila's and the Condor's heads suddenly appear as if propped upon their necks, while the Domo's head ripples, then rigidifies as if cast.

At such times, it can happen that I spill wine when pouring it. I then stop taking notes.

*

Attila's question about the myth-making power of animals went far beyond Rosner's scope. The dimensions it aimed at were not those of big game, but those of the cosmic hunt.

For what great figures can stars and constellations be named? Since Chaldean times, astrognosy has responded to this question with an unerring instinct: they should be named for gods and animals; outer space is not for human beings, with few exceptions, such as Palinurus.

Nevertheless, the professor was not at a loss. Folklore, manners, and mores as well as totems and heraldry are within the domain of positive science. Rosner had traveled the Andes from Quito to Cape Horn, learning all sorts of things in villages and towns, and also from the primitives—"Even though, when I was in Tierra del Fuego," he said, "I was pursuing a different bird, namely the southernmost hummingbird.

"In point of fact, the condor was the object of religious worship by the natives. They attributed supernatural powers to it. Unfortunately, its numbers have decreased dramatically; guano dealers have decimated the population out of greed, and Indians for the plumage.

"Once, in the highlands, I came upon an old man hauling a bagged condor on his shoulders; he praised it as a morsel fit for a king and distinguished three sorts of condor flesh, one tasting like beef, one like horse, the best like condor; he also said that the bird's stomach and heart provided a miracle drug."

Rosner then detailed the tricks for catching the great tyrant. A hunter lies under the skin of a freshly slaughtered bull, with the bloody side up. Once the condor perches on it, the Indian, using the hide like a sack, wraps up the bird's claws and ties them with a string. Then the other men come dashing over.

In many districts, they stuff llama cadavers with narcotic herbs. The vultures, intoxicated by their meal, hop around in a circle. They are subdued with bolas, or else a poncho is thrown over them.

On the plateau of Huascarán, the Indians place dead mules on the rim of a very deep crater. When the condors yank them back and forth, they push the carcass over the edge and plunge after it. From there, they can no longer rise up and so they fall prey to the hunters.

Other things are reported by old travelers: Alexander von Humboldt, Pöpping, Tschudi, Jerry and Libby McGraham, and also a poet, Pablo Neruda, who has sung the condor's praises.

Rosner continued: "Once, in Peru, I participated in a ritual fiesta that involves the sacrifice of a condor. It always takes place in February. These people are truculent; though worshiping the bird as a god, they slowly torture it to death. More than anything else, however, the condor is kept for a bullfight. First, they let it starve for a week; then they tie it, like a rider, to the back of the bull, which has been stabbed bloody with lances. The populace is thrown into a paroxysm while the condor, with outspread wings, rips the mighty animal to pieces."

*

The professor now made his point, which he had obviously prepared with great skill, I must admit, during his lecture: "I may assume that this spectacle conceals a totemic encounter. The sacred bird of the aborigines vanquishes the bull, the symbol of the Spanish conquistadors.

"In Mexico, incidentally, there are no condors, but only their closest relative, the splendid king vultures—what we zoologists call a vicarious species. The king vulture enjoys the same respect here as the condor in Peru. As we know, the eagle is Mexico's heraldic animal—the eagle holding a serpent in its claws. This refers to the plumed serpent, an Aztec image.

"During my travels in the interior, and also when I saw Mexicans sitting around a bowl in their harbors, I often had a peculiar thought, although one forgivable for an ornithologist: they could just as easily have the vulture in their coat of arms—it would be appropriate. All that is missing is the king, who, having regaled himself, allots and carves. Perhaps he shows up every so often and comes down to them, recognized as the first among equals, like that Juárez, who had the emperor shot. That, too, was a totemic encounter: between the king vulture and the Hapsburg eagle—he avenged Montezuma."

*

The professor had almost talked himself into a frenzy; I had, of course, been mixing drinks, as demanded. The vaporizer was running at medium speed; the room felt cozy. The specialist had spoken—*The Wren* could not compete. At the same time, the specialist had flown beyond his limits, the ornithologist's, perhaps with a not-so-clear conscience; but his institute was richly rewarded.

26

It had grown late; up in my room, after the bar had closed, I lay in bed, thinking about the conversations. By and large, the participants do not fully realize what they are saying—that is, the words are weightier than the opinions. Sense is hidden in even the most banal intercourse. When someone enters the room and says, "Good morning," this is a polite cliché, perhaps also a cordial wish. At the same time, it heralds a cosmic event.

They had captured the political structure of Eumeswil more sharply than they realized—perhaps only Attila knew how sharply. He was the farthest from the center. Granted, the Condor lived off leviathan. But this leviathan was a corpse. No longer a gigantic toy for the world spirit to have fun with, it was already a cadaver, washed up by the tides. Granted, the king vulture was stronger than the eagle, but this eagle was hardly more than a stuffed, moth-eaten fowl. Rosner had scored a good hit by mentioning Maximilian, one of the last epigoni of Charles V.

*

Juárez had killed one of the rulers of decadence; the Condor had swept out the final tribunes. There was still the eagle, a dismal bird, splaying empty claws, stripped of crown and scepter. In his shadow, they had their sessions, half Catos and half Brutuses; both unanimous and quarreling, they succeeded one another in their powerlessness. It all collapsed like a house of cards, and my dear old dad is still mourning the loss.

Once authority is worn down to the final thread, then the tyrants or despots come. *Auctoritas* yields to *potestas*, as Don Capisco explained. Often, the intermezzos are more rewarding, especially at the great fracture points. Ingrid was doing her postdoctoral dissertation on one of those topics; we summoned Pompey the Great to the luminar. His royal features are unmistakable, as were his efforts to restore the monarchy. This trauma haunted the Romans through the centuries.

Accordingly, Pompey and not Caesar was the ideal figure for Brutus to protest against.

*

Caesar, stabbed by Brutus, fell at the foot of the statue of Pompey; such images normally succeed only in dreams. I will resist the temptation to lose myself in them. Let me therefore only briefly mention one of the models of the intermediary period that we reviewed in Vigo's garden. Bruno was also present.

Our theme was a comparison between a Russian revolutionary named Trotsky and Peter the Great: both were confronted with the problem of coordinating a spatially limited revolution with the current state of the world, especially Europe. The czar's solution worked, Trotsky's failed. Perhaps he had staked too much on the cliché of 1789, thereby, like Brutus, misjudging the situation. Nevertheless, the Fourth International contained the stronger thrust toward a world revolution.

I do not wish to expatiate. The discussion was shaken to its core when Bruno gave technological development the priority over economic development; Trotsky accused Stalin of "Thermidorism." He himself, with Lenin, called for "Socialism plus electricity," but, according to Bruno, "got stalled at midcourse." The materialists of the eighteenth Christian century were more consistent in their thinking than those of the twentieth.

Still and all, the First World State would have been inconceivable without the leveling impact of technology, especially electronics—one might also say (again according to Bruno), it was their byproduct. Vigo, who innately despises technology, heartily agreed.

*

If the Condor is overthrown by the tribunes, little will change, for they, too, would need to practice violence. Only the style will differ. The tyrant is replaced by demagogues. The demagogue remains at the helm by orienting the plebiscite according to his wishes. The art lies in the posing of questions; if they are put successfully, then the response is overwhelming, not only in its massiveness, but also in its intellectual uniformity, which goes all the way to the top.

The Condor tries to avoid plebiscites; they would be a foreign language to him. On the other hand, he makes use of popular demonstrations. If an opposition becomes too blatant, then the Domo is always capable of raising and subduing violent storms along the waterfront or in the marketplaces. For the curtain raiser, a semi-tolerated underground press, in the style of *L'Ami du Peuple*, wants heads to roll—this usually suffices. Otherwise the popular anger seethes and becomes virulent.

During such eruptions, one glimpses neither the military nor the police, not even well-known partisans. Quite the contrary: the Domo does not deploy them until the mob does more than smash the windows. The mighty Condor then takes his adversaries under his wing.

*

Power is not entirely absorbed in politics; personal elements unavoidably seep in. This is the limit at which both tyrants and demagogues stoop to despotism. Mania forces its way in, outstripping power and often verging on the comical. Despite his weak voice, Nero wanted to rank first even as a singer. Recently I watched his grotesque performance at the circus in Naples, where five thousand hippies were distributed in gangs across the tiers in order to applaud. The cheers began with the "humming of bees" and intensified into a "hollow-brick sound," until it surged as a "kettle resonance" into the arena.

Another, Commodus, who claimed to be a descendant of Hercules, personally killed wild beasts in the Colosseum and guzzled from a cudgel-shaped glass. Incidentally, I find this Commodus strange: the embodiment of the anarch manqué. I am not alluding to details reported by Lampridius—say, that he gathered noblewomen in the palace, ordered them to strip naked, and then examined them like a buyer at a brothel. What was unusual was that he had this and others of his obscene exploits recorded in the government protocols.

The anarch's study of the history of the caesars has more of a theoretical significance for him—it offers a sampling of how far rulers can go. In practice, self-discipline is the only kind of rule that suits the anarch. He, too, can kill anyone (this is deeply immured in the crypt of his consciousness) and, above all, extinguish himself if he finds himself inadequate.

*

The tyrant, even when degenerating into a despot, supplies a richer selection of anecdotes than the demagogue. Sulla and Marius are cases in point.

A large-scale demagogue, who turned up when the planet Pluto was discovered, dabbled in painting just as Nero did in singing. He persecuted painters whose works he did not like. He dabbled in other areas, too—for instance, as a strategist who doomed many people, but was technically perfect; as a chauffeur in all directions, who eventually had himself cremated with the help of gasoline. His outlines melt into insignificance; the torrent of numbers wipes them out. The pickings are slim for both the historian and the anarch. Red monotony, even in the atrocities.

Unlike that demagogue, the Condor stays within the modest borders of Eumeswil. Progress is completed; domestic unrest drives events in a circle, like the hands of a clock.

"There is no progress," I often hear my genitor say; he seems to regard this as a misfortune. He also says, "Standing still means going backward." The little people, in contrast, are satisfied if everyday life remains constant; they prefer to see their chimneys smoking, not their houses.

*

Furthermore, the generals usually work in a less fantastic manner than the demagogues. Almost as children, they are integrated in the hierarchy and accustomed to orders and obedience. They are trained in dictatorship, not dialectics, which can join together in a single person; Trotsky is a good example. (The belief that Jews cannot command was a prejudice.) *Dicto* and *dico*—that is the difference. Experiencing power at an early age, they are familiar with its statics and dynamics; they know how to move others without budging themselves. If a professor, an attorney, or a littérateur comes to power, he finds it intoxicating. He gets lost in inordinate projects; he exaggerates their implementation.

The fact that the Condor has "no ideas" is one of the things for which my genitor reproaches him. But when ideas, even good ones, enter such minds, they usually spell misfortune for the world. Mankind has experienced the most absurd things in this area.

The egalitarian mania of demagogues is even more dangerous than the brutality of men in gallooned coats. For the anarch, this remains theoretical, because he avoids both sides. Anyone who has been oppressed can get back on his feet if the oppression has not cost him his life. A man who has been equalized is physically and morally ruined. Anyone who is different is not equal; that is one of the reasons why the Jews are so often targeted.

Equalization goes downward, like shaving, hedge trimming, or the pecking order of poultry. At times, the world spirit seems to change into monstrous Procrustes—a man has read Rousseau and starts practicing equality by chopping off heads or, as Mimie le Bon called it, "making the apricots roll." The guillotinings in Cambrai were an entertainment before dinner. Pygmies shortened the legs of tall Africans in order to cut them down to size; white Negroes flatten the literary languages.

*

The anarch, recognizing no government, but not indulging in paradisal dreams as the anarchist does, is, for that very reason, a neutral observer.

The historian in him, like an arbiter, sees men and powers marching into the arena. Time gnaws on every regime, and even faster on the good ones.

Drawing on this knowledge, the Domo seems to be oriented more to the present than to duration; he has gained yet another day when the guards have marched up after the evening report. Though he often skips dinner, he never misses out on the night bar; I have to telephone him when the Condor shows up there unexpectedly. A short time later, I see him sitting to the tyrant's right; even late at night, after a long workday, he seems alert and precise, yet not tense.

27

I am still en route to the central bank—but the foregoing was no digression. I have even had to keep it short. These are thoughts that cross the mind during such démarches, or even any other activity. They echo the overall theme. That is why I find perfunctory work so easy; I fade it out, while upstairs I've got a home theater playing for free, and often even simultaneously on different stages. Moving my legs, tending the bar, ripping up a copy of *The Wren* at the street corner—these actions are marginal. Sometimes I return to the moment in order to enjoy it thoroughly.

Arriving at the central bank, I obtain my orders. A few will be sealed; others will follow, depending on the situation. Perhaps they will be transmitted to me on the way.

I assume that the Domo had his reasons for picking me of all people for this task. An academic, a university teacher, is ordered to go unescorted to a place where huge amounts of gold are stockpiled. Naturally, the bank guards will have reinforcements. I am apparently expected to perform a service that calls for intelligence and, presumably, tact. The Casbah, I must here point out, considers the free flow of cash more important than, say, freedom of the press and other postulates which, as the Domo always says, "are all well and good, but won't buy you anything." He also says: "The first thing people here ask is whether the books are balanced."

Hence it goes without saying that the central bank is one of the sore spots. In critical situations, the tellers should go about their business as usual; this provides a sense of security. Advance notice is required only for major withdrawals. The treasury can be replenished at any time from the vaults of the Casbah; they are greater than any possible demand.

*

I must now devote a few words to the finances. Their stability is the main reason why the tyranny has endured for a relatively long time. A precondition is the Domo's lack of imagination. There are obviously two things he has thought about very carefully: police and money.

As an anarch I may find this subject thoroughly uninteresting, but as a historian I had to help him with his studies. Sometimes he would call me late at night: "Manuel, I need a pamphlet by a fellow named Karski: 'Inflation, Commodity Prices, and Gold Production.' It must have been published in ancient times, before the First World War. Please get me the text tomorrow. His name may possibly be written with a *-y*."

Tracking down and getting hold of such things, either up here in the Casbah or down in the institute through the luminar, is child's play. The next evening, upon arriving at the bar, the Domo found the photocopy on the table. Out of dutiful curiosity, I had already taken a peek.

In point of fact, the available stock of gold was an important issue. The Domo had started out with the problem of need: he had ordered an investigation into what the average man requires to be content.

A certain excess is indispensable when demands are refined or—this is not the same thing—spiritualized. The dissatisfaction of the spiritual man is even more dangerous than that of the starveling. A magical bond exists between gold and art. Private excess should benefit aesthetic life and finer handicrafts all the way to bookbinders and cooks, while government excess should benefit the comfort of the masses, especially in the form of games. Distribution of bread is to be avoided; even superfluous buildings are preferable. Of course, these should be artworks; and that is precisely our problem.

A city without wealth is as shabby as a city without poverty: it is delightful to see what life has to offer. Harbors where rouged girls beckon to strangers, and peddlers hawk superfluous wares: it is nice to land here; life must be good. I bought a parrot and let it fly away; the Africans laughed and invited me for a drink.

*

Gold is available beyond demand; that is the chief reason why it must be hoarded; its invisible might lies in its hoarding. Besides, the prices rise if there is superfluous gold. Inflation hits especially those who live from hand to mouth.

The gold mines are located deep in the south; they have rich lodes. These veins have been exploited for a long time, so that the growing shortages during the tribunate seem peculiar by comparison. Despite this wealth, people got to see nothing but paper, smooth bank notes, hot off the press. Even the smallest coin, the copperlet, was adulterated.

After that era, it seemed utterly incredible that the Condor was paying with gold. This miracle was due to his judging people objectively, indeed skeptically—unlike the tribunes, who had stylized the word "human" into a sublime concept. It is the guiding light for their pedagogical efforts, their promises of happiness, even their messianic prophecies. Needless to say, all this costs money, which, however, they collect from concrete and not ideal human beings. Since they deal in illusions, hard currency soon vanishes; money, too, becomes fictive. This is a conjuror's trick. Yet, like my dear old dad, the tribunes can still be of good faith.

It is no coincidence that precisely when things started going downhill with the gods, politics gained its bliss-making character. There would be no reason for objecting to this, since the gods, too, were not exactly fair. But at least people saw temples instead of termite architecture. Bliss is drawing closer; it is no longer in the afterlife, it will come, though not momentarily, sooner or later in the here and now—in time.

The anarch thinks more primitively; he refuses to give up any of his happiness. "Make thyself happy" is his basic law. It is his response to the "Know thyself" at the temple of Apollo in Delphi. These two maxims complement each other; we must know our happiness and our measure.

*

State bankruptcy, despite a huge natural wealth of agriculture and mineral resources (again, Mexico supplied an example), has multiple causes, such as corruption, overspending, poor planning. Populaces have to pay through the nose for the building mania and bellicosity of rulers and tribunes. Modest, by contrast, are their personal pleasures, although these are resented more deeply. The great ideas blast loudest through the chimney.

*

The Condor can pay cash because he has few ideas. Money in hand is persuasive. At worst, he may be accused of squandering on the navy; however, he owed to it his decisive victory in the civil war. Hunting is done on a lavish scale—not only for his own enjoyment, but as a kind of tribute to the Yellow Khan. And, finally, there are the minions.

Eumeswil is a nest of fellahs. This saves money on armaments, yet requires a supple politics between the great powers. An army in this situation would be a senseless provocation.

*

Our monetary structure is rooted in principles that have stood the test in the greatest times of Heliopolis. Calculation is based on two systems: the buying and selling of either goods or energy. Payment can be demanded in gold for houses, land, machines, tools, all forms of commodities—anything, in short, that is visible and tangible. This unit of currency is the "condor," a coin almost entirely restricted to banks, if only because of its weight. There are one hundred scudi to the condor—a scudo constitutes a good daily wage, while one can live extravagantly on a double scudo. For an erotic service in the harbor the charge is half a scudo, in the three-star lupanars a whole scudo.

Energy—that is, machine work, compulsory labor of people and animals, the broadcasting of games and news—is paid for in soldi. But gold is expected for song and poetry, for writings and artworks—and, as I have said, for erotic services. There are distinctions between salaries and honorariums. Basically, these are simply two forms of accounting, since the amounts can be freely converted. They overlap in the automatic machines, in that the inserted coin can be translated into either values or services. Heliopolis had an even higher category in the form of metals that radiated energy directly. In Eumeswil, this technology has grown obsolete—for one thing because it proved to be highly dangerous, and also because people have forgotten how to use it. On the other hand, it was perfected in the catacombs. This is to be inferred from modest samples "for peaceful purposes," which, like the mechanical pencil or the thermal rings, have been introduced in the city. They recall the mirrors and glass beads for the natives along the Slave and Gold Coasts.

*

Thus, we have the soldo for energy services, the scudo for goods. Now, why the distinction, since either can be converted at any time and at any counter?

Our currency expert is Professor Scavo, whom the Domo occasionally brings to the night bar. His marginalia yield an item or two for my notes. Most of his remarks deal, of course, with practical concerns—say, the gold drain, which has always been a problem for mercantile societies; but still he inevitably has to touch on fundamental issues.

Once again, I am astonished by the Domo's restraint, his sangfroid in restricting himself to rational and measurable dimensions. What counts for him is the weight of gold, not its magical prestige, which fascinates men like Bruno. In one of our nocturnal conversations, Bruno said that there were three "revealed secrets": the Serpent, the Jews, and gold. "In each of them, salvation and disaster still cleave together, which spells doom for reason."

An expert like Scavo does not venture behind the scenes—something that delights the historian. Facts, not ideas, are his staples. Obviously, Scavo feels that the existence of two currencies is important in practice as well: "There has to be a money that is rapidly used up. The soldo permits this circulation, as it is cyclical; the scudo, in contrast, is vertical. This force of gravity explains its efforts to vanish into the ground until grass grows over it."

That was not bad; it was complemented by a different kind of drain—namely, hoarding. Gold is socked away. The Condor hoards the biggest piggy bank under the Casbah; this creates a counterweight. Gold must be shown on the money changers' table. Nothing succeeds like success.

*

By their functions, the soldo could be likened to a checking account, the scudo to a savings account. In daily practice, as I have said, the distinction vanishes—not to mention that payments have reached a high degree of abstraction. Anyone in possession of a phonophore—in other words, nearly everyone—is always solvent. His account is kept up to date automatically. The arrangement is complicated, but the procedure simple; through the phonophore, I pay more quickly and more easily than with a check.

The leveling of society through automation—the way in which cardinal issues of wages and labor are revolutionized—that is a story unto itself. Here in Eumeswil, it seems as if the system occasionally falls asleep and the city begins to dream. The ship founders on a sandbank and then gets back afloat. Electric power stops; after a while, the machines start up again. During such recesses, the anarch measures his own strength and autonomy.

*

After observing Scavo at the night bar once or twice, I attended his course when I happened to be at the university. I saw that my notion about current was not accidental. Electricity has exerted a much stronger impact on property, and thereby on money, than steam has.

Scavo said, "The equivalent value of the soldo is energy. The scudo's value is intrinsic. It therefore has purchasing power for both objects and energy. The relationship remains hidden, since either soldi or scudi can be taken in payment.

"The soldo is, however, if not fictive, then effective—tied, that is, to the performance of services. This is made obvious by disturbances inside the world of labor. In the worst-case scenario, a blackout, the soldo becomes worthless, while gold retains, and even increases, its value."

*

This is roughly the skeleton, which he filled out with historical flashbacks: inflation resulting from extravagance, as after wars; hoarding of potential services through reserves of the unemployed; currency manipulations; rate and price controls; adulteration of coins; the cowry shell; the Dutch tulip panic; the Abbé Galiani; Law and the Spitzeders; the Panama Canal scandal; and so on.

A good historical fundament, a lavish yet controlled association. I found inspiration for my field and also for developing his theories at the luminar. Say, the idea of the historian as a neutral, nonjudgmental observer. The anarch, however, is (I am simplifying) on the side of gold: it fascinates him, like everything that eludes society. Gold has its own immeasurable might. It need only show itself, and society with its law and order is in jeopardy.

The anarch is on the side of gold: this is not to be construed as lust for gold. He recognizes gold as the central and immobile power. He loves it, not like Cortez, but like Montezuma, not like Pizarro but like Atahualpa; these are the differences between plutonian fire and the solar brilliance worshiped in the temples of the sun. The supreme quality of gold is that of light; it bestows through its sheer existence.

*

The movement generated by gold ("everything strives toward gold"), even when it rests deep in vaults, is merely a reflection of what Agrippa calls its "dignity." This is its value; its price is merely the latter's expression.

The value is stable, the price variable and dynamic, and also contingent on fashion. The preeminence of stability comes out in Scavo's theories and even in our daily practice, albeit imperfectly.

A conversation that the Domo and Scavo had about these matters is fixed in my memory. They were talking about the actual meaning of work, which the Domo called its "genius." He said that whenever genius flows into work, whether a cabinetmaker's, a painter's, or a silversmith's, then such work is "worth its weight in gold" and should be remunerated accordingly.

A great deal had already been drunk; Scavo livened up and came out of himself. I helped a bit with the vaporizer. The professor clearly noticed what was bothering the Domo. First he pointed to the destruction of values by the economic era. It had, he said, been a paraplegia hindering any superior movement, a paralysis from which no one had recovered.

I can only sketch his ideas, and roughly at that. In essence, he went on, only time and piecework were remunerated, quality was replaced by standardization. "What you call 'genius,' Excellency, is outside of time; it therefore cannot be rewarded appropriately, much less according to set criteria. Whenever it goes far beyond talent, it is recognized either inadequately or not at all. An artwork fetches high prices long after the death of its creator, who may have died in poverty. Yet the very highest price can signify only that genius is priceless. Hence, even when patrons or rulers spoil a genius, he labors for free. In this respect, he resembles the gods, who bestow freely. The world as Creation is not beyond but outside of things. That is where its immutable Being is to be found."

*

An advantage of the night bar is that experts reach beyond their grasp here. It has an ambiance; that is why I would rather tend bar than serve dinner, although excellent music is offered there.

The professor brought his hand to his mouth; he seemed embarrassed by his own brio. But the Condor enjoys seeing his guests let go. Thanking the professor, he added a final remark. He tends to express himself simply; unfortunately, I did not record his exact words. I was too, absorbed in the conversation; it touched on distinctions that I ponder both as a historian and as an anarch.

The Condor has a sense of history and its entanglements; this is attested to merely by his putting the luminar at my disposal. His leaning is one that is especially prevalent in periods of epigoni and fellahs—I mean the wish for "historical equivalences." Tradition, with its works and documents, is then taken as a reproach. The restoral of Creation—that is a primal problem. Now the wish may be father to the thought, but not to the artwork, even the humblest poem.

In this connection, the Condor had been struck by Scavo's maxim that genius exists outside of time and can do nothing but affect it. This implies that genius is also outside of society and independent of it—with which the anarch can only concur. At times, I suspect the Condor of hoping to turn Eumeswil into a small-scale Florence; he would then have his Machiavelli in the Domo.

When the good spirits have left the house, no invocation can lure them back. Their absence troubled him. Attila had recognized the mistake in this reasoning.

"If genius were inside time, it would never manifest itself in Eumeswil. But this way, we never lose hope."

He touched the Condor's hand: "Nor is a miracle inside time."

*

What could he mean by that? This was not their first debate about genius; they merely had different names for it. From the outlines I jotted down during the nocturnal conversations, I could piece together a mosaic, which, of course, like any artistic work, has its cracks and flaws.

If Attila were a Christian, then I would have interpreted his statement about miracles accordingly, say, as an echo of old hymns. Such things, like any transcendence, would never occur to him. For Attila, a miracle is possible at any time; it can be experienced—it dwells among us. Transcendence is the side track of reason. The world is more miraculous than as depicted by sciences and religions. Only art has any inkling of it.

He seems to regard genius as a finely distributed energy that can appear at any time, in any place. An animal develops other organs, it begins to fly, it changes its species and genus, or else an individual crops up and gives world history a new direction—faith did not create the miracle; rather, the miracle preceded faith. New surprises keep occurring, especially in periods of decline.

Attila spent a long time in the great forests beyond the desert. He must have had strange encounters there.

*

When it gets late, an underwater atmosphere pervades the night bar; I grow more alert when observing my aquarium. As in every discussion, the same word may cover different contents. The Domo is the most intelligible. For him, "genius" is an extraordinary achievement, not just in art or science, but also in craft. His reasons for equating it with gold, for honoring it with prizes and awards, are obvious. He knows that a hierarchical society is more easily governed than a leveled one; this is already true in the physical world. The serpent is more dangerous than the millipede.

In Eumeswil, where demagogues and fortunate soldiers spell one another, every social distinction has been wiped away. Almost no store is set by medals, yet nobody would refuse a hundred pure-gold condors. So anyone who wants to hierarchize must relate gold to performance.

Furthermore, the Domo has tried to enrich his palette by making education less compulsory—indeed, even abolishing it altogether for certain professions. For this, the shepherds and fishermen are grateful to him, as are their children. The other day, when I was sitting in one of Rosner's bird-watching stations on the Sus, two shepherd boys were driving their sheep past me. They seemed to be talking about a friend; I heard one of them say, "He has to go to school." He did not exactly sound envious. I was glad that I, as an anarch, renouncing any bond, any limitation of freedom, also reject compulsory education as nonsense. It was one of the greatest wellsprings of misfortune in the world.

*

The Condor, too, would like to remunerate works of genius with gold, yet he seeks them in vain. He emulates the Baroque princeling in his capacity as a good paterfamilias. Everyone should be as content as possible in his own way. Politically, the Condor cares less than the Domo about order and security. Rather, his personal well-being depends on them. This is the point at which egoism becomes amiable.

To each his own: no discord should disturb the Condor's circle. This is indicated by the mere fact that he—and in this he agrees with the Domo—listens to music during his repasts. Thus, unlike colonial masters, he could not maintain an imperturbable conscience when breakfasting on a kilogram of beefsteak and waited on by starvelings. His musicality lends him a grace that is transmitted to his minions.

*

I gaze into my aquarium as into a mirror that brings me remote times, perhaps times that never were:

> Whatever never happened anywhere,
> That alone is true.

Sometimes a moment of happiness disrupts history like a magic spell. Order subsists, with its distinctions—and yet these move in a different way, from the king to the kitchen boy to the convict who shows his chains. They dance instead of walking, they sing as at the opera instead of speaking, they exalt their pleasures in songs, they deepen their suffering in hymns.

This, I suspect, is Attila's standpoint; genius is transmuted into visible harmony. This is its identity, its immediate link with the masterpiece that is the world. Genius dwells not in some afterlife but in our midst; anything is possible, now and here.

*

A gloss on compulsory education: the anarch learns how to read and write if and when it pleases him. Many children are drawn to a book by innate curiosity. Charlemagne was still illiterate after many years of ruling his tremendous empire. Even when associating with scholars like Alcuin and Peter of Pisa, he had not gotten very far with writing; after all, he had more and better things to do.

It is unlikely that Homer knew how to write; the letter inhibits free singing. At any rate, caution is indicated when a boat leaves the sea and glides into the canals—the most dangerous thing of all is numbers. As a historian, I depend on the written word; as an anarch, I can do without it. Incidentally, people in the catacombs have supposedly devised methods for making script superfluous; the luminous pencil is a sample of this development—but that is a different story.

Compulsory schooling is essentially a means of curtailing natural strength and exploiting people. The same is true of military conscription, which developed within the same context. The anarch rejects both of them—just like obligatory vaccination and insurance of all kinds. He has reservations when swearing an oath. He is not a deserter, but a conscientious objector. I owe that expression to an old poet whom I summoned to the luminar: Gustav Sack.

The anarch can kill anyone, and this is the basis of his self-confidence, yet he kills only where and when he likes—in any case, far more seldom than the criminal, the chauffeur, or the state. The archaic figure of the mercenary is more consistent with the anarch than is the conscript, who reports for his physical examination and is told to cough when the doctor grabs his scrotum.

"Give me gold and I'll defend your cause, but I can give notice at any time." This may happen out of necessity, out of boredom, or because one likes a man and his cause. In any event, the anarch will reserve his decision when a demand is placed on him—even by his own family.

If a weapon is forced on him, he becomes not more reliable but even more dangerous. The collective can shoot in only one direction, the anarch all around.

*

Gold and soldiers who have sold themselves are made for one another. Eumenists like Kessmüller, narrow minds and nit-pickers, do not know the magic of language. In fact, it makes them uncomfortable.

Serpent—a hissssing of the passing second. In *gold*, the unslaked craving, in *sold*, the slaked craving emphasizes the shiny yellow vowel.

When I pay Latifah (whom I will get back to) for lying on the mattress, the fee is in gold. She would find paper as repulsive as the mercenary does. When life strips bare—in nakedness, in pillage, and in the ancient sacrifices—people pay with blood and with gold. The man knows that gold is his due, the woman knows even more so that it is her due; and this knowledge will outlive states, no matter how many of them fall or rise.

To wrest gold from the individual, to rob him of his claims—these are the strivings of the states; while he seeks to hide his gold from them. They "only want what's best for him"—that is why they take it away from him. They hoard his gold in deep vaults and pay with paper that loses more value every day.

The more domesticated human beings are, the more easily they fall for any swindle. But gold is credible. It contains its own value, hence it never inveigles. The fact that it is shown openly here is one of the merits of Eumeswil.

A Day in the Casbah

28

It is time I outlined my daily schedule to the extent that it is helpful to my narrative. I would do better to start with the night, for my day is merely its reflection. I infer this simply because I do not like to wake up; every morning, I have to don my armor anew.

The night is dark, the day is bright. According to Bruno, this light is only a siphoned, only a weakened, filtered darkness. There must be some truth to that. When I close my eyes, everything becomes not dark but bright, as if the stage lights began shining while the curtain rolled up. Gently sinking flowers appear, particolored wheels turning, countless faces striving for individuation, my own face among them. All that before I even fall asleep. Then I penetrate deeper.

*

The hooting of the owl with its tender wing is more familiar to me than the crowing of the cock. I prefer the strings to the woodwinds. Intermission: that is the darkness. The light feels like a vague scratching; it is malaise rather than pain. I am glad to sink back into darkness.

The dreamless sleep after midnight is the deepest; the mind then enters the land of dreams as its lord. Not only does it orchestrate the events, it also fabricates them at whim and will, drawing sets and characters and decors from its inexhaustible reserves.

This is a living possession. The mind is transformed into a torrent; it inundates its mise en scène. It can open its eyes anywhere—in people, things, animals, or plants; it gives breath to its creatures and makes them speak: it acts as their prompter. Yet it is astonished by anything they say, as if its words were intensified by those echoes. "In a dream we are gods," a Greek said, and he was right.

*

Toward morning, sleep becomes fitful, absurd strands weave into its texture. What could have moved me, when this day was dawning, to summon a soubrette to my mental stage, a mestiza who displayed herself, singing in a husky voice? She crooned a series of ditties that did not appeal to me although I must have composed both the tunes and the lyrics. She therefore apologized to me, saying she performed such items only for her *culture physique*. She was lying, of course; she merely wanted to flaunt her breasts and her behind. Which she did, flourishing her top hat with simian agility.

Such scenes flash by like lightning. I suspect they develop out of timelessness; we then interpret them more or less precisely. They recall the New Year's Eve fire-crackers that blow apart after we've ignited them with a female partner. Out pops a rather flimsy aphorism. The ancient, primitive interpreters of dreams were more reliable than the modern ones.

Life in the Casbah triggers infiltration by erotic dreams. This is understandable, but that is all. A painter would say: the motif does not make an artwork.

*

My work is irregular; a week can go by without the night bar being used. It remains open only as long as the Condor visits it. The Domo probably wants to prevent the formation of any small sedentary cliques.

The mocha has already been served in the mess hall; often the meal is followed only by a digestive. Then again, it can last until dawn. I enjoy such nights; they yield a great deal. Once I have closed the bar and sealed it, I go upstairs and, while sipping a glass of wine, I try to decipher my luminous script and think about the conversations.

When tending bar, I do not touch a drop, even if the Condor is in a good mood and asks me to have a drink. Nor do I drink water, even if I am thirsty. I "do not touch a glass" except to serve; there are a number of reasons for this—aside from my wishing to express myself accurately.

People are careless here; they say things like, "I'm sleeping with her," even when they have anything but sleep on their minds.

On this score, I concur with the Domo, who, as I have pointed out, likewise values precise speech. I see him nodding in approval when he notices that I stand my ground even with the Condor—yes, I *am* reliable. Nor do I mean this ironically.

*

Late to bed, and late to rise; the day belongs to me. The sun is already blazing upon the Casbah; the air is flickering above the euphorbia. The room gets torrid when the cooling system is turned off. I usually switch it back on when I wish to work. Incidentally, the technology is unreliable, even though a staff of electricians and other workers are on call. At times it seems to me as if the technology were both developed and neglected in a dreamlike manner. In any case, it is no longer taken so seriously; and even the Domo seems to prefer a *juste milieu* to technological perfection.

If he becomes grumpy, then it is caused by the failure of workers rather than of machines. The outlook recalls princes in the age of periwigs: they viewed the rifle chiefly as an instrument for drills.

*

After I have stood behind the bar all night, it may already be light out, often close to noon, by the time I awaken—but I am still lying in the dark, for I sleep behind a thick curtain in the alcove. I then spend another quarter hour in bed before getting up.

If I say, "in order to pray," it may sound strange. Of course, this word is quite worn, and it has been corrupted by the padres. *Religio*, as we know, harks back to a word (*re-ligo*) meaning "bond"; and that is precisely what the anarch rejects. He does not go in for Moses with the Ten Commandments or, indeed, for any prophets. Nor does he wish to hear anything concerning gods or rumors about them, except as a historian—or unless they appear to him. That is when the conflicts begin.

So if I state, "in order to pray," I am following an innate instinct that is no weaker than the sexual drive—in fact, even stronger. The two are alike insofar as foul things can happen when they are suppressed.

Regarding this need, the anarch is again no different from anyone else. But he does not like to attach himself. He does not squander his best energies. He accepts no substitute for his gold. He knows his freedom, and also what it is worth its weight in. The equation balances when he is offered something credible. The result is ONE.

There can be no doubt that gods have appeared, not only in ancient times but even late in history; they feasted with us and fought at our sides. But what good is the splendor of bygone banquets to a starving man? What good is the clinking of gold that a poor man hears through the wall of time? The gods must be called.

*

The anarch lets all this be; he can bide his time. He has his ethos, but not morals. He recognizes lawfulness, but not law; he despises rules. Whenever ethos goes into shalts and shalt-nots, it is already corrupted. Still, it *can* harmonize with them, depending on location and circumstances, briefly or at length, just as I harmonize here with the tyrant for as long as I like.

One error of the anarchists is their belief that human nature is intrinsically good. They thereby castrate society, just as the theologians ("God is goodness") castrate the Good Lord. This is a Saturnian trait.

Natural law has been twisted every which way—from legitimation to brutal violence to a paradisal idyll. This is grounded in the possibility of reading anything at all into nature. "It is everything at once." Well, fine; then let every human being get his own bit from Being.

The random and the arbitrary begin in the realm of molecules. There must be a crack in the universe from the very start. The very word "nature" contains a "nay." Genesis offers marvelous hints—but only rumors, as if a shepherd had been listening at an unclosed door.

Lawfulness must be sought in the atoms and even deeper, including our own atoms. From these depths, the ethical and aesthetic judgment reacts to the finest variations. That is why injustice usually appears as ugly. The dangers increase in the ascent, as on a tightrope without a safety net, or as on the Sirat, that sliver of a bridge across the chasm of hell. Never is the temptation to summon the gods more powerful and never is there greater merit in resisting it.

As a historian, and only as such, I am a positivist. Lawfulness is valid so long as it is observed and can be observed. A good conscience—though not, of course, in the form of moral arrogance—is one of the prerequisites. It is not only the fit who survive, but also the honest. The fact that these two survivals do not coincide in time goes back once more to Genesis, to the separation of the Tree of Life from the Tree of Knowledge.

*

Needless to say, when praying, the anarch neither requests nor thanks. Nor does he seek a magical force in prayer. How many ardent prayers have not been heard? As a historian, I linger in the cells of the condemned; as an anarch, I would like to offer them posthumous solace; and I know that the guilty need this even more than the innocent.

I was in the dungeon with Boethius and in the temple with Marie Antoinette when her hair turned white. I was there when the mob was howling outside and the father put on his prayer thongs. The child groped for his hand. But neither the father nor the child was heard.

*

Nevertheless, prayer comes from an innate drive. It is more important than food and drink, since it testifies to more than transient life. It takes us behind the bleak stage set with which knowledge disguises the universe. Water is seen differently in retorts than in the aqueducts leading to big cities, and differently again in the ocean—and as the water of life in prayer.

The padres set great store by addressing prayers to personal gods: "Genuine prayer exists only in religions in which there is a God as a person and a shape and endowed with a will."

That was stated by a famous Protestant. The anarch does not want to have anything to do with that conception. As for the One God: while he may be able to shape persons, he is not a person himself, and the *he* is already a patriarchal prejudice.

A neuter One is beyond our grasp, while man converses with the Many Gods on equal terms, whether as their inventor or as their discoverer. In any case, it is man who named the gods. This is not to be confused with a high-level soliloquy. Divinity must, without a doubt, be inside us and be recognized as being inside us; otherwise we would have no concept of gods.

"For a God reigns within us" (Hölderlin). "ONE is the start of everything" (Philolaus). "A God is the greatest among gods and among men, not comparable to mortals in shape or thought" (Xenophanes). "A whirlwind of multiple shapes detaches itself from the Totality" (Democritus).

And, over and over again, Heraclitus. We should not make a fuss about the numinous; it lights on everyone—every man has his Sinai and also his Golgotha.

29

The floor outside the alcove is inlaid with hexagonal tiles; they fit together as in a beehive. They are still cool, agreeable to the feet. Their pattern is evident to the rested eyes in a special way. Its impact would be even stronger if I had never heard of mathematics.

There is an adjoining bathroom. It has no windows and is illuminated by indirect lighting from the ceiling. I step in front of the mirror and gauge the degree of my presence by my reflected bust. Like everyone else in the Casbah, I am well tanned. The blue of the walls makes my body stand out in relief.

Thus, usually I see myself sharply outlined; there is no doubt: this is a mirror image. The day beckons with its tasks. Whatever turns up, I will easily handle it. I will find the proper detachment from things and people. I promptly notice this in the exercises. If I were to play pool, I would rack up many wins. This is the overall mood in the citadel—especially the Condor's when he dismounts after his early-morning ride.

Then again there are days when my reflection blurs as if the mirror were misted over, and yet the image keeps gaining more and more reality the longer I stare at it. My body loses reality to the same extent. Caution is then indicated for the day; one becomes accident-prone. On the other hand, motion in mental space becomes more fluid. Studies prosper both in the libraries and at the luminar.

I also notice that it is easier for me to be spoken to and to speak to others. The gates of friendship open. Eros rolls out a carpet before me. Even the Domo smiles if I make a mistake, which can happen in such a mood. The Condor's "Emanuelo" then sounds especially pleasant. I have to make sure not to overcommit myself.

*

Consulting the mirror is worthwhile, though perilous; it is also a charge, a passage from existence to Being. Such issues could, among other things, strengthen the female element, the influence of moon and sea, of dream and night—of the other side, pure and simple. The words of an ancient sage are valid here: "By day, everyone sees the same thing; in a dream, everyone sees something particular."

This could estrange us from the calculable world, from language, which we cannot forgo. We would lose our sense of discrimination. For me, say, this would mean a farewell to the science of history, which my family has cultivated for generations.

Eumeswil's sanitariums and *maniconia* are crowded with patients who have gotten in over their heads. They did not even have to experiment with drugs. This occasionally happens to one of my students; the populace then says, "He studied too much." There is some truth in it: too much light is blinding; it provokes the darkness. I like visiting these inmates; one hears words as in the ancient oracles or Scardanelli—a murmuring of earth-spirit strength.

In the teeth of all dangers, it is valuable—I would even say invaluable—not only to believe in but also to experience the possibility of being both here and elsewhere at once. I resisted this all the more stoutly the further I shifted toward materialism. It was, above all, Bruno who helped me overcome this phase—particularly with his course on optical and electromagnetic phenomena. The details would take me too far afield. I will content myself with his maxim: "Primal image is image *and* mirror image." His actual strategem was to reduce the platonic idea to phenomenon, thereby reanimating matter, which had been emasculated by abstract thinking. A miracle, he said, could not be expected from above or from the future—say, from a world spirit ascending from level to level; despite its variable elements, he said, a miracle always remains the same, in every blade of grass, in every pebble.

*

The mother hears the shouting of her son, who is drowning in the Pacific, at the antipodes. This is no mere invocation. How many people have heard similar things. For all the vexations caused by religions, one must credit them with not only cultivating this knowledge but also acting upon it. Passages can be practiced. True, there is no monopoly here, since anyone can manage to do this, and innately at that; however, there are differences in know-how. This can be observed in dying people.

*

The bath. The pipes bring cold water and hot, fresh and salt. The fresh water comes partly from the Sus and partly from the rain that gathers in the large cistern hewn into the rock. This cistern lies above the vault, which it could flood within seconds.

There is also an emergency device for desalinating the ocean water. It would enable us to hold the Casbah for as long as Eumenes held his cliff castle Nora, which, according to one historian, "starvation alone could force him to surrender."

While I was shaving, the tub filled up. I prefer seawater. Pumped from a great depth, it is significantly cooler than at the beach. The Domo has its chemical and biological quality tested; it is intact. Since all rivers flow into the sea, its water must have more curative power than any wellspring. In addition, there are the tiny organisms on which others feed, all the way up to the whales, and which shine in the breakers with phosphorescent power. No physician knows what they also mean to us—in any case, I break my fast with a hearty swig of seawater and I gargle. Nothing, in fact, is better for the teeth; I once heard that from the fishermen and simple people who dwell by the shore. Their lifestyle is the old thrifty one that is pleasing to the anarch. They also harvest their salt from the ocean by scraping it from the cracks and hollows in the rocks where it crystallizes. This was prohibited under the tribunes; they regulated everything down to the last detail. Salt, at the hundredfold price, had to be bought in their government stores. They also mixed in additives that their chemists praised as useful, even though they were injurious. The fact that men with such minds consider themselves thinkers is forgivable; but they also claim to be benefactors.

The beach was patrolled by customs officials, who ambushed the poor. This measure was particularly odious, for gold and salt ought to be every man's untaxed due as the pure equivalent of his labor, just as he pans gold from the riverbeds or scrapes salt from the cliff. The Condor made both legal, and this was one of the first measures that established his popularity.

A little generosity is worth more than a lot of administration. The tribunes were redistributors; they raised the prices of bread for the poor in order to make them happy with their ideas—say, by building extravagant universities whose jobless graduates became a burden to the state (hence once again to the poor) and never touched another hammer.

The pauper, so long as he does not think parasitically, wishes to see as little government as possible, no matter what pretexts the state may use. He does not want to be schooled, vaccinated, or conscripted; all these things have senselessly increased the numbers of the poor, and with them, poverty.

*

Next come the hot and then the ice-cold shower, both with fresh water; finally, my exercises. If I am scheduled to tend bar, I normally shave once more in the evening—indeed, take care of my overall exterior. Before going down, I stand before the mirror and view Emanuelo: clothing, physical appearance, smile, and movements must be casual and pleasant. It is important—we can learn this from women—to look the way others picture us in their wishes.

Exercises. The Condor goes horseback riding before breakfast; he is accompanied by a few of his courtiers and the minions. This keeps them in shape. Aside from my preferring to spend mornings alone, my subaltern position excludes my joining them.

Besides, I find it better to gaze at a painting or listen to music. As for the interior personnel, many people exercise, and for various reasons: a few to lose weight, some to strengthen their muscles. Then again, others, like Kung, the Chinese, despise both goals: "Why sports? I'd like to grow old. Besides, I'm best in bed if I move very little and eat a lot." He has his personal recipes for that—and not much else in mind.

I have to keep myself intact so that I can take my forest flight at any time. In this regard, I focus more on my joints than on my musculature. I do circles with my body from neck to toe, skip rope, and juggle balls; I practice "conscious" inhaling and exhaling. You have to sink the conscious mind down into the diaphragm and suppress any thoughts, which cluster in ravenous throngs. This is difficult—if it succeeds, it also aids normal breathing; it spiritualizes it. It might be better to say it exposes its spiritual strength. That this spiritual strength exists and establishes all Existence was taken for granted in good times and was linguistically attested to by special words like *pneuma*. Russian pilgrims followed its trail with "perpetual prayer." Prayer becomes breath, and breath prayer.

Your breathing is more successful if the mirror is deep, just as, more generally, your vegetative, instinctual disposition increases. To be sure, this disposition must not gain the upper hand in everyday life. In the depth, the animal spark must keep glowing, as on the fuse leading to the powder keg. One can learn that from the samurai: the leap from a motionless state, the deadly thrust with the sword flying from the sheath.

*

Prior to summoning the cabin steward, I put on my robe and my slippers in order to make myself what people call "decent." My babouches are leather; beneath my robe I wear a linen suit such as is worn in the tropics. Dressed like this, I can show myself in the corridor.

The day's menu is rich, as on good passenger ships. I have already mentioned that there are two cuisines: a European one with a Mediterranean accent and a Chinese one that seldom appears on a normal day. It is meant as conspicuous consumption for banquets and important visits; in this respect, the Condor is a match for the khans.

Breakfast is my chief meal. It is my only meal if I tend bar. Otherwise I also eat dinner, sometimes with one of my staff colleagues. Occasionally, I drop in at the great mess hall, but I generally avoid flaunting my academic position; my restraint pays off. If I have a lot to do, I report to the head steward or the purser; they then usually say: "That's all right, Manuelo, you can stick to your studying." I am regarded as a hard worker. This is difficult to conceal, even though people luckily have only vague notions about the nature and direction of my activities.

*

My selection from the menu is modest; I am lavish only with fruit. The Condor's table is supplied with fruit from three continents. I prefer the varieties that are grown here and now—that is, the local ones in season.

Walking through the weekly market, which lies right on the edge of the city, is a festival. The piles of incredibly fresh fruit stand out against the hot, russet earth, which recalls Attic soil. The vendors brought this produce here at the crack of dawn from the oases and the lowlands by the Sus. Then there are the pushy voices of the hawkers, the chimes of the water carriers, the flutes of the snake charmers—why, even the flies swarming around the butchers' stalls: the market creates a greater exaltation, a whirlwind of freedom and pleasure. It is the real center of society—the goal of the state is to strip it of its freedom and superfluousness. One need merely visit the marketplace and the graveyard to determine whether a city is in both physical and metaphysical order.

*

In my office, baskets of fruit stand next to the luminar. I have the stewards fill them up. Perhaps someday I will live entirely on fruit—not as a vegetarian, but as a frugal eater. Attila ate little else when he went astray in the great forests. He did, however, have the Golden Lamb, and not just to satisfy his hunger.

Fresh fruits bestow solar cheer; no fire but that of the sun has touched them. They also quench the thirst with their juices, in which water has been filtered and enriched while losing nothing of the spirit of the soil and its own specific nature. This is borne out by the variety of grapes and their wines.

The dry fruits, by contrast—figs, almonds, nuts—give the muscles unbelievable strength. I noticed this during the gazelle hunt, when provisions consisted solely of carob and dry dates. Despite the blazing heat, the hunters remained tireless and barely seemed to sweat; it was as if their muscle fibers had solidified into wires.

In a situation like mine, which can lead to a forest flight at any moment, vegetables, needless to say, are not enough. I would lose my aggressiveness. All animals that kill need flesh, and even the warrior caste of India ate meat.

These are issues not so much of diet as of overall adjustment. Carnivores have canines and incisors; they use a knife for cutting—that, incidentally, is one reason why bread should be broken and not sliced.

The carnivorous man recognizes the existence of the world of slaughterhouses, warfare, bloodshed. If he denies them, then he is sitting on the wrong horse. He must give up either his beefsteak or his thinking. On the other hand, the world lives on erroneous ideas. Here in Eumeswil, one sees tremendously potbellied sheiks who would not hurt a fly. Yet someone somewhere is slaughtering and thinking for them, too.

This was simpler for the ancients. The gods divided the ethical cosmos among themselves. Ares was given bloody offerings. This was also expressed when warriors sat down for a meal. Other foods were sacred to Demeter and still others to Aphrodite, especially if they came from the ocean. This is how people still dine in Eumeswil, although the gods no longer participate.

30

In the Casbah, I have close personal contact only with the chamber stewards, who bring in breakfast and serve in other ways as well. Some are only temporary, most permanent; their official title is "cabin steward."

Aside from my general typological interest, I normally feel them out if only because I will have to share the command post with them. Kung, the Chinese, is concerned chiefly with his comfort; Nebek, the Lebanese, is a stalwart warrior, but unpredictable. Someday, perhaps, I may have to aim, over open sights, at either man or both. But I am in no hurry to do so.

For about a year, I was served by Knut Dalin, a Norwegian. We were on and off duty at the same time because our work schedules were both tailored to the school semesters—he was studying chemistry. After sounding him out for a long time, I was surprised that he could have slipped through the nets of the psychologists since he embodied the classic type of the unsafe personality.

It is, of course, possible that a man's character reaches a critical point, at which a "tilt effect" occurs. One fine day, after thirty years of loyal service, a cashier runs off with the cashbox; an irreproachable burgher kills his entire family. This eruption can occur suddenly, or only after lonesome brooding has undermined the moral foundation drop by drop. It has secretly hatched the misdeed.

So, fine, or not fine—but one could assume that the psychologists, if one cares to take them at all seriously, could detect and warn against such a predisposition. In Dalin's case, his physical state had clouded their judgment. The Casbah greatly esteems a good appearance. On the other hand, as I know from my own experience, the testers are able to create situations in which the face is removed like a mask.

Dalin looked wonderful; his picture could have graced the covers of magazines like *Ladies' Life* or *The Bachelor* as a model of what thrives under the midnight sun. He also had a bohemian streak. Dalin would have cut a finer figure among the illustrious guests at the night bar than as a member of the staff. But he preferred the latter. In this regard, he personified a favorite motif of novelists: the corrupt aristocrat. If such a man cannot assert his role as lord among his peers, then he feels he can do a better job of it several degrees lower. He enjoys getting mixed up in dubious matters or visiting the tropics. The master among coloreds. His face appears in his mestizo sons.

Peeling Dalin's strata away down to the core was not easy; they contradicted one another. To judge by his eyes, he seemed capable of anything. This was not the blue of the Adriatic, nor that of the Aegean, which can turn violet; it was the pale steel blue of the fjords, such as one sees on calm days.

His left eye seemed smaller than the right because of its slightly drooping lid. This minor irregularity could scarcely be called a defect; it grew more blatant whenever Dalin pulled off stunts that he considered daring.

Sometimes I felt he was trying to test me to see how far I could be provoked. It first struck me when he was recounting one of his nocturnal adventures. After sleeping with a woman in a hotel, he had gone downstairs in the morning and settled the bill with the desk clerk:

"If you want to go up—she's still lying there—that'll save me the tip."

And he winked at me. His caper struck me as even harsher in that the woman was no one-night stand. I soon realized that such behavior was intrinsic in him. He strove to do harm at any price, as if a demon were whispering to him.

My failing to bat an eyelash (which would have been a mistake) increased his confidence. He gradually opened up. Bruno had already told me that Dalin played with drugs and explosives. But he had turned his back on him with their very first conversation. "One of these days, he's going to blow himself up." This was a good forecast; it came true in an unusual and unpredictable way. Such are the genuine prophecies.

Whenever he carried in my breakfast, I would get into a shorter or longer conversation with him, as with the other cabin stewards. He had sound attitudes. I am referring not to his morals, but to his trenchant way of formulating his views. Like many young men with time on their hands, he occupied his mind with the "perfect crime"—about which he also had a theory.

"Every crime, with almost no exception, has a weak spot, a flaw in the weave. I mean the interest, the focus of the '*cui bono?*' as the basic question of criminology. When the rich aunt dies, her nephew is closely scrutinized; the circumstances do not even have to be suspicious. If a hiker is killed and robbed in the woods, they look for the mugger; presumably he's already in the police register."

"Fine—but what's your point?"

At the Casbah, we used the familiar form with each other, which was normal between staff members, but not if I bumped into him at the university.

"My point is that interest and perfection are mutually exclusive. The more suspicious I look a priori, the more meticulously I have to work out the plan, especially the alibi. This creates a huge amount of evidence before I even get started. If you go through a bunch of suspects with a fine-tooth comb, you have to focus on the one who knows exactly where he was at the time in question. And you have to delve into it all the more painstakingly, the more time has worn by."

Dalin must have pored over the matter thoroughly—all too thoroughly, I felt. Another time, he began talking about arson. If you've lit a fire, it's especially important not to have been at the scene of the crime. Arsonists therefore have to make ingenious preparations. Burning glasses, timing mechanisms, and similar devices are then found among the ashes.

"If a man is in a bad mood and he sets fire to a barn that he happens to be passing, he is seldom found out. Just like someone who walks into the forest and kills the very first person he runs into, but without robbing him."

I said, "He'd have to be crazy."

Dalin did not care to go into this: "A lunatic would already be on file or about to be. Crazies don't count. There must be nothing special about the crime, nothing specific."

*

So, art for art's sake—the joy of not only composing a criminal act but also perpetrating it? Everyone asks, but only Rumpelstiltskin knows who it was. And then there's the thrill of danger.

By an odd coincidence, I had been studying pre-revolutionary writers for some time—Encyclopedists, playwrights, novelists. In this context, I had obtained details from the eighteenth, nineteenth, and twentieth Christian centuries—encounters between literature and politics, which now interest only historians.

If a society is encrusted and a new consciousness is trying to break out, it recognizes itself in artworks; this explains their violent impact, which frightens not only the rulers, but often the artists themselves. A "new man"—basically, of course, always the same old one—is presented in his active and passive form. A vast gamut: the individual recognizes himself, from *The Sorrows of Young Werther* to Schiller's *The Brigands*, from *The Marriage of Figaro* to *The 120 Days of Sodom*.

The topic emerged from my studies of anarchy—or, in more banal terms, from the question of why the individual is always taken in. It also contained dissertation subjects for Vigo's institute. Few of them, incidentally, pleased the master, who was more enthralled with a Sybaris of the sixth pre-Christian century or a Venice circa 1725.

*

But I do not wish to digress; I was talking about Dalin. When he said there must be "nothing specific" in the crime, I recalled one of the dissertations at the institute; its title was *Raskolnikov—The Werther of the Twentieth Christian Century?* It was still being written—by an unusually gifted Eumenist.

Raskolnikov, a character in a novel by a Russian author named Dostoyevsky, who lived during the czarist period, plots a murder on a purely experimental basis. His problem is power; a man who proves he can shed blood has thereby ordained himself in the first holy orders. An old usurer becomes his victim, as random as any pedestrian who is run over in the street. He robs her of some jewelry—but even that is merely symbolic: he buries the loot under a rock and pays it no further mind.

Thus, I thought of this Raskolnikov and mentioned him during that breakfast conversation. To my surprise and also malaise, Dalin had read the novel. He could have gotten it only from the Eumenist who was working on the dissertation; it did not sound like an accident.

Dalin rejected the Russian as a superman gone awry. "Why does he kill that usurer, of all people? Because he considers her useless, as superfluous as a louse. But that is highly specific, an ethical corset. That alone nipped the matter in the bud. Manuel, you did not understand what I told you."

*

Initially, I had regarded him as a vandal such as is concealed in every man. In the young, the vandal comes out when they are in high spirits, especially after drinking; this manifestation can range from a beery prank to mayhem and assault.

But Dalin's system was too intricate for such juvenilia. So then was he a socialist revolutionary, the sort that keep popping up and that were called "nihilists" during that final stage of czarism? A misnomer, incidentally—although they did wreak destruction preferably with dynamite, which had just been invented. They operated somewhat like big-game hunters; just as hunters go after "royal" heads, they went after crowned heads. They were liquidated either by the system they fought or by the one that followed. The true nihilist will not lift a finger to change, much less improve, the world; he is related more closely to the philosophers than to the politicians.

Dalin loathed and, no doubt, disdained society—not just a given one, but any society, as a matter of principle. His appearance was very casual, but not unpleasant, since he set great store by his exterior. He read a lot; I would also see him in Vigo's history library. I noted, as a minor yet characteristic trait, the way he clutched the book so hard with both hands that he damaged the binding. There was nothing he respected.

I had already heard from Bruno that Dalin's experiments were suspect. I once asked Dalin whether he observed the necessary caution; he said, "I work in one of the abandoned bunkers on the Sus," which, of course, I did not like to hear.

The direction of his experiments fitted in with his leanings. His ruling principle seemed to be a *perpetuum mobile* of destruction. His train of thought, if I understood him correctly, was roughly as follows. Destruction must live on itself—gaining ground. This should be attained with the least possible exertion. If, for instance, someone wanted to destroy a forest by chopping down trees, he would have to hire an army of lumberjacks. Yet all it takes is a feather shaft.

"How's that?"

"I fill it with the eggs of a wood-eating moth from Australia and introduce it in the forest. Reproduction does the rest."

Such things are possible; a child can set a whole city ablaze with a match. Dalin's doctoral thesis dealt with problems of antimatter. His insights into the molecular world, said Bruno, could not be disputed. This, he went on, required a special ability to see in three dimensions. But there were few if any practical results. He experimented with mordants, caustics, and corrosives, hoping to achieve highly dangerous potencies that would continue the destruction automatically.

*

One morning, after listening to him enthuse about those experiments, I said, "You could do something beneficial by spraying your essences over large dump sites and polluted beaches. Perhaps you could tackle it biologically—grow bacteria that digest oil and rubber."

I said that to annoy him; it was the exact opposite of what he had in mind. His heart, his thoughts must have been stirred by something manifested in corrosion, in gradual decomposition. It did not appear to suffice for a Luciferian spirit, since, oddly enough, his plans excluded fire.

For a while, he experimented with substances that could produce cancerlike alterations in cellulose. They could be used for infecting books and starting tumors that could devour whole libraries. He did not seem to be making much headway; nevertheless, once or twice,

Eumeswil postmen discovered that the contents of mailboxes had turned into a kind of gelatin—now just who could have done that?

Dalin yearned for greater disruptions. Yet he never so much as dreamt of joining a party, say, as a partisan; instead, he hoped for more freedom for his own mischief.

"If *I* rub someone out, I'll do it only from the back; I've already picked out a couple of bastards."

"But if I understand you correctly, you intend to hurt *everyone*, don't you?"

"Of course—I wouldn't think twice about it."

"Then you could just as easily knock off someone on the other side—the effect would be the same."

"No, Manuel, there's a fundamental difference."

*

Mulling it over that evening, I had to agree with him. Dalin embodied the anarchic nihilist, a type that is not all that rare. What was special about him was that he not only reacted with a general malaise, he also thought about it. Of course it made a difference whether he shot someone from the front or from the back—a difference not in the effect, but in the self-affirmation.

I have noticed that a cat will turn up her nose at a piece of meat if I hand it to her, but she will devour it with gusto if she has "stolen" it. The meat is the same, but the difference lies in the predator's delight in recognizing itself.

The anarchic nihilist is not to be confused with the socialist revolutionary. His aversion is not toward one person or another but toward order per se. Asocial and apolitical, he represents the destructive workings of nature. He would like to accelerate them. Compared with even the modest methods of our tyranny, Dalin seems like a kind of Don Quixote tilting at windmills. What was accomplished when a train derailed, a bridge exploded, a department store burned to the ground? True, one has to see this in different terms—say, as a paltry sacrifice to the delight of the powerful Shiva. A chemist seldom knows precisely what he is doing.

*

While I did owe Dalin a number of insights, I nevertheless had to keep him at arm's length, if only for my personal safety. I would therefore divert the conversation about theory whenever he hinted at turning it into practice.

But how did he come to be so openhearted in my presence? He must have whiffed the anarch in me, a man with no ties to state or society. Still, he was unable to sense an autonomy that puts up with these forces as objective facts but without recognizing them. What he lacked was a grounding in history.

Opposition is collaboration; this was something from which Dalin, without realizing it, could not stay free. Basically, he damaged order less than he confirmed it. The emergence of the anarchic nihilist is like a goad that convinces society of its unity.

The anarch, in contrast, not only recognizes society a priori as imperfect, he actually acknowledges it with that limitation. He is more or less repulsed by state and society, yet there are times and places in which the invisible harmony shimmers through the visible harmony. This is obvious chiefly in the work of art. In that case, one serves joyfully.

But the anarchic nihilist thinks the exact opposite. The Temple of Artemis, to cite an example, would inspire him to commit arson. The anarch, however, would have no qualms about entering the temple in order to meditate and to participate with an offering. This is possible in any temple worthy of the name.

*

I believe I have already mentioned that Dalin was originally detailed for my battle station at the duck shack. This put me in a quandary, for he could be expected to cause me headaches. Yet it was equally certain that he would not do so for long; he would have to be stopped, if only for my own safety.

At that point, either the Chinese or the Lebanese was slated to be the third man—whoever happened to be on duty when the alarm was sounded. The Lebanese was aggressive; at my faintest nod, Dalin would be taken care of. On the other hand, I could not bank on the phlegmatic Chinese; I would have to take care of it myself. This would be safer and also consistent with my own responsibility. The latter is the anarch's ultimate authority.

31

I am reminded of an anecdote that, while only remotely connected, gave me pause to think when I heard it, or rather overheard it, from Attila. After all, for my own edification, I unobtrusively tap the stream of conversation, drawing things off into my own conduit.

It was already early morning, a time when the night bar is most revealing. The men—I no longer know why—were discussing abortion. In Eumeswil, abortion is one of the actions that are punishable but not prosecuted. They include, among other things, gambling, smoking opium, and—strangely enough from the Casbah's viewpoint—pederasty. Nearly everyone gets involved in an abortion, everyone knows about it, people even boast about it. But the authorities look the other way. I, too, would have fallen victim to my dear old dad and been flushed down the toilet if my mother had not insisted on having me.

*

"Everyone knows": this is especially true of the Domo and the police. Bizarre hieroglyphs are pierced into their files; they lead to a *chronique scandaleuse* that is carefully preserved in voluminous dossiers. The Domo observes the principle that not every crime has to be prosecuted. But if it *is*, then not only must it satisfy the terms of a statute, it should also throw off something for the journalists. Only then does it also gain political clout. That is why he sets great store by piquant details. This attitude will be perceived in any absolute regime; one of the first reports of the day is delivered by the chief of police, who always has immediate access. That was the Sun King's practice with d'Argenson.

Thus, an action that is actionable in itself is graciously overlooked. This changes, however, if someone has incurred displeasure. He is "prosecuted to the full extent of the law."

Greasing palms is customary; it even facilitates trade and traffic, as their names indicate. Yet bribery is illegal; if it is shouted from the rooftops, one can also reckon with envy. But if, say, the Domo wishes to trip up *The Wren*, he will not indict Zerrwick for seeking to denigrate the Condor as a scavenger. Instead, Zerrwick will be tried for bribery or extortion. All these editors use informers to penetrate the inner sanctums of the rich and powerful; this pays off in the form of sensations or private transactions. The victim either coughs up or exposes himself to moral indignation.

*

The same is true of abortion. It is tolerated here, if only to keep the economy stable. The cake is always sliced up into the same number of pieces, even if some are smaller and some bigger. Poverty does not come out of the blue; it is bred. "There were periods when abortion was even rewarded." This was an aside from the Domo during the debate that I jotted down.

Proletarii were the citizens who served the state not with money but with children. Ever since progressive ideas and nationalist ethos lost their vigor, at least in Eumeswil, two children are enough for rich or poor. My dear old dad would have contented himself with one.

*

As I see, I have inserted a digression into my digression. At times, the quill simply runs away with itself. This can do no harm, inasmuch as I have taken on the secondary task of describing the order or, if you like, disorder of Eumeswil. Nevertheless such meanderings should not degenerate into a game of Chinese boxes.

Thus, my outline of my daily schedule has gotten as far as breakfast and the cabin stewards who serve it: first of all, Dalin, who might someday get so dangerous that—to put it in the Casbah's straightforward lingo, which is popular even with him—he would have to be knocked off. I have also noted that—to use still another of these quaint phrases—one had best "take care of it personally." This was meant to illustrate an anecdote I had heard from Attila in the night bar when they were discussing abortion.

I am trying to piece together the biography of this physician from the various sections of his life, and to do so I must rely on whatever I pick up in conversation. It appears that his life has often verged on the fantastic, or even gone over the brink.

*

The historian is therefore confronted with a peculiar problem. I will call it the *inclusum* and sketch it briefly.

History is not simply what has happened; it is the arrangement of those events. This arranging is done first by the chronicler, then by the historian. Needless to say, not only does a selection take place, but the style of the period also plays its part. Some facts are overexposed, others not even glimpsed. They vanish forever, or are fished out one day by a resourceful mind: for instance, the lead content in Roman plumbing and its influence on the mortality rate.

Recently, I stumbled on a history of Norway from the final days of the second Christian millennium. A major demagogue had invaded this country and oppressed it. This period filled three quarters of the text; the previous two thousand years, including the Viking era, were compressed into the first quarter of the book.

Fine, those are foreshortenings, which are corrected within a few generations. But *inclusum* means something else—that which is "altogether different." There are phases within the course of events that the historian can barely cope with, if at all. He contents himself with shrugging them off as "dark," like, say, the witch hunts of the sixteenth Christian century; but what lies hidden in the darkness?

*

People certainly have explanations. But they barely go beyond causes and mechanisms. These persecutions were, no doubt, occasioned by *The Witches' Hammer* and the infamous bull issued by Pope Innocent VIII, the very model of a persecutor. There is no denying that the madness of the inquisitors infected the defendants bit by bit. This is corroborated by the judicial records.

Nevertheless the overall complex rises like a bubble from the murky bottom to the surface—a mirror of history. People have always believed in witches and will always believe in them; their faith corresponds to a concrete type that changes with time. Just recently, an old crone was apprehended here; she had taken straw contaminated with a virus and thrown it into a neighbor's stable.

A demonological literature à la *The Witches' Hammer* still exists, but underground. Whenever it has an effect, whenever it turns virulent, one can assume other causes—above all, a cosmic angst in search of objects.

The *inclusum* can expand. Hence the savage's terror during a solar eclipse. He is afraid that the huge star will be swallowed up.

Most people regard the night as an *inclusum* of the day; very few, like Fechner and Novalis, believe the opposite.

> Must the morning always return?
> Will the sway of the earthly never end?
> ......
> Time was meted out
> To the light
> And to waking—
> But timeless is the reign of night.

*

An *inclusum* can be brief, even flash by like lightning, and yet transform the person and thereby the world. One example was provided by Saint Paul on the road to Damascus. His experience should not be confused with the return of mythical figures to history; rather, it opens up a new kind of phenomena.

Incidentally, there can be no doubt about the Resurrection; the emptiness of the tomb undermines certainty rather than strengthening it. According to Celsus, some gardeners did not want their cabbages trampled by the mourners and so they removed the corpse at night. An argument for the simple-minded. A phenomenon in this sense, a resurrection, presumes the existence of a corpse in the first place. The primal image is image *and* mirror image.

*

According to Saint John Chrysostom, the Resurrection is denied only by the vicious; according to Saint Gregory of Nyssa, it takes us back to divine nature. He pictures it more or less like a savage slipping out of the fur, from which his body is liberated in its full perfection. Since the body retains its form, the organs must have a different purpose than physical necessity. The painter sees this more clearly than the anatomist.

If Saint John Chrysostom was right, then vice must have become quite popular in Eumeswil. Nevertheless, every individual is haunted, indeed tormented, by "this topic." In my exercises, I, too, am confronted with problems that I can scarcely resolve, but that have an effect precisely by surfacing.

It is, I feel, well attested that image and reflection, body and astral body, can be simultaneous. A reflection and a corpse can also appear simultaneously, but, no doubt, only for a short time. The dying or even dead man sees himself at his bed while his near and dear are already lamenting his demise and the physicians are still bustling around him. It may be possible to summon him back to his body; that would be roughly the opposite of resurrection, and all the people to whom it has happened claim they regretted it.

In the moment of death, many people reach beyond their earthly being and bear tidings about this; there are a thousand testimonies. In the glowing of sunset, a now invisible star reaches into the visible as if with arms.

*

Insertions, it seems, were laid bare at the start of the third Christian millennium. People must have grown ever wearier with the ciphering of the world. On the other hand, a desire for spiritualization was palpable; but it could make no headway against bulldozing ideas. These failures suffice for the formations of sects, for works by artists who starve to death or take their own lives, for technological and political mistakes in the style of Brobdingnag.

The historian has a hard time defining the contours of this Tower of Babel with its cracks, breaches, and oubliettes; even contemporaries had not known what was happening. But these insertions proliferated, and we wonder: Are they rumors, dreams, or facts buried by catastrophes?

This is the spirit of Atlantis. Here in Eumeswil, the optics have been simplified, inasmuch as the dreamlike elements have increased and are weakening reality. As a historian, I cannot take them seriously—though I can as an interpreter of dreams. Through them, I gaze down at history with its cathedrals and palaces as if at a sunken Julin, which was swallowed up by the ocean. I hear the tolling of bells from the deep; this is a painful pleasure. I am shaken not by the roar of battles now but by the brief, dreadful hush when armies stand face to face. The sun glitters on their armor.

*

Equalization and the cult of collective ideas do not exclude the power of the individual. Quite the opposite: he concentrates the wishful thinking of millions like the focal point of a concave mirror. He becomes their mime, their tragedian; his theater is the world. He can draft titanic plans, be it for the common good or for his own delight. They come pouring in—to haul, fight, and die for him. Nero, in order to construct his Golden House, tears down a portion of Rome and pierces through the Isthmus of Corinth—two works he never completed.

*

In the phase I have mentioned, such plans, including misdeeds, were raised to a higher power by automation. They were joined by plutonian might. The accounts multiply here, and in checking them, I waver between what happened and what was dreamed or concocted. It also appears that immense hypnotic forces were released. This is useful for insertions.

Back then, as in the days of witch trials, terror must have been widespread, along with the concomitant persecutions. The tableau includes a subterranean system: drillings, excavations, catacombs—all sorts of plutonian activities. The preliminary labors for the luminar also began—the Alexandrian gathering and stockpiling of data, plus the appropriate technology.

Nero said, "My predecessors did not know what risks can be taken." This is a mood that recurs when the radiant circle around power becomes rigid. Wishes must come true at once; the world becomes a puppet show. The masters frown at the slightest delay. One of these modern rulers wanted to have a meditation chamber for hatching his plans in solitude; he had his men hollow out an Alpine peak and carve an elevator inside the massif. This reminded me of the invincible stronghold of old Eumenes. Moreover, the private individual has similar cravings, only he cannot fulfill them. That is why he projects them, half with pleasure, half with fear, onto the powerful.

Another ruler—or was it the same one?—transformed an entire mountain chain into a fortress containing huge stores of provisions and tremendous arsenals. It was meant to ward off an encirclement or an assault by superior forces. He also brought in treasures and artworks and constructed lupanars, baths, and theaters. In this way, they could hold out for fifteen years, in a kind of deliciously extended twilight.

The pyre in Nineveh, where Sardanapalus had himself burned alive with his treasures and his wives, blazed for only fifteen days.

*

After the first lunar landing, there were few if any problems that could not be solved by technology, so long as money was no object. Those space flights had left behind a disenchantment that, in turn, gave latitude to romantic fancies. They were reinforced by the potency of dynamics.

Reports on a strange island in the North Sea were equated by many with the periodic tales of sea serpents. Navigators whose ships had struggled through the ice floes of the Arctic night claimed they had been terrified by the miragelike vision of a radiantly illuminated palace. Some maintained they had sighted a huge tower on a cliff that was inaccessible on all sides; others said that the rows of windows had been broken into the rock and that light was streaming from its interior. The rock must have been hewn like a beehive.

I delved into these accounts. Vigo's institute has collected a huge number of relevant items—especially clippings and articles from occult periodicals. In addition, I have consulted the luminar. It was also alleged that astronauts from other planets were landing on ours. Many people had seen them.

*

Every rumor has a more or less concrete nugget. What got me thinking was that no pilots flew over that area; they avoided it because airplanes kept vanishing there and were never heard from again.

I am willing to admit that as an anarch I was lured by the image of this castle, shining in the polar night like the residence of the Flying Dutchman. If a Croesus, or better yet a Crassus, of that era, a man bursting with political power, had created his *buen retiro* here, then he certainly had a flair for ultimate contrasts.

The landscape was filled with howling storms that until recently would have been lethal to anyone venturing to explore the storm center. The ocean was covered with floes that the surf shattered on the basalt. No *wasteland* could be more inhospitable. Inside, the opposite:

the light, the warmth of baths and winter gardens, the orchestral music in festive halls. And overall, the tremendous, almost godlike arrogance: Anything goes here.

We also hear about moonlit nights with curtains of aurora borealis. Outdoors, blue icebergs silently drift by. The storms fall still; an equilibrium, as if immense forces were hovering there, creates expectation, but without dread.

32

How did I come to surmise that Attila might have occupied a position there similar to the one he has here with the Condor? I could only speculate. His travels had certainly led him to the farthest north. He loves islands, deserts, jungles. Like Ahasuerus, he dwelt in cities that have burned to the ground and whose names are snuffed out. He knows the frontiers where illusion and reality abolish each other.

When his tongue loosens in the morning hours, I stand behind the bar as a hunter: the harder I focus, the more I expect the appearance of animals whose names are not in the books.

He knows the island, I am fairly certain; he once mentioned the entrance, which resembles Fingal's Cave. Yet not a word about the celebrations on the brink of nothingness, when the basalt was crowned with Saint Elmo's fire. Though Attila has probably seen a great deal, including somber things, he retrospectively prefers the splendor of silence, the moonlit clearings.

*

That island—whether the same or a comparable one—lay far beyond the Arctic Circle; the sun would revolve around the horizon for weeks and weeks without grazing it. The summer transformed the island from a place of terrors into a mythical world. It was icebound and therefore shielded. Legions of birds and sea animals had flown over or swum under this barrier, frolicking on, above, or below the surface of this icy-clear ocean.

I enjoyed hearing Attila talk about his fishing expeditions. He knew less and more about animals than Rosner did—less about measurable data, more about their virtues, their divine power. The Condor found this reassuring.

If and how far a mind penetrates matter, and whether it grasps the crown of the root from which the details branch off—these things are perceived even in practice. "He's no general, he's a special," I once heard the Domo comment when rejecting an application. The born commander requires neither an office nor a diploma; he is recognized by his gaze and his voice. And the man predestined to create is recognized by the dreamlike mood he emanates. That is the effect of artworks, their immeasurable, incomprehensible enchantment, and also their power to console.

While listening, I was reminded of my profession; the historian must keep both feet on the ground—the ground of time in history, the ground of space in geography. But the earth is beautiful. Occasionally it seemed as if Attila, by blending color into his words, were discussing a period of painting: from Early to Late Romanticism, from Impressionism to Magical Realism and beyond.

*

I could see him nosing out of the basalt. He was sitting in a kayak, and behind him an Inuit with yellow skin and red hair was clutching a paddle in both hands. On the water, ice was drifting in white flakes and blue floes with seals resting on them. The seals would wait for the kayak to come very close before they glided into the sea.

The space was inundated with light; the ice crystals splintered it up. Amidst the slivers, multicolored planes shone in soft hues: teeming life of suspended animalcules—soup for leviathan. He wallowed in the food, moved through it like the ancient hunters in the "clouds of game."

Attila seems to have felt more like an observer there than a hunter; he was charmed not so much by the giants as by the creatures that were their pasture. Of course, the wealth, the plethora of forms, increases as they get tinier. The phenomenon gains in meaningful density the closer it gets to nonextension. This reminds me of one of the pointless conversations I had with my dear brother about *origin*. Perhaps I will come back to this later on.

*

Returning from the far north, Attila had brought along a primordial delight in superfluousness. The latter, he said, represented the capital whose interest nourishes the world, harvest by harvest. That was how the hunter lived amidst tremendous herds, which kept multiplying without his interference, long before the earth was notched by the plowshare.

"The hunter has companions, but tillage brought slavery, killing became murder. Freedom ended; the game was driven away. In Cain a descendant of the primal hunter was resurrected, his avenger, perhaps. Genesis supplies only a rumor about all this. It hints at Yahweh's bad conscience regarding the slayer."

I enjoyed hearing these things when I poured the refills long past midnight. Those were spoors that the anarch repeatedly tracks down—and the poet, too; no poet is without a touch of anarchy. Where else could poetry come from?

*

Attila felt that superfluousness requires its control. When the word comes surging, the poet has not yet formed it into a poem. Countless shapes slumber in marble—but who will bring forth even one? Hard by the rich pastures, Attila had run into nomads who arduously dug their food from the earth: worms and roots.

Oolibuk—that was the Inuit's name—was still a good hunter; he knew how to wield his bow. Once Attila asked him to shoot a black-throated diver swimming some eighty feet from their kayak. The bird eluded the first arrow by diving; the second pierced its head through both eyes when it resurfaced.

Otherwise the Inuits were thoroughly corrupted by dealing with the whalers, who, next to the sandalwood skippers, were notoriously the worst villains ever to plow the seas. From them, they had learned how to smoke, drink, and gamble. They gambled away their dogs, boats, weapons, and also their wives; a woman might change hands five times in a single night.

*

Yet Oolibuk also knew about the days before any ship had ever penetrated these climes. Grandmothers who had heard about the past from their grandmothers would tell their grandchildren.

The big day in an Inuit's life comes when he, still a boy, kills his first seal. The men gather around him and his booty; they hail his dexterity and praise the seal—never has anyone seen such a strong animal and such good meat.

Killing a seal is difficult; a man is not a hunter if he fails. He has to content himself with female food, with fish, seaweed, and crustaceans. Strange tales are told about such men; one of them, finding no wife, had to make do with a mussel, and he lost his member because the shell closed up.

The hunter, in contrast, is a free man, around whom the world arranges itself. He alone maintains the family, richly providing it with meat and hides, as well as blubber, which provides light and warmth in the simply endless winter night. The hunter is bold and cunning, and, like all early hunters, he is related to the game he tracks. His body is plump and brawny like a sea mammal's, it is rich in blood and fat and has the same smell as the animal. The hunter will brave even the whale and the polar bear.

*

But the winter is long. It can come early and wear on interminably. Nor is the hunter always lucky. Though the pantry and storeroom of his ice dwelling can be chock-full at the start of winter, the crossing of the Arctic night remains a unique venture.

Incidentally, prior to setting up my bunker on the Sus, I studied construction plans that Captain Ross had found among the Eskimos of New North Wales. A basic theme for the anarch is how man, left to his own devices, can defy superior forces—whether state, society, or the elements—by making use of their rules without submitting to them.

"It is strange," Sir William Parry wrote when describing the igloos on Winter Island, "it is strange to think that all these measures are taken against the cold—and in houses of ice."

*

If the prey is inadequate, then the family will not survive the winter. It will waste away with hunger and scurvy in its glass palace. Polar bears will break open the igloo and find their meals. They will be followed by foxes and gulls.

Frost is a harsh master. Even while the Greenlander is struggling with death, the others bend his legs under his loins to make the grave shorter. If twins are born, the hunter kills one so that the second may live. The food would not suffice for both. If a mother dies in childbirth, the newborn is buried with her, or a bit later, when the father, at the end of his rope, can no longer stand the baby's bawling. "The father's grief is, of course, unbearable, especially when it is a son"—so goes Parry's account. Sometimes infants are exposed on desert islands when winter comes.

*

Why did Attila stress such details in his reminiscences of the polar night? What was his "guiding thought"? (That is what the Domo always asks when checking instructions.)

Was Attila bent on offering examples of the "power of necessity"? When worse comes to worst, a man is forced to make decisions that are hard, cruel—yes, even deadly.

Naturally, the Arctic tribes, or whatever is left of them, have long since been perishing in comfort. This is a gradual dying, over generations. But the fateful question remains in its harshness, even if time gives it a different mask.

With the discovery of oil in northern Alaska, high rises shot up there as everywhere else in those days. A traveler walled in by fire on the twentieth floor of a hotel has to choose between burning up and leaping into space. He will jump; this is documented by photographs.

*

But this did not seem to be Attila's point. His guiding thought in that discussion (which, as we recall, concerned abortion) was, more or less: It is reprehensible to delegate a misdeed. The hunter takes his son to the mother's grave and kills him. He does not assign the task to anyone else—not his brother, not the shaman; he carries it out himself.

If a man here in Eumeswil has "made a child," he usually hands his wife or girlfriend a check and feels he is off the hook, certain that she will take care of it. Attila obviously means that if the man personally killed his son like the Inuit, then he would know what he was doing.

As an anarch, who acknowledges neither law nor custom, I owe it to myself to get at the very heart of things. I then probe them in terms of their contradictions, like image and mirror image. Either is imperfect—by seeking to unite them, which I practice every morning, I manage to catch a corner of reality.

*

My mother wanted me. She knew me when she was carrying me under her heart. She knew me better than I will ever get to know myself, even if I live to be a hundred. She wanted me, no matter how I would develop physically, mentally, ethically; she wanted me as I am. Had I been born an idiot, a cripple, a murderer, she would have loved me even more fervently. Her tears are worth more than the father's pride when he sees his son crossing the threshold in a wreath of laurels.

My father hounded me when my life was frailest. This may be our most exquisite time. My mother concealed me from him in her womb, like Rhea hiding Zeus in the grotto of Ida to shield him from the clutches of a voracious Cronus. Those are monstrous images; they make me shudder—conversations between matter and time. They lie as erratic boulders, uninterpreted, beneath the surveyed land.

Uninterpreted, no doubt, but the field is active. I picture myself appearing to my father when he is approachable—in a dream, that is—and demanding an explanation. I would then get to hear what they all say: about the situation of the poor, ill-paid teacher, and a married man, to boot.

Such are the standards in Eumeswil, a fellah society that periodically suffers moral harassment from demagogues until generals come and insert an artificial spine. Some ration, others squander gold, salt, and blood. *Et ça veut raisonner et n'a pas cinq sous dans sa poche.* One does best to pay back with small change. For instance: "Hey, Dad—couldn't you have been a little more careful in the map room?"

*

Perhaps he, for his part, might talk some sense into me, albeit in a discussion such as is conducted only in dreams—in realms, that is, where individuality, though not yet eliminated, is strongly diffused. (*Diffundere*: "to pour out, to tap wine from the cask." Pliny. But also "to cheer up, relax." Thus, Ovid, for instance: "*Jupiter nectare diffusus.*")

Prudence is indicated here: a basic issue, the anarch's relationship to his father, is broached. The discussion can, as I have said, be conducted only in a dream; for had my father taken my advice back then in the map room, I would never have materialized in the first place. So our conversation would be impossible in the geographic Eumeswil, but not in the dream city of the same name, for dreams can include not only the dead but also the unborn.

*

There is no doubt that I owe my father my existence—assuming that existence actually deserves gratitude. The tremendous wastefulness in the universe gives one pause to think. After all, aside from me some ten thousand others were awaiting their turn in the map room.

My father could give me existence, but not Being. I was in the latter before my birth, nay, my conception, and I will "be" in it after my death. Being comes into being through Creation, existence through procreation. The father "provides" existence by procreating. In procreating the son, he demonstrates Creation symbolically. He is given a priestly office; a great appeal is propagated through time, echo by echo.

An obligation to the father cannot be denied. It is normal for the father to sacrifice the son; this establishes the basis for myth, religion, history. It is normal—but it is not my job to decide whether it is right; such questions lead away from the main path. As a historian, I have to deal with the order of facts. They abide—what is right and legal changes. In this regard, I benefit from freeing myself from moral and religious bonds. Even Moses, when I summon him to the luminar, must answer to me.

*

The father shakes the foundations when sacrificing the son. The Inuit cited by Attila was aware of this. Zebaoth himself held back the father's arm as it brandished the slaughtering knife on Mount *Dominus videt.* Although the Lord of Hosts had demanded the offering symbolically, he would not allow it pragmatically.

I summoned one of the old city kings, who lost hope after a long siege. Unable to see a way out, he took his son to the rampart and sacrificed him to Baal. This spectacle horrified the foes; they gave up the siege and quit the land.

This recurs in history; in all countries and all ages, the father appeals to the son when he is at the end of his tether: ancient and modern princes, party chiefs and clan chieftains, high priests, parliaments, senates. Whether the father is waging a just or an unjust war, planning vendettas or pillages, having him fight for provinces or for ideas—the son steps in for him.

It also happens that a son will settle accounts with a father; he topples him from the cathedra, the throne, the altar.

If things should reach the point of my collaborating on Vigo's historical opus *Historia in nuce*, as he occasionally suggests, I would incorporate the chapter on "Father and Son" in the basic structure.

*

It is not that I as an anarch reject authority *à tout prix*. On the contrary, I seek it, and that is precisely why I reserve the right to examine it.

I come from a family of historians. A man without history is someone who has lost his shadow. At the same time, he becomes repulsively flexible. I can observe this only too well in the Eumeswil professors. Half are crooks, half are eunuchs, barring very few. These exceptions are outdated men like Bruno and Vigo or, like Rosner, solid artisans.

I can count my dear old dad among the eunuchs, the speechifiers. It is impossible for us to have a conversation about facts without his puffing it up with social and economic platitudes and spicing it up with moralisms he derives from them. Saying what everyone else says is a delight for him. He comes out with things like, "I am simply expressing the public opinion." And he actually plumes himself on such things. A journalist, even though he disagrees with the current editorials. "He is controversial"—for him, as for all eunuchs, that is a put-down. The exact opposite of an anarch; God bless him—but why is he a historian?

*

Great conversations have taken place between father and son, even here, and as far back as the period of the Diadochi—conversations between the powerful and also between losers. The anarch is fascinated by both; the imminence of death sharpens the outlines. We had, if I am not mistaken, an Antigonus; he led the elephants in the center; his son, in the right flank, led the cavalry. Both men died in battle: the father was not found until several days later when the vultures were already at work; however, his dog was still guarding his corpse.

Later on, an admiral likewise perished with his two sons: they went down with the fleet. My dear brother, who misses no chance to mouth something stupid, opined, "It was foolish for all three of them to sail out together."

Then the father's conversation with his son prior to the latter's execution under the wall—a conversation that laid the foundations of a regime that endured for forty years. And finally the conversation before the murder of the tyrant—a conversation that, of course, as is the nature of things, usually occurs between brothers.

Naturally, I know that neither war nor civil war has any historical sense here. War is waged by fathers, civil war by sons. Here in Eumeswil, the mercenaries have to be kept on a tight leash and in high spirits and the officers under strict surveillance. For these reasons alone, the government is reluctant to get involved in foreign quarrels. And revolutions lose their charm if they become permanent fixtures. Tyrannicide, the killing of the *tyrannus absque titulo*, presumes the existence of underdogs of quality. It would resemble the beheading of the Hydra; for every tyrant, thirty more would sprout, as long ago under Lysimachus.

*

A conversation with my father would be as pointless as wallowing in the mud of the lagoon. Getting fired up, as he does, over long worn-out buzzwords, he is even more closely bound to tradition than I. Yet his way is necrophilia.

I am an anarch in space, a metahistorian in time. Hence I am committed to neither the political present nor tradition; I am blank and also open and potent in any direction. Dear old Dad, in contrast, still pours his wine into the same decaying wineskins, he still believes in a constitution when nothing and no one constitutes anything.

A conversation with the FATHER could orient me. Why is it always night when I imagine it?

We are standing on deck; the sea is hollow—he is the steersman who stays on course even when the constellations are veiled. "Father, how far are we from Actium?"

Or else I stand next to him in a very old astronomical observatory, trying to find out about the weather. We have left the final sign of the zodiac behind us; the influence of sea and waves is very strong now. The mother's influence, too? The animals have lost their rank, which was not equal but superior to that of human beings. Even the fish were suspect. They appeared neither in shoals nor as leviathan.

We can exterminate the animals but not annihilate them; they withdraw from manifestation to the primal images, perhaps to the stars. The men who explored the moon could not tell that there was life on it, for they brought wasteland along.

The earth cleanses itself periodically, new shapes will come thronging. They are heralded by tremendous birth pangs. Then new Prometheuses will be their midwives. Or will we find our way back to the animals after a chain of spiritualizations, as after a sleepless night? Thus, the lamb could return on a higher level, as Capricorn, a sign uniting happiness and power.

But could that happen with the empirical father, who has lost his rank?

33

How did I get on this topic? I am still at breakfast, waited on by Dalin. Right—I was saying that he could mess things up for me personally—say, as part of my team at the duck shack, to which he would be detailed. There he would be in clover. Then he would be knocked off. I was saying that instead of delegating this job to the Lebanese, who would enjoy it too much, I would take charge of it myself—like Attila's Inuit.

When Dalin expatiates. I listen to his nihilistic tirades. They are instructive, yet I find the trust he places in me dubious. I eat my breakfast as if I were not listening.

"The tea is cold. You've been dawdling in the corridor or else you've been laying one of your rotten eggs again."

That is unlikely, however, for here in the Casbah he is on his guard. Though noteworthy as a type, he will scarcely do more harm than a mosquito. Some of his machinations are not altogether pointless. I dislike the mailbox scheme because I suspect that it recently claimed a letter I had sent to Ingrid. As for any other mischief he causes in Eumeswil, I am unconcerned.

I mention my indifference because it illuminates the gap between positions. The anarchist, as the born foe of authority, will be destroyed by it after damaging it more or less. The anarch, on the other hand, has appropriated authority; he is sovereign. He therefore behaves as a neutral power vis-à-vis state and society. He may like, dislike, or be indifferent to whatever occurs in them. That is what determines his conduct; he invests no emotional values.

*

Dalin will not get very far. Such types try to hoist a boulder that is much too heavy for them. They are crushed when it slides back. Moreover, they draw attention; often they fall victim to the first cleansings. They do not know the rules, they even scorn them. They are like people who deliberately drive on the wrong side of the road and want to be applauded for doing so.

The anarch, in contrast, knows the rules. He has studied them as a historian and goes along with them as a contemporary. Wherever possible, he plays his own game within their framework; this makes the fewest waves. Thus, Dalin's liquidation would presumably be consistent with the system that he defied. But that is not the basis for my legitimation.

One might erroneously assume that I take bloodshed lightly. Not by a long shot! I simply stay free of moral judgments. Blood has its own laws; it is as untamable as the sea.

The historian is familiar with many examples of the inadequacy of moral judgments. Over and over again, especially after crushing defeats, history brings forth constitutions because of which one does not dare touch a hair on the heads of even cannibalistic sorts. And the retort is inevitable: "The government didn't have the courage to have me shot—the feeling is not mutual." First the rider slackens the reins, then the horse bolts.

The extremes meet. Some people lavishly squander blood, others shy away from it. This contradiction is probably based on a telluric equilibrium; the Romans knew why they gave the arena an oval form and draped the divine effigies before the start of the games.

*

There are jurists and even theologians who advocate capital punishment as the last resort of justice. Others reject it as immoral. Both sides have good reasons. Both call upon statistics, which, as usual, can be exploited every which way. Numbers should be kept aloof.

This controversy passes the anarch by. For him, the linking of death and punishment is absurd. In this respect, he is closer to the wrongdoer than to the judge, for the high-ranking culprit who is condemned to death is not prepared to acknowledge his sentence as atonement; rather, he sees his guilt in his own inadequacy. Thus, he recognizes himself not as a moral but as a tragic person.

On the other hand, authority will do everything it can to make him repent. But hats off to the man who remains true all the way to himself and to his cause. Here, too, there is a difference between tactics and strategy. The cornered man can deny his guilt and risk some dodges, he can sacrifice his pieces until only the king is left on the board. That was how Jacques de Molay, the last grand master of the Knights Templars, behaved when retracting the confession that had been tortured out of him; he was then burned to death very slowly.

Incidentally, the charges that Philip the Fair leveled against the Templars do not seem entirely concocted. The study of this order, combined with the study of the Old Man of the Mountain, is a gold mine. Alamut *and* Famagusta, Baphomet *and* leviathan.

For the anarch, the death penalty makes no sense, but it does have meaning, for he reckons with it. This is among the realities that heighten his tension and alertness. A maxim I heard at the night bar points in this direction: "One should not spoil the game for the man who is gambling his life; one should take him seriously." It was the Domo speaking; the subject was a pardon, to which I will come back.

*

It does not look good, whether someone is put to death in a classical fashion or otherwise. An uncleared battlefield is likewise a repulsive sight. The images were denser when united fronts and squadrons were led into combat. Plainly, such things were more easily disregarded. Executions were public; they were well attended.

With the spread of atheism, death grows more horrible, since annihilation is total and irrevocable. Death is overrated, both by the person suffering it and by the person inflicting it. Repentance, too, is secularized. It no longer relates to the evildoer's salvation before he passes away into the cosmic order; now it signifies his obeisance to society and its legislation.

My dear brother exhibits photographs to demonstrate the odiousness of executions. Since, as I have said, the association of death and punishment is absurd for the anarch, my brother is wasting his breath with me. Besides, he is making a fool of himself, since, as a historian, he ought to know that one can prove anything with photographs, even the very opposite, especially if it is odious.

Art has the privilege of showing the ultimate horrors, and also the glory of martyrdom.

*

The anarch knows the fundamental law. He also knows its falsifications. He realizes that atonement is his due for misdeeds against it. The state has tricked him out of the right to pass this judgment; it is obligated to carry it out on his behalf.

Instead, one sees eunuchs convening in order to disempower the populace in whose name they presume to speak. This is logical, since the eunuch's most heartfelt goal is to castrate the free man. The results are laws demanding that "you should run to the district attorney while your mother is being raped."

They cheat a man out of the blood that expiates murder, just as they rob him of the gold attesting to his share of the sun, and spoil the salt that, as the spirit of the earth, unites all free men.

Against this background, the nihilism of a Dalin is understandable, even when he employs abstruse methods. He feels an urge to blow up something; these are the beacons of the impotent.

*

The populace consists of individuals and free men, while the state is made up of numbers. When the state dominates, killing becomes abstract. Servitude began with the shepherds; in the river valleys it attained perfection with canals and dikes. Its model was the slavery in mines and mills. Since then, the ruses for concealing chains have been refined.

The anarchists would like to change this; their ideas are inherently wrong. Man should be not the sun's friend, but the sun itself. And that he *is*; the mistake lies in his failure to recognize his place, his home, and thereby his right.

In its late period—that is, when it has already fully consumed the populace and alleges to be acting purely at its behest—the state either renounces killing or else overkills. This must be connected to the building of dikes; now and then, there are floods.

Killing is delegated. A eunuch who could not harm a fly administers any number of killings from his desk. The victims are innocent (so is the eunuch). The verdict no longer intervenes; the number reigns. The gods have gone home.

*

I have studied the revolt of the Vendéans in the luminar. Their war was bizarre, a Gothic relic. It was waged by the three basic estates: knights, peasants, and clerics. The relationship to the king was still personal and intact. The republicans were far better equipped and vastly outnumbered the royalists.

That is the classical situation for the forest flight, the kind achieved some two centuries later against leviathan, albeit in swamps and tropical thickets. In Brittany, the forest was reduced to a gridwork of hedges. Under their cover, the Chouans trailed the regiments marching along the roads and intimidated them with shrieks. These peasants, who, as one historian says, "could barely distinguish their right hand from their left," had very few rifles, mostly bird guns. But they were good shots; they crossed themselves before firing.

Very ancient reserves must have survived there in both the earth and the people. Napoleon eventually built military roads through this countryside. Vigo mentioned this as an example of constellations that he calls "faded reminiscences." Long, long ago: Bronze against the Neolithic.

*

I mention this because of the five thousand captured republicans of Saint-Florent-le-Vieil. After various skirmishes, they had fallen into the hands of the peasants; the prisoners had to be gotten rid of. The mood was not favorable to them; they had left a trail of burned villages, castles, and churches, and the news had come from Paris that the queen had been guillotined. Commander Chollet had brought the captives here. *C'était un homme fort dur*; during the march, he had had nine of them shot for attempting to escape.

When their fate was deliberated, everything was repeated that tends to be voiced on such occasions. Finally, the decision was left to Monsieur de Marigny, who said that such a butchery went beyond his strength, he did not feel up to it. Monsieur de Lescure, who, being heavily wounded, had participated only silently, murmured, "*Ah, je respire.*"

Incidentally, these prisoners soon got hold of some cannon and, predictably, shot at their liberators. That is why Monsieur de Marigny's decision deserves all the more respect. Presumably, the captives wanted to ward off any suspicion of having royalist sympathies and to put themselves in a good light for the Convention. The army was accompanied by republican commissioners. The knowledge of such fears is soon lost; for anyone studying them, the biographies of revolutionary generals are informative.

In such conflicts, the knight is at a disadvantage vis-à-vis the demagogue, because his responses are chivalrous, hence old-fashioned. Such is his nature; he will perish along with it.

Monsieur de Marigny could have opted for execution; this would have conformed to the period style, degrading him into the adversary of a Fouquier-Tinville. In any case, he had no intention of delegating his responsibility or evading it by merely signing his name.

Responsibility is the bottom line of a soliloquy. A tragedy makes it concrete by distributing the responsibility among several characters.

34

My anxieties about the headaches that Dalin might cause me were needless. Every man destroys himself—albeit each in his own style. Bruno's forecast in this matter was accurate. If prophecies come true in some unforeseeable way, then they are all the more convincing.

Sebastian Carnex, a lawyer known throughout the city, was exceedingly fat. His natural aggressiveness was beneficial to his profession, but whenever he tried to fast, he grew bilious and made mistakes.

Attila took him in hand, prescribing a regimen that would both help him slim down and strengthen him. To this end, he put him on a nut diet. A nut, by its very substance, forces you to chew meticulously; that is only one of its virtues. So Carnex was to eat as many nuts as he wanted, but also to go walking—namely, barefoot along the beach.

Diet and exercise are the classical remedies in such cases; Attila thereby weaned him away from meat and a sedentary lifestyle. He also made sure that Carnex usually had something between his teeth and was not bored. He dutifully chewed his nuts, even developing a taste for them. He ambled along the tideline, now on the wet sand, now on the fringes of the waves; light, air, water, and especially earth contributed to his sense of ease. When court was not in session, Carnex would stroll every day; he lost weight slowly but steadily.

*

The shore is animated near the city. You see tents, with horses and camels being rented out in front of them; vendors peddling their wares. After an hour's walk, you run into only fishermen shoving their boats into the sea or a net-caster standing waist-deep in the water. The mouth of the Sus is a lonesome area; Rosner has his flock of birds there, the district is considered unsafe. That was where Carnex would refresh himself with a swim when the sun was highest. Then he would take an extended siesta; he also slept better than before.

Aside from his bag of nuts, the lawyer would also be carrying a briefcase on these strolls. After waking up, he would unlock it with a small key and study case files. By sunset, he was back in town.

Carnex had already slimmed down quite a bit the first time his briefcase vanished and could not be found no matter how hard he looked. The loss was all the more annoying because the briefcase contained some documents. Carnex put up a reward, but in vain. It was obvious that he had been robbed. The theft was repeated twice.

Initially, Carnex assumed that the thief had been after his dossiers, but now he felt that a hateful enemy was at work. If someone was playing a joke, he had picked the right victim, for Carnex was extremely touchy, and when retaliating, he tended to overdo it. This was true now: after missing his briefcase for a third time, he planted an explosive inside it.

He had procured one of the flat bombs that partisans use for assassinations—virtually a parlor game in the city. Every lawyer in Eumeswil has ties with the underground.

These bombs are no larger than dessert plates. They are packed in cotton so as to make no sound when they fall to the floor during a meeting or a demonstration. They are also used with timers and remote-control devices. Carnex had set his bomb to a specific wavelength.

The plan worked smoothly: Carnex had not yet ended his cure when the briefcase disappeared once again. This time, the thief had stolen it during the lawyer's ocean dip. When he re-emerged from the water and noticed the loss, he twisted the small transmitter that he was wearing on his throat like an amulet. There was a bang in the dunes, not much louder than, yet different from, Rosner's shotgun. Carnex nodded; he was satisfied—but it was unwise of him to boast about his deed. He was not accustomed to hiding his light under a bushel.

These bombs, though weighing little, are effective. The coroner and his staff had their hands full piecing Dalin together from the jigsaw puzzle that had arrived at their laboratory. It was what used to be called "a job for the king of Prussia," for, like most of their labors, it vanished into the strait between the penal islands.

*

I had warned Dalin at almost every breakfast: "What you're doing is going to turn out badly in the long run." Nonetheless he would never do the same thing twice in the same place. This time, his luck must have run out. Presumably he had not even heard about Carnex's annoyance; he had most likely noticed the briefcase as he happened to wander by. He must have been en route to the bunker where he was doing his experiments. He would have thrown his booty into the river or gotten rid of it in some other way, for his goal was only to damage. Any profit would have been a break in his style. But the lawyer came back early from his dip.

If Carnex had not boasted about his deed, no one would have thought of him. The police would have assumed that they had picked up the trail of one of those anarchists who dabble in explosives. But now Carnex was indicted for a capital offense. There was no question that this was murder; the charge was borne out by the cunning preparation and the absolutely deadly methods. Even the illegal use of explosives would have sufficed. The Casbah is very touchy about such things, and rightly so. The death penalty was appropriate.

It seemed odd that an astute jurist like Carnex would have stuck his neck out so irrationally. Still, it was well known that his judgment abandoned him whenever there was a chance of profit; this was something he shared with nearly all the citizens of Eumeswil.

*

The handling of the case was extremely thorough—not only when the court officials reported to the Domo and the Domo to the Condor, but also in their subsequent nightly conversations. These gave me sound insights into their views on capital punishment as they have evolved in practice and in theory at the Casbah. I was able to complete my notes.

Let me repeat that the discussion about the death penalty does not concern the anarch. Since he dictates his own law, the word "punishment" is one of the prejudices on which society lives. Here, everyone is set to punish everyone else.

Killing, by contrast, is one of the fundamental facts. It reaches deep into the organic, nay, inorganic world. Every moment is deadly for every other; it becomes its heir—Cronus survives by devouring his children.

Like gold and salt, the state has also usurped killing. At times, the state deals with it extravagantly, then again avariciously. Hecatombs bleed to death in the struggle over a ditch or a patch of forest; a butcher of children is coddled as a patient.

The anarch cannot go along with this game. He knows he can kill; on the other hand, it matters little whether he ever actually does. Perhaps he will never go through with it. And it must also be stressed that he grants this possibility to everyone else. Each person is the center of the world, and his unconditional freedom creates the gap in which respect and self-respect balance out.

*

I was attentive yet neutral when they were discussing Carnex. His life was at stake. The year was drawing to an end and no death penalty had as yet been implemented. Usually the Condor commutes the sentence to deportation to the islands. The Domo feels there has to be at least one execution a year; he clearly views it more as a power demonstration and less in juridical terms. Once, when he was talking to Attila, I heard him developing a quasi-hygienic system.

"It is enough to show, now and then, that we do not hesitate to deal with the person himself. Blood is a powerful arcanum; its homeopathic use is enough. If the patient gets feverish, some bloodletting is advisable; if pus forms, a quick cut is unavoidable."

I found these comments bizarre inasmuch as I heard similar things from dear old Dad. Both men see crime as a disease of the body social; my dad with the eyes of the internist, the Domo with those of the surgeon. For the former, the patient dies because of an internal complaint; for the surgeon, because of an operation.

35

Anything that spoke in Carnex's favor ultimately worked against him. There was sympathy for him in the city. After all, he had reacted to an anarchistic aggression. He was a prominent citizen, well respected and of a good family. He was even distantly related to the Condor. But all these things contributed to the demonstrative character of the verdict and its implementation.

At the time of Carnex's trial, someone else was facing the same doom. For months, Eumeswil had been terrorized by assaults on lone girls and women. People spoke of little else around their hearths and in the taverns.

These attacks took place at twilight and—at some distance from Eumeswil, say, around the Sus—also in broad daylight. The victims included maids, prostitutes, girls from good backgrounds, even a female professor—in short, any woman wearing a skirt, especially a long one.

The perpetrators were known as the tulip twisters and they triggered a citywide mood in which people huddled together and whispered. Yet there were also sympathizers: when Dalin had brought me my tea in the morning, he would sometimes rub his hands and announce, "They twisted another tulip yesterday."

These assailants operated as a pair on the side streets and along the edge of the forest. One man would speak to the woman as if he happened to be running into her, while the other would play his trick from the rear. He would rip open her skirt, and they would tie it up over her head. Then they took their pleasure on the rest of her body.

Normally, they would stop there; but even so, they wreaked their havoc. One peasant woman, whom they had surprised at her milking, lay stabbed to death in her cow pasture. The police conjectured that she had recognized one of the men, and they investigated this lead. Two of the other victims, likewise farm women, had suffocated in their skirts. They wear heavy homespun cloth here.

The tulip-twisters did their dirty work for nearly a year; eventually few lone females could be seen walking in remote places or after dark. Fashions also changed; women now wore trousers or knee-length skirts.

Raids and undercover work proved fruitless. But in the end, a female officer managed to do what the entire police force had failed to bring off; Kun San, a delicate Korean. She had been trained since childhood in the niceties of self-defense. A long skirt, jutting breasts, a baby cap, and a small parasol—that was her getup as she minced along the Sus, not very conspicuous, but more as if she were late or had missed an appointment.

She had costumed herself as a delicacy. Not to mention that Far Eastern walk. But the bait had no lack of hooks. Her figure was squeezed into an impenetrable corset. Her cap likewise had a metallic insert. The top of her parasol was armed with a lead knob and the bottom with a three-edged steel point. I will ignore details that were subsequently concocted by the populace; such items belong to hero-worship. It is, however, documented that her skirt concealed a spring mechanism that could instantly roll it up so that it girded her hips like a belt.

The trap was sprung the very first time. Kun San had refused any protection. Behind the dunes, an expanse covered with tall broom stretches away, offering Rosner one of his best preserves. The two men jumped out from this thicket, pouncing on the policewoman, one in front, one in back; they were dumbfounded when her skirt instantly rolled up and she changed into a vengeful Artemis.

The assault proved deadly for the front man, since the three-edged tip sliced through his throat. The other man would likewise have been doomed had he been hit full force by the lead knob, which Kun San, whirling swiftly, aimed at his head; but the knob only grazed it. While he was still reeling, she threw herself on him with her iron grip and hurled him over her shoulder. Then she poked her fingers into his eyes. "Hey, pal, you didn't expect this, did you?" He was very glad when she delivered him to the city.

*

Two postilions had been indulging in these pranks. The title is actually used for stableboys, but the Condor loves such designations. He cultivates not only the naval legacy but also his cavalry tradition. While the horses have no military function and, aside from the mounted patrols, little significance for the police, there is a hierarchy of ranks—from the *grand écuyer* to the man who picks up the droppings. The postilions wear blue uniforms with yellow piping and boots with braiding; some have been promoted to minions. They often have duty at the Casbah for weeks at a time, and needless to say, they store up fantasies there.

The prisoner, Salvatore, was a lithe, graceful boy with a small black beard; it spoke for Kun San's superior technique that she had managed to flip him over.

*

Eumeswil now suddenly had two causes célèbres, which were treated with the usual pomp: spirited debates in front of overcrowded auditoriums, where ladies from the West End could be seen next to pimps from the waterfront. During the examination of the witnesses, the female professor fainted. Kun San, who demonstrated some of her holds, was the heroine of the day, but Carnex and Salvatore also aroused sympathy. On the other hand, the postilion was very nearly lynched outside the Palace of Justice. Such is the chaos when the populace gets riled up. I was rather glad that little was said about Dalin; after all, I was virtually his accomplice.

*

Both cases were tried as capital offenses. I was in the courtroom in order to hear the summations for and against Carnex, and I was surprised by the deployment of rhetoric. Plainly, the Domo's emphasis on grammar was already bearing its fruits. Naturally, Carnex's attorney pled self-defense, for while there could be no doubt concerning the "unlawfulness" of Dalin's offense it was debatable whether the other condition, namely that of a "clear and present danger," had been fulfilled. Needless to say, if the "clear and present danger of an ongoing action" is questionable, then the fighter with a command of the tenses has the edge. I do not wish to go into the niceties. In any event, the demands that law must place on logic were satisfied.

At this point, I feel tempted to discuss the merits and perils of education in times of decay. Whenever education is expressed in language, it brings an invisible legacy into the present. In decadence, it is enjoyed; in a time without history, it is still perceived, still sensed. One sees the fish swimming even when one no longer knows how it manages to do so. This restores an old relationship, but on a new level: the relationship between the illiterate and the literate.

*

As a historian, I felt content when leaving the courtroom because I found that the presentation of the defendant and his actions had succeeded. In this respect, great trials verge on becoming artworks. Guilt is not thereby extinguished, but it gains something within the composition. Defense attorney and prosecutor are then no longer adversaries, they work together on the image that emerges from light and shadow.

No Last Supper can forgo a Judas. This hints at one of the perspectives of the anarch, who does not acknowledge guilt: namely, the arrival of an era in which death and terror are not reduced, but newly conceived. For this, the world must be dreamed once again, and in a godly way.

36

Both Carnex and Salvatore were sentenced to death almost concurrently. The Casbah has a rule that an execution must be done by hand and that blood must flow. Criminals are decapitated, politicals shot. The public viewing is guaranteed, but limited.

I believe I have already said that the death sentence is very seldom carried out, and that its implementation has not so much a legal and moral character as a logical and administrative one. The year was waning, and an execution was due—if only so that, as the Domo said, "Pedro should not get rusty." Pedro is the headsman for criminal cases.

The surprise was great when it was announced that it was Carnex who had been refused clemency. Salvatore, in contrast, was exiled to the islands. I overheard most of the decision taking shape at the night bar, and I also took notes.

The Domo had carried his point, although he was obviously over-insistent about his principles. This bordered on art for art's sake. He probably wanted to avoid any appearance of what used to be called "class justice." Salvatore was a stableboy, Carnex a respectable citizen. Furthermore, Carnex had struck a sore point; the Casbah's dislike of private possession of explosives.

Above all, I believe, Salvatore owed his life to the Domo's secret sympathy with criminals. I notice that his head begins swaying almost benevolently whenever the conversation turns to major felonies. This happens less with fraud and property offenses than with armed robbery and violence, which have stirred the imagination since time immemorial. In spreading terror, the forces they unleash confirm the ruler and his justice. Such observations could support theories that power per se is evil.

*

Boys like Salvatore always find benefactresses with a taste for high meat. One of them, Lady Pelworm, had managed to get in to see the prisoner; she had money and influence. I heard the Condor telling the Domo: "Visiting his cell without supervision, and for two hours to boot—that's pushing it."

"I had her thoroughly searched. She didn't even have a nail file."

"On the other hand, he was togged out in his uniform and all the paraphernalia."

The Domo laughed. "He was in pretrial custody. What would a postilion be without boots, whip, and horn? Incidentally, she wants to accompany him to the islands; she's already submitted her request."

My dear father regards the Domo as a "humorless sort." This is debatable; in any case, he is not lacking in wit—a wit based essentially on shortcuts. It is amusing when someone skips a few steps. Thus, the Domo jumps over two or three possible objections. To this end, he, of course, requires intelligent interlocutors.

*

So Salvatore was banished to the islands. While they are very close to the mainland, one hears as little from them as one heard, in the past, from hospitals for incurables, where lepers wasted away for the rest of their lives after receiving final benediction. This may be the right time for a few remarks about "treatment of prisoners" as it has developed in Eumeswil. I have repeatedly emphasized that for the anarch there are no punishments, only measures taken among equals. If I start by quoting the Domo—and on the basis of my rapid jottings at the night bar—then I am merely providing a sketch.

*

Any incarceration lasting more than two years is a waste of time; it is throwing good money after bad. "Life imprisonment" is absurd. Better death. Which most convicted men prefer, anyway.

*

If forced to choose, anyone would favor a brief detention, no matter how perilous, to twelve years behind bars. This lies in the nature of the thing; one favors a dangerous crisis over a chronic languishing.

*

It is the instant of despair that brings the change; this is true not only for imprisonment. But imprisonment can aim at that instant. Three months should be enough; six would be too much. Hermits knew the recipe: fasting, waking, and working to the limits of one's strength.

*

Above all, a trained and well-paid staff. Distance. Three feet from the person—this applies not only to the prisoner but also to the guard. Physical contact is permitted only in self-defense, against bodily assault.

*

Witnesses are to attend every confrontation, every interrogation. A coerced confession is worthless, even damaging; it must be obtained like the "mate" in chess.

*

If someone absolutely insists on risking his life, then his game should not be spoiled, he must be taken seriously. This applies also to a hunger strike. If a man wishes to do battle, he has the right to be treated according to military law.

*

Anyone who disposes of another's man time holds not only his sorrow but also his joy in his hand. He can lessen or heighten them as he sees fit. There have been penitentiaries in which the inmates were allowed to waste away in dreadful bleakness until the end. They died of consumption and wound up in cemeteries where a cross was marked only by a number.

How different it is, if for a night I either grant him or withhold his wife, his girlfriend, a streetwalker—even the hardest man will soften. Yes, Condor, in this way he can become your friend. (This insight came from a discussion about Salvatore that I noted. Incidentally, Latifah told me that she sometimes refreshes a prisoner in this manner, albeit not without a fee: *honorarium*, "the honorable payment.")

*

"An egg of Columbus for justice. It is laid again every year."

The Domo was speaking as they came from dinner recently. He was referring to one of the suggestions that arrive by mail. There is a special letterbox for them. He particularly values the anonymous missives.

"Most offenses can be taken care of quickly and painfully with a flogging. Who would not prefer that to a longer incarceration? Everyone is unanimous on this issue—the culprit, the judge, the *opinio publica*. Certain offenses simply cry for a flogging. It clears the air. While the deterrent effect may be arguable for capital punishment, it is beyond all question for corporal punishment. Besides, the latter makes reparation possible—compensation makes more sense for pain than for false imprisonment."

"All well and good," said the Domo, "but why is it obvious a priori that it will not work? Why is life still more bearable in a state that executes than in a state that flogs? And even with a total consensus? This, incidentally, is an example of the fact that unanimity and lawfulness are apples and oranges."

"And even more so unanimity and morality. If everybody is of the same opinion, then it is best to sign oneself into a madhouse. The dislike of painful penalties has not existed always and everywhere. Perhaps it is a sign of decadence. In China, even high-level officials supposedly received the bamboo, and the Yellow Khan still maintains this practice today. In the great periods of the British navy, the cat-o'-nine-tail menaced even highborn cadets; its cords were as sharp as for the common sailors, but the handle was swathed in velvet."

That was Attila speaking from his experiences. I also noted: "Morality has its own evolution, though not in a rising line. But eventually, some things become impossible. We similarly lose our taste for a specific dish, perhaps because it once tasted too good."

*

Further notes, stemming partly from the Domo, partly from Attila—the conversation was lively; it sped by so quickly that I could not attribute the comments properly.

Opinions on the cruelty of capital punishment are relative. The Duke of Châtelet said, as he was being led to the guillotine, "This is a pleasant way to die."

His remark was no cynicism if we recall that, only a bit earlier, people had been broken on the wheel, drawn and quartered, and burned at the stake. In fact, Guillotin's invention had humanitarian aims. Then, too, perhaps the duke was suffering from an incurable disease. He was over seventy when he was beheaded for a bagatelle. Suicide demonstrates that there are worse things than death. The obvious detachment toward death that lingered could have been an afterglow of the heyday of the baroque. When Sillery was being dragged to the scaffold, he said, "Up there, my gout will be cured."

It is understandable that this detachment survived more among Christians than among philosophers—for instance, the Carmelites of Compiègne, or Madame de Laval-Montmorency, the abbess of Montmartre, who, with bound hands, said upon seeing the decapitation machine, "I have been craving you for a long time; this is a precious death."

Attila quoted this and other utterances from people condemned by the revolutionary tribunal; he also allowed the cynics to speak.

Item: "Photography falsifies the problem by limiting itself to the ephemeral. The appearance of cruelty could easily be mitigated, even transformed into its opposite, say, through drugs that bring euphoria. Is that the task of justice? Justice holds not only a sword but also a set of scales; the relationship between sin and atonement has to be balanced. The point is not just to get rid of the perpetrator; in that case, it would be better to banish him. People used to say, 'Justice has been dispensed.'"

And then: "The topic should be discussed only by people who have lingered in the vestibules of death, close to the serpent that gives death and life. The contact can be transmitted and rediscovered. Pericles rebuilt the Temple of Eleusis after many years of its deterioration. This can happen at any time and in any place."

Before the Condor could respond, the Domo said, "What for? It is better for us if they are afraid of death."

*

If a perpetrator has had three sentences of at least one year each, he vanishes in the islands and thereby forever from the city. There are exceptions, along the lines of that mythical Captain Dreyfus, whose case I have studied in the luminar. Along with Giordano Bruno and others, he is one of my dear father's saints.

The "islands" were not invented by tyrants or generals; republics and democracies also like to use them. The rulers change, the prisons abide; they are even overcrowded with each new regime. I recall that Father and Brother rubbed their hands together when the Condor's predecessors were sent to the islands by the tribunes; they even viewed this as an act of clemency. Today, they think otherwise; indeed, they think too much altogether.

As a historian, I deal with the necessity of this institution. Banishment is one of the ancient methods by which communities try to cleanse themselves. It can take the form of expulsion—say, of the leper after a meticulous examination by the priests, as prescribed by Moses: the unclean "shall dwell alone; without the camp shall his habitation be."

Banishment as an attribute of society is a symptom of its imperfection; the anarch accommodates himself to it while the anarchist tries to eliminate it. These are theological residues. Only in a perfect condition "shall there be no more anathema" (Revelation 22:3). "But the throne of God and of the Lamb shall be in it; and his servants shall serve him." Those are dismal prospects. Even anarchism ultimately leads to someone whose feet must be kissed.

*

Insula, isola, island—that which is surrounded by water; *sal* is salt water, the sea. *Campi salis* is Virgil's term for the ocean. *Insularis* was the exile, also the occupant of one of the many-storied tenements known as *insulae*. Islands are places that lend themselves prima vista to isolation, insulation—whether as residences for toppled caesars or as penal colonies for social or political undesirables.

Of course, one cannot get along without surveillance even at the Antipodes. Saint Helena was more conveniently located than Elba, which lay too close to the mainland. "Napoleon was solar, he was born under the sign of the Lion; Helena is the moon goddess. Triumph ends beyond the Hesperides." That was Vigo—these words transcend science.

In Eumeswil, the islands are similarly near the coast; before the sirocco, their outlines are visible from the mountains: an archipelago of more than twenty atolls, the largest of which are barely smaller than Elba. The tiniest are hardly indicated on maps; they are more like reefs on which a hermit's shack and the smoke of his fire can be seen from time to time.

This group of islands was, as I have said, used for banishment by the tribunes and even before them. They were populated first by batches of reactionaries, militarists, bloodsuckers, torturers, or whatever they were called—with disempowered persons and their followers who were on the proscription lists and were glad to get off in this way. The supplies were replenished as needed.

The punishment was carried out according to the classical model of penal colonies—that is, strict surveillance in situ, barracking, supervised labor, frequent roll calls. There were high-ranking specialists in criminal law who saw the overall procedure as optimal, or at least as the lesser evil in an imperfect world. This, no doubt, contradicts the maxim "Only the dead never return"—one of the misconceptions of despotism.

The dead do return, and not only as ghosts; they also dun us in the political reality.

*

The Domo went along with the spirit of the procedure but not the letter. His attitude touches on the distinction between theoretical and practical emancipation, between liberalism and liberality. He transferred the guards from the interior of each island to the sea. Their stations were set up on the outer reefs and they had speedboats. No swimmer would have ventured into the channels, anyway—if only because of the big fish. Protection against aerial landings was assured by permanently revolving projectiles, which had come down to our era along with other remnants of the age of high technology. The catacombs supply them according to need, but never beyond.

So escape from the islands is virtually hopeless. Nevertheless, inmates very seldom do manage to flee, thereby providing material for the conversations in the night bar. The Domo usually draws the final conclusion: "My compliments, we are rid of the guy."

*

The soil of the larger islands is fertile; the exiles can live off it. Aside from produce, they also plant grapes, poppies, and hemp for good fellowship and dreams. They raise cattle and they fish off the cliffs. Building boats is prohibited. That is the sole restriction; otherwise, anything goes.

The selection of inmates for the individual islands has led to sociological experiments. But, whatever the mixture of deportees, the initial "anything goes" situation soon developed into an authoritarian system.

*

The island simplifies things; it provides a stage for mounting the drama of society with a small cast. Poets have been repeatedly inspired to depict the island, philosophers to contemplate it. Robinson Crusoe: the loner—first in despair, then in action. Master and servant: Friday joins him. The mutineers on Pitcairn Island: after the massacre, the special treaty on a Biblical model; Titanic order is followed by divine order, Cain by Abel.

Odysseus is the born islander, Sindbad the Sailor is his Oriental counterpart. They represent the loner who, through cunning and boldness, overcomes the elements and holds his own against humans, demons, and deities. They change crews (who perish) and they return alone to Ithaca or Baghdad. Such is the course of life.

The one-eyed Cyclopes, the fatal song of the sirens, the charms of sorceresses who turn men into beasts, the sleeping potion of the *lotophagi*, the whirlpool between Scylla and Charybdis—models of our encounters not only on the most remote islands but also on any street corner in any city. The constraints of customs, the terrors of despotism, are reduced to tersest formulas. Sindbad lands in a city whose citizens view marriage as so holy that a bereft spouse is buried with the deceased. Sindbad nearly falls victim to the sheik of the ocean, who mounts the stranded man, almost riding him to death as a submissive slave while soiling the mariner's back with his excrement.

*

Here, authority has crystallized on every island, albeit in a distinct way each time. One island was named Rock Castle after a forgotten novel by a German baroque author, Johann Gottfried Schnabel. His book, a utopian *Robinson Crusoe*, predated Rousseau's *Contrat social*, in which, as we know, natural man, coming of age as a citizen, delegates part of his freedom to the collective will. The harmony of individual interests leads to a democratic constitution of the state, the internal concordance of wills to the ideality of the state.

Summoning Schnabel's novel from the inexhaustible repertoire of the catacombs, I reviewed it at the luminar; I concluded that the Rock Castle is founded not so much on the social contract as on a contract of submission, to which, however, the free will of not only the individuals but also their majority can contribute. A helper, a leader, a father is desired, recognized, and elected, particularly during an emergency. Soon the elected turns into the elect. All who toil under heavy loads transfer their burdens to him; they jubilantly hand over their freedom.

*

Whenever the will of the collective is replaced by the will of the masses, the individual's luster begins to dazzle; technology, of both propaganda and killing, contributes to this irresistibly. Here on Eumeswil's Rock Castle, the ruler appeared as the classical model of the "kind father." It was a promising start, but it resulted in unforeseen abuses. Rock Castle is the richest of the islands, a true Cockaigne, affording a comfort that was half lotus-land, half land of plenty. The young, both male and female, revolted out of sheer boredom. The kind father had to become strict. He started to weed out; the trouble-makers were banished to the reefs.

"They're too well off," said the Domo when he found out. He cannot be accused of harboring Rousseauistic tendencies.

*

Nevertheless, Rock Castle had a kind of Periclean Age. There were even artworks. The other islands endured partisan fighting. Rival groups rallied around bosses or *capitanos*, one of whom carried the day. He would then distribute work and profit. "They could have had the same thing under us, and even better," said the Domo—this is one of the formulas that I have often heard him voice.

Potentates like making such comparisons. The anarch cannot worry about that; he retains his freedom for himself, however good or bad the regime. He assigns it neither to the legitimacy of the kind father nor to the legal claims, which change in every land and every period. They may all want what's best for him, but the very best, his freedom, is something he keeps for himself. It remains his impartible property.

For the historian, of course, an inexhaustible field opens up. The less partisan he is, the better he understands his job; the red poppy shines no more weakly for him than the white lilies; pain shakes him no less than pleasure. Both are ephemeral, the flowers of evil and those of good, but he is permitted a glimpse over the wall of the garden.

*

If history does have an overall theme, then it is probably not will but freedom. That is its gamble. One could also say, with some reserve. That is its mission. Freedom is common to everyone and yet impartible; it is the will that adds the manifold.

Some time ago, I had to conduct a seminar at Vigo's institute: "Lucius Junius Brutus and Marcus Junius Brutus—A Comparison of All Aspects." The topic brought me a fairly heterogeneous audience.

The original and semi-mythical Brutus killed the last Roman king, his historical descendant killed the first caesar—both with their own hands. One commenced and one concluded the five-hundred-year history of the republic. Solid distinctions can therefore be linked to both men—say, distinctions between the will of the collective and the will of the masses or between justified assent and vote on the one hand and acclamation on the other. The transitions were captured by literature in Mark Antony's renowned funeral oration.

I do not wish to go into details. The sympathy of the students with both tyrannicides was instructive. (Brutus is also one of my dear old dad's heroes.) But they found the distinctions difficult. I admit they are not simple, touching as they do on the problem of freedom.

We are already on the wrong track, for freedom is no problem. It is impartible and therefore in no place that can be counted, measured, or pondered—that is, not in time or space. It is understood in time, say, in a sequence of political systems; it is felt in space—by the bird fluttering against the bars of its cage and by the nation battling for its borders. Over and over, the individual offers himself as the agent of freedom, as a conquering hero or as a martyr who is inevitably felled by freedom and perishes.

This is where the historian's tragedy begins. He must distinguish, but he cannot take sides. His office is to judge the dead; he has to balance the freedom of a Brutus against that of a Caesar.

*

Still, my seminar was not entirely fruitless. Though I sometimes wondered what I was doing (one has fits of self-alienation while standing at the lectern), the seminar helped me to assess my situation and probably also served to discredit me politically. The way in which history is selected and interpreted by the intelligent middle class is a prognostic. A crater, long cooled, starts rumbling. Brutus reawakens. Spartacus returns. Barbarossa has stirred in the Kyffhäuser Mountains. Then the solfatara, the suburbs, likewise begin seething.

At any rate, I went on more and more of my outings to the upper Sus. I also took along parts of my manuscripts. This, incidentally, explains some of my repetitions. Time has not only a thematic but also a technical impact on such works. When the creditors looted Balzac's estate, the street was carpeted with loose pages. But so what? The writing suffices; it is conceived by the universe. Ultimately, there is no difference between paper that is charred and paper that is written on, between dead and living substance.

> Great Caesar, turned to day, henceforth
> Stops up a chink in the far north.

*

On the other hand, I had two or three students who did not succumb entirely to being up-to-date, and who touched not only the *nomos* but also the ethos of history. I took them to Vigo's garden, and their active interest made up for everything. We also had that silent rapport when the moon hung over the Casbah. Every teacher knows that select few.

Vigo's capacity is acknowledged by the elite, so far as an elite exists in Eumeswil. Their acknowledgment speaks for it, I mean, the elite: people of the day after tomorrow and the day before yesterday—hence, people of no importance. For them, Vigo's name is a *mot de passe.* To be sure, his intellectual capacity is also noticed by the collective awareness—somewhat like a splinter in the flesh. That is his relationship to the faculty.

It is no doubt pleasant for a contemporary to be carried by a great wave; confirmation echoes from all sides. It leads to collective self-satisfaction. But when something that was already boring in the editorials read at breakfast is passed off as elite wisdom, then you feel annoyed.

*

The earth is always involved. The ancestral Brutus was the "Imbecile." That was his nickname because he pretended to be a moron whenever he felt threatened. He accompanied the sons of Tarquin to the Oracle of Delphi, where they asked who would be the father's heir; the answer they received was "Whoever kisses the mother first." On the way home, Brutus, in a mock accident, fell to the ground and touched the earth with his lips; the prophecy was fulfilled.

Perhaps I have dwelt too long on the islands; but for the anarch they are a major theme, for he leads a solitary, an insular existence. When

Sindbad sails from the Tigris, through the Persian Gulf and the Arabian Sea, and into the Indian Ocean, he leaves the historical, nay, even the mythical world. This is the beginning of the realm of dreams, to which he gives the most individual shape; everything is forbidden and everything allowed. The sailor is terrified by his dreams; he triumphs over them as their inventor, their creator.

The sand of the islands is dazzling; corals ground down into atoms by the surf. Yet the strength of their gardens has survived; it passes, indestructible, through the great mills of the world. This island: it may also be a fish drowsing in the sun, with palm trees growing on its back.

*

To return to Eumeswil: our islands are populated with malcontents whose communities soon turn out to be the same old societies with all their sense and nonsense. They regard the island as an interregnum, a stopover on the journey to a better world. So they prowl through the institutions, eternally dissatisfied, always disappointed. Connected with this is their love of cellars and rooftops, exile and prisons, and also banishment, on which they actually pride themselves. When the structure finally caves in, they are the first to be killed in the collapse. Why do they not know that the world remains unalterable in change? Because they never find their way down to its real depth, their own. That is the sole place of essence, safety. And so they do themselves in.

The anarch may likewise not be spared prison—as one fluke of existence among others. He will then find the fault in himself. Did he sail too close to Scylla, too near Charybdis? Did he trust the song of the sirens? Odysseus did not stop up his ears, he let the crew stop up their own; but he had himself tied to the mast so he could enjoy the enchantment. He locked himself up. In this way, the prison becomes an island, a refuge of free will, a property.

*

At this point, we ought to touch on origin—that is, heredity and milieu, both of which are overrated. They are the first accidents that we have to confront upon seeing the light of day, whether as bastards in a saloon or as legitimate heirs in a palace. A beggar's staff or a scepter: the handsel of fate; frequently, one has been traded for the other. King Lear roams the heath, a female serf becomes empress. And over and over, Odysseus, the divine endurer, who triumphs now as beggar, now as king.

Origin—a thousand meanings and only *one* sense. The German word *Erbe* (heir, legacy) is cognate with *labor*; the anarch accepts the labor, while any compulsion is contrary to his nature. He is familiar with only one kind of serfdom: the discipline of subordinating his body.

The root of *milieu*, in contrast, is *medius*, and "*médius est celui qui est au milieu*." The anarch recognizes himself as the middle; that is his natural right, which he also grants to everyone else. He recognizes no law—but that does not mean that he despises law or fails to study it meticulously. If his milieu is water, he will move his fins; if it is air, he will spread his wings; he subdues the surf as a flying fish. He knows when to submerge; nor does he shrink from fire.

We are touching upon a further distinction between anarch and anarchist: the relation to authority, to legislative power. The anarchist is their mortal enemy while the anarch refuses to acknowledge them. He seeks neither to gain hold of them, nor to topple them, nor to alter them—their impact bypasses him. He must resign himself only to the whirlwinds they generate.

*

The anarch is no individualist either. He wishes to present himself neither as a Great Man nor as a Free Spirit. His own measure is enough for him; freedom is not his goal; it is his property. He does not come on as a foe or reformer: one can get along with him nicely in shacks or in palaces. Life is too short and too beautiful to sacrifice it for ideas, although contamination is not always avoidable. But hats off to the martyrs.

It is harder to distinguish the anarch from the solipsist, who views the world as the product of his own devising. This attitude, though stepmothered by the philosophers, is widely tenable, as borne out by dreams. The world as a house with its scaffolds is our conception; the world as a garden full of flowers is our dream.

Of course, the solipsist, like all anarchists and as the most extreme one, is hoist by his own petard, since he arrogates to himself an autonomy whose responsibilities are too much for him. If he as an individual has invented society, then he bears the sole guilt for its imperfection; and if it spells his doom, then he bears the sole guilt mythically for his impotence as a poet and logically for an error in thinking.

*

Birth and birthright can destine the anarch to rule; this is one role among others that he has to master. Ruling is a *corvée*, especially for the ruler; a Louis XIV lives in a golden cage with less freedom than the least of his stableboys. Tolstoy, in his history of the Russian campaign, rightfully says that of all the actors Napoleon had the least freedom.

One can judge the caesars by the extent to which they achieved self-realization despite the constraints of fate. In the life of Tiberius, there must have been a turning point, when the glory and misery of ruling became burdensome and he forsook the Capitol for the island—his Capri, which, as Suetonius says, he chose "because it was ringed by steep, sky-high cliffs and deep sea."

This turning point must have predated Tiberius's journey to Campania, from which he never returned to Rome. It was foreshadowed by contradictory actions. Thus, a few days after reprimanding Sestius Gallus in the senate for his debaucheries and revelries, Tiberius invited himself to the man's home, ordering him to modify nothing in his table habits and to have the meal served by naked girls.

The historians have noticed this ambivalence; they have pulled him to pieces, at least regarding the second half of his life. They say he chose Capri as a place where nothing was forbidden and where he could satisfy his cravings on a fantastic scale without being noticed by the public.

They may be right; but for the anarch, this is secondary. The island is a model for the realization of any sort of character; someone else could have picked it in order to live a holy life there when he was repelled by the baseness of the world. There are examples of that, too.

37

I am still having breakfast; Dalin no longer worries me. A suitable death: he atomized himself. In the channels, the little fish are even more aggressive than the big ones; they come in bloodthirsty swarms that even the barracudas avoid.

Dalin's conversations had been instructive although not undangerous; that was why I had reined him in as much as possible, even contradicting him in case my room was wired. His successor's prattling could be heard by anyone. It consisted of intimate disclosures; a tyranny likes it when the individual cultivates his most private secrets. This distinguishes it from despotism, and also from the censorial instincts that prevail in a perfect democracy. Eumeswil has developed a climate that is not unfavorable to the epicure, the artist, the criminal, and even the philosopher. One should be careful only *in politicis*; otherwise, one can get away with a lot. I have demonstrated this in regard to the fate of Salvatore on the one hand and Carnex on the other.

Once, behind my counter, I jotted down a dialogue between the Condor and the Domo about two candidates, one of whom was morally suspect, the other politically. The Domo said, "He would like to saw leisurely on our branch; and he expects a salary and a pension to boot—I don't think he's quite right in the head."

I knew the man, he was a friend of my dear brother's; eventually he became an editor at *The Wren*. Still and all, the journalists who "come to power" have a head start over the professors; they are used to working in the *derrières*.

*

Dalin's successor was one of the cooks, Kung, who had been detailed as a cabin steward. As I have mentioned, the Condor's meals are simple; the Chinese cuisine is his gastronomic reserve for official visitors, especially the Yellow Khan. At such times, it unfolds its arts, which make it superior to any other cookery. In Eumeswil, the Provençal style comes closest, at least in regard to the spices.

Kung is a cook with all his heart and soul; he misses his kitchen and repeatedly sneaks over for a spoonful of something or other. He is in poor shape. In the morning, by the time he waddles into my room, wearing his knee-length robe, he is already wiping his forehead on his sleeve. Around this time, when the senses are well rested, I am especially sensitive to smells—I am not saying that he smells bad, but his odor *is* foreign. Dalin had always brought in something of the bleary-eyed vagabond who fiddles around with acids. Kung smells fishy, though not obtrusively so. His favorite spice is *dayong*, which he blends according to his own recipe. If I run into him during the afternoon, I find it pleasant.

Otherwise he is a good waiter; after setting down his tray and pouring my tea, he stays on for a conversation, with his hands in his sleeves.

His subject matter gravitates toward two poles: one, of course, is the art of cooking, the second his girlfriend Ping-sin, who keeps house down below in the city and waits for him with mounting ardor—he is blatantly intent on convincing me of that.

*

His patter becomes all the more intense the closer we get to the end of his shift. This is true of the Casbah altogether. Just as Salvatore's emblem is the horse and Nebek's (I will get back to him later) the whip, Kung's is the casserole. His two areas of expertise complement each other: hearth and bed. All he lacks to be part of ancient Mandarin culture is literary refinement. He does not miss it; nor is he dependent on concubines, Ping-sin is quite enough for him. I have often seen her in the city when she came prancing out of one of the garish, parti-colored shops. She had on scarlet makeup and was wearing the black satin cap of Kiangnan, an area renowned for its beautiful prostitutes. Trained in music and fancywork, and also in the amorous arts, they are sold practically as children by their parents.

Cookery, as Kung understands it, should foster embonpoint and libido alike. It must be both delicious and arousing. Hence his predilection for gelatinous soups and spicy ragouts, as well as any fish, mussels, holothurians, and crustaceans that come from the ocean. Eel pâté is his pièce de résistance. He also praises certain methods of smoking food, rubbing in ass's milk and camel-hump fat. Supposedly, these procedures are wondrously salubrious.

I usually check my tray to make sure he does not smuggle in his specialties. One morning, before the arrival of his relief, he brought me a blend of honey and pulverized almonds with indefinable ingredients. "Manuelo—you have to drink this on an empty stomach, then you won't be able to stop."

"That's all I need—I don't even want to start."

"Manuelo—you don't live sensibly, you take cold baths, and you're studying your eyes out. Believe me, it's not good for you. Besides, you're not like the other Mediterraneans" (that is his term for dissociating himself from us). "They take pills so they can do it as often as possible. Then it's puff-puff-puff like a choo-choo train."

But he, Kung, was a man who worked in a deliberate fashion, cooking over slow heat until it was done—everything at once, number played no part.

"I won't change my mind; they are rams and you are a salamander. And now, get going—I want to work."

*

Kung could not be offended, or else he did not let on. Willing or not, I also had to listen to what was awaiting him in the evening. Anticipation is part of his pleasure. Ping-sin was inconceivable without her servants; she had to keep her hands soft. She groomed her fingernails and also her toenails. She did the cooking ahead of time. Kung would bring ingredients that he managed to get hold of at the Casbah and also from the innkeepers with a red crab in their signs. They know and honor him as a master chef. Besides, there is always a certain traffic between cooks and innkeepers. The Domo has said, "They get away with anything they can carry inside their coats—but if it's a fish, I don't want to see the tail."

*

Ping-sin has burned incense and put on the lamps; their light is so dim that the only response comes from the intarsia of the chests and armoires. It is strange that, while partial to silk and bamboo, they prefer dark, heavy furniture.

"You know, Manuelo, I want to see the skin clearly, but not sharply." His distinction is not bad; that I must admit. Kung gives his instructions, then the very hot bath comes, and the kimono. They sit down at the table, the domestic waits on them. After serving the soup as the last course and thanking them for the honor, she vanishes for the night. They linger over their tea.

"Get down to business already so I can be rid of you!"

Not on your life. First comes the ceremony of disrobing; he caressingly strips her, leaf by leaf. At last, she sits across from him in the armchair; he feasts his eyes on her. How much time wears by before he reaches toward her without touching, then quickly pulls his hand back, like a fish frightened by bait. Fondling her arms, her shoulders, her knees—he puts everything off until long past midnight.

I hear nothing about the breasts—which I owe less to his discretion than to a dizzy spell that overcomes him. It is like a curtain dropping when the image becomes so intense as to strike him dumb. His permanent smile twists into a grimace, such as one sees on the faces of temple guardians.

*

After Dalin's death, Kung was assigned to me for the duck shack, and he could cause me headaches there—a different kind, but in his fashion. No one can be trusted here when the red color is shown: fire and blood. In this respect, the breakfast conversations are not without value.

I have little faith in national characters—for one thing, because all they yield is the rough average, and also because they grew blurry in the era of the fighting nations and the world state. Chinese are found everywhere and with any skin color. Thus, little can be done with what was said about them by Sir John Barrow, an old traveler and sharp observer, who could make thorough comparisons: "This nation's general character is a singular mixture of arrogance and baseness, of artificial gravity and true contemptibility, of refined courtesy and crude boorishness." One of his contemporaries, a forgotten yet excellent anthropologist named Klemm, said, "This is a description that fits every civilized nation on earth. In a country of millions of individuals, good and bad can be found in all shades."

At the time when Barrow and then later Huc were traveling through China, countless monasteries, all the way into deepest Mongolia, were living by the catechism of Buddha's disciples. It starts with an explanation of the word *shama*, which means "commiseration." The first of its ten commandments is: "Thou shalt kill no living creature, not even the slightest insect." This sounds different from the words of Zebaoth.

*

What struck me as Far Eastern in Kung was the relationship between time and sensuality. Mandarins groom their hands, they let their nails grow incredibly long, they like surfaces that feel pleasant—silk, porcelain, and jade, ivory and lacquer. They twirl fine brushes in their auditory canals. Their physicians have charted a system of sensitive points, a dermatological map.

Supposedly, they also invented the fuse and tell time by means of smoldering cords. Their art of torture has always been notorious. On the other hand, meditation is their forte—spiritual calm against the torrent of surging worlds of images. Their temples are filled with enthroned gods the sight of whom sets you dreaming.

Kung limits himself to matter. Even opium is too spiritual for him; it also blocks the libido. He is a Fabius Cunctator of his desires, a retarder par excellence. He will also know the precise moment for turning his back on the duck shack. He has mulled this over no less thoroughly than I.

"Old friend, you could get into a lot of trouble if you should vanish before I allow you to."

"Emanuelo, I'm surprised at you—I would rather suffer the death of a thousand cuts than run out on you."

38

Nebek is easier to judge in regard to the duck shack. He will cause the least headaches when the killing starts. If I abandon the post, he will continue fighting in the city, especially once the looting begins.

Nebek is Lebanese; he studied in Beirut. He serves in the Casbah during school vacations, and I know him fairly well since he works as an Orientalist at Vigo's institute. Still without a title and ill paid, he ekes out his salary by working as a steward. A small check comes from Beirut every month; he is, or rather was, married.

Vigo sees him only at the institute, not in his garden; he clearly finds this type unpleasant. On the other hand, Vigo respects his knowledge. In the archipelago of history, Nebek has settled on an island where discoveries can still be made even today. Top-drawer Orientalists are rare; the great ones can be counted on the fingers of one hand. This field is enormous, and, as in gnosis, there is something diffuse about it. An innate proclivity is indispensable, if only to overcome the philological barrier. This opens up an immense treasure trove of manuscripts and incunabula, in which the pearls must be separated from the theological donnybrook.

Nebek has the requisite qualities. I, too, found him unpleasant—if only because he kept trying to wrangle his way to my luminar, which, along with my immediate observations at the night bar, forms the bait that holds me in the Casbah. When conjuring, I need utter silence—there the object and here the eye, in lonesome wedlock; the presence of another person would add an obscene touch.

Besides, his subject matter would be distracting. He is researching the great khans—Genghis, Kaidu, Kublai, Bãbur, Timur, and others. They fascinate me only peripherally—where their hordes invaded cultures. There is something elemental, something pulsating in the way they spread out from Outer Mongolia, devastated lands and nations, and then vanished like a bad dream. Perhaps, like ebb and flow, it is one of the tides regulating the earth—but where is the moon? For the historian, in any case, the pickings are slim.

*

One night in the garden we were discussing Nebek, and Vigo confided in me: "I really do not know whether he deserves the title of Orientalist. Actually, he is more of a detective, studying footprints in the sand. And these traces were marked only in cultures. Mongolian horseshoes can still be found along the Rhine. The things that Nebek excavates in the lamaseries are worthless. But he does peruse the Chinese, Persian, Indian, and European sources with a delight in the scars caused by our burns. Here in Eumeswil the masses are ahistorical, an elite is metahistorical, most people vegetate, a few think—but he is antihistorical and he will not feel good until the city starts burning."

*

Vigo lets everyone be; that was why his criticism astounded me. He then spoke more generally: "Whenever the hordes burst in, historical time is snuffed out. Like the crashing of meteors, this lies beyond reckoning. The firmament is left with black holes where one may suspect the presence of, at most, interstellar matter. Our stacks contain a dusty Muscovite chronicle from the reign of Ivan III shortly after he freed himself from such a horde. This backward glance is meager, nor could it be otherwise; I was particularly struck by the conclusion, which naïvely expresses the destruction of time: 'And this intolerable condition endured for four centuries.'

"Yes, nations without homes or calendars, yet sensitive to changes in the weather, lunar nations, without contours sharp enough for the historian. That may be the basis for the aversion that one of our people, a very ancient man, feels toward the Turks."

*

Like any faculty member, Nebek had access to the great luminar—but only down in the institute and for restricted periods. The Great Luminar is a greatly desired passkey, similar to the Gold Phonophore. The users work on apparatuses with limited keyboards.

A comparison with the Freemason lodges suggests itself; there is progress from apprentice to journeyman and then master; a man recognizes himself by his words and handshakes. Many are felled sheerly on account of the technology; memorizing the ideograms until they are effortlessly read and used is an arduous process. The data are more numerous than the molecules in an adult brain. There are also tests.

Up here, Nebek was deprived of the great instrument. I could empathize. He had to make do with a reception that was fed by the stacks of the Yellow Khan; this fitted in with Nebek's specialty, but not with his need for stereoscopy.

His specialty also explains his field trips, which have taken him to those areas, and it thus explains his—albeit modest—political clout. He often hints that the khan granted him an audience. In any event, he participates in the morning rides: not among the followers, like Salvatore (with whom he was well acquainted), but in the closer retinue with the minions and the bodyguards.

His interest in sharing my hours at the luminar also signaled a wish for closer contact. This is something he has in common with the other stewards who wait on me. They sniff neutral soil and come capering out. One hears things that they keep even from their wives, one gets the most intimate glimpses into their private spheres. And what would a historian be without knowledge of human character: a painter equipped with only the pencil, but not the color. On the other hand, I have to be careful. As with every neutrality, one must avoid commitment.

*

Nebek is of medium height, with a good physique, broad shoulders, a narrow waist, and then a wide pelvis—a horseman's figure. His boots, breeches, and leather belt contribute to this image. Upon entering, he was already dressed for the ride and he brought in a whiff of Russia leather. Well groomed, though a bit puffy as after a steam bath—I do not know how many times a day he changes his shirt. He does not like to shake hands.

His hair, not blond as he would like it to be, is pale and waxy; despite his scant beard growth, he is meticulously shaved. I do not know whether he depilates himself; in any case, he did depilate his little dove, as he soon informed me.

Such confessions were preceded by a staking-off of territory. I want to note this, though as a *quisquilia*, because they shed light on the interior staff. After getting up, I am, as I have said, hypersensitive to certain smells—say, leather, horses, and dogs, which I usually find unpleasant, anyway. To which was added the cossack outfit. It was obviously deliberate. Although the subalterns normally use the familiar form with each other, I addressed him formally.

"Tomorrow I would like to see you in the service uniform."

Nebek has a wan face, and not only because, like me, he can never leave the luminar on his nights off. He avoids the sun, his eyes are the palest blue. His features are nervous, they flicker like a brewing storm; for brief moments, they take on a Sarmatian sharpness. The moon is in Sagittarius; at such times, it hits the mark with dreamlike confidence.

He replied in the polite form: "You know as well as I that you are not to give me orders here."

"It would be better, though."

He raised his chin, tried to throw out his chest, began attitudinizing. Then he picked up the tray and left. The next morning, he arrived in a striped smock and with the skiff on his head. He had removed his spurs.

*

Est modus in rebus—one must know the rules, whether one is moving in a tyranny, a demos, or a bordello. This holds, above all, for the anarch—it is his second commandment, next to the first: "Know thyself."

Nebek, no anarch but a man of violent action, had flouted the rules. He was too intelligent not to realize this promptly, and so he adjusted accordingly.

The Domo has a sharp eye for anything concerning greetings and clothing, and rightly so, for therein lies the start of insubordination. If a man is not reprimanded for leaving his top button open, he will soon walk in naked.

Furthermore, down in the institute, I, as Vigo's right hand, was Nebek's superior. And finally, Nebek had his hopes pinned on my luminar. So we soon got along.

Now, it might look as if Nebek's transgression resulted from rudeness; nothing of the sort. Quite the contrary: he had the finest manners imaginable. They were probably linked to his tactile acuteness, his highly sensitive character, which kept him instinctively aloof. In this regard, he moved like a dancing master.

On the other hand—if the dance led out into the dooryards, the mask would drop away.

*

One night, when, after tending bar for a long time, I was sitting with my wine, he walked in unannounced. The moon was full; his face was aquiver. He too had obviously been drinking as well; I poured a glass for him. He was wearing a frogged *litevka*, partly unbuttoned, a fantasy costume. Very white skin underneath. He, likewise, had been working somewhere.

After we had done a lot of drinking, I moved over to him and put my hand on his arm: "Nebek, what's eating you?"

Nothing good emerged. The scene changed. I was sitting next to the degenerate son of an Orthodox priest, in a tavern with cockroaches scurrying across the floor; soiled icons hung on the walls. "La Paloma" was being played on a zither. It was one of the instruments that lie on sheet music; the hand follows the printed cliché.

He had lost the white dove that he had worshiped as a saint—and lost her in an insidious manner. There was no doubting her; she had passed the test to which he had put her. He had told her his dream.

"I am suffering in the lowest hell, which I deserve, but you are resting on the Lord's shoulder. You glance down at my torments. A mere drop of water would ease them, if only for a second; I plead with you. You do not waver—you poke out God's eye and drop it on my tongue—that is salvation: tell me, would you do it?"

He brushed the hair from his forehead: "Yes, Manuel, she promised she would—there was no doubting her. I kissed her feet."

*

I disliked his dream; it brought bad air into the studio. A man may lose his composure, but not his courtesy. Nebek had tendencies in that direction; hence his cleanliness—indeed, his compulsive washing.

It was hot; I pushed the window open and heard the guard's footsteps on the granite. There are sounds that have a cooling effect. A variant of the story of the rich man and poor Lazarus. Very early on, this text had been one of those that especially bothered me in Scripture: Father Abraham in his legalistic arrogance prohibits Lazarus from even slightly moving his finger in order to cool the tongue of the now impoverished man suffering torture in the flames. Swarms of teachers have lived off this drivel.

I sat down opposite Nebek again: "Get to the point. Just what happened?"

*

Beirut is a hot town, where Muslims, Christians, and Jews live cheek by jowl, further split up into sects. Just as there are soils with Uranian virtues, which may have contributed more to evolution than we may allow ourselves to dream, so, too, there are landscapes with incessant religious turmoil. Time is not as productive there as in secular history; it is produced.

The sects include the Druzes and the Maronites; the former trace their origins back to the divine Durûz, the latter to the holy Maro. The two groups have been attacking each other for centuries.

When Nebek had begun his studies there, he rented a room with a Maronite family consisting of a widow and two children: a daughter—that little dove—and her baby brother. They lived in a one-story house near the beach, by the road to Maʿameltein.

The little dove had enchanted him on the very first day—with her shyness, her pallor, her obedience toward her mother, the way she looked after her little brother, the way she adorned the icons and prayed to them.

What had to happen did happen, on a moonlit night like this one; I will skip the classical details—"this child, no angel is so pure."

And, needless to say, the widow promptly noticed it; she did not even seem to mind. It was likewise self-evident that she insisted on marriage before the consequences became visible. Nebek left the house one night and moved to Eumeswil. He was still a student; I met him when he introduced himself to Vigo. We were fascinated by his initial visit. The extremely arcane facts that he presented were joined by a kind of passive suggestiveness, a smiling silence that literally challenged agreement. There was no question that he would receive a scholarship. Besides, he came highly recommended.

*

He soon noticed that he could not get over his little dove; she haunted him. She was more intense in his memory than she had been in his proximity. One day, he went to Vigo: "I would like to get married. We are expecting a baby."

Vigo said, "Congratulations. A child is a great thing—I can only encourage you."

Nebek flew to Beirut and got married according to the Maronite rite; then he returned with his little dove. Although we had little contact outside of school, I once visited his home. It is hard to distinguish between what a man sees in a woman and what dreams he places in her—especially when he sits there with a face that says something like: "Well, what do you think?"

I, in any case, remember her as vaguely as a pastel that one politely puts back after viewing it along with a dozen others. She poured the tea and listened to our conversation, accompanying it with an occasional smile. "Another lunar creature—perhaps she should apply some rouge."

The child came a short time later. It died after taking a few breaths—a boy with an open skull. The Domo had given Nebek some time off; when he returned to the Casbah, he was paler than ever. Of all the horoscopes that he had cast, this was the worst; Mars was rising, Jupiter was down—it was best this way.

*

Of course it was best—I soon found a simpler explanation. With all the things weighing on the wife's mind, she was unable to carry a healthy child to term.

Two circumstances struck me as utterly incredible: she had kept the secret for such a long time, and he, a born policeman and a highly sensitive bloodhound, had discovered it so late. Granted, he had been in a trance that moonlit night, but there had been no lack of evidence before and after. Plainly, this was the blind spot in his eye, something that everyone knows from his own experience.

At some point, however, he must have felt the end of a thread between his fingers; and he pulled himself up like a spider. The rest was mere routine, a torturous inquisition. By his very nature, Nebek was the sort of man who pries into a woman's past; no speck of pollen is allowed on the myrtle. "Damn it, there has always been someone else—the cousin in the arbor or the uncle who took her on his knee."

In this case, the man who had been there first was a student who had lived in the widow's home as Nebek's predecessor. And, just like Nebek, he had departed at night when little Benjamin announced himself—the little dove's baby, and not her baby brother.

*

That sect—*Haeretici ad libanum montem*—is ruled by Old Testament notions. Ascetic rigor enjoys the highest esteem. As do an intact hymen and a blood feud. Hence, Nebek was in the right place.

The widow had claimed to be pregnant and took off for the mountains with her daughter; there the little dove gave birth to Benjamin. When they returned to Beirut, they passed him off as her baby brother. If her father had still been alive, he would have killed his daughter. Even a distant male relative would have done the job.

The fact that the secret was kept so long was something I could attribute only to the docility of the little dove and the strictness of the widow, who, no doubt, had drilled every last detail into the daughter's head. But the tension must have been unbearable.

I learned all this from Nebek when I sat facing him during the moonlit night. He obviously could not stand it anymore. I asked, "Why didn't you—"

"Cut her throat right away?"

"No—why didn't you send her back home? Nearly everyone would find out about such a thing—if not under such gross circumstances. And you're no saint, either."

"Thank goodness. But I am her devil after she was my angel. She more than deserves it. She shouldn't get off that cheaply."

"Nebek, believe me: She is exactly as you sensed she was at the very outset—you saw her substance, those other things are accidents. She is the born sacrificial lamb."

That was precisely the challenge. Deep down, he enjoyed what had happened to him.

*

First he had put pressure on the widow. Flying to Beirut, he subjugated her physically as well. He overpowered her right in the kitchen, satisfying his rage in front of the open fire. "There was no shilly-shallying—she knew instantly." Then came the pension he squeezed out of the widow: her vineyard bit by bit, then eventually the house. The little dove remained in his hands.

Whenever he came down from the Casbah, he would put her on trial; he sat in the armchair—she had to kneel before him. I would rather skip the particulars. He interrogated her more and more narrowly. He had to probe everything deeper and deeper—especially the night when his predecessor had gone to her room. He grilled her down to every last fiber and in slow motion. He must have been suffering from a primal angst that he satisfied through torture.

"Nebek, you won't wipe it out; you're going to kill her. Then you'll mourn her at her grave as a saint and string yourself up in the attic. Just send her back home."

Magma from the Archaean, an overwhelming weight. "Suddenly an awakened fly began to buzz and it fell silent on the ceiling. The prince jumped. 'You did that…?' he finally managed to whisper. 'I—did that,' said Rogozhin just as softly and looked down."

*

"Nebek—this is not the finale: you have to sound yourself out. Tell me—you had early dreams like anyone else, reveries that we indulge in until we know what's at stake—daydreams?"

Yes, he knew what I meant. His parents had enrolled the little boy in the Koran school—a sort of kindergarten for the scions of wealthy families. He had attended it only briefly during a hot, lazy summer in Al Biqa, the fertile valley between the Lebanon and Anti-Lebanon Mountains. I had noticed that he knew how to sit cross-legged; that is something one learns early or never.

"The schoolmaster—his name was Mustafa—was an ignoramus who had no right to have raised his turban; he could read, but only barely. Nonetheless, there wasn't a peep out of us when he strode in; he wore high boots, had his writing tools in his belt and the Book under his arm. The ends of his skinny mustache dangled down to his chest. Mustafa was strict; the parents liked that.

"He planted himself behind his desk, glared at us like an equerry, and launched into the prayer, whereupon we joined in. Next came the recitation, on which he, like all obtuse teachers, placed a supreme value. It wasn't hard for me; I was his favorite pupil, for even back then I could repeat a text flawlessly if someone pronounced it slowly. Bending over down to my waist, I could recite even the second sura, the longest, the one about the cow, as if I were reading it from the page. And I was barely six years old. I was his showpiece. And you know how polite I am.

"Some of my classmates recited more or less well, others badly or not at all. I would then mentally rub my hands together, for I knew what was coming. Mustafa would stroke the ends of his mustache and frown. If he was any sort of master, then it was in punishing. The culprit had to go to the front, loosen his trouser string, and bend over the desk. Then he would get the cane. We would see his face contorting like a gargoyle.

"It struck me that the teacher would favor certain pupils for these reprimands—and not even the worst reciters. His victims were good-looking boys, spoiled sons of effendis, who already sensed what lay in store for them and who began stuttering the instant he eyed them. They were the same boys that I preferred.

"It was already hot in the morning; I would stay in the shadows as I walked to the mosque with my slate, reeling off the assigned sura, but only moving my lips—and I also indulged in agreeable thoughts. One boy or the other would probably get it again.

"And my hopes were seldom dashed. Mustafa would never inflict less than two or three punishments, especially when he was in a good mood.

Strangely enough, my concurrence did not escape him. Whenever he summoned one of our favorites to his desk, he would wink at me—oh, was that good."

*

"Mustafa was my role model; I identified with him. There was an arbor in our garden, and I would go there in the evening to dream about him. This arbor, which was out of the way, was luxuriantly overgrown; even its entrance was concealed by a curtain of vines. Two creepers had interwoven: a bottle gourd and a squirting cucumber. One had been planted by the gardener, the other had settled in as a weed.

"I would sit there like a bird in a green cage until the moon rose. The heavy calabashes were dangling from the trellis by their necks."

Nebek's face had regained its contour; he splayed his fingers as if weighing a gourd.

"And then the squirting cucumbers. Curious fruits, like certain plums, yellow when they ripen. By then, they are tense, like cocked pistols—your finger barely has to graze them, you practically only have to think about them, and they burst open and hurl out their juice and seeds. I had fun with them; the taste was bitter when the charge hit my lips.

"There I became Mustafa, rising to the rank of pasha in him. I called our favorites to the desk in order to interrogate them and I was more severe than he. I did have a variant, however: I also summoned girls. I used to watch them in the neighboring gardens; they were already watched by eunuchs at an early age.

"The girls, too, had to undo their trouser strings; I then ordered them to step forward in pairs so I could investigate what they had done with each other—no amount of denying helped. Just what it was they were supposed to confess—their secret eluded me although they were guilty beyond the shadow of a doubt.

"That was my favorite game in that garden; I often played it until the first birds stirred in the bushes; then I stole back into the house. I am a night person; by then, my pallor was already blatant. My father believed I was studying too hard; he was worried about me."

*

That was Nebek's story. It is strange to see how early the composition of life emerges, to be repeated in destiny. I had already sensed it: he and the little dove were made for each other. It was not her guilt—it was her secret that no torture could wrest from her, a secret that made her guilty and was causing her doom.

The night was brightening, the horses were pawing the ground in the stables, the dogs were baying. I said, "You can't forgive her—I realize that. But recite the divorce formula three times—you have to send her home."

It would be too complicated to describe how I brought this about—indeed, managed to get it done; I had the means at my disposal. Incidentally, it was a wasted effort. *Oleum et operam perdidi.* Scarcely had the little dove arrived in Beirut than the news of her death came from her mother.

Even though the widow cursed him, Nebek flew to Beirut again; there was no dissuading him. He came back even paler than usual; however, there was something—how shall I put it?—inspired about his features. I learned what had happened.

In the winter, people in those climates warm themselves with a *mangal*, a clay or copper basin containing coal; it is placed under the table, from which carpets hang down. It is not hard to poison oneself with the fumes from the coal; such deaths are not rare. That was precisely what the little dove had done and, as Nebek especially emphasized, so cleanly. She had donned festive garb, winding a cloth around her head to avoid tousling her coiffure. Now she was the saint.

*

"Do you smell something?" asked the prince.

"Maybe I do smell something, I don't know. In the morning, people will definitely smell it."

The anarch's relationship to ethos has already been touched on. We must distinguish between ethos and morality. The warrior follows his ethos; this can be morally challenged. Being and custom conflict with each other.

While I may disapprove, I do understand the carryings-on of the commanders and the subalterns in the Casbah, especially the stewards who bring breakfast and are slated to fight at my side in the duck shack.

My disapproval should not color my historical viewpoint. The latter should, above all, avoid guilt and punishment. Guilt and atonement are a different matter. Every man pays for his uniform, every man atones for his guilt.

On the other hand, the anarch has to maintain his aura; this is a need, like the need for pure air. In the street, you likewise avoid stepping on turds. The further behind you leave law and custom, state and society, the more concerned you are with your own cleanliness. The distinction is as great as between the naked and the clad. The uniform sustains only holes; the body, injuries.

I have noted that when they gather in my dear father's home in order to improve the world, the air soon turns bad. No incense helps, no air freshener—you have to go outdoors. Once again, as a historian I am obliged to be there occasionally; this is as indispensable for everyday life as for scholarship. The air smells worst among the anarchists—and they can be found in Eumeswil, too, as they are everywhere and always. I gain access to them through my students, although they regard me as suspect.

The bad odor is related to their intrinsically correct maxim that everyone should live according to his taste—but their taste stinks. One finds types among them who deliberately step on turds and flaunt it as an intellectual achievement. Vigo, although affected by their machinations, is not unbenevolent toward them. "In ten years, they will all be lawyers with stylish haircuts."

*

Fine—just what do they suffer from? An underdeveloped notion of freedom? It is corrected by facts. If they were to dig in one story farther down and recognize themselves as anarchs, they would be spared a great deal. They would seek freedom in themselves and not in the collective.

At first blush, the anarch seems identical with the anarchist in that both assume that man is good. The difference is that the anarchist believes it while the anarch concedes it. Thus, for the anarch it is a hypothesis, for the anarchist an axiom. A hypothesis must be confirmed in each individual case; an axiom is unshakable. It is followed by personal disappointments. Hence, the history of anarchism is a series of schisms. Ultimately, the individual remains alone, a despairing outcast.

The goodness that guides the anarch's conduct is not an axiom in Rousseau's sense but a maxim of practical reason. Rousseau had too many hormones and Kant too few; the former moved the world through confession, the latter through cognition. The historian must do justice to both.

39

Breakfast is over; Nebek removes the dishes. I have gotten slightly ahead of myself: he has not yet recited the divorce formula—if we move to the duck shack beforehand, I will have to weigh the possibility of knocking him off.

It has already grown hot; the cicadas are strumming in the thornbushes on the hillside of the stronghold; the parasitic kite circles above the slaughterhouse at the eastern edge of the city. Despite the distance, I see the bird distinctly in the clear air.

I have the evening off; unless I get a call, the day belongs to me. I bolt the door, close the shutters, slip out of my robe. The armchair stands at the right distance from the luminar; next to my chair lies the indicator with its keyboards, various card files, and other instruments. The arrangement is well known, but the wand I hold in my hand is a secret. It is even rarer in Eumeswil than the Gold Phonophore. However, any child knows how to use the phonophore, whereas here years of training are required merely for the technical aspect. Nor does the latter suffice if the instrument is forgotten. Then the wand functions as an extension of the hand. It becomes magnetic: the facts leap across.

The material is inexhaustible; it was accumulated over centuries that can be regarded as the great era of historiography. The overview grew to the same extent that the political impulse waned along with its passions. Countless scholars found their final haven here—an illusionary refuge. One of the best legacies of the world state is the fact that these efforts formed a collaboration. Granted, there were variants, but they heighten the stereoscopic pleasure. In the palace of Tiberius, the imperator and the slave, the captain of the praetorian guards, the cook, and the fisherman have equal rights. Everyone is the center of the world. If I dwelled on that point, I would get lost in the mazes of an opium night.

*

First, literature. What we call a "source" is actually fixed, an era's sediment in its written signs. But just one hammer blow, and the water spurts from the rock.

A letter of the alphabet also contains an immediate secret, like the corals in the petrified reef. The molecules have remained as they were shaped by life and they can be reanimated.

A supratemporal core can be discovered in matter and liberated from it. These are resurrections. Here, the view leads beyond knowledge—indeed, beyond art—to the high noon of the present. The hand that wrote the text becomes one's own. At the same time, quality becomes less important; the drama of history is woven entirely from the yarn of the Norns. The distinctions are created by the interplay of the folds, not by the cloth. People used to say, "Before God all are equal."

*

Normally, answers to the previous day's inquiries lie in an open mailbox. They concern my own works or those I supervise, like Nebek's or Ingrid's. Plus what Basleda, a Swabian, calls "a sheer pastime."

An inserted question may be: "Re: rue Saint-Honoré. Who aside from Robespierre lived in the house of the cabinetmaker Duplay? What became of him and of Eléonore? Extract from the 1789 speech in which Robespierre demanded that the National Assembly abolish slavery in the colonies and capital punishment in the kingdom itself. How high were the towers of the Bastille?"

And so forth. The apparatus spits out the answers in the required format. The height of the Bastille was seventy-three feet and three inches. Almost no light fell into its courtyard. The promenade on the towers was better; it was considered a privilege.

As for Duplay, there is no need to leaf through the property records and address cadastres—he is instantly found among ten thousand namesakes in the central population register. If he has even the slightest importance, then references lead to further indexes—say, the Archives of Correspondence or the bibliographies. A petrified memory, tremendous—and on the other hand, the sphinx that responds.

*

Without budging from my chair, I can manage this mechanical part by means of analytical adjustments from the Casbah. I scroll the texts on the monitor, pulling out whatever documents I need. In Eumeswil, there are scholars, like Kessmüller, who fabricate their works in this manner. They are not worth dwelling on.

Those underworlds that have survived all the firestorms must have minds that can associate in an original way—men who may even have united in a kind of republic of scholars. And I suspect it might be possible to get to them when the studies up here have reached their ultimate degree. Perhaps only a single word will suffice, a sign—but this is guesswork.

At times, I have made futile efforts at playing a game that secret services instigate with and against each other. Information comes that can scarcely be located through record offices—but it is always anonymous and machine-processed. It never involves a personal dialogue—only information that is unthinkable without intuition. For example:

Question: "The collective spirit can be stimulated to a certain degree that compels unanimity. The problem would be simple if assent were imposed, but in extreme cases there has to be a demand that allows no other choice and that heaves up and subjugates the individuals like a wave. I need a striking example."

Information: "Paris, rue Saint-Honoré, 2:00 to 3:00 A.M., August 10, 1792, of the Christian era. Cosmic time follows."

Even those words seemed to go beyond mere numerals. Were they hinting that this was the first time I was dealing with that street? An initial feeler? It could scarcely be a coincidence. Then came the example: an excerpt from the memoirs of the Marquise de la Rochejaquelein.

This woman, a close friend of Princess Lamballe, whose atrocious death was imminent, had played a heroic part during the fighting in the Vendée. A peasants' war was raging there; aside from its name, it had little in common with the one that had devastated Germany almost three centuries earlier. The Vendéan uprising came later chronologically, but earlier morphologically—it was still Gothic; it was fought by the three primary estates in unison; knights, peasants, and clerics. In Germany, by contrast, an estate in a new sense had stirred, still unclearly. The German peasant had come too early, the Vendéan too late. The German banners had shown bread and boots, the French the lilies.

The Vendéans made a good choice; the marquise was indubitably the paragon of a both intrepid and reactionary person. That night, she and her husband crossed the Champs-Elysées, where more than a thousand people had been massacred during the day. They saw fires at the barricades, heard shots and shrieks. At place Louis XV, they were stopped by a drunkard who boasted of killing many people that day; he was now charging toward the Tuileries "*pour aller tuer les Suisses.*"

There are nights when the air is virtually charged with gunpowder. There are also squares and streets, the major arteries of big cities, where terror is repeated. No matter what the wise men say: blood works more changes than a thousand debates at the Convention. The distinctions fuse together.

Her husband was unable to calm down the marquise, who was beside herself. She began screaming: "Long live the sans culottes; to the lanterns, smash the windows."

Clearly, this lady was not only courageous but also honest, for she includes this incident in her memoirs, even though others would have suppressed or simply forgotten it.

*

So much for the transmission of texts and their combination. The Tower of Babel was dismantled brick by brick, quantified, and rebuilt. A question-and-answer game leads to the upper stories, the chambers, the details of its appointments. This suffices for the historian who practices history as a science.

However, the luminar offers more. Not only was an encyclopedia of inconceivable dimensions created in the catacombs, it was also activated. History is not only described, it is also played. Thus, it is summoned back into time; it appears in images and persons. Both scholars and artists must have been at work, even clairvoyants who peered into crystal balls. At midnight, when I call up one of the great scenes, I am directly participating in what is virtually a conjuration.

Certainly there are objections. My dear old dad generally refuses to employ this part of the luminar; it offends his sense of historical precision. But then how precise is historiography—say, Plutarch's? The great speeches of kings and generals before a battle? Was he present? He must have put the words into his heroes' mouths. And why not? Besides, I often hear better things from the luminar. And the sources of the era that introduced speaking machines are terribly meager.

40

Both the texts and the spectacles in the luminar are beneficial to my study of anarchy, which is my secret focus. I summon the leading and marginal figures of theoretical and applied anarchism from *The Banquet of the Seven Sages* to the *dinamiteros* and bombthrowers of Paris and Saint Petersburg.

Let me make a general comment on the luminar. Whenever people appear in the spectacle, remarks and replies are put into their mouths, often brilliantly. However, the catacombs must have an elite that tries to reach further. The people are supposed to answer on their own! This would not be altogether impossible, even technologically; it would constitute a supreme level of automatism. There were early efforts—in the automated chess games, the artificial doves and turtles, the Point Office in Heliopolis. Clearly, more is intended—namely, resurrection. This touches on other networks: reminiscences of Faust, Swedenborg, Jung-Stilling, Reichenbach, and Huxley—of constantly reiterated attempts to degrade the material not metaphysically but...yes, this is where the problem begins.

*

Words that are to be intensified by the suffix *-ism* reveal a special demand, a volitional tendency, often hostility a priori. The motion becomes tumultuous at the expense of the substance. These are words for sectarians, for people who have read only one book, for those who "pledge allegiance to their flag and are unconditionally committed to their cause"—in short, for traveling salesmen and peddlers of commonplaces. A conversation with someone who introduces himself as a realist usually comes to a vexatious end. He has a limited notion of the thing, just as the idealist does of the Idea or the egoist of the self. Freedom is labeled. This also holds for the anarchist's relationship to anarchy.

In a town where thirty anarchists get together, they herald the smell of fires and corpses. These are preceded by obscene words. If thirty anarchists live there without knowing one another, then little or nothing happens; the atmosphere improves.

What is the basis of the mistake that claimed countless victims and that will operate endlessly? If I kill my father, I fall into my brother's hands. We can expect as little from society as from the state. Salvation lies in the individual.

*

These encounters at the luminar could fill a book. There would also be repetitions. The guiding thought—the anarch's relationship to the anarchist—is simple, despite all the variants. Besides, the distinction is merely one of degree, not one of principle. As in everyone, as in all of us, the anarch is also concealed in the anarchist—the latter resembling an archer whose arrow has missed the bull's-eye.

Whatever we may ponder, we have to start with the Greeks. The polis in its multiplicity: a test-tube system that risked any and all experiments. It contains everything—from the topplers of the Hermae and the killers of tyrants to the utter withdrawal from the quarrels of the world. In this respect, Epicurus can be considered a paragon with his ideal of painlessness founded on virtue. There is no intervention from the gods, who enjoy human efforts as a spectacle; the most we can hope for from the state is security—the individual should stay as free of the state as possible.

*

I soon had to abandon my plan to group the personnel around two poles. Say: on one side, the dreamers, the enthusiasts, the utopists; on the other side, the thinkers, the planners, the systematists; the demarcation is not sharp. Feelings and thoughts correspond, person and thing, state and society melt into one another. The wave, irresistible in the surf, dissolves into foam because of both its own fatigue and the external resistance. This is demonstrated by practice—for example, the schisms of the Anabaptists or the Saint-Simonians. Caution is especially called for when messianic claims are voiced.

I reviewed Fourier's world plan in the luminar. It was presented as implemented in a surrealist version. There were no more towns or villages. The planet bristled with gigantic high rises, the phalansteries. These white towers were separated by their attached agricultural areas, which were run and farmed as cooperatives. I must admit that the sight had something majestic about it, as Fourier had dreamed. Indeed, there were approaches to his ideal in the course of history. Dreams and images always precede reality.

Some features that seemed utopian back then have actually been surpassed; in that era of the Physiocrats, when agriculture still predominated, there were men who foresaw the technological worlds; these too were, after all, founded on dreams. Granted, the blueprints often resembled palaces without stairs, but some plans were carried out.

The environment was already taken into account; thus the collaboration of the phalansteries has produced a difference in climate, and indeed a favorable one. An agreeable, harmonious temperature prevails everywhere, as under a glass roof. Seawater has become potable, the wild beasts are tame. The whole earth becomes habitable—even the deserts, and also the poles, above which heat radiates from torrents of light. The population will grow to three billion. People attain a height of six-foot-eight and live to be 150. The number three plays a major role; it reveals a harmonious spirit. Work is subdivided into necessary, useful, and pleasant. Yields are distributed to three classes: capital, labor, and talent. A woman can live with a spouse, a lover, a procreator, or even all three at once. A man has the same choices. Children are raised by their grandmothers.

Fourier's basic idea is excellent: namely, that Creation failed in its very casting. His error is that he considers Creation reparable. Above all, the anarch must not think progressively. That is the anarchist's mistake; he thereby lets go of the reins.

Not even Fourier can do without authority. A phalanstery is ruled by a unarch, a million phalansteries by a duarch, the totality by the omniarch.

A phalanstery is tenanted by four hundred families. Considering what goes on in just a two-family house in Eumeswil, one can imagine the chaos. It soon starts to smell; then the unarch has to intervene "with an iron rod." He may even have to summon the duarch.

Fourier found a patron who supplied land and capital for setting up the first phalanstery. The enterprise collapsed at the very outset.

*

Two reefs tower in front of the anarchist. The first, the state, must be overcome, especially in a hurricane, when the waves soar. He ineluctably runs aground on the second one, society, the very image that flickered before him. There is a brief intermezzo between the fall of the legitimate powers and the new legality. Two weeks after Kropotkin's funeral cortege, in which his corpse had followed the Black Banners, the sailors of Kronstadt were liquidated. This is not to say that nothing had happened in between—Merlino, one of the disillusioned, hit the nail on the head: "Anarchism is an experiment."

Hence also the endless squabbles between anarchists, syndicalists, and socialists of all stripes—between Babeuf and Robespierre, Marx and Bakunin, Sorel and Jaurès, along with all the others whose names, but for the luminar, would have been effaced like footprints in sand.

Aside from maxims that occasionally flash through the fog, reading these things is like reading the Church Fathers: sterile and often annoying for endless stretches. Moreover, just as all their roads but led back to Rome, here all roads have but led to Hegel ever since the nineteenth Christian century.

When I summoned Bakunin to the luminar, other problems arose. First of all: how to explain the role of the *jeunesse dorée* in the worldwide activities of the anarchists? There is no lack of princes, of sons and daughters of the upper bourgeoisie and the high military, as well as students, who have never held a hammer.

And how can we explain the link between pity and extreme brutality in their actions? These may be combined in a single person or split between several. A classical encounter between left-wing and right-wing aristocrats is that of Florian Geyer with his brother-in-law, who felled him with his own hand. The peasants did not even want to have the nobles join their uprising.

During his wanderings, Don Quixote hears the yammering of a servant whose master has tied him to a tree for some delinquency and is punishing him cruelly. The knight releases the unfortunate and inflicts a penance on the tormentor. No sooner has the knight ridden off than the servant is tied to the same tree and disciplined even more horribly. The knight has made enemies of both men.

Time and again, these stories include the conflict with the father and also with the brother. I believe it was Bakunin from whom I heard the following anecdote. During a meal, the father was annoyed because the servant had broken a dish or made a mistake while serving. Next came what the children feared and shuddered at: the father penned a note to the nearest police station, demanding twenty strokes for the servant. When the note was dispatched, the children hugged the servant in order to weep with him—but he shoved them away; he refused to have anything to do with them.

Being excluded is bad. It leaves scars. Similar things can be found in Tolstoy. Back then, people ran gauntlets.

*

Taking part in civil but not national wars is consistent with anarchist logic. There are exceptions, also transitions—an uprising, for instance. Bakunin combines anarchism with Slavophilia. Garibaldi, a national hero with a dash of anarchism, toured the theaters of war on two continents. It stood him in good stead that he had practiced the use of weapons at sea and on land. By contrast, a dismal spectacle is offered by the pure ideologist who "seizes power" for days or weeks.

For the anarchist, too, war is the father of all things; he rightfully pins great hopes on it. Clausewitz's maxim that war is a continuation of politics by other means holds for the anarchist but in a converse sense: at every declaration of war, he sniffs morning air. In the world civil war, a diffuse army of anarchistic partisans operates between the fighting nations and parties. These partisans are used and used up.

There are few anarchic maelstroms that whirl in the torrent of history for weeks or longer; they presume a political stalemate. The classical example is the Paris Commune within a Gallo-Germanic war in the late nineteenth century of the Christian *saeculum*. It was cited by both socialists and communists.

We can also warm our hands at the fires of history, albeit from a prudent distance. Timeless things, seeping uncannily into time, can be felt. Just as war is the father of all things, so, too, is anarchy their mother; a new age is ushered in.

41

Pain is the historian's portion. It strikes him particularly hard when he ponders the fate of the do-gooders. An endless lament and an eternal hope are handed down through the generations like a torch that keeps going out.

In the luminar, the images are three-dimensional; according to my whim, I can sit with the Montagnards or the Girondists in the Convention, occupy the seat of the chairman or the concierge, who may have the best overview of the situation. I am at once plaintiff, lawyer, and defendant—whichever I like. My passion flows into the parties like an electric current.

This topic often takes me to Berlin. I visit this city shortly before Hegel's death, moving about there for roughly two decades—more precisely, until the uprising of 1848 of the Christian era.

This revolution is bizarre in that throughout the European countries where it took place, it achieved the exact opposite of its goals, thereby damming up the world torrent for nearly a hundred years. The reasons have been examined from different vantage points. In medicine, such a process is known as *maladie de relais*: a disease providing new impulses—in this case, say, Bismarck and Napoleon III. That would be a verdict such as Kaunitz would have issued had he lived until that period. From the viewpoint of the first German parliament, which met in 1848, the crisis did not lead to a recovery; instead, it launched a chronic illness. Naturally, they lacked any sense of self-criticism. I believe they failed because idealistic prattlers like my dear old dad were in the majority. Such people economize with that "special sap"—blood.

*

At first blush, the choice of place may seem inappropriate for this topic. Sunday morning, Unter den Linden: Berlin impressed me as a royal residence tenanted half by soldiers, half by philistines. The relief guards headed toward the castle and the Brandenburg Gate, goose-stepping whenever a frogged officer heaved into view; in the center lane, the cavaliers were returning from their morning ride through the Tiergarten. Gentlemen in high hats and ladies in leg-of-mutton sleeves were coming from the Church of the Trinity on Mauerstrasse. Schleiermacher's sermons were still well attended. The Brandenburg air is dry; Schelling had disappointed them, Schopenhauer had been disappointed.

I did not turn toward the castle on the river Spree, although I would have liked to visit the monarch in his private apartments. Here again we have the difference between anarchist and anarch: the anarchist pursues the ruler as his mortal enemy, while the anarch's relationship to him is objective and neutral. The anarchist wants to kill the monarch, while the anarch knows he *could* kill him—but his reasons would have to be personal, not general. If the anarch is also a historian, then the monarch offers him a highest-ranking source—not only for political decisions, but also for the typical structure of the epoch. No two pharaohs are alike. But each mirrors his time.

*

The anarch can face the monarch unabashedly; he feels like an equal even among kings. This basic mood affects the ruler; he senses the candid look. This produces a mutual benevolence favorable to conversation.

I want to touch on the external forms—say, the manner of address. Was it necessary for the poet Georg Herwegh to employ an insolent tone in his letter to Friedrich-Wilhelm IV of Prussia? There were teutomaniacs who deliberately soiled their boots before entering the Congress of Vienna—those are resentments.

People like hearing themselves addressed personally—whether by surname, first name, nickname, or by title or distinction. Sire, Excellency, Doctor, Monsignor, Comrade Jones, my sweet bunny. "It takes a title to arouse their confidence"—this provides a good start for the meeting. Metternich was a master of such niceties.

"To each his own"—not the worst of the Prussian maxims. In this context, the anarch, sure of what is his own, indulges in a smidgen of irony.

*

The talk I would have liked to have with that ruler concerned one of the recurrent figures—namely, the way an ideal shatters against the power of the Zeitgeist, which degrades the ideal into an illusion. Such failures are repeated in the romantic interludes that separate the historical scenes.

I knew he was poring over the writings of Donoso Cortés, whom he soon accredited as the Spanish chargé d'affaires. Spain is one of the great strongholds of reactionism, just as England is a bulwark of liberalism, Sicily of tyranny, Silesia of mysticism, and so forth. "Blood and soil"—this inspired muttonheads, who amused blockheads.

Herwegh and the king were united in their ideal: that of the Christian crown menaced by the atheistic socialism that was being heralded. And both men saw liberalism as the stirrup holder or, according to Saint-Simon, the *chausse-pied*, the boot hook of the new titans, the future lords of the world.

Only the Spaniard saw more sharply than the Prussian; he gazed a hundred years farther and realized that the catastrophe threatening the sacred order could not be staved off. His basic attitude was not idealism, but despair.

"*Je marche constamment entre l'être et le néant.*" This did not become modern until a century later. Along with all the usual exaggerations voiced by all ultras and radicals, there are crystal splinters, such as the fact that the abolition of the legal death penalty was the signal for illegal butchery.

Fine, the historian should not take sides. He must also see the zoological and the physical terrain under the social humus. For him, reactionism is a movement like any other—indeed, one indispensable to progress, which it accompanies as shadow does light. In harmonious times, this can assume the form of a dance. The parliaments were unthinkable without oppositions; even today, I still play intellectual duels in the luminar—such as those between Pitt and Fox.

*

Like some members of his family, the Prussian monarch was a good speaker—which is a dubious gift for a ruler. In his dislike of parliaments, he was one with Donoso: he refused point-blank "to transform the natural bond between ruler and people, a bond drawing so much power from its inner truth, and turn it into a conventional, constitutional relationship."

Using the luminar, I inquired about the advice that Donoso could have given him. In the archives that administer the past, good minds had pondered this question thoroughly. Without a doubt, Donoso would have propagated the coup d'état. However, the legitimate ruler is least qualified for this vocation; by resorting to it, he retreats from the focus of his power. Dictatorship is not hereditary.

Conversations between utopists and idealists—even when merely driven by reality without affecting it—are highly appealing to the historian: seedlings in a glass house before the hailstorm. Donoso had to seek his enemies in other utopists—say, in the anarchistic socialism of a Proudhon, while he failed to perceive Marx. He did regard Hegel, however, as a "devastator of brains."

Yet every new chimney that started smoking was a contraindication. The machine-stormers had realized this earlier and more clearly. After all, they celebrated their return in the twenty-first Christian century.

*

These reruns of the great games, now on one side, now on the other, increase the historian's pain. He plays not against one, not against the other, nor even against both; rather, he plays against the mighty Cronus, who devours his children, and then against Chaos, who gave birth to Cronus.

*

My stroll across the decades in Germany before the Revolution of 1848 does not, as I have said, lead me to the castle; instead, at the Café Kranzler with its famous smoking room and its "service with a tender hand," I turn off into Friedrichstrasse. My goal is Jacob Hippel's wine garden, established at house no. 94 for decades now.

I linger almost as often on this street as on rue Saint-Honoré. At various times, I have stood not there but between the barricades—for example, during March 1848, after the fateful shot was fired in front of the castle, then again at the end of the two great wars between the red flag and the swastika. I was there when the barricade hardened into a wall and once again when it was razed. I marched under various monarchs and presidents to the drill grounds and back to the barracks. I accompanied the tanks from the Reich Chancellery until they were blown up at the Weidendammer Bridge. I also visited the garrets—Schadow's northern room, where he drew; the student digs where Friedrich Hielscher brooded about the autonomy of the self. Across the street there was a cabaret, the Bonbonnière; I conversed with the women who were walking their beat.

So this time, Hippel's wine garden was my goal. In those years, it was the meeting place for a circle of men who, enjoying some modest attention from both the educated public and the police, were known as "the Free Men." They were categorized as part of the "far left"; their common traits were intelligence, intellectual independence, and discontent with the status quo. Otherwise they were very different in their views and designs—an explosive group.

Another shared feature was their encounter with Hegel; it had left scars or neuralgic points. Bruno Bauer, having been dismissed from the university faculty and now running a publishing house combined with a cigar shop, was widely known and feared as a Bible critic. He had studied under Schleiermacher, for whom he had attacked Strauss and his "historical Christ." The reason for his dismissal was provided by his "Trumpet of the Last Judgment," which he had blasted against Hegel. Altenstein, his protector, had dropped him because of that pamphlet, saying he "was developing too far to the left"—the typical blunder of a government minister unable to survey the overall climate.

Like those of the peasant's insurrections, these quarrels were tied to the Gospels. For the first stirrings of the theological current, the place of freedom must be determined and secured. The Free Men sought this place in the individual person. Through its own "self-awareness," freedom would become the focal point of action. Personal freedom, they said, had to be safeguarded on all sides, be it against the state, the Church, liberalism, or the growing socialist movement. For those men, all these things were part of the "masses," restricting and inhibiting the "absolute emancipation of the individual."

*

A regular customer at Hippel's was Buhl, if he happened not to be incarcerated. A critical mind: I glanced through the few issues of his journal, *The Patriot*, in the luminar. He may have been the first man to formulate the maxim that one should reject not the current form of a state, but its essence. This is an insight that the anarchist lacks; it can be applied to capital as well. State capitalism is even more dangerous than private capitalism because it is directly tied to political power. Only the individual can succeed in escaping it, but not the group. This is another reason why the anarchist fails. Perhaps it was this insight that moved Bruno Bauer to proclaim "lack of conviction" as the ideal of the Free Men before he returned to his studies of history.

In the beginning, Marx and Engels, who were to play a worldwide role later on—albeit dead—frequented the get-togethers of the Free Men. In the long run, needless to say, the atmosphere was not to their liking; they wanted to take over the state, not abolish it. Gradually, yet more and more distinctly, the Free Men distanced themselves from them. Apparently, Marx and Engels suspected them of paving the way for what was known some hundred years later as "an artillery position."

The dislike was mutual; it was recorded in, among other places, a pamphlet issued by the Marx-Engels Dioscuri after their departure from Berlin: *The Holy Family, or Critique of Critical Critique, against Bruno Bauer and Consorts.*

Such encounters make it obvious that the socialists recognize their archenemy not in the state or in the Church or in capitalism; all those institutions, clarified by scholarship and refashioned by propaganda, can be replaced. Their struggle is waged not against but for power. Their deadly foe is anarchy, represented on the one side by the idealistic anarchist and on the other by the lumpenproletariat, which, in a crisis, casts off the final trappings of law and order, and even humanity, and closes the debate. In order for them to resume under a new constellation, all those entities, indispensable at absolute zero, are the first that must be liquidated.

42

The air was bad, as it is wherever people are debating. One must put up with it. My goal in visiting the Free Men was not to observe one of the great minds about whom whole libraries were then written. Indeed, a personal encounter only weakens the impact.

I was researching a customer who seldom participated in the conversations. He sat silently in front of his glass, smoking with visible relish. Supposedly, a good cigar was his sole passion. In any case, he had accomplished little in his profession (he taught at a finishing school), his marriage, or his literary efforts (with a single exception).

His wife, interviewed by Mackay in London many years after the divorce, had nothing good to say about her ex-husband. They had wed in their Berlin apartment under what were then scandalous circumstances, with Buhl and Bruno Bauer as witnesses. When the clergyman, a high-ranking councilor of the consistory, appeared, Buhl emerged from the next room in his shirtsleeves. The bride, too, arrived late, without myrtle or veil—they had neither a Bible nor wedding bands. Bruno Bauer contributed two brass rings that he detached from his purse. The Berlin rumor mill turned them into curtain rings. After the wedding, they all remained together, drinking beer and returning to the card game that they had been playing beforehand.

The couple had met at the get-togethers of the Free Men. The wife, needless to say, was emancipated; her ideal was George Sand. But in London she turned sanctimonious. She no longer wanted to hear about her marriage, and she told Mackay that her husband was crafty, cunning, and underhanded—she summed him up with the English word "sly." She had brought some money into the household, but he had drunk it up and gambled it away. Her statements were probably valid to the extent that he had squandered it on bizarre projects. Like many literati, he was impractical but had bright ideas that he would have done better to use in novels than in commerce.

Thus, he realized that the dairy industry, which was still being run in a medieval fashion, would be improved if centralized. But he had not reckoned with the housewives: they were accustomed to their farmer, who would appear with his dogcart at the crack of dawn. The customers stayed away. The milk turned sour and flowed into the gutters. But the idea was good, as demonstrated by a shrewd businessman, who shortly carried it out, thereby raking in a fortune.

*

I can see him sitting there and smoking, a delicate profile. The sketch that Friedrich Engels drew from memory in London captures only the middle part of the face: the straight nose and the fine mouth. It was revised by the media service in the luminar. The new version also had the high, though less receding, forehead, which is *Stirn* in German. And indeed, he, Johann Kaspar Schmidt, had been nicknamed Stirner by one of his fellow students at the University of Königsberg; later on, he used the pseudonym "Max Stirner."

His signatures are likewise delicate; one notices that the final stroke sinks with the years. Incidentally, he died not by his own hand but from a fly sting that became infected. A banal life: misspent in profession and business, a failed marriage, debts, a regular tavern table with the standard blabber preceding the German revolution, a high-level philistine—the usual stuff.

His literary output—essays and critiques in newspapers and journals—is equally unimportant; it was already forgotten during Stirner's lifetime and would have been consumed by the firestorms had it not been preserved by the luminar. Yet these little leaves, which, in times of crisis, sprout like mushrooms from the humus and then perish, are invaluable for the historian who wishes to study ideas *in statu nascendi*. They are covered by the rubble of revolutions.

And the Marx-Engels pamphlet attacking Stirner—*Saint Max*, a folio manuscript of several hundred pages—also very nearly disappeared. By the time it was excavated, it was already well gnawed by the mice. Engels had entrusted it to a cabinetmaker named Bebel. The luminar restored the text.

The manuscript was begun in 1845 of the Christian era, the year when Stirner's magnum opus, *The Only One and His Own*, was published. This study is the exception I mentioned above. Thus, the polemics must have sprung from an immediate impression.

*

All derision contains a speck of truth, as does the epithet "Saint" Max. Stirner found his Saint Paul in John Mackay, who took saintliness very seriously—for example, when he put Stirner's tome above the Bible:

> Just as this "holy" book comes at the beginning of the Christian era in order to carry its devastating effect to almost every last corner of the inhabited earth, so, too, the unholy book of the first self-aware egoist comes at the start of the new era—to exert an influence as beneficial as that of the "Book of Books" was pernicious.

And then he quotes the author:

> A tremendous, ruthless, shameless, unconscionable, arrogant crime, perpetrated against the holiness of *every* authority.

*

Such claims are not new. Even Franciscans have dared to maintain that the earthly life of Jesus was "notably surpassed" by that of their founder. De Sade was elevated to "the divine marquis"—a similar approval is given to every border-crosser. In regard to Helvétius, who put personal happiness above all else, and whose book *De l'esprit* (1758) was burned in Paris, a clever lady said that this work had "bared every person's secret." I heard this in Auteuil, at the luminar, from the author's both intelligent and charming wife.

The characteristic feature of the great saints—of whom there are very few—is that they get at the very heart of the matter. The most obvious things are invisible because they are concealed in human beings; nothing is harder to evince than what is self-evident. Once it is uncovered or rediscovered, it develops explosive strength. Saint Anthony recognized the power of the solitary man, Saint Francis that of the poor man, Stirner that of the only man. "At bottom," everyone is solitary, poor, and "only" in the world.

*

It takes no genius to make such discoveries, only intuition. They can be granted to a trivial existence, they are as clear as day. That is why they cannot be studied like systems; they are revealed through meditation. To get back to the art of archery: it is not certain that the most skillful archer has the truest aim. A dreamer, a child, a crackpot may be the one who pulls it off. Even the bull's-eye has a midpoint: the center of the world. It is not spatial, it is hit not in time but in the timeless interval. One of Stirner's benign critics (he had few of these; but lots of enemies) called him the "metaphysician of anarchism."

Crackpots are indispensable; they operate gratuitously, weaving their fine nets through the established orders. While skimming these forgotten journals, I came across a surprising item. A psychiatrist had taken the trouble to decipher the notes of a "mentally disturbed female," a "serving-girl who was declared legally incompetent because of her idiocy." While interpreting them, he had been struck by acutely logical maxims that fully coincided with Stirner's cardinal points.

Paranoia: "The illusion generally evolves into a coherent logical system and is not to be refuted by counterarguments." *Spiritus flat ubi vult*—the spirit blows where'er it will. This recalls a certain philosopher's judgment of solipsism: "An invincible stronghold defended by a madman."

Stirner, incidentally, is no solipsist. He is the Only One, like Tom, Dick, or Harry. His special trait is simply that he recognizes himself as such. He resembles a child playing with the Koh-i-noor he has found in the dust. His keeping the diamond for himself is consistent with his nature; it is peculiar that he has told others. Fichte, teaching in Berlin one lifetime earlier, also discovered—or better, "exposed"—this jewel in the self-setting of the self; unnerved perhaps by his own boldness, he wrapped it in philosophical obscurity. Nevertheless, he too was disparaged as a solipsist.

*

Now just what are the cardinal points or the axioms of Stirner's system, if one cares to call it that? There are only two, but they suffice for thorough reflection:

1. That is not My business.
2. Nothing is more important than I.

No addenda are required. Needless to say, *The Only One and His Own* immediately triggered lively protests and was so thoroughly misunderstood that its author was declared a monster. When the book appeared in Leipzig, it was instantly confiscated: the minister of the interior reversed the ukase, saying the book was "too absurd to be dangerous."

Stirner's response: "Let a nation do without freedom of the press. As for Me, I will hit on some trick or act of violence in order to print my work; I will obtain the permission only from Myself and My strength."

The word "monster" is also ambiguous. It derives from *monere* (remind); the author set up one of the great monuments. He made the self-evident evident.

The rebukes against him concentrated—nor could it be otherwise—in the reproach of egoism, a concept with which Stirner himself never fully came to terms. Still, he annexed it, often replacing *Einziger* (Only One) with *Eigner* (owner, proprietor). The owner does not fight for power, he recognizes it as his own, his property. He owns up to it, appropriates it, makes it his own. This process can be nonviolent, especially as a strengthening of the self-awareness.

"Everything should be my business, but never My business. 'Fie on the egoist.' However, God, mankind, the sultan have all based their business on nothing but themselves, and it is from these great egoists that I wish to learn: nothing is more important to Me than I. Like them, I too have based My business on Nothing."

The owner does not fight with the monarch; he integrates him. In this respect, he is akin to the historian.

*

The discoverer has his delights. When I began dealing with *The Only One*, I could not help discussing it with Vigo. He showed interest; sitting under the cypresses in his garden, we delved into this topic while the moon hung over the Casbah.

What had touched me so deeply? Stirner's arrow grazed the point at which I suspected the presence of the anarch. The dissimilarity presupposes a very subtle distinction, and, I believe, Vigo is the only person in Eumeswil who could make it. After all, he instantly caught the difference between owner and egoist. It is the same as the difference between anarch and anarchist. These concepts appear to be identical, but are radically different.

Vigo felt that the subject should be treated in a series of dissertations. If Eumeswil has a group to which the problem could be submitted, then it is his circle; it includes loners like Nebek, Ingrid, the Magister, and others who do not need gloves to play with fire. We never got beyond the plan and the general outlines, which I stored provisionally in the Archive.

*

How should it be tackled? Usually, such projects begin with a historical overview. The self-evident is timeless; it keeps pushing its way up through the tough historical mass without ever reaching the surface. This also obtains for the consciousness of absolute freedom and for the realization of that consciousness. In this sense, history resembles a fragment of magma in which bubbles have petrified. Nonconformity has left its trace. Approaching it differently, one could picture the crust of a dead planet struck by meteors. Indeed, astronomers have wondered if the craters are to be interpreted as scars left by such impacts or as extinct volcanoes. But whichever, from above or from below—cosmic fire was at work.

One would have to determine where anarchy's self-understanding in acting, thinking, or poetic creation occurred—where it coincided with man's attainment of self-comprehension and was pinpointed as the basis of freedom. To this end, we authorize the use of the Great Luminar: pre-Socratics, Gnosis, Silesian mysticism, and so forth. Among the bizarre fish, large ones also remain in the net.

*

The Christian century from 1845 to 1945 is a sharply outlined era; it also confirms the inkling that a century achieves its true form at midpoint. I would not deem it mere chance that *The Only One and His Own* came out in 1845. Chance is everything or nothing. In the luminar, I skimmed the mass of critical literature on Stirner, including the memoirs of a man named Helms, who depicts Stirner as the prototype of the petit bourgeois and his ambitions.

This judgment is valid to the extent that the Only One is concealed in every person, including the petit bourgeois. It was particularly true in that century. However, the importance of this type is overlooked—this alone reveals his robustness. Since my dear brother and his fellow students use cardboard figures as bowling pins, any four-letter word is proof positive. That is one of the reasons for their disappointments.

How come the petit bourgeois is treated as either a bugaboo or a whipping boy by the intelligentsia, the grand bourgeoisie, and the trade unions? Probably because he refuses to be forced from above or below to run the machine. If push comes to shove, he himself takes history in hand. A tanner, a joiner, a saddler, a mason, a house painter, or an innkeeper discovers in himself the Only One, and everyone else recognizes himself in him.

How come a snowball turns into an avalanche? Initially, like everything around it, the ball has to be made of snow; the incline takes care of the rest. Likewise, the men and the ideas of a final period, leached out as it is by history, must conform; they can never be singular and by no means elitist.

That was why Vigo balked at delving any further into the problem. A historian needs characteristics, dates, facts; he needs drama, not apocalypse—I fully understood.

*

It is especially difficult to tell the essential from that which is similar to and indeed seems identical with it. This also applies to the anarch's relation to the anarchist. The latter resembles the man who has heard the alarm but charges off in the wrong direction.

However, the anarch lurks in the anarchist, as in anyone else, and so, in the wasteland of their writings, they often score a hit that confirms that statement. At the luminar, I plucked out utterances that could have been signed by Stirner.

Take Benjamin Tucker, a true don Quixote, who, in his *Liberty*, one of the small anarchist journals, tilts at the windmills of the "riffraff of future governments":

> Whatever the state socialists may claim or deny, if their system is accepted, it is doomed to lead to a state religion whose expenses must be borne by everyone and at whose altar everyone must kneel; a state medical school by whose practitioners everyone must be treated; a state system of hygiene that prescribes what everyone must eat and drink, what everyone must wear, and what everyone may or may not do; a state code of ethics that, not satisfied with punishing crime, will suppress everything that the majority may describe as vice; a state system of education that will outlaw all private schools, academies, and universities; a state elementary school, where all children are educated collectively at public expense; and finally, a state family, with an attempt to introduce scientific eugenics. Thus, authority will reach its peak, and monopoly the supreme display of its power.

*

That was penned in the Christian year 1888, way before a like-minded Irishman sketched the horrific image of such a future. Poor Tucker—he died very long in the tooth, during the first year of World War II; he had lived to see the triumph of the authoritarian state in Russia, Germany, Italy, Portugal, and Spain.

Throughout his writings, I stumbled upon statements that were unusual for an anarchist, such as "Anarchy is order" or "Attend to your own affairs; this is the only moral law." That is why he regards all efforts at "suppressing vice as intrinsically criminal." Here, an anarch smashes through the anarchist system. By comparison, individualist anarchists like Most, who rejoices whenever a ruler is blown up, are mindless firecrackers.

Bakunin would like to replace the church with schools; Pelloutier would like to infiltrate the trade unions; some want to work in the masses, others, like Emma Goldman, prefer elitism; a few wish to propagate with dynamite; a few by nonviolent means—one gets lost in labyrinths. Prison trustees, prison stokers; all they share is the fact that they roast and perish in their own fire.

Eumeswil, too, had a core of activists; such people love to die, but the breed does not die out. They have an officer for whom they go through fire and water. The rank and file includes Luigi Grongo, a waterfront trucker, who does errands for me—a sturdy, stocky guy, muscular all over, with a low forehead above a good-natured face. When he shakes my hand, an electric current shoots through me. If his boss told him that I was obstructing the happiness of the world, Luigi would joyfully kill me. One cannot help loving him.

Stirner does not deal with ideas, especially those of universal happiness. He looks for the source of happiness, of power, property, divinity, within himself; he does not wish to serve anything.

"Unconsciously each man strives toward his own intrinsic self. However, an unconscious action is only half an action, and you always keep falling into the hands of a new faith—but I smile as I watch the battle."

I, here and now—there are no detours. One of the first dissertations ought to focus on Mackay's rediscovery of Stirner. Mackay understood Stirner's uniqueness, but could not see the fire for the smoke. This is even revealed by the epigraph of his *Settling of Accounts*: "He who speaks the truth does not forge his happiness."

That widespread penchant for gratuitously making oneself unpopular is not found in Stirner. He would say: "Truth? None of my business." It remains his own property. He does not accept it, he does not want to serve it; instead, he disposes of it freely.

Mackay's writings are haunted by the "association"—a word he took over from Stirner. The difference is that the association—to use Thomas Aquinas's terminology—is substantial for Mackay, but only accidental for Stirner.

"Could a free man then ever take a part or join a party? Yes—but he cannot be taken himself or be taken over by a party." He creates an association "that will last as long as the party and the self pursue the same goal."

Mackay is more consonant with Stirner in the maxims he aims at the "masses." For example:

> "The masses remain as stolid and apathetic as before; and the now empty place is occupied by someone else from the inexhaustible arsenal of those who are always ready to exert any kind of repression."

*

Vigo had added a gloss on this passage in my outline:

"At this point, you ought to investigate the differences between communism, anarcho-syndicalism, and individualist anarchism. Development from Fourier to Sorel."

Dividing this hornets' nest into its cells would fill a tome and still be unsatisfactory. More vinegar than honey would be gained. This is the crossroad of the demands made by the state, the collective, and the individual—not to mention the basic issue of whether the "ultimate" goal is economy or freedom.

The syndicalist view of profit as belonging to the enterprise that achieves it sounds reasonable. But what about a subtle yet indispensable achievement outside the enterprise—say, a poem? The enterprise would have to assume the role of patron—but when the state takes charge of the artist, then bad taste triumphs all too often. A pleasant thought: no state, no armies, peace at home and abroad as among brothers—but this goal is to be attained only through violent overthrow.

Sometimes we detect glimmers of nostalgia for ancient times: "When Adam delved and Eve span." Yet the more reasonable an idea, the more hopeless its realization. In those days, it would have been better to wager on the Synarchs, something like high-level Mauretanians, whose doings, mostly shrouded in darkness, unfolded at the end of the above-mentioned epoch. Their arguments were not reasonable, like those of the syndicalists, but rational. Planning, brain trust, technocracy were their buzzwords. I summon them to the luminar through Saint-Yves. Social progress and technological progress are interwoven, both Babylonian; they foster and hamper each other, creating a mutual equilibrium. In hindsight, it is hard to determine which has wrought the greater havoc.

*

Stirner was unfazed by such problems; he flicked them off like the ashes of his imported cigars. They were "not my business." He was taken up with other issues, such as the rights that the Only One had over life and death. He would kill and die not like the soldier for king and country, not like the anarchist for an idea, not like the martyr for a faith, but only if his own cause demanded it. He cited the example of the vivandière who bled to death in the snow on the shores of the Berezina. She died next to her baby, after strangling it with her garter.

*

To draw an important demarcation, we had envisaged a comparison between the Only One and the Superman. It would make little difference whether, as Mackay assumes, Nietzsche, Old Gunpowderhead, was acquainted with Stirner's work—ideas float in the air. Originality lies in rendering them—in the strength of the tackling and shaping.

First of all: The Superman recognizes the world as the will to power; "there is nothing else." Even art is a will to power. The Superman joins in the rivalries of the world while the Only One is content to watch the spectacle. He does not strive for power; he dashes neither after nor ahead of it, because he possesses it and enjoys it in his self-awareness. This recalls Far Eastern empires of images.

Naturally, because of external circumstances, power can fall into the hands of the Only One as well as the anarch. But power is burdensome for the Only One. Periander, tyrant of Corinth, "inherited it like a disease" from his father. Incidentally, it strikes me that certain features of Periander and also Tiberius, especially in their good times, are to be found in our Condor, though in the effete and ahistorical framework of Eumeswil. I have already said that the anarch and the monarch have a polar resemblance; basically, each contains both.

Secondly: the famous "God is dead." By then, Old Gunpowderhead was forcing an open door. A universal awareness was unveiled. That explains the sensation he caused. The Only One, on the other hand: "God...is none of my business." That leaves all doors open: the Only One can depose or impose God or let the matter rest—whichever he likes. He can show him the door or "form an association" with him. As with the Silesian mystic, "God cannot be without me." Like the Biblical Jacob, the Only One can wrestle for power until dawn. That alone is the message in the history of God's redemption plan.

*

Vigo had penned some marginalia here, too. For example: "Porphyry: Only the individual exists." And also: "This takes us back to the nominalism debate. Our institute has limited means."

Nevertheless, Old Gunpowderhead remained a nominalist in this matter—until the encounter in Turin. The debate is still unsettled, unless *nomina* and *res* coincide in the gods. Besides, the historian must not exhaust himself in cerebral processes; his field is facts. That is why at the luminar I act mainly as a physiognomist.

When that old fox Eumenes, the founder of our city, was declared dead after an engagement, his brother had nothing more urgent to do than seize the throne and marry the ruler's wife. When the two men did meet once more, the supposed deceased embraced his brother and whispered to him, "Next time don't marry till you've seen my corpse."

It must be noted that Eumenes' brother came toward him at the head of the guards and with a spear in his hand. The performance was fine—especially the sweeping way he lowered the spear. The start of the third

Christian millennium produced a breed of actors who abandoned psychology or absorbed it entirely in their actions; their achievements have been preserved in the luminar.

*

I admit that it is not easy to detach oneself from the present and refrain from evaluating it. Yet a barren Eumeswil that has been charred by nihilism provides the right setting. Your eyes descend from the extinct crater to the ocean. Down there in Pompeii, the markets are filling up; soon Pliny the Elder will come sailing in from Misenum.

Anyone who takes on the risk of history must, like a Proteus, be transformed within its element, must unreservedly conform to the spirit of the time in which the decision has been rendered and to the character that has rendered it. Passion without participation. Life throbs, unbroken by the verdict; the spirit rises with the billow and sinks with it. It feels fine in the surf. A ruler, a commander, a tyrant, his executioner, his victim, and his murderer are summoned and questioned—but only in the interrogator's mind: that is what you are.

The results: there were many possibilities—knowing the bottom line, we can check the figures. The right flank should have been stronger. And yet the Zeitgeist was powerful, the character compelling; the decision, good or bad, wrong or right, could not be otherwise. That is why nothing is learned from history. The doer imagined he could determine the future; but he was sucked in by the future, he fell prey to it. At the crucial moment, what was necessary happened. It is subsequently mirrored in its own irrevocability.

Now things become sinister. The nameless force, to which even gods must bow, dims the vision.

43

Another long day has ended; in the city, lights trace out the pattern of the straight principal avenue and the twisting streets. The boats at sea also have lights; a few craft are circling the islands, others linger on the surface mirror—those are the lamps of the fishermen who hunt the *loligo*, the squid.

Whenever he seeks pleasure with the woman,
Who, just like him, gives off a pearly sheen
Resembling the veiling of the iris—
The cunning fisherman approaches him.
He tosses glass spheres in the sea, they menace
With sharp points and they shine like you, *loligo*,
And now, deceived by light that stirs throughout
The sea, the swift one comes and plays with glass,
And bloodily he tears his coat apart.

Downstairs in the hall, the Condor has terminated the dinner; this is the moment I am to wait for. He may wish to carry the conversation into the night bar. This is not on the agenda, but I must be prepared, and usually I have an unwonted gain. But no one telephones; I can now drink my wine.

The luminar has an aftereffect; I can indulge in a pleasure shared by all historians: metacriticism. Somebody or other is summoned; I put myself in his shoes and weigh his decisions. In so doing, I must avoid an almost universal mistake: *post hoc* judgment. Thus, my dear old dad, harking back to better days, censures the corrupt standard of Eumeswil. But it is precisely the historical necessity of this corruption that eludes him. It is a condition like any other. The milk of human kindness has gone sour; no Cato will make it fresh again. Besides, any present time is grim; that is why better times are sought partly in the past, partly in the future.

*

Toward midnight, it is time to retire. The play of the retina commences. The luminar images recur, sharp in their outlines but with complementary colors. Pages of text slip in between; I could read them. The human mind must house a tremendous archive that loses nothing.

The faces come alive; they change as supplely as plasma and rigidify once more. Then alien things join in: a green bronze head, *en face*, after spending ages in Etruscan soil; it has an aureole of hair. Reality grows stronger, but not dreamlike. Plus voices.

"Neverman has died."

Then another.

"Ball is dead."

I do not know them. The voices seem to be coming not from outside, but directly from my ears. Presumably a catacomb medium to which I am connected willy-nilly. I hope it is only a crossed wire.

*

My sleep is preceded by either thoughts or images: thoughts, if, in the morning, reality prevailed in the body; images, if it prevailed in the mirror.

It strikes me that these combinations focus primarily on balance. How does the interplay of influx and erosion maintain the salt content of the oceans, keep their calcium level constant; in what rhythm do the rocks crumble into dust and scree and then tower up again as mountains?

Through millions of years, the masses of meteors and cosmic dust that keep peppering the earth must add enormously to the planet's weight. Its centrifugal force is bound to grow, increasing its distance from the sun. Still and all, we may assume that the sun is likewise charged to the same degree by various objects, so that the overall proportion is restored.

The great mill: grain becomes flour, flour becomes bread. Bakers like to give bread the shape of wheat grains or, as some people think, genitalia. But there is no difference.

Aggression and reply. Periander, upon seeing the first catapult arrow, which had been brought to him from Sicily, exclaimed, "Good God—a man's courage is a thing of the past!" But then the walls were reinforced, and the soldiers shot back with catapults. This was repeated; when Richard the Lion-Hearted lay siege to a vassal's stronghold, he leaned comfortably against a wall until he was mortally wounded by a bolt in his shoulder. He did not realize that English craftsmen had managed to build a crossbow that could shoot farther. It may have gained an advantage of only a few ells, and so the odds were soon even again.

This recalls the hourglass: as the upper part empties, the lower fills up proportionately—but the weight remains constant. This notion is so simple that it defies the imagination. It was the work of a time-maker, not a clockmaker. Any calculating is a *re*calculating. If the numbers look right, we feel a gratuitous peace of mind, as if we had managed to complete a game of solitaire. Then the cards are laid out again. The hourglass is used until the curtain falls.

My sleep becomes light: I move on in overhead illumination, not with precise thoughts but in a pensive mood. In my drowsing, the weights keep shifting, but without substance, without cohesion. It is different if the mirror image was stronger in the morning. Then I feel scattered throughout the day, I have to concentrate on my work. But at night, the mind passes unhampered into the splendor and terror of the world of dreams.

*

Everyone knows what it is like to jump up from sleep. Escape from the early morning hours seems impossible; they are a labyrinth. Nearly always there are worries, often only minor ones—but now they are hopelessly entangled; how can I find my way out?

At such times, I mull over my situation—what am I doing in Eumeswil? Here, I am a suspect waiter on the one hand, a historian without a system on the other. I am unconcerned about how people judge me; but how shall I stand the test of my self-criticism? It is hard when a man summons himself to the bar.

The change in the imminent power struggle will place me in jeopardy; but I find the prospect agreeable. The bunker on the upper Sus is prepared—for all the trouble I went to, it was more of an intellectual game, like winter plans for a later vacation. You get hold of a tent, a faltboat, a rifle. If things get serious, off I go on my holiday. I will return after a while. That is how all romantic excursions wind up. You escape either not at all or by the skin of your teeth.

It makes no difference to me whether Eumeswil is ruled by tyrants or demagogues. Any man who swears allegiance to a political change is a fool, a *facchino* for services that are not his business. The most rudimentary step toward freedom is to free oneself from all that. Basically each person senses it, and yet he keeps voting.

Inside the polis, everyone is on a treadmill. The slave is free only in his sleep; he becomes king in his dreams, even on the night before his execution. At these tables, more is served than our daily bread. This, too, is basically sensed by everyone; prophets and popes have lived on this hunger. Princes of the night, garbed as magi, want to lay hands on our very dreams.

*

Two steps, or rather leaps, could get me out of the city in w
lution has run its course. Boutefeu realized this early on, but w
on evolution all the same. When appraising an experiment, one m
ignore any possible usefulness, avoid any value judgments. An experiment enriches only our knowledge; like nature, it has neither an aim nor a goal such as we project into it.

An experiment always "succeeds"; as such, the Superman, akin to the proconsul, has found his place, his group, his fossil rank among the primates; a family tree also has its dead branches. "Like many fossil anthropomorphs, the proconsul has likewise been raised to the level of man's forebear" (Heberer). *Why "raised"?* one might wonder.

As little can be expected from evolution as from any progress. The great change transcends not only the species, but the entire bios. It is a crucial loss that mere fragments have come down to us from the most ancient documents. The difference between the forests and the catacombs seems to be that in the former one experiments at the Tree of Knowledge and in the latter at the Tree of Life.

*

Attila is familiar with the forests; he lived there for a long time as at many outer limits. That is why I listen very attentively to his words and even more to his silences.

Likewise, more is happening in the catacombs than the hoarding and administering of knowledge. It is the foundations of the species and not of consciousness that are being shaken. In the forest, a new Isis ought to be engendered, and Prometheus liberated from the Caucasus by the subterraneans.

In our epigonic world of languishing empires and degenerate city-states, aspirations are limited to the crude needs. History is dead; this facilitates a historical retrospective and keeps it free of bias—at least for those who have suffered pain and put it behind them.

On the other hand, the things that gave substance to history and put it in motion cannot have died. They must have shifted from the phenomenal world to the reserves—on the night side. We dwell on fossil soil that can unexpectedly spew fire. Everything is probably inflammable, all the way to the core.

The fact that some places are heating up is perceived not only by visionaries and crackpots. While political and economic problems are touched on only peripherally, the Domo has to deal with them ex officio. The intelligence he receives from border patrols and the information he gathers elsewhere are things he keeps top secret, because he considers them dangerous and also because he would like to suppress them: they do not fit into his system. He would prefer to treat them like the tales about sea serpents. At the night bar, I occasionally catch a remark that sheds light on his appraisal of the situation. His assessment, in accordance with his nature, is realistic and could be formulated roughly as follows.

"There is no doubt that these rumors, while exaggerated, indicate the existence of specific neuralgic points. In a tiny number of centers, knowledge has become autarchic, independent of even the empires. This autonomy of both the technocrats and the biologists is based on the hoarding of knowledge and on its secrecy. Their independence is expressed in the luminars, which transmit news and indispensable data. Towers have been driven downward and turned into cisterns that weather the assaults of political might.

"Such constellations have always existed—say, in the history of the secret orders or the way the Old Man of the Mountains at the fortress of Alamut influenced the policies of Oriental kingdoms.

"If my evaluation is correct, there are two schools at work: one wants to pile higher stories on the cerebrum, while the forest school wants to sink it back into the thalamus. One group cannot get along without fire, the other cannot get along without the animal.

"We in Eumeswil are little people and so we have to steer clear of these quarrels. It is more important to have bread on the table every day. Then again, scuttlebutt about sinister things does us no harm. People huddle together as on the brink of an abyss."

*

Such are the Domo's thoughts. Attila, by contrast, seems to feel that the Condor should get involved in the forests. I once heard Attila say, "The Condor and the lamb."

As a historian, I infer the existence of a still aimless movement that could be called the "pre-current"—a spiritual disquiet that spreads out before tangible things appear. Parties have not yet formed, but are adumbrated. Something is going to happen. Even nuclear fission was preceded by whispers.

On an island without dogs or cats, one could still determine who, if these animals were ever introduced, would go for dogs and who for cats, and who would remain neutral. Thus there are people who are scared of snakes without ever having encountered one. This can be applied to Montezuma and the White Gods.

*

Thus, in Eumeswil, Vigo strikes me as being predestined for the forest, Bruno for the catacombs. They are also the only people with whom one can converse about those matters. As I have mentioned, I took the job at the night bar chiefly because of Vigo's advice. I am grateful to him for his exegeses of the bits and pieces I bring back.

In regard to what I told him about the Domo's ruminations, Vigo said:

"The man is good in his place. His tread is sure because he does not see or wish to know what is going on below or above the surface. Otherwise he would not take science so seriously. The fact that science is a puppet show, especially in technology, would be an absurd thought for him. Yet science does not have a light of its own. The theft of fire: first by Prometheus for the hearth, then by the Uranians for leviathan. Clearly a third stage is in the offing: the transmutation of fire into mind. At that point, the earth will not make do without gods."

*

Such reflections are typical of Vigo; they have caused him to be discredited in the official establishment. For him, Herodotus is the greatest man; without a precise study of myth, says Vigo, there can be no well-grounded historiography. While venerating him as I do, I cannot go along with this point. Whatever man may devise, it will fall back on him.

I waver between Vigo and Bruno, who, in turn, has a different standpoint. Bruno is closer to the catacombs and has haunted at least their antechambers. One of the areas he studies is the ability of human intelligence to reach a level of supercommunication, which will make the mind independent of technological media. This development would have to be preceded by vast reductions. The Titans restrain freedom, the gods grant it.

*

I am still in the night, still pondering the possible ways out. Perhaps I will see them more sharply in the bunker, in solitude. I have also equipped it with a pure crystal mirror. I expect the catastrophe not to move the political weights around, but to abolish them altogether. Lightning clears the air.

I must also mention a different category of appeals, unlike those from the catacombs—a sudden collision with the human substance, a nocturnal *de profundis*.

Saint Silas was startled out of his sleep by similar voices and he believed that dead men were calling to him. He then got up and prayed for them. I am thinking rather of contacts with disarticulated suffering, and I trace it back to my studies.

At times, when at the luminar or reading, I stumble upon unthinkable atrocities and I would rather that the witnesses had refrained from communicating them. I am not thinking of the horrors that make up our shared Cainitic heritage. Murder has an indivisible quality. Anyone penetrating it will kill one person or even many thousands if he has helpers and means. However greatly technology may contribute, those murderers cannot hold a candle to Cain. With his fist, he accomplished more than the greatest khans with their armies.

I stumble upon crimes that would make one strive against the reformers of systems, the gods, the inventors of hell, the trailblazers. Herodotus once said that the gods are keeping the final horrors for themselves; accordingly, man would have to be better than they and set a standard for them. Also, are certain animals, especially insects, that kill in a highly refined manner, but only if necessary. The earth needs murder, its economy requires it; but if the earth knows the punishment, it rejects the revenge.

It is not the nearest being but the most distant—Prometheus on his rock—who taps on my door at night.

A Day in the City

44

A day in the Casbah, from one morning to the next; and yet I have said little about my work.

The length of a day is not fixed by the clock. It hinges on our imagination, on the playing of our thoughts. Images make time pass since they banish boredom; they also increase the contents. The ideal would be the moment in which time concentrates, even annihilates itself, and everything becomes possible. Light becomes more intense, it becomes absolute.

On this as on every morning, my relief comes. I relinquish the night bar and everything in it, I turn in my key and my uniform at the office. During my absence, the studio remains locked; the Great Luminar is top secret.

Now I can head for the city; the stronghold mountain is already warm. The descending footpath, cutting through the curves of the paved road, is a red arrow pointing at the harbor. Green lizards whisk across it, vanishing in the euphorbia. They are indifferent to the tufts of spines. My pay is in my pocket, and I jingle the gold pieces. I will stop at the harbor.

Latifah is expecting me; I notified her through Madame Poser. Latifah cannot receive messages directly; all she has is the gray phonophore, which is limited to official announcements from the Casbah, and with which one can hear but not transmit. If any vestiges of a class or caste system have survived in the atomized society of Eumeswil, they are expressed in the phonophore. The rights are of a dynamic nature; they are based on power and not on property.

Latifah—just between you and me—was the next best woman to come my way. I spotted her the very first time I went off duty. Her beat is over the waterfront, among the brokers, ship chandlers, and small taverns. That is where she walks up and down; halftime is marked by Madame Poser's *albergo*—a cramped, shabby *hôtel de passe* with narrow stairs going up several stories; outside the taproom, two round tables and some chairs are set up on the sidewalk. Madame rents out by the hour; few patrons wish to spend the night.

Latifah approaches no one, but her slow steps and querying looks reveal that she expects to be approached. And then there is her gray phonophore. This area has a better clientele: steersmen, pursers, chief stewards, even a notary or an effendi with a sudden urge. It will not hold him up for long.

I have grown accustomed to her. Basically, I prefer the women in the lower harbor—galleon figureheads with protruding breasts and Medusas from the river basin with their impudent stares and swaying buttocks. But one can seldom avoid a ruckus. The harbor police have their hands full, especially when a big ship is lying at anchor.

*

We sit at one of the round tables; a pattern of holes is punched into its metal. If you spill something, no traces remain. Madame serves the aperitif. The sun is already above the rooftops, the light is good. I peer at Latifah like a slave trader before the gavel comes down; there is something ancient about her, something of the early Persepolis. The teeth are of prime importance: they tell about the bone structure. In the left upper row, a gold tooth, which does not really bother me. The tooth is exposed by a smile that lends a mysterious depth to the features. It is an ineradicable male error to treat this as a sign of intelligence.

Latifah never applies rouge, only lipstick; together with the black hair that dangles into her forehead, the lipstick makes her face seem even paler; her facial skin has large pores.

"You wear long skirts. I bet you have ugly legs."

"You'd like to see everything right on the street, sir?"

Not a bad comeback. Altogether, she eyes me in an appropriate way, critically, as if I were a fish caught in her net. My striped phonophore reveals a man from the Casbah; these are brisk customers, who demand no extras and avoid romantic soft-soaping. And, above all, they are solvent.

"Fine. Then up we go—Madame, I'll take care of the room right away."

"The aperitif is on the house. *Professore*, you'll be satisfied."

She seems to know more about me than I suspected. This is unavoidable; Eumeswil is a village.

*

We pause on the stairs.

"*Comme hors d'oeuvre?*"

"*Des crudités. Trousse, trousse, garce.* You're in for something."

"Oh, yes, I can tell—the Condor keeps you Casbah boys on a tight leash."

Sometimes it is not bad if one is honored "in the group." It normalizes a situation; little is wasted on individuality.

Upstairs in the room. A bed, a fireplace, the usual. Drawn shutters, the sun filtering through the slats.

"You do know how to treat a lady?"

She sounds like a novice talking on a tape and rehearsing. I reach into my pocket and place a scudo on the mantel.

"Oh, that's generous."

"And now, take it off!"

"*À vos ordres, à votre service.*"

Outside, the gulls sweeping past the gable are shrieking. The light here is neither too dim nor too bright. For an instant I see her standing at the fireplace—free and easy, her hands closed and on her hips. Her breasts: not voluptuous, yet well shaped. Archaic style, detracting from the atmosphere.

*

The Leyden jar, also known as the Kleistian jar, an apparatus for electric condensation. A glass cylinder, partly coated both inside and out with metal foils. It would be better if it curved upward like a vase. The glass layer isolates through spatial separation; it operates as a restraint on time. When the circuit closes, a flash, a spark proclaims the annihilation of time. Whether a man dies or a mosquito—it does not matter.

The atoms contain the mystery exploited by bios and psyche; they make the most of their talents.

*

Latifah is to be taken as seriously as any other woman. Now she is leaning on the mantel again. I can gaze at her leisurely—the wan body, the dark delta, the black hair falling deeper into her forehead. My first impression is confirmed: she must have been conceived under a lucky star. In our lupanars at the upper edge of the city, one finds any and all hetaerae, from the classical ones of the Periclean Age to the Hellenistic ones of the Diadochic era. There are albums to choose from. Or else Madame claps her hands—"*le choix*"—and they present themselves *en groupe*. But Latifah would have seemed archaic even when Eumenes founded this city.

She smokes a joint, touches up her lips in front of the mirror, prepares herself for the next customer. She is about to get dressed. She wears little on her body.

The atmosphere is pleasant, clear contours, like a mountain after a storm. I might now focus on a problem. Down below, a fishmonger is calling out his mackerels: "*Tutti freschi*." It is still early. Here in the harbor and in the side streets, every ware is chanted, by the market women, the kitchen lads, the soft-drink peddlers. Perhaps the Condor will hold out longer than I assume. I'm in a good mood.

"Latifah, you're worth your weight in gold—do you make every man as happy as you do me?"

She is again wearing a dark triangle around her hips, a thing of woven air.

"Hey, I'm a joygirl—but some guys even cry."

"They're married."

"Oh, but they're not. They bawl because they can't do it, or because they've done it. You boys from the Casbah never make a fuss."

She disappears in the *escalier*, waving her handbag.

*

These conversations have become habitual, recurring whenever I go off duty. I am curious by nature. Bit by bit, I piece her life together—how it all came about, how it continued, who the first man was. Was it her seducer or her rapist? Almost like Nebek, but *sine ira*, I want to know the details. She is of average intelligence, yet imaginative; a human being is revealed more in his lies than in his banal truth—his measure is his wishful thinking.

Once, when she was standing at the fireplace again, something eerie occurred. The light began to flicker as before a short circuit; instead of darkening, however, the room turned dazzlingly bright. I raised my arm to cover my eyes; the light shot between my ulna and my radius. The walls were virtually blasted away; only the frame stood out. I saw a skeleton at the mantel, a scaffold of bones with the gold tooth; next to its thighs, the garter clasps and the scudo; which she had already stowed away; the small spiral inside the vulva.

An experiment from the catacombs—either a failure or a flaunting of power. Sometimes, these interventions unnerve the city, provoking a kind of paralysis. The clocks stop; a blackout follows as if time were blocked. They can also generate quakes and darknesses. A brief shaking of the power of the khans, quickly forgotten like a nightmare.

I heard Latifah: "Should I come again—to you?"

This was the first time she put it that way. We were lying under the blanket, almost skinless, two embryos in the belly of leviathan. Yes, it was good; a relapse into humanity.

After she left, I found the scudo on the mantelpiece. She had put it back. Well intended, but against the rules. At my next relief, she found two scudos. She took them without batting an eyelash. A smart child. Still and all, we became intimate.

45

Latifah also serves as my lightning rod—Ingrid dislikes brutal embraces, she sticks to the absolute necessities and even then, I assume, more as a favor. She never stands on ceremony, but she respects herself without being prudish.

In our Eumeswil, she seems like a girl from abroad, like a far-northern bird of passage in its winter quarters. Her figure is shorter than average, but nicely proportioned. If one saw her face in an anthropological museum, the label would say, "Female Swede." Why was it that the word "twin" flashed through my mind the first time I encountered her at the institute? It must have been due to those nice proportions, which seemed to have emerged from a foundry cast. In such instances, race wins out over individuality.

Her color is blue; she wears linen, which shades from an almost whitish blue to very intense aquamarine, with some lavender. Scant jewelry, aside from a cameo and sometimes a necklace, but no ring. At meals, as in all her habits, she is simple; fish soup without saffron, and naturally without garlic—*con pepe*, if we dine together; I follow her example. She and Latifah know about each other; I do not keep them secret. Besides, Latifah's base of operations is very close to the pied-à-terre where I recover from dealing with my dear old dad. Ingrid is not jealous; Latifah has no right to be jealous.

Ingrid is reliable in her work; in this context, I am what is known as her doctoral adviser. Her devotion is almost filial. It culminates in incest. That was what I scented at our very first encounter.

Vigo is the kind of prophet who is greatly honored save in his own country. Among insiders, his name, to the secret chagrin of his colleagues, is regarded as a *mot de passe* from Beirut to Uppsala. That is why his courses are always attended by students from far away.

Once, when I was saying good-bye to him after one of our evenings, he said, "Incidentally, another snow goose has reported to me; she wants to work with us. She's got good marks, and she's also discovered a thing or two at the luminar. I'd like you to take her off my hands."

He acts as if these responsibilities were burdensome; in reality, they increase his prestige.

*

The next morning, Vigo introduced us to each other at the institute. He also suggested a thesis: The differentiation of authority in the ancient empires. The research was to include the colonies of the Western powers, especially proconsular autonomy.

Sometimes the warrior caste is disempowered by the demos or by the senate and it then migrates to remote territories. That is how the motherland gets rid of its agitated minds, aristocrats, and reactionaries; in those areas, as in nature reserves, they can wage old-fashioned wars against nomads and mountain tribes. Adventures in service. On the other hand, they can turn dangerous when they, like Caesar, create their Gaul or, like an Iberian general named Franco, return with their legionnaires during a crisis.

That was roughly how Vigo pictured it. He said: "It is a vast domain. One ought to extract a leitmotif—perhaps the extrapolation. (Mathematically: the extrapolation becomes less certain the farther one moves from the original field—in some cases, right upon leaving it.) Now see what can be done with this...." And he left us to our own devices.

He was right: it *was* a vast domain. Still, distance has scarcely mattered since the development of airborne troops. Ingrid worked at the small luminar in one of our rooms—almost a cabin. I noticed that she attuned the blue of her clothing to her lavender sprig.

And indeed, she was quick at making good discoveries; thus in the Archives of Correspondence, she found a new version of Lord Clive's suicide. It also helped me in my definition of the anarch. She managed to dig up something fitting the theme in the *Twelve Articles* that an Anabaptist had set up during the Germanic peasants' war. The text said that warfare between Christian nations and thereby the arrière-ban ought to stop. If any men were still left with an uncontrollable lust for war, they should be packed off to fight the Turks.

*

During my service at the Casbah, I let Ingrid use my office at the institute—with Vigo's permission. This gave her access to the Great Luminar. A year passed, but we realized that the topic was unraveling. After I spoke with the professor, we hit on a suggestion that was more to her liking. It concerned the Goldfinch Plan—I can only sum it up. As we know, the Jews are drawn time and again to the Promised Land. As far back as during the Egyptian and then the Babylonian captivity, and during the scattering of their nation after the destruction of their city. Age-old quarrels, like those with Ammon, are revived.

"O Zion, high-built city." Through changing times, this remained one of their great dreams; Zionism tried to make it come true, reaching its goal during the era of the world wars, despite both external and internal resistance. Someone said: "This shows me that we are no smarter than the others."

Religious and cultural Zionism cut itself off from national Zionism. As in all problems involving wishful thinking, there were fuzzy aspects;

the edges blurred into one another. The Goldfinch Plan, by contrast, was down-to-earth, a program on a mercantile basis.

I had heard only rumors about it; the term was not to be found in Herzl's or Bialik's correspondence. It had obviously been chosen as the symbol of a multicolored, disparate unity. The various countries were to give the Jews small, even minuscule territories, either leasing or donating them. Here a free city, there an island, a scrap of Yemenite desert, the tip of a peninsula, and so forth. The plan also was to provide Zion with a corridor to the sea. From there, the twelve tribes were to ply their commerce by means of a federal fleet, and shipyards and refineries were to produce their wares.

For the various governments—it was still a long way to the world-state—the contributions would have been minor compared with the advantages. Everyone knows about the stimulating effect that neutral free-trade zones exert on large, closed empires. Often the merchant has achieved more in this context than the armies. The same applies to civilization, to the whole range of values. Such a situation could lead to a universal monetary framework.

Vigo instantly pounced on this subject. I have already noted that he has a predilection for Venice. "It could turn out very nicely. The Jews, gold, and the serpent—these are revealed mysteries."

*

Ingrid was soon finding material in small journals and notes by students at the Archives of Correspondence. She was now quite adept at the luminar. Above all, she grasped the gist of the Goldfinch problem: we had to go back to the Semitic roots. Early Mediterranean civilization is an inexhaustible model of all later systems, a foretaste. Thus the Goldfinch Plan had already been implemented by the Phoenicians. Their voyages between their settlements, the trading posts they set up on barrier islands, the secret mines they worked even beyond the Pillars of Hercules, their commerce in highly desired items such as ivory, glass, purple, silver, the amazing abstraction of their currency system—all those things seemed more concentrated in their origins than in their repetitions. They demand a boldness, though more that of Odysseus and Sindbad than that of the conquistadors.

At this juncture, vast prospects opened up. For example: what would the Mediterranean be like if Hannibal had triumphed over Scipio the Elder or an Emir Musa over the Cross?

It was also good that Ingrid went back to the bios: navigation was secondary. There are plants, especially grasses, that spread out over steppes or prairies. Others thrive in isolated places that are remote from one another. Thus, the Phoenicians were Semites first, then seafarers. Whether wind, air, or ether—the challenge was to maintain the identity of the species at whatever distance. After the destruction of Jerusalem by Titus, that challenge was successfully met worldwide. Naturally, here as everywhere else, the gods had to be taken into account: "No matter what, God is the Lord of Israel."

Here, one might suspect, lay the weakness of national Zionism: it had oversimplified the biotope, removing it from the magical consensus and degrading it.

46

That was our theme on the day that we were spending together like many other days at the luminar. But it was to go down as a special date.

Private sessions with top students like Nebek are agreeable, often exciting. One forgets all about eating or drinking, even about the body. A problem surfaces; it is thrashed out and illustrated by a historical reference. Flavius Josephus; a synagogue on the upper Rhine during the Crusades; the Prague Cemetery; Dreyfus, his epaulets torn off, his saber broken. The book of hours is illuminated—often with merely a glowing initial.

I see Ingrid at the luminar. Her delicate figure, her narrow hands, her intellectual devotion. I do not know whether Jenny Lind played an instrument. The Swedish Nightingale: this was what she would have looked like at the piano—say, around the time when she was festively welcomed by the Göttingen students.

"Ingrid, I have a feeling that Hesiod mentions a Phoenician merchant?"

She begins to play; the keys appear to sink before her fingers so much as touch them. No one here can hold a candle to her memory. As if skiing down a forest lane, she cuts a trail straight through the thicket of numbers. Soon I see the stranger at the well and next to him the girl; she follows him onto his ship. She does not return with her jug in the evening. This is an ancient song, like that of the wind and the wave.

The luminar is a time machine that simultaneously abolishes time by leading out of it. This is not true always or for everyone; but in some passages, one hears only the melody and forgets the instrument.

*

Ingrid had rented a room near my father's house; I was accompanying her to her front yard in the moonlight. We continued our dialogue; in the shadows I saw only her face and hands—she was wearing her darkest dress and a more intense lavender.

At this point, I should mention an ambivalence that surprises even me: the scent of lavender is usually off-putting. That was how I had perceived it at the institute; but now I felt a strong attraction. However, it was shortly before the blossoming of the oranges, and several trees were already in bloom. They were brighter, and heady fragrances were wafting from the gardens, mingling with the lavender. It all blended on my skin.

Part of my ambivalence is the fact that a precise female intelligence is likewise off-putting. Then again, this is not true of the top female minds, as borne out by a number of great encounters. At our academies, of course, the apple of Paris is scarcely weighed, and happy marriages are exceptions here.

Fine—but during that walk I felt a tension that threatened to become unendurable; we lost the thread of our conversation. The pauses were strenuously overcome. It was harder and harder for me to hold back.

Granted—I was not only her teacher, I was also her ideal. I had often perceived this during the year; nor had she made any bones about it. But what would happen if I touched her? I could picture it: the incredible surprise, the deadly hush in the moonlight while our faces turned pale, perhaps teary; the image was destroyed.

So I walked her as far as her front yard. "Till tomorrow, then." I avoided her hand. As I have said, I would be close by whenever I stayed with my dad. I walked up and down in front of his house, cooling my forehead; then I went in.

No sooner had I shut the door than someone knocked. Ingrid was standing at the threshold; the light was still on in the hall. She handed me a note; I was able to read it: "Please do not stand on ceremony."

I put out the light with my right hand and drew her in with my left. My father was upstairs, working late as usual; my brother had already retired. The floor was plated with marble. A hard bed; but we did not stand on ceremony. She had made all necessary preparations. The surf of that moment foams even over the memory.

I must have fallen asleep on the spot. When I awoke, I found myself alone. I felt as if I had been dreaming.

*

Strangely, little changed between us. Our conversations grew more intense as if a barrier had fallen. Whenever I am in the city, I spend my mornings at the institute. I report to Vigo, give my lecture, visit the advanced students at their workplaces. As for my own research, I find time enough at the Casbah.

My tour ends in Ingrid's cell; we discuss the current problem and play at the luminar for an hour or so. The conversation develops further as we walk to the harbor; for a while, we sit by the dock where the boats are moored. It is high noon at the marina; I take her to my sparsely furnished room. Not a word is said about this, just like during that nocturnal stroll; we glide through the streets and up the stairs as if on rails.

I have often wondered what, if anything, she feels at these times or whether she considers it a duty—not as an act of submission, but more as an inherent matter of course. In any case, words are superfluous; we limit ourselves to the necessities. Accordingly, I have never seen her naked although I feel her body through the cloth; she bares only her thighs and fleece. On the other hand, it would be presumptuous to say that the matter at hand predominated. Naturally, I have to control myself to avoid whispering indecent words to her as I love doing with Latifah.

*

Rosner's museum has a room devoted to the birds that make their nests on the northernmost cliffs; many of these birds are astonishing for their splendid plumage, their colors, their shimmering brilliance. Some of them were bagged by Attila, who tracked not only the fish up there. Life is concentrated in the polar night.

I enjoy listening to him at the night bar during the wee hours, when he starts talking about his voyages beyond the pack-ice belt. His face then takes on Neptunian features: I can see the trident in his hand. He ventures into the crevasses that split the iceberg, he forges all the way into the blue grottoes polished by the swell. The plunging of glaciers reverberates in their cathedral. Lavender-blue ice crystals crackle under the bow. Even Iceland is down south; we are alone.

*

We continue our dialogue about the Goldfinch Plan. According to a Cabalist exegesis, leviathan dwells on towering citadels that are remote from one another, perhaps on cliffs; the Jews are scattered among them as strangers. From those heights, leviathan battles behemoth. Behemoth defends himself with his horns; leviathan tries to suffocate him by stuffing his fins into behemoth's nostrils—"which, incidentally, is a lovely example of defeating a land by means of a blockade." The simile comes from don Capisco—Ingrid discovered it in the luminar.

Like any fundamental corpus of work, the Cabala contains prophetic nuggets. This struck me in that depiction of leviathan, which is also one of the Titanic symbols of the catacombs.

The people of Eumeswil think that the catacombs are subterranean; the reality is more subtle. Bruno is reticent with his allusions, but I suspect that he has lived in hollows made by plutonian and human efforts. They contain extensive gardens with a flora more splendid than that of the upper world. The constant warmth and the strange rays of light produce wonders. Botanists have released previously unknown forces of nature. I asked Bruno, "Doesn't that seem odd, since the biologists are on the side of the forests?"

"Now, you know that when Proserpina was picking flowers on a meadow, she was abducted by Pluto and carried off to the underworld."

Of course; his answer pointed to times when luminaries of science fell into enemy hands, because of either cunning or force, and were "turned around."

The catacombs may be subterranean, but they vault up with the mountains. The resulting cones are filled with chambers and hermetically insulated like termitaria. These strongholds—and this recalls both Fourier and the Cabala—rule the intermediary spaces. The strongest, Fort Rhadamanthus, also functions as a satellite control center. From here, projectiles and spaceships are kept on their courses and guarded on cosmic ramps. Depending on the situation, they are steered toward or away from the earth. Beyond the stratosphere, space is taboo, even for the great empires.

Vigo feels that this would provide material for a Dante. Yet, as he adds, Dante had the frame and could make up the Inferno, while metatechnology must first build this frame. Accordingly, it seems to aim more at limiting itself than dominating.

*

When we play at the luminar, sometimes with four hands if I join in, then a childhood memory surfaces in me. My dear old dad was concerned about my education—that I have to admit. He particularly succeeded in two areas. One was speed-reading, which is indispensable at the luminar. Beyond skimming or reading stenographically, one can gain a qualitative evaluation of a text from the various handwritings, the distribution of the capitals, the accents, the punctuation, which indicate not only what but also *how* to read. Otherwise the immense amount of material could not be coped with.

The other area was my piano lessons. The best hits we score are flukes. In our neighborhood, Signora Ricci was the undisputed music authority; she was an *émigrée* from Smyrna: Greek, Lebanese, Jewish?—our city is a melting pot. She taught piano in the summer and dance in the winter. A brunette with a full figure and gentle features that recalled a Murillo painting. There was down on her upper lip; whenever she grew energetic, and during dance lessons too, there was something of a circus about her—for instance, when she clapped her hands: "The ladies alone—*Messieurs, à genoux!*" Precise decorum, as demanded by her profession.

I went there reluctantly, like a young dog who has to be carried to a hunt. That was the period of my dismal hours in the attic. I was about to be tormented once again by Diabelli's minuet. By the fifth measure, I invariably fluffed a note; then came the slap on my hand.

The slap was the best part of the lesson; it was light, even gratifying. Plus that dark voice: "Muttonhead, butterfingers, you're incorrigible."

There is a technique to everything; I practiced the minuet at home, as if typing letters of the alphabet. In this way, I produced a correct, listless text—the slaps stopped, the lessons grew boring.

The left thumb must sink on the E. I failed to do so and was unmasked *a tempo*:

"Are you trying to get my goat? You did that on purpose!"

And she wove her fingers into mine. You can imagine what came next. Now I could hardly wait for my lessons and I would often hear "Butterfingers!" and also, "You're incorrigible." An ambivalent word.

My melancholy faded as if blown away; I got over my mother's death and also became a good student in my other subjects, learning not by heart but with my heart.

The signora claimed to be thirty-five; today I believe she was going on fifty. There is no better age for an initiator into the mysteries. "The teachers will shine with the brilliance of heaven."

Just why have I brought her up? Oh, right: I am playing four-handed duets with Ingrid at the luminar, Now it is I who put my hand on hers. I pass along what I have learned. These are crisscross interweavings, a parti-colored carpet, woven not only for one's own pleasure.

*

When describing my free evening at the Casbah, I neglected to mention the chess game. The board is near the wine and the fruit; it must not be touched.

The game has only an opponent, but not an enemy. It is played as an agon between equals. Hence it is created no less for the anarch than for kings—the bold attack, the cunning snare laid for the player, arouses Olympic contentment in him. He can, as I do here in the Casbah, play against himself.

The match goes on throughout a service period. To save moves, I first build up one of the opening gambits that have stood the test since Philidor. Then the game begins. It is limited to one move per day; the interval is enough to make me forget the motives that spurred me the previous day. The man who plays against himself must not look over his shoulder.

The pleasure is archaic; I move the pawns and noblepieces, the agile bishop, the cunning knight, the powerful rook, the king, the queen. The Casbah is hushed; destiny is concentrated. I achieve a state in which the figures are no longer important, but meaningful. They become autonomous; the simple soldier turns into the commander; the marshal's staff he was carrying in his kit bag becomes visible.

Whether ivory or wood, day or marble, the material is concentrated. It reduces itself to its final denominator, no matter if the stakes are hazelnuts, kingdoms, or "merely honor." Ultimately, we always play a game of life and death.

I am still with Latifah: the game did not go beyond the opening gambit. A girl from the river basin—Aphrodite is in her as in Cleopatra and every other woman. I could lead her through the black and white squares all the way to the far edge: a pawn becomes queen. Had I taken back the scudo, I would have made the first move in that direction—but why her, of all women? In each man, a shepherd slumbers, and the goddesses appear to him as they did on Mount Ida.

Concerning the Forest

47

I return to my job in the Casbah. From the bar, I can see the Condor; he looks nonchalant and nearly always cheerful, sometimes exhausted, too. At his right, the Domo as Odysseus with a mossy goatee that sharpens rather than conceals his profile. At his left, Attila, the unicorn with the white, undulating fleece. When drinking, he runs his hand down the flow of his beard. I would count him among the centaurs—not dichotomous, but twofold. The guests change from day to day. A few are summoned late at night through the phonophore if the discussion requires their presence. On the side benches, the minions; each one's eyes are glued to his master. If he has drained his glass, the minion brings it to me without being asked and carries the fresh drink back.

First the chef. The dinner was as simple and exquisite as ever. He submits the suggestion for the next one. The Condor crosses out the dessert, substituting another. A small band has been playing on the estrade, and sometimes its leader comes in. The Domo sends for him when he is particularly satisfied, but also if he is bothered by anything. He is hard to please. They discuss nuances that are beyond my ken.

"I would like to hear the note, not the instrument. The note should flow more lightly."

"The violinist was not in form tonight. He's got problems at home."

"That can happen."

It is easier for me to follow when the critique touches on principles of physics.

"You have to show more respect for the preceding pause."

"I do not quite know what you mean, Excellency."

"I mean the pause that comes before you start playing—not the interval within a performance."

"That pause is indicated by my raising the baton."

"No, that is already a visible sign. Imagine a ladder. When you raise the baton, you have already reached the first rung; what comes before is the preliminary pause."

Why did that make perfect sense to me? Most likely because it touched on a general artistic problem. The painter, too, stares at the white surface for a while, the poet ruminates silently until his tongue loosens. Perhaps during this hush, they are closer to perfection than in the execution—however the work may turn out.

The Domo apparently meant that one should wait for the *euphon*, or rather wait to be prepared for it. Of course, this applies to the composer more than to the performer, especially before a dinner.

*

I still have no concept of Attila's age or background. Sometimes I categorize him among the mythical figures; this involves timelessness. Then again, he reminds me of a certain Comte de Saint-Germain, who claimed to be in possession of the elixir of eternal youth and also told about feasting with Alexander the Great.

Initially, I thought Attila was one of those doctors who cultivate an uncouth tone while associating with officers. Whenever his tongue loosened, anecdotes like this one contributed to my assumption:

"Beards change with the fashions; men often imitate the current monarch—well, I'm beyond all that." He nodded at the Condor.

"I have often worn a beard like this one, whether on a patriarchal impulse or on an anarchic one. During the first war I fought in, I was a beardless youth; it was the only time I swore an oath of allegiance prior to military service. I mean the only allegiance that I observed. After that, I swore a lot of oaths, either to gain an advantage or to sidestep a disadvantage. Even the Hippocratic oath was more of a general guideline. Oaths are like virginity.

"It was after a lost war that I began wearing the beard I have today; it was already white. As a doctor, I had seen and learned a lot; a great military hospital station is a kind of gateway to hell. The city was occupied by the Yellow Khan's troops and it was already relatively calm. My beard helped me; it made me a venerable personage in the eyes of the Tartars. They were soon referring to me as The General.

"On the other hand, I noticed that our young men found me offensive; they viewed me as a kind of protest figure. They would insult me, yell curses at me. It did not faze me. I lost patience only once, when a man stood in my way and seized my beard with both hands. I grabbed his shoulders, pushed him around, and kicked him through a store window. The only damage he could do was to the glass, since the shelves were empty and sporting no more than a picture of the Yellow Khan.

"After that, I felt unsafe. The boys formed groups and did violent things. I got anonymous threats. I asked to see the commander, and he received me benevolently. He was enthroned among a luxurious medley of looted furnishings. I kowtowed to him.

"In this connection, I must remark that I was way past the time of esteeming resistance as a moral achievement. Those are liberal reminiscences, recipes for suicides who save the police some work. Here there is only one kind of behavior—that of the chameleon. This Greek word means 'earth lion.' I swore allegiance once, I 'resisted' once. Nation and king have no further claims on me."

*

"'General, what brings you to me? What can I do for you?'

"'Commander, I'm being threatened. They resent me for treating your wounded, for tending them. I would like to continue my work, and so I am asking you for a weapon to protect myself with.'

"He shook his head. 'It would be better if you gave me the names of these pests; you can count on never seeing them again.'

"'Unfortunately, I don't know them.'

"I did know them, of course, and I also owned a weapon that I had stowed in a safe place. But one sticks to the rules, and indeed plays on both sides, as long as one can. Besides, I had done a discreet service for the commander; a physician is something of a father confessor.

"'Very well, my friend—I'll make an exception in your case.'

"And so I got a pistol and, most important, a gun permit. One should resort to illegality as late as possible. The city park lay between my home and the military hospital. After a long workday, I was crossing the park in the darkness. The guy I had catapulted through the window stood in my way. I released the safety catch.

"He held a cigar toward me in his left hand.

"'Hey, old goat—do you have a light?'

"'Sorry, I don't smoke.'

"Next came a haymaker that knocked me to the ground.

"'*Pardonnez-moi, mon vieux*—here's my lighter.'

"And sprawling there, I fired through my pocket and gave him something to remember me by. The memory would linger on: shots slanting up from below leave complicated wounds.

"I then went over to the others and ordered them to lie on their bellies. They had become as meek as lambs; I touched the back of each neck with the mouth of the barrel. The Tartars use this approach during an interrogation in order to break resistance—just as the Romans made their defeated pass under a yoke, and a single time was enough.

"I had nothing more to fear from them, at least so long as we were occupied. However, most of these young men are offspring of prestigious families. They revolt against the fathers who let themselves be conquered; and that was how they pigeonholed me. I would have gotten along with them if they had understood me. But life is short, and I prefer wine to cider.

"After a while, I felt it was advisable to fold my tents. One night, taking two pistols, I crossed over to the other side. There, I had friends and patrons—we went back a long way. A Mauretanian finds a set table everywhere. Moreover, there are natural gifts. A talented doctor, singer, hetaera are popular with both friend and foe. Like Bias de Priene, they carry their belongings with them; they are born with a global passport in their mouths."

48

During these late-night conversations, Attila acts the bon vivant, like someone recounting youthful pranks that he no longer takes seriously, but with which he occasionally entertains others. The peculiar thing about it is the frankness of his comments on tyranny; this may be due to his position of authority. Besides, he is speaking to messmates who are sure of themselves; the Condor and the Domo unabashedly go along with this tone. Something similar can be found in the self-irony of intelligent Jews; it eases, nay, brightens the conversation.

I have gathered a number of such anecdotes as are heard in veterans' groups. Oddly enough, Attila barely mentions the period of his studies; yet he must have spent many years in laboratories. They are bound to be registered in his papers; the Domo sometimes alludes to them. Attila must have played a major role in the era of transplants, when medical science attempted grafts on natural growth. It was not only as Uranians that the new sons of Prometheus realized their hour had struck.

There could be two reasons for Attila's reticence. Either he views his experiments as excesses that had a repulsive outcome and should therefore be hushed up, or else they were successful beyond all measure. Silence is also called for with the discovery of a gold mine. Perhaps the answer was mightier than the question—a miracle snuffed out the experiment. A master tried to outfox nature, and an explosion corroborated his work, destroying it at the same time. Such is the course of evocations. The preliminaries are intricate. When the mind enters, the intricacies become superfluous. And people would rather forget the technical detail.

*

I perk up my ears when Attila, at a late hour, ventures beyond the boundaries: into the polar sea, the great deserts, the forest. I can barely distinguish between geography and dreams; but that already applies to our Eumeswil. The reality of everyday life blurs, it merges into the reality of dreams; now one reality, now the other penetrates the consciousness more sharply.

I have reconstructed some of these places from fragments—for instance, the Gray Castle of Transiceland. Guesswork, even mistakes are inevitable; those are some of the weaknesses of our science. Wellsprings spurt only once in time.

*

"It was after one of the great devastations. Years had gone by. The desert, which had already been sparsely planted, was now thoroughly burned out. The caravan trails were lined with human and animal skeletons. The bones gleamed like opals in the sun; they were calcined. It was not decay that had bleached them. The flesh must have been devoured instantly. The earthen huts in oases, the houses around drilling rigs had melted in a similar fashion; the clay and the stones were vitrified. The walls bore the silhouettes of palms, camels, and people as shadows cast by the radiation that had followed the fire. The upper drill pipe of one derrick dangled as if a fountain had petrified. A cannon barrel was twisted like a hose; steel drops lay in the sand underneath. Catastrophes, too, have a style of their own.

"I was alone. Some of my companions had given up after the early marching because they could not deal with the horrors. A lot of them must have died of thirst or perished in the contaminated valleys. Once again, I was the last; this is one of the experiences of old age; a man grows tired of outliving.

"I don't know how I reached the forest. Cloudbursts must have filled up the old water holes. I was also moving away from the eye of the destruction; the first vultures were circling in the air. Then I saw plants and animals, including some that were new to me. A few of them evoked pictures in old fable books, as if a demiurge had patched them together.

"It is well known that people on exhausting marches have visions. On the other hand, these creatures reminded me of experiments I had dealt with for a long time, and perhaps this memory projected them into the desert and magnified them. Such recollections can also become realities; after all, every experiment is a realized reminiscence."

*

"The forest stood like a rampart; no axe could ever have touched it. The cataclysm must have intensified the growth of the forest, as if the breath of the fire and the subsequent deluge had liberated its primal energy. This would speak for Cuvier's theory.

"Seed trees had shot up to an acme surpassing the highest towers. Others had spread foliage that could have provided shade for a whole army. It was not until later that I noticed something bizarre in their interweaving: the branches had copulated. In and of itself, this is nothing new for the botanist, or for the gardener who inoculates. I once knew a man in Saxony who had grown seven varieties of fruit on a single trunk. But the extraordinary thing about the forest was the promiscuity of the mixing. Entirely alien species had coupled, and their fruit would have made Linnaeus tear his hair out had he seen them.

"That, too, reminded me of the laboratories. We had succeeded—if I may call it that—in begetting gigantic growth, multi-armed creatures like Hindu gods, multi-breasted females like the Diana of Ephesus. Groping our way through genetic mazes, we had awakened forebears that we had known only from marlpits and slate quarries."

*

"But protean winds were blowing here, and throughout the forest they had achieved something that we had spent so much effort trying to attain in our laboratories. I sensed it directly, almost like an alchemist who, already despairing of the great transmutation, sees solid gold shining in his kiln. I felt myself drawn into the metamorphosis—into a new world, and my experiences did not confirm the details until later.

"The road back from the Tree of Knowledge to the Tree of Life is a sinister one. But there was no returning to the desert that lay behind me. There, death was certain. Despite the risk of getting lost in the forest, I had to cross through it to reach the open sea. Like every jungle, the forest was surrounded by a girdle of dense, partly thorny underbrush. It was more negotiable in the deep shade. But there the foliage covered up the sun, the only thing that could indicate my direction.

"I must have wandered in circles for a long time, naked and with ripped skin like a castaway. The thorns had shredded my clothes and my body. I found springs and brooks from which I could drink, and also fruits and berries that I took a wild chance on. Perhaps their virtues were imbued with the visions produced by fever, imposing imaginary trials of strength on me.

"Once I had to avoid an army of termites. They were enormous and they were marching toward an obelisk that was shooting sparks from its tip. The snakes that traveled the trees overhead were also huge. They seemed neither to glide nor to fly; the edges of their skin were shimmying. They were obviously demonstrating the transition to dragons. They mated with the trunks, enclasping them. Blood-red resin or resinous blood flowed from the cracks struck by their claws. I did not miss my binoculars; every scale was stamped on my mind.

"It also appeared that the kind of sensitivity that we only see in mimosas had become universal there. One of the trees had fruit like that of our maples; our children pin them on their noses and call the tips 'little wings.' That is a pure metaphor; in the forest it became operative: the fruits did not whirl to the ground, they fluttered. A tumult of tiny bats was celebrating a wedding around the trunk. A man could strike roots here and become a tree.

"In a clearing, a sunbeam fell upon a ramlike shape. Its left front leg was propped on a lamb with a human face. Both dissolved in light as if the vision were too powerful."

*

"Then once again islands of thicket along the windbreaks. A path had been trodden into one, an animal trail. Lethally exhausted, I blindly groped my way along. The path led to an open space; a cypress was growing there, its height beyond imagining. Had the sky been cloudy, I would not have seen the tip of the tree. Its trunk was hollow; the entrance to the interior was not weathered, a rectangle had been cut into the alburnum, like a gateway. Trees are our best friends; I ventured inside.

"Through the darkness, I reached the interior on all fours; the floor was covered with furs, or rather a fleece that seemed to have grown as if on the back of an animal. A marvelous bed; I stretched out and instantly fell into a deathlike sleep.

"I don't know how long I rested there. When I awoke, I felt reborn, as if I had bathed in the fountain of youth. The air was delicious; it smelled of cypress wood whose resin is smoldering into incense.

"The morning sun fell through the wooden gateway. I sat up; my skin was shiny, the blood had been washed away, and there was no trace of the thorns. I must have been dreaming. But meanwhile someone had taken care of me. What is 'meanwhile'? A pause between two instants or even between two forms of existence.

"A garment was lying at my side, a kind of burnoose; it was woven of the same gold as the carpet. Next to it there were sandals and a tray with bread and wine—a large and undeserved bestowal. Wherever it came from no response was possible but prayer."

*

Attila seldom reaches this point, and then more often in monologues. Gaps are interspersed—in the "meanwhile." Sometimes he even gets lost in scientific or mythological digressions. For instance, about cedar wood, which was once considered indestructible. It used to be employed for temples and ships, for cradles and coffins, and even for the burning of the dead. However, it strikes me that for him its mythical significance outweighs its botanical significance. Cedar, cypress, arborvitae, juniper were confused, just like mountains such as Atlas, Zion, Sinai, and also ranges in the New World. Apparently he considers Yggdrasil not an ash tree but a cypress. Thus the word has less of a biological than a cosmogonic meaning for him. I note this detail because I initially found it hard to delve into the background of his language, until I finally realized that it makes things simpler rather than more complicated; he takes them back to their synthesis.

That is how I explain the impact he has on the round table. A silvery figure, he constitutes its center. Even the Domo is illuminated. They have drunk a lot; I am the only sober person here. I concentrate on his forehead, I see the horn arching forth as if from a bud. He strokes the Condor's hand, almost like a father—it could also be the gesture of a father-in-law.

He stops talking about the forest; when he gets to the sea, he will become more loquacious. It could not have been that far away. The path led from metahistorical to ahistorical landscapes, from the forest to the chaotic shore. What he reported did not sound good, it even sounded hopeless.

One of the symbols of places without a history is refuse. Space is menaced by garbage. Waste is no longer coped with as in civilized countries; it outgrows the structures. When a ship founders, the wreckage drifts ashore. The mast, the planks are used for building shacks or as fuel. People live on and from the refuse—among garbage heaps that they exploit. Naked hunger follows bygone wealth and its lavishness. Growth fails to keep pace.

At first, thoughts are twisted, then actions become ominous; there are foretokens. One such sign, according to Attila, is the passion—a humanist legacy—for excavations. "Something like subterranean cargo cults began back then; only the graves contributed artworks. The disempowerment of the gods progressed at the same rate. Then came the exploitation of fossil remains, followed by earthquakes and the destruction of primeval forests by the hunger for energy. Even the ocean became a dumping ground. The ash tree was no longer bent, it was chopped down."

*

The degenerates, whose behavior Attila studied in the Great Dump Site, lived there in dugouts; they were virtually unclad and unarmed. "That is how mushrooms live on the chlorophyll of other plants." As gatherers and hunters, they grubbed for roots and set traps for small animals. Unable to work either stone or wood, they used them in whatever way they fit into their hands. That was also how they utilized the vestiges of metal utensils and machine parts. They seemed barely alive, drowsing in a dreamlike state, as in the days before Prometheus had given them fire. "The heir to the Last Man is not the primitive, but the zombie."

Clearly Attila had given them medical attention, but without success. Now and then, pirates would land and hunt them down in order to try out the weapons that they had obtained from uncontaminated bunkers. And they carried off a few people in order to reconnoiter those same bunkers. As slaves, the captives were useless.

49

Today I was faced with a decision that may herald my departure from Eumeswil. When Kung brought in my breakfast, he also had the work schedule: the Domo was commanding me to report to him at eleven o'clock—"in mufti."

Still in my bathrobe, I mulled it over while the Chinese laid out my things. This order could spell trouble; perhaps they had overheard conversations in which Dalin had boasted to me of his nihilistic attacks. Or had they discovered my bunker on the upper Sus? I would present the former as a curiosity, the latter as a private pleasure. There was nothing to reproach in my work; I had served that night as usual, and the Condor had dismissed me benevolently. So there was nothing serious to fear; besides, in such cases, one is not summoned, one is taken.

*

The Domo received me at his desk; he was obviously very busy, but concentrating as always. That morning, as it happened, I had recognized my real image in the mirror. It stared at me as though receiving some pleasant news—I had perused its face during many nights.

"Venator, you know how much we appreciate you—both in your work up here and as a historian. You read nothing superfluous into history. The Condor knew what he was doing when he allowed you to use the Great Luminar. It was a sign of trust and also reliance."

Then he got to the point:

"The Condor has decided to go on a Great Hunt—it will take him beyond the desert and into the woods. I am now arranging the preliminaries; we will set out shortly. Along with the hunters and the usual escort, I have decided to take along a small staff of scholars, including Rosner as zoologist and you as historian. 'The donkeys and the scholars in the middle'—you know the quotation. But joking aside—we regard you as our Xenophon; that is, if you are willing."

He may have wanted to add something, but then limited himself to a hint:

"I feel uneasy about the whole thing; it could go almost anywhere."

He was alluding to Attila. The fact that the Domo had thought of a zoologist and a historian indicates that he wants to keep the hunt within both natural and human boundaries, whatever the dangers. This is also evidenced by his own participation, given how indispensable he is here.

He turned to the side in order to get the phonophore for his next report; I saw his head in profile. The close beard sharpens and elongates the chin slightly; that is where the horn seems to start—not on the forehead as with Attila. The Domo's beard shone moss-green as demanded by the red rock of the citadel mountain. Life is a chain of optical illusions, but this one fitted him; if any of us escapes, then it will be the Domo—he will not get involved with gods.

He gave me time to think it over; for tactical reasons, I agreed to sleep on it, though I had made up my mind on the spot. This opens one of the two roads leading out of the city, if only into an intermediary realm, an antechamber. I will stick not to the Domo, for whom the catacombs are more suitable, but to Attila. He will precede the Condor, functioning as a marriage broker.

*

Vigo was the only person whom I might consult before saying yes. I got time off from the Casbah and went to see him in his garden that evening. He promptly understood that this hunt is more than an expedition. Of course, every hunt has its Calydonian background.

Vigo's assessment of the situation had a historical foundation. "The great goal of the political will is leviathan. This goal has been more or less achieved—it is necessary in late eras, as under the caesars, or in the world-state as the consequence of technological perfection. Two peaks: one grew from the personal will, the other from the collective will. In the one, the god-caesar; in the other, *homo magnus* as titan; one is tied to the animal, the other to plutonian energy. This is shown in the symbols: eagle and lion as opposed to colors and tools.

"The world-state is shattered into its parts, just as Boutefeu predicted. We are left with Diadochic realms and epigonic city-states. The keynote proclaimed by the nineteenth Christian century was a permanent, indeed qualitative growth; this seemed to be realized by *Homo faber* in the twentieth century. Next, new distinctions split off from progress—and they can be roughly described as the differences between economists and ecologists. The former thought in terms of the history of the world, the latter the history of the earth; the former thought in terms of distribution, the latter in terms of administration. Conflicts erupted between the human milieu and the natural environment, and they were exacerbated by the apocalyptic atmosphere that recurs at the end of every millennium.

"The concentration of power likewise occurs toward the end of an era. This time it was inevitably of a technological nature. Again, speaking roughly—that is, in the framework of classical science—we might say that on the one side biologists were rearming and on the other physicists. One side strove toward the organic grid, the other toward the material grid; genes versus atoms. This led below not only the historical but also the human fundaments—forest versus underworld.

"People were skeptical about everything but science. This was the only thing that developed unswervingly and worldwide; it ultimately consumed the state. Science managed to do something that had been reserved for the Great Titans, who had existed before the Gods, indeed created them. In order to recognize these goals, which were hidden even from science itself, it had to reach a limit at which death and life offered a new response."

Vigo said: "Martin, I have never doubted that you prefer the forest. Yet I also know that you regard it as a passage—not as a goal, like Attila, or as a fiction, like the Domo. But what are fictions? A dream comes true in each of our great transformations. You know this as a historian. We fail not because of our dreams but because we do not dream forcefully enough."

50

Attila has calculated the favorable moment; we will march at night, starting tomorrow in the full moon. The advance units have already gone ahead with the tents. Meanwhile I have paid my good-bye visits, also calling on my dear old dad, who naturally tried to talk me out of going. He sees this undertaking as halfway between adventure and charlatanry. Bruno likewise expressed doubts; he would have preferred my heading toward the catacombs. I also went to see Latifah and Ingrid and took another dip in the ocean with its warm and cold currents.

Latifah received a bouquet of flowers this time instead of a scudo. My choice hit home. I felt it in my very marrow. Inner warmth was released. Ingrid likewise amazed me by shedding her clothes for the first time. I did justice to the surprise.

I then bid farewell to my refuge on the upper Sus. The entrance was already overgrown, soon it will be spun shut. I had gone there to stow away the notes I have gathered at the night bar; they can be deciphered at most by Bruno. I am leaving my scholarly works at the institute; they are chiefly sketches.

In regard to these jottings, I considered burning them; they weigh on my mind if only because they are incomplete. A sense of inadequacy casts a shadow on my existence both as a historian and as a man. Nevertheless, the destruction of a manuscript is a kind of spiritual suicide—whereby I am not putting down suicide. However, I was held back by an experience that concerned that very shadow.

During those days, I worked intensively at the mirror in order to prepare myself for the forest. I thus managed to achieve something I had always dreamed of: a complete detachment from my physical existence.

I saw myself in the mirror as a transcendent suitor—and myself, confronting him, as his fleeting mirror image. Between us, as always, a candle burned; I leaned over it until the flame singed my forehead; I saw the injury, but I did not feel the pain.

When Kung arrived with my breakfast, he found me stretched out naked on the floor. The Chinese are masters of both killing and reviving; he brought me to with hot towels and powerful essences. He swore he would keep silent. Had it not been for the stigma on my brow, I would have thought I had been dreaming.

Epilogue

My brother, Martin Venator, who vanished years ago with the tyrant and his retinue, has now been declared legally dead. Our father was correct in urgently warning him not to join that undertaking. We already saw it as the last resort of a ruler who had lost the game.

Meanwhile, a great deal has changed in the city and, if I may say so, for the better. The Casbah is now desolate; goatherds pasture their goats inside the walls of the stronghold. The exiles have returned from abroad and the prisoners from the islands; the henchmen of the tyranny have traded places with them.

As my brother's sole heir, I have the responsibility of administering his posthumous papers. They include the studies that he deposited at the historical institute, of which I have now become director. He described them, perhaps all too modestly, as sketches; I am having them edited.

We were surprised by the papers just recently discovered in the wilderness along the upper Sus. Hunters pursuing a buffalo found them in a bunker, next to weapons and provisions. If the party had not included a scholar, they would no doubt have burned the manuscripts. But this way they came into my hands.

We deplored and disliked the subaltern work he performed in the Casbah. However, this hiding place, which cost him a great deal of effort, testifies to his skepticism and his spiritual resistance. He would certainly have also resisted in deed. It would have been better had he confided in us and our friends.

The bulk of his papers consists of a throng of dated or undated scraps: accounts and jottings about his nocturnal activity, interspersed with passages in hieroglyphic style. Bruno, to whom he specifically refers, has emigrated. Supposedly, he has an important position in the catacombs.

And then these notebooks, to which I am adding the epilogue. They are more readable, despite the often rapid penmanship. However I am almost as familiar with his handwriting as with my own. There are things people simply have in common that cannot be denied.

Reading these pages has thrown me into an inner conflict—between the private man and the historian. My brother did not love his family. Such was his peculiar character. But we loved him. His presentation is larded with judgments and, in my opinion, misjudgments that would justify my burning it as a private person; I have thought about it. Burnings take place with every legacy, perhaps to purge the deceased's image in our memories, perhaps for the sake of his family.

I, however, am a historian and come from a family of historians. My dear brother—one of the titles he loved was "historian by blood."

There is an archivist's conscience to which a man must sacrifice himself. I am submitting to it by sealing these pages and storing them at the institute.

Also from Telos Press Publishing

The Forest Passage
Ernst Jünger

Sturm
Ernst Jünger

On Pain
Ernst Jünger

The Adventurous Heart: Figures and Capriccios
Ernst Jünger

Theory of the Partisan
Carl Schmitt

The Nomos *of the Earth*
in the International Law of the Jus Publicum Europaeum
Carl Schmitt

Hamlet or Hecuba:
The Intrusion of the Time into the Play
Carl Schmitt

Germany and Iran
From the Aryan Axis to the Nuclear Threshold
Matthias Küntzel

The New Class Conflict
Joel Kotkin

Confronting the Crisis: Writings of Paul Piccone
Paul Piccone

A Journal of No Illusions:
Telos, *Paul Piccone, and the Americanization of Critical Theory*
Timothy W. Luke and Ben Agger, eds.